GODS & MONSTERS

JANIE MARIE

Book One
of the
Gods & Monsters
Trilogy

Second Edition

Illustration & Cover design by Thander Lin
Editing by Murphy Rae and KD Phillips, www.murphyrae.net
Proofreading by Emily Vaughan
ISBN-13:
9781686005602

The Gods & Monsters Novels

GODS & MONSTERS
Book One

THE FALLEN QUEEN
Gods & Monsters Book Two

THE LIGHT BRINGER
Gods & Monsters Book Three

WHO'S AFRAID OF THE BIG BAD WOLF?
A Gods & Monsters Novel

For Tifani

✧

PROLOGUE

Glowing emerald eyes stayed fixed on the two women who conversed in hushed tones across the bedroom. The pair had no idea they were being observed so carefully. In fact, they were unaware another was present at all.

It would stay that way, too. Unless, of course, the green-eyed *man* wished otherwise.

It appeared, though, he had no intention of letting the two friends know their conversation was no longer private.

Leaning his muscular back against the wall opposite the bed one of the women lay on, he crossed his arms and listened.

They talked of nothing important, nothing he didn't already expect in such times for mortals. Death had a way of causing the same conversations again and again.

So, after a while his gaze began to wander. He had no interest in the flowers, cards, and balloons displayed on the dresser and side tables, but he did pause as he came upon a set of picture frames and medications.

The medication was no concern to him, but at the pictures his eyes flashed.

There were various groups of people in each photo, but each one contained the woman who currently lay in bed. Only, she no longer resembled the young lady seen smiling in all the pictures. Cancer had a way of doing that.

He returned his attention to the woman but instead of observing her, all his focus shifted to the brunette sitting on the chair. Her hand was shaking as she applied lip balm to her friend's chapped lips.

He let out a breath and continued to study the brunette. She was no longer looking at her friend, though. She was staring right at him. If he allowed it, she would realize her hazel eyes were locked with his.

"Jane?"

The brunette, Jane, blinked and returned her attention to her friend. "Sorry, Wendy. I thought I saw something."

The corner of the male's lips twitched, but he made no other outward reaction to her words.

"Thank you, again," said Wendy.

Jane shook her head. "I already told you not to thank me."

Wendy frowned. "But you're still sad."

Just weeks before, Jane had signed Wendy's "Do Not Resuscitate" order because it required a non-family member as a witness. And the green-eyed man had seen it all.

He had witnessed the shock in her eyes when every head turned to Jane after Wendy asked her for the grim favor. Jane had been given no warning or time to think over what was asked of her. She had looked fragile, yet when it seemed she would refuse, those hazel eyes that seemed to captivate the green-eyed man burned brightly with determination, and she agreed.

He glanced over at the unopened bible sitting beside the bed. It was still in the exact spot where Jane had left it three weeks ago.

"Are you mad at me?" is what Wendy had asked Jane that day.

The green-eyed man had stood silent and unseen by the pair as he listened to the exchange. Wendy had already resembled a talking corpse, and Jane's anguish shone in her eyes every time she looked at her friend.

"I could never be mad at you," Jane said. "I love you, always. This doesn't change that. I'm just afraid I won't see you when I die. I don't know if what they always say is true. About not going to Heaven if you don't believe in God. I just want to know I'll see you again."

His expression didn't reveal any sign of emotion, but his eyes followed the tear that slowly slid down her face. When it finally fell from her chin, he looked back to Wendy.

"It's a nice idea. It would be wonderful to go to such a perfect place." Wendy stopped and watched Jane for a moment. "I just don't think there's anything after we die. It's just what people say to make themselves feel better. At least, that's how I see it."

Jane seemed to sort through the comment before she looked up. "What are you going to tell your boys?" she asked.

"They're going to pick out a star with my mom. They'll be able to look up at night and think it's me. They'll talk to me that way. I think it'll help my mom, too."

Jane smiled sadly. "You know we came from stardust—so it's entirely expected that we would return to the stars when we die."

"I've never heard that before," Wendy said, looking almost lost in a daze. "Where did you hear that?"

"I heard it when I was little. I think my mom told me."

Peaceful smiles formed on both women's faces.

"I think it's a beautiful way for them to be able to remember and talk to you," Jane said quickly. "I think I'll do the same—talk to you when the stars come out."

Wendy looked at peace, and Jane had appeared happy for being able to accept her decision. Jane didn't have to force her beliefs on her friend, she had given them both something to hold on to—a place for them after they left this world.

"Stardust," Wendy had murmured. "I like that."

After that day, Wendy's condition worsened. Now, she was a shell of a person, barely able to stay conscious. She tried, though. Whenever someone sat beside her, she tried. Even if the medications she was on altered her focus, she said what the brave ones did on their final days. Reminding her loved ones to live after she was gone.

The green-eyed man glanced up as a few family members entered the room. They all greeted Wendy, and Jane sat up. She always left quickly whenever someone came to visit. It hurt for her to go, but she did have her own children and husband to take care of.

Jane looked down at Wendy. "I'll come see you tomorrow, okay?"

Wendy managed to nod and gestured for Jane to come closer. Jane glanced around at the small group of visitors and then bent down.

A weak, raspy word left Wendy's lips, "Blood."

Everyone looked around, confused, including Jane.

"Blood?" Jane asked. Wendy nodded, yet she was still baffled. "What about blood?"

"Your blood."

Jane frowned. "You want my blood?" Wendy nodded again, and this time, Jane smiled as she clarified, "Like a vampire?"

Wendy made a small biting motion with her teeth and Jane laughed softly. The others joined her laughter and even he smiled, knowing why they would bring this up. The girls loved vampires. Both were silly with their beliefs in fantasy and other magical beings. They had each led difficult lives, but they held an innocence that many did not possess.

"You want to drink my blood so you can become a vampire?" Jane asked, obviously amused, but the green-eyed man watched her eyes light up, as though she was actually wishing for something so magical.

Wendy's head bobbed, but her eyes closed. Her medicine had kicked in.

"That would be cool," Jane muttered as she smoothed Wendy's thinning hair back. "I'm going to go now. I love you. I'll see you tomorrow."

As a red glow lit the space beside the green-eyed man, he sighed and addressed the new presence without looking away from Jane. "What is it?"

A new male, also invisible to those around them, observed the scene in front of him before answering, "Our brother is missing. There is something amiss with Earth's immortals as well."

They both watched Jane lean over and kiss Wendy's head. She moved back, holding her breath as she gave the others an awkward wave and quickly left the room.

The two unseen males turned toward each other. Brothers they may have been, but they looked nothing alike. While the green-eyed man had black hair that was spiked upward, tanned skin, and green eyes; his brother had long, fiery red hair, amber eyes, and golden skin.

"Who was the girl?" asked the red-haired brother.

"Which girl?"

"I honestly do not care, brother," said the red-haired brother with a smile. "I am merely curious to know what you are doing here since you seem more interested in the one that left, rather than this one."

The green-eyed man shrugged as his brother inclined his head toward Wendy. "I simply watch them from time to time."

"Right, brother. Well, we should hurry."

As the green-eyed man nodded, his gaze lowered to the dresser he stood beside. There was a picture of the two girls when they were teenagers. They had been working at an animal hospital and were both wearing scrubs while they smiled and held several puppies in their arms. Next to that picture was another one of the two friends. They were older in this one, early twenties, sitting side by side with several other mothers who each held small children on their laps—a playdate. Jane and Wendy were smiling in the center of the photo. Jane held a little boy and girl while Wendy held two boys.

"*Hm*, that's all, is it?" The red-haired brother chuckled as he traced his large finger over Jane's face in the playdate picture. "She must be an entertaining little thing. I do not recall ever witnessing you so intrigued by a human—or anyone, for that matter. No one will believe me."

The green-eyed man's face remained neutral, but he knocked his brother's hand away from the picture. "Leave it."

"Of course, big brother. Are you ready?" He paused and looked over at Wendy. "Or—"

The green-eyed man shook his head but said nothing.

His brother nodded, and in a glow of red light, he vanished.

As the green-eyed man let out a breath, he looked toward the dying girl but quickly returned his gaze to the picture. He slid his fingers over the curve of Jane's face before lowering his hand.

Then, in a glow of emerald light, he was gone.

CHAPTER 1
JANE

One Year Later

Gasping, Jane opened her eyes and tilted her head to the side where the dimly lit numbers of her alarm clock came into view: 5:59.

"It was just a dream," she whispered, turning her head so she gazed up at the ceiling. A tear slid into her hair. "Just a dream."

That was a lie. They were never simply dreams. Only her memories terrified her this much. Not even sleep could offer escape from such horror.

They were becoming more frequent and intense, too. Not that Jane could break down for more than a few tears when no one was looking. Because she still had to get up every day, and she did so without complaining to anyone. She woke up and lived.

Well, she was alive. Not quite living, but she found strength from the air in her lungs, and though her heart always beat a little faster than most, it always slowed enough to assure her she wasn't *there* anymore. That was enough to get through each day.

Still, even the most rested people wished for extra sleep on a Saturday morning, and nightmares spawned from truth or not, Jane was no exception when it came to fatigue. She'd almost happily welcome the darkness of her past if that meant obtaining unconsciousness. But sleeping in no longer existed for her. Any moment now, soft footsteps would come to a stop beside her bed, and her day would have to begin.

Sure enough, shuffling footsteps greeted her ears. Jane rolled her head to the side and smiled at her five-year-old daughter. Natalie, who was practically a miniature version of Jane, with her pale skin and dark brown hair, stood quietly as her mom caressed her cheek.

Jane sighed and pushed some of the girl's curly locks behind an ear. Life would be so much simpler if Natalie had her straight hair, but she loved her daughter's unruly curls.

Natalie rubbed her chocolate brown eyes. "Mommy, I'm hungry."

Jane sat up and glanced over at Jason, her husband, who hadn't stirred. It took some effort, but she kept herself from throwing a pillow at him. If he hadn't helped with the kids in the past five years, she shouldn't expect him to help now.

Despite being exhausted and feeling the start of a headache, she swung her legs over the edge of the bed and got up. "Do you want waffles or cereal?"

"Cereal," Natalie said before skipping down the hall.

Jane nodded and went to the kitchen. She pulled down a box of Natalie's favorite cereal and poured it into a plastic princess bowl.

Her daughter had gone into the living room and turned on the TV, so Jane poured a cup of orange juice and carried everything to the coffee table.

"I'm going to lie back down, okay?" Jane said.

Natalie nodded without looking away from her cartoons.

On her way back to her room, Jane stopped in the hall and listened for signs of Nathan, Natalie's twin brother. Hearing nothing, she breathed a sigh of relief and returned to her room.

She quickly got back in bed. Falling fully asleep was unlikely, but she hoped to enter that halfway state, the place where she could push back the menacing smile that resembled hers.

She enjoyed these in-between moments in her consciousness. Here she could feel calm. Here she felt a warmth that tingled across her skin before seeping into her soul. Here is where she saw a smile that did not resemble her inner demon's. Still dangerous, she did not doubt, but more comforting than anything she'd ever experienced. The smile was what constantly renewed her belief that one day everything would be okay. The owner of that beautiful smile, never fully visible to her, always pulled her close with strong arms and promised to keep her safe.

Finally feeling somewhat relaxed, she shut her eyes. She felt as though she could call her protector to her, and just as her mind reached out, she gave up.

Hearing a distant bedroom door opening, Jane sighed and sat up for round two.

If ever a genuine smile could be found on Jane's lips, it was for her children, and her son held a special place in her heart.

"Hey, bubby," she greeted Nathan. "What do you want for breakfast?"

Nathan didn't bear much of a resemblance to his petite sister. He was heavier set than his twin, and his olive skin was a shade lighter than his father's. While Natalie had inherited her father's curls, Nathan had inherited Jane's straight hair.

"Want breakfast," he said.

He'd been diagnosed with autism a few years ago, and he struggled to communicate with words, but Jane had her ways to get responses.

She spoke to him again and made sure to prompt him this time. "Do you want a waffle sandwich?"

"Sandwich."

He ate the same thing every morning, but she always asked him the same way, hoping one day he would respond without a prompt or, by some miracle, ask for something else.

They didn't speak as Jane put together his sandwich: a slice of microwaved bacon tucked in a folded waffle. Unlike his sister, though, he sat at the table and ate. Occasionally, he'd look up to watch her, but Jane had to feed their pets, so she quickly kissed the top of his head and went to the pantry.

Jules and Belle, the two cats, took turns rubbing along her calves, meowing loudly, like they usually did until their bowls were filled.

After she fed them, she grabbed dog food and went to the back door to feed Kuma and Rocky.

"Dogs," she said. Such a simple way to greet them, but they seemed to understand her affection in that small word. They jumped up, licking her hand as she filled their food bowls.

She stood there as they scarfed down their meal and then glanced up at the stars fading from the morning light.

Her gaze drifted to the brightest of stars. Even if someone had stood behind her, they wouldn't have heard her whisper, nor would they be able to see the pain caused by the twinkling starlight. "Hi, Wendy."

Her eyes stung, and the inside of her nose burned as a pain in her chest grew, but she smiled as best she could before looking away.

She did not cry. She only rubbed under her eyes to ease the pressure before going back inside the house.

After locking the door, she debated whether she should prepare breakfast for Jason but decided to wait until he woke up. She quickly ate a granola bar, went to the refrigerator, and drank from the jug of orange juice. She peeked at the kids as they played, and then went to her bathroom.

As soon as she shut herself inside, she looked in the mirror and frowned. She couldn't remember the last time she'd felt satisfied with her reflection. There had been a time when she'd considered herself pretty, but now she didn't know how to describe herself. She only knew she didn't like what she saw.

It didn't matter how many compliments she received from strangers and acquaintances on how lovely she was. She didn't believe their kind observations and often realized afterward she hadn't even replied with a generic thank-you.

At least my eyes are still pretty, she thought as she turned the water on to wash her face. Something about her hazel eyes pleased her. Mostly, she admired the green in them.

Jane never acknowledged how envied she was for her long, dark eyelashes, high cheekbones, sun freckles that sprinkled across her nose, pink lips—all enhancing a clear complexion. It didn't matter what anyone said.

Jane saw a monster.

✦✦✦

New Influenza Virus Spreads Across the Country

Jane leaned back in bed, squinting at the news headline that appeared when she opened the internet browser on her laptop. She'd heard about this flu epidemic yesterday. It had apparently originated in the United States, and reports showed it had already spread to several other countries.

Over the past several decades, major outbreaks of the flu virus had ravaged the planet, so it no longer shocked her. She ignored the rest of the articles and checked her email. This was more of a habit, really. She didn't receive personal messages anymore, not that she ever had an excess, but there was no chance now. With Wendy dead, there were no more friends to stay in touch with.

Without her only real friend, a hollow feeling spread through her more every day. Of course, she had her children but even before she had them, for as long as she could remember, she'd felt like part of her had been carved out.

She needed someone to hold her hand because she honestly felt lost in the dark most of the time. Of course, Jane had Jason; they were friends, but not like they had been in many years. And it had been a long time since Jason could be considered a "good friend," which only worsened the fact he was her main adult contact on a regular basis.

Wendy had told her to go out and make new friends when they found out she wasn't going to survive. Jane always wanted to please her friend, but she couldn't do this. People didn't understand her. Even Wendy, as amazing as she was, didn't fully grasp all that happened to her. She accepted Jane, though. She never gave up on her. Jane didn't think there would be another person like that in her life. If by chance there was, she feared getting close to them. Losing people was all she knew, after all.

Jane let out a breath and closed her laptop as she glanced at Jason. He was still dead to the world. He always seemed to be so at ease and had no problem achieving a peaceful night's sleep. Not that she wished her nightmares on him, but it hurt that he never noticed hers.

She wished she didn't resent so much about him and their relationship. While she loved him, and knew he loved her, it always bothered her they weren't what they should be.

Jane gave herself a little shake to get rid of her unpleasant thoughts and turned on the TV. News reports about the flu were unavoidable, and this time, she paid more attention. The ill were instructed to make their way to the nearest medical facilities and avoid contact with others. The reports continued to repeat symptoms: fever, body aches, trouble breathing, coughing blood, and popped blood vessels in the eyes.

What sucked for her was that more than likely she'd end up with this flu; she always got sick. So she was relieved when both children entered the room and climbed on the bed between her and Jason. They nudged their dad, but he didn't move. Jane smiled, changed the channel to one of their favorite cartoon networks, and listened to their giggles while she waited for Jason to wake.

✦✦✦

After a long day of doing nothing special, Jane and her family made it to the grocery store. They were already in the checkout line, and while Jason loaded their items to be scanned, Jane stood lost in a daze. Life really was a blur sometimes. Again, like something wasn't right inside her—something was missing.

"She bit me!"

The shout broke Jane from her trance, and she turned her head toward the commotion. There was a man in the middle of a growing crowd near the store's exit. Firefighters and medics assisted the hysterical male while others attended a different person already strapped to a stretcher.

"Did he say someone bit him?" Jane asked Jason.

The cashier looked up from scanning items and responded to her when he didn't. "Yeah, I think so. The woman on the stretcher passed out; that man was helping her. When she woke up, she attacked him. I guess she bit him somehow. The medics arrived quickly, though. I think they'll be okay."

"That's a weird thing to do," Jane said, glancing at the medics wheeling the now screaming and thrashing woman out of the store.

✦✦✦

"Why do you think someone would bite another person?" Jane asked on the drive home.

Jason shrugged, not taking his eyes off the road. "I don't know. Maybe she had a seizure."

From Jane's experience as an animal medical technician a few years back, she recalled seizures with animals. She'd even been bitten by a small dog after it had been poisoned, but she thought it was strange a person would allow themselves to get bitten.

Those were good times. Not being bitten, but her time doing something she loved around people who liked her. Around Wendy. They worked hard, but they and their coworkers never passed up a chance to goof off.

It was rare Jane found herself reminiscing about the wild and carefree Wendy. The healthy and alive Wendy. There was no such thing now. She was gone. Forever.

She sighed and looked out the window. There were too many sad things inside her head and heart; she didn't want to put more there.

The cars and businesses they drove past suddenly blurred and flashbacks from her past began to play like a terrible movie in her mind.

She gasped and stuck out her hand for Jason's. His sigh touched her ears before he held her hand. Tears distorted the world passing by outside, and she couldn't bring herself to look at him. He never liked seeing her like this, so she stared out the glass and hoped to slow her rapidly beating heart.

"Is Mommy okay?" Natalie asked from the backseat.

"She's fine," Jason replied.

Jane squeezed his hand to show her thanks and teared up further when he didn't return the gesture; he never did.

Breathe–it will pass, a comforting thought promised.

She squeezed her eyes shut tightly, trusting the sweet assurance while a lone tear made its way down her cheek, and it wasn't alone for long. A faint tingle was quick to follow the trail her tear left behind and, as always, her pained heart received a moment of peace as a warm sensation spread throughout her chest.

"You fine now?" Jason asked, not looking away from the road or giving any other comfort.

"Yeah." Jane wiped the tear away and held her breath for a few seconds. The tingling feeling spread out and smothered the constant sting tormenting her heart. It replaced it with magic, and a sad but grateful smile spread across her lips. "I'm okay."

CHAPTER 2
THEM

Jane wasn't a fan of Texas summers. It wasn't that she was used to cold weather; she'd only ever lived in Texas, but the one-hundred-degree temperatures and high humidity were hard on her. It even made it difficult to keep her flowers alive. She tried, though. The flowerbed didn't look like the pretty ones in magazines, but it was alive. Barely.

Staring at the wilting blooms of a morning glory vine that had wound around one of her small bushes, she listened to Nathan and Natalie giggling as they played in the small sandbox next to her flower garden. Their laughter was the real reason she made the effort to come out. She'd try for them because she never wanted them to be like her. She wanted them to be what she would not be.

As she went to wipe the sweat from her forehead, a siren made her jump. They lived fairly close to the highway, so it was common to hear passing emergency vehicles, but this one sounded closer than that. Along with the first siren, more could be heard farther away.

Jane glanced around for a few seconds but went back to her garden. The morning glory called to her, and she reached out to touch one of its wilting petals. The heat was too much for the pretty flower. She glanced around and found a good size rock, and moved it next to the flower, giving it enough shade so it wouldn't wither away. "There. Maybe I can keep you alive."

A helicopter flying over the house ruined her accomplished moment, and she looked up, surprised to see seven military helicopters all going in the same direction. They were low, too. So low, in fact, she almost believed they might land in her backyard. It made the continuous blaring from the various sirens in the distance more alarming and had her heart rate spiking.

"Mommy, it's loud." Natalie came running to her side. "Why are there so many?"

The frightened look on her daughter's face made the situation seem worse than it should probably be, but Jane grew worried a manhunt might be the cause of the air searches. It was standard to search by air if a criminal was on the loose. That didn't explain the military aircraft, though.

Jane smiled anyway, hoping to calm Natalie. "There must be a bad accident, that's all. But get your toys; we should go in."

Not a second later, screams on their street ripped through the air. Jane's eyes widened because it was the kind of scream that made your heart race. A genuine, blood-curdling scream that only a person fearing for their life would be able to produce.

Something was most definitely wrong, but she kept calm so as not to scare her children. "Hurry. Let's go inside." She picked up toys and led them into the house.

The sensation of someone watching them had her peering over her shoulder. No one was there, but she still felt as though she wasn't quite alone. Strangely, this feeling didn't frighten her. In fact, she felt almost safe because of it until the screams rang out louder, only to be abruptly silenced.

Fear grew as she peeked through her windows. There was no sign of anyone or anything, but she locked her door before turning on the television to find out what was going on.

Austin, Texas, was a busy city, but they lived on the northern side of town where things were calmer. People screaming in the middle of the day as if they were being murdered, sirens, and military helicopters flying over her house—far from normal. Nor was it normal to find panicked reporters on the TV speedily reading from prompts in their hands.

Jane stepped closer to the television to listen.

"The virus initially believed to be a new strain of flu has now been confirmed by WHO to be a brand-new virus. The Zev-Virus, named after the first confirmed fatality, Zev Knight, has already spread across the nation and is ravaging Europe, Asia, Africa, and Australia.

"The CDC is working together with the World Health Organization and other health agencies in hopes of developing a vaccine. So far, all confirmed cases have been fatal."

Jane tightened her grip on the remote as the reporter continued, her voice shaking.

"As I mentioned earlier, health organizations have joined together to find a cure, but due to the short incubation period and transmission involving violent attacks, they are making slow progress. For now, they urge everyone to reduce or avoid contact with the public. They also warn to expect delays from authorities due to the influx of emergency calls coming in. If a family member or friend is showing symptoms of this virus, isolate them from all others in your home before contacting emergency services. Under no circumstances is it recommended you attempt to treat, transport, or remain in contact with anyone showing symptoms.

"Local law enforcement agencies are reporting an increase in the number of assaults resulting in injuries over the past two hours and have called all first responders into action. Attacks involve bites and scratches from those who appear to be suffering from this new illness."

The reporter wiped her forehead and coughed. "Let me go over the symptoms again: fever, fatigue, body aches, trouble breathing, coughing up blood, broken blood vessels in the eyes, and hostility. At this time, there is no indication that the virus is airborne as all confirmed cases have involved direct contact with infected individuals. We will keep you updated as more information is made available."

The screen flashed with a list of business, school, and government office closures before resuming the show that had been on.

"Are we gonna get sick?" Natalie asked.

Jane squatted and comforted her with a small hug. "No, we'll be okay. We'll just stay away from anyone who's sick, okay?"

✦✦✦

Jason was late. He got off at four, and it normally took him fifteen minutes to get home every day. If he was going to be late, he would text her. It was six, and he hadn't contacted her once.

The news had stopped coming on, making her anxiety a hundred times worse. The only thing running now was the Emergency Broadcast System. Jane couldn't stand the blaring noise it continued to make, so she'd put on a movie in all the rooms.

The last image she'd seen before the channels went off was police in riot gear, barricading the entrance of a hospital. There had been people attacking the officers, but it was hard to understand why the attackers were being prevented from getting medical care. She'd assumed it was due to the hospitals overflowing with patients, but then she watched several officers pushing back the mob as they swarmed a man carrying a bloody child while he yelled, "We're not bit!"

The newsfeed had cut back to the anchor she'd seen earlier in the day, and Jane watched in shock as the reporter fainted in the middle of her report. The feed had blacked out, and that station, along with other local and national stations, had gone off air.

The sudden whirring sound from the garage door sounded, causing Jane to jump up. She quickly ran to the door and saw Jason getting out of his truck.

"What's this?" she asked, stepping into the garage.

He held his finger up to his mouth and pulled the emergency lever to pull the garage down without using the automatic opener. Jane stood perfectly still, watching him carefully move around their car, then slide the manual lock over.

He breathed out and walked to the door he'd left open and picked up several grocery bags. She was surprised to see the seats filled with bags and items rolling on the floorboard.

He barely looked at her and kept loading his arms with bags. "Did you watch the news today?"

"Yes, I watched. It stopped coming on, though." She stepped closer to the truck. "You should have called. I kept texting you."

"I saw them," he said softly.

Jane studied his worried expression. He was sweaty and darting his eyes around the garage, not making eye contact with her. "What do you mean, them? Someone sick?"

"Well, yeah, I guess. But it's weird the way they acted. I've never seen anything like this. They were crazy. They kept—I don't know—biting and scratching everyone."

"Were you bitten?" She scanned his body.

"No," he said quickly, and she let out a breath. "People are going nuts. Police and ambulances are on every street. People are crashing into each other, running red lights—I saw someone steal another person's car when they were loading it with supplies. It's chaos!"

She didn't know what to say. He kept looking around their empty garage as if someone might jump out at any moment.

"It's almost like a zombie movie," he added suddenly.

She stayed quiet and waited for him to laugh. He didn't.

When he picked up the bags again, she considered everything he'd told her as well as his strange behavior. His theory actually made more sense than some flu, that was for sure. What sort of virus made people violent other than those you saw in zombie movies?

"What should we do?" She helped him with the bags. "Before the news went off, they said everyone should stay inside."

More sirens and helicopters sounded before Jason spoke. "The guys at work were talking about gathering their weapons and shit like that; I don't have any guns, so I figured supplies and food were the most important step. When I left work and realized all hell had broken loose, I stopped and got what I could. They were—" He shook his head and didn't finish.

She nodded and carried what she had picked up inside, and he followed her without saying anything else. When they entered the kitchen, barking from her dogs sent her into a panic.

"Crap, the dogs," she said, dropping what she had on the floor without caring if it broke.

She ran to the back door and looked out the window. Kuma and Rocky pawed at the door, displaying the same behavior they did whenever there was a thunderstorm. Usually, Jason didn't allow them inside, but she opened the door and led them to the playroom.

"Why are doggies inside?" Natalie asked as she passed her in the hall.

"Mommy wants to keep an eye on them. They're scared of the noise, that's all. Daddy's home. Go say hi."

Natalie needed no other prompting; she took off, hollering to welcome him home like she always did.

After Jane locked the dogs in the playroom, she returned to the kitchen. The kids had already eaten dinner, and she figured Jason had told them to go play before bed since they were in the living room.

She watched him as he stared at their children play. His silence irritated her, but she kept her frantic thoughts to herself and put the groceries away.

"There's a plate in the microwave," she told him.

When he didn't make any effort to get up, Jane went to the microwave for the cheeseburger and fries she'd made for him. She placed it in on the table and waited. He still didn't look up, but he did start eating.

As each minute passed, she grew more annoyed. How was he going to leave off mid-sentence during a time like this? Jason didn't like to be bothered, though, so she kept her mouth shut.

Only after she'd put everything away did she join him at the table. He didn't react. She wanted to scream at him but controlled herself and spoke in a calm voice. "What were you going to say earlier?"

He continued chewing his food in a daze, and her anger dissipated when she realized he was as much a nervous wreck as she was.

Horrified, but eager to hear him answer, she scooted closer and lowered her face so she could see his brown eyes. "What else did you see?"

The strain on his face made him appear much older than his twenty-eight years, but he finally answered her in a low whisper. "There was a little boy and girl in the parking lot. I heard them screaming." He lifted his hands to cover his face. "I thought they were screaming for their mom and dad, but they were screaming for their parents to stop hurting them." She moved back and stared at him with wide eyes. "The mom and dad were doing more than just attacking their kids. There was blood—so much blood—and their screams. They were—they were eating them."

Jane didn't realize she was hyperventilating at first. Too many images were rushing through her mind: the scene at the grocery store over the weekend, the scream, the sirens and helicopters, the fainting reporter—the man yelling that he and his child weren't bit.

A pulsing hum in her ears grew louder. For a second, she heard her panicked breaths before the hum mixed with the disturbing blare of a siren.

It wasn't a normal siren. It was a creepy, terror-instilling sound.

"What's that?" she asked, her breathing quickening.

Jason looked around. "It's the warning system for the city."

They kept growing louder in a high-pitched wail before fading, then high again. It reminded her of war movies when they were preparing for bombs to drop over towns, or when a tornado was close.

"Jane, breathe!"

She didn't know he was talking to her. There was so much pain in her chest.

For a tiny moment of awareness, she knew what was happening; she'd had too many panic attacks to not know—but it never stopped her from thinking she must be dying. "It hurts—I'm dying . . . D—"

"Dammit, Jane." Jason's face came into view. She didn't know she was lying on the kitchen floor now. "It's a panic attack. You're not dying."

She heard him, but only barely. The pulsing sound in her head continued to mix with the sirens as Jason's words kept coming back: they were eating them.

CHAPTER 3
DAVID

Yukon Territory, CANADA

The castle doors opened with a bang as a well-built male with black hair and vibrant sapphire eyes entered. His heavy footsteps echoed off the polished marble floors, and though the halls were lined with gilded portraits depicting ancient battles from legend and myth, so detailed you'd be a fool not to look at them, the man didn't bother.

After all, they weren't myths to him. They were history he was well aware of. History that this man had been a significant part of.

His name was David.

Several of the castle's occupants who had been talking in small groups halted their conversations, bowing their heads in David's direction. They always treated him like a god, both with fear and desire. A few women even smiled while they made obvious attempts to enhance their figures. The temptation was certainly enough to make the most devoted man stray, yet David made no acknowledgment of those around him. He never did.

Even with rumors about his sexuality and lack of interest in women did he bother with them. Despite his disinterest or how many times he refused their advances, women continued to throw themselves at him. It was hard not to. According to all who saw him, he was the most beautiful male of their kind.

His beauty didn't make him look soft. He oozed masculinity. With his chiseled features, a strong jaw, high cheekbones, straight nose, he stole your breath. His sapphire eyes glowed against his golden skin, and his smile melted your heart.

If you managed to draw your stare from his gorgeous face, you'd have the urge to run your fingers through his thick black hair, which, at the moment, lay messily over his forehead. He suddenly jerked his head to move that hair from his eyes and blissful sighs sounded from every female who watched.

At an impressive six-foot-five, he was pure muscle, and those muscles could be seen through his plain gray T-shirt. It fit tight across his wide back and arms. With every step, his leg muscles flexed and bunched under his black cargo pants.

"Perfect," they whispered as he passed. "Deadly."

Even though he looked to be in his mid to late twenties, something about him made most people wary of coming closer.

Out of all the stunning features on his face, the most distinct were his vibrant blue eyes, the faint glow illuminating his skin, and his slightly elongated canine teeth. Those particular markers warned the normal person that he was much more than a human man, and he was. He was something beautiful and frightening.

He and those he lived amongst went by many names. They were legends, heroes. Gods. Beautiful, strong, and brave beings who traveled the world, fighting evil and aiding mankind. But other labels followed them as well: demon, cursed, vampire. Monster.

They were the myths our world hid in the back of our minds, and when spoken about, were mocked and called impossible. They were the forgotten truths to our story as men and children of God. They were the Immortals.

Once David crossed the grand hall, he passed two men standing guard outside the door without a word and entered the next room.

✦✦✦

David looked around the circular room briefly and nodded to the twelve others already seated at the round table.

"Arthur," said David, greeting the man to his left.

"Welcome back, brother. News?" Arthur asked.

David glanced at the empty chair beside him but looked back to his brother-in-law. "The Greeks are gathering to divide into groups. Scouts are locating key areas to start the extermination. They are going to select cities with high concentration of infected mortals to start with and work outward."

"And Lance?" Arthur asked in a slightly more agitated tone.

Shaking his head, David answered, "No one can find him."

"Anything about the risks to our kind?" asked Gawain in his usual, less than serious manner.

"No," said David, ignoring Arthur's anger. "There was a report Sin decided to attack a horde of the infected by himself."

"And?" Gawain asked with a laugh. "What happened to the reckless devil?"

David eyed his best friend, who also happened to be second in command of his personal team, and smirked. "What usually happens when Sin gets off his ass: a naked, victorious warrior walked out unscathed."

"I think we will work our way south, rather than select cities," Arthur said, bringing David and the other's attention back to him. "Best if we concentrate on pushing them back."

"The Norse are planning that as well," David said. "But they have no concern for the rest of the world, merely their own feeding grounds."

Gawain let out a sharp laugh. "That figures."

"And the Hounds, what of them?" asked Tristan.

"No word on the Hounds yet. And besides the rumor about Sin, nothing from Nyc and his wolves," David answered. "No one has heard from them in months. I believe I was the last to see them."

Arthur stood, causing all conversation to halt. "We set out as soon as we can gather our supplies. I will not wait around to discuss what others are planning. Our duty to the mortals will not be ignored. First, we secure Canada. The guards will ensure the kingdom's continued safety. Canada alone will provide adequate feeding for those here. Gwen will speak for me while we are gone and relay news from our allies."

"David, what about the South? Any word on what they are doing?" Gawain asked.

"They do not seem to have any plans to work against the plague," he said. "They are frantic in their feeding habits, and there are rumors of rogues doing the same. They are not making attempts at hiding their identities anymore."

Uproar erupted around the table. "Stupid fools," Gawain bellowed as he slammed his fist on the table. His laid back personality was easily shed to display the fierce warrior he was underneath.

"We will deal with them later." Arthur quickly quieted his men. "Our mission is to eliminate the plague. Should we come across any rogues, they will suffer God's law."

David's lips twitched when Gawain returned to his previous easygoing state, leaning back in his chair and folding his arms behind his head, a wide grin taking the place of the angry scowl he'd worn moments ago.

"Kay, see that the plane is prepared," said Arthur, looking at his adoptive brother briefly. Kay nodded, and Arthur made eye contact with each of them. "Gather your supplies and bid your wives farewell. We leave at once and will not return until the threat to the mortals is eliminated. Bors, make sure we are stocked with blood to get us through the first month. We will not feed publicly." He didn't bother saying goodbye and left the room with unbelievable speed.

The rest stood. Some left at the same inhuman speed as Arthur while a few spoke quietly and exited at a more human pace.

Gawain walked over to David and slapped him on the back. "Bidding anyone farewell, David?"

"You know the answer to that by now." David shook his head. "Quit worrying about me, will you? Go see your wife."

David never took what Gawain said on the subject regarding his lack of female companionship to heart. Apart from Arthur and David's sister, Guinevere, Gawain was the only friend who knew of his sacrifice. They all understood that when the time was right, he would be granted the woman of his dreams, the other half of his heart, and at the same time, fulfill his destiny.

"Come on, David," said Gareth, Gawain's younger brother as well as the third and final member of David's personal team. "Surely one of them is worth consideration after all these centuries."

They chuckled, but David stayed quiet as he continued walking to the door. He knew his friends were teasing, but it was a constant reminder of how alone he truly was.

"He has his standards, brother," Gawain spoke up. "None have proven worthy of a second glance from our David. Let's get ready, shall we?"

Gawain winked at David and playfully shoved Gareth on the back.

David nodded to him, relieved to be done with the conversation and followed them out of the round room. He wasted no time and ran upstairs to his quarters.

After entering his room, he went to his closet and selected his necessary clothing items, then several handguns, a rifle, and ammunition for both before examining a large, ornate sword. Even though it was a much older weapon, it remained his favorite, and if using a gun could be avoided, he did so.

David quickly placed everything in his bag. He wanted to see his sister before leaving, but a delicate knock on his door made him forget all about stopping to see her. All he could wish for now was to be on the plane, a thousand miles away.

Several impolite words came to his mind, but he held back as he reminded himself that, in just a few short moments, he would escape the daily pressures he encountered at the castle.

He opened his door. "Hello, Melody."

The breathtaking immortal smiled up at him. Her wavy, blonde hair hung to her slim waist. She could have any man she wanted. But not him.

She peered at him with green eyes as her bell-like voice and the golden glow of her skin sparkled. Most were enchanted by her sweet voice, but David couldn't stand to hear her talk.

"Hello, David." Melody smiled. "They say you are setting out on a mission for the mortals?"

"Yes. We are leaving as soon as we get everyone prepared." He quickly dismissed her presence and returned to the bed for his bag. When he turned to leave, he almost growled as he realized she'd let herself into his room.

Melody reached out to take his free hand, but he only looked at it before looking back at her face. She withdrew quickly, masking the hurt in her eyes, but he caught it.

Often, David pitied the women who he ignored, but she was one of the many females who refused to take no for an answer. Unlike the hopeless romantics who desired his heart, Melody was only after power and status. And everyone knew she hoped David would claim her as his Other.

"I haven't time to entertain you, Melody."

She stuck out her chin. "I merely came to inform you that you have nothing to worry about. I will wait for you, as always."

With a frustrated sigh, he gave her a firm look. "I have told you before, there is nothing for you here. I urge you to find another. I do not want you to hold on to any false hope. My decision will not change."

Anger burned in her eyes while her pride took yet another blow of rejection. In a bold attempt to stare him down, her eyes swirled with varying shades of green. He couldn't believe she was trying this shit on him. Her ability to manipulate and control others allowed her to get whatever she wanted, but her power never worked on him.

To show her that her attempts were futile, he returned her stare and let his eyes change from their hypnotizing sapphire color to the palest glacier-blue, reflecting his cold feelings for her.

With a huff, she turned, leaving without another word.

He knew she wasn't finished and wouldn't put it past her to return. So, silently bidding his lonely room farewell, he left to meet the others for their departure.

They all lived to fight, but he knew his comrades enjoyed being home. He, however, welcomed the bloodshed he was about to encounter. He knew one day he would find the woman he was told about during his creation, but for now, he needed to embrace what he was made for.

Battle.

CHAPTER 4
MONSTERS & SWEET DREAMS

"Jane, you can't pack this shit," Jason said, holding up Nathan's dinosaurs.

She pulled the toys from his hand. "He needs them."

Jason sighed and continued digging through the bag she'd packed, then held up two DVDs. "Really?"

Jane glanced over and saw Nathan and Natalie's favorite movies. "They like them."

"Jane," he said, tossing them on the floor next to her. She grabbed them and put them on her lap as he ranted. "You are supposed to pack stuff we need in case we have to run. Toys and movies are not going to help us survive."

Her eyes watered as she stared at the plastic dinosaur in her hands. "I just want them to be happy. If we need to leave, that's it. They won't have anything left. And Nathan will have a hard time with everything if he's taken away from what he knows."

"I know, but we have to think about surviving."

"I'm sorry." She wiped her tears and more fell as she listened to him groan because she was once again crying. She'd been crying for two days since the plague had broken out. They'd boarded up all their windows and doors as they listened to gunfire and screams, even explosions, and she'd broken down each time, afraid the infected people would break down their door.

"I'm sorry," she repeated. "I don't know what you expect me to do. I'm trying to pick what I know makes them happy. If it's such a big deal, I'll take my stuff out and put their toys in my bag."

He stared at her like she was a moron. "Instead of food and supplies, you'd rather take toys and movies?"

"Yes," she snapped, even as he gave her a look that made her feel pathetic.

"Get it together, Jane. You're acting like a baby, and they need you to think about them. Food, clothes, medicine–that's what is going to help them. Not this!" He held up another movie. "Do you really think if we have to leave here that we'll be able to play these?"

Jane looked up. "I got the portable player out."

He looked at her like she'd lost her mind. "Where did you put it?" She didn't answer him, and he dug into the bag until he found it. "Dammit, Jane. I'm not carrying this. Be an adult for once." He stood and dropped the portable DVD player on her lap before stomping away with his bag.

She cried and double-checked to make sure the player was intact. It was, and she placed the movies on it before getting her backpack. She pulled out most of her clothes, medicine, and toiletries, then added the toys and movies. There was a little room to re-add a few things, so she started to put her medicine and toiletries but stopped when she realized she'd also pulled out a photo album.

More tears clouded her vision, but she picked up the album. She flipped it open and first saw a picture of her and Wendy, then one of her and Jason, then one of her holding the babies when they'd just been born. Closing it up, Jane looked back at her bag, then removed her toiletries and replaced them with the album.

"Mommy?"

Jane zipped her bag shut and turned to see Natalie watching her. "What's up, baby?"

"Why are you crying?" Natalie asked.

She smiled sadly. "I just have a headache. I'm okay."

"Oh. Will you come help Nathan sleep? He doesn't like having our beds in the living room."

Jane nodded and got up. "Yep. Let's go help him sleep." She held out her hand and went to the living room to see Nathan frantically looking around the bed.

Natalie let go of her hand and ran to jump on her mattress they'd placed there as Nathan sat up.

"Di-saur," he said, pointing to her bag.

"Oh!" Jane knelt on the mattress next to him and opened her bag. She pulled out his favorite brachiosaurus and handed it to him. He clutched it to his chest and lay back down.

Jane sighed and looked over to see Jason standing by the living room entrance. He watched her for a moment before walking away.

Nathan's fingers touched her hand, and he started scratching her skin. He always did this when he was a baby. He often opened her skin on her arms, but she let him because it was just something that he did to fall asleep.

Lying down beside him, she put her arm over his chest and watched as he kept scratching her forearm with his eyes closed.

She needed to sleep, but she couldn't. Instead, she stared at his other hand clutching his toy. Jason may not realize how much their son needed these toys, but she knew how hard it would be on Nathan without them.

Jane closed her eyes. It had been two days since they'd boarded up their windows and doors. Two days since the news had gone off the air. Two days since she'd had her last panic attack. Two days since she'd felt any sort of peace.

She had tried calling Wendy's husband and mother, but there was no answer. All grim possibilities played through her mind as she worried over her friend's children. She wondered if they'd made it somewhere safe, then she began to reflect on how little she'd done for them since Wendy's death.

Now, they were likely dead, and she'd only gone and seen them once since Wendy passed. And that was all because it had been too hard to learn her best friend's husband had already moved on. That didn't mean that the children had, though, and Jane should have sucked it up to at least check on them from time to time.

"I'm such a terrible friend," she whispered, trying her hardest to not disturb Nathan as she cried. She hadn't been there for them, and she was probably going to fail her own children, too. Jane bit her lip to keep herself from making noise. She hated being like this.

As her body began to tremble, a faint tingle slid across her mouth, and she sighed before slowly releasing her lip from her bite. Her breath came easier, and she rolled on her side to cuddle with Nathan who still dug his fingernails into her arm. The tingling feeling on her lips spread to her face, then down her spine until most of her back felt a strange warmth that seemed to dance between fire and ice.

Her trembling eased and her chest stopped aching from her cries as the strange sensation moved down her arm to where Nathan still scratched. He abruptly stopped, and the stinging cuts left by his fingernails warmed.

Jane hugged her son, feeling an increased pressure around her, then drifted off to sleep.

✦✦✦

Three loud gunshots woke Jane from her peaceful nap. She tensed, looking around the darkened room before noticing Jason peeking out the cracks of one of the windows.

She carefully slipped out of Nathan's grip, grip, covering him with the blanket before going to Jason. "What's happening?" she asked him as her heartrate sped up as shouts and cries grew louder.

"I think the truck ran out of gas or something. I'm not sure," Jason muttered with his eyes glued to the scene out on the street.

Though hesitant, Jane mustered the courage to look. The scene terrified her. Their quiet neighborhood had become a war zone, and even more so when she noticed an Army Humvee stalled across from their house.

Several more shots went off, and Jane's heart pounded as she watched two soldiers come into view. One struggled to lift an unconscious comrade from the ground, while the second offered cover fire.

With a shout, the assisting soldier dropped the now conscious, snarling man to the ground. Fear was in his pain-filled eyes as he backed away from his wild friend. He clutched his neck tightly and disappeared from her view as he stumbled away. Jane knew it was too late for him. He was infected.

The scream had distracted the other soldier from the swarming, infected mass for just a second. An infected woman grabbed his arm and bit down to the bone.

He cried out as he tried to free himself, but despite being larger than the woman, he couldn't get out of her grasp. So he aimed point blank at her forehead and fired. She fell to the ground, finally dead, but the damage was done. He was also infected now. But unlike his friend, he fell to the ground as two other infected bit and began ripping him apart.

His bloodcurdling screams caused Jane's eyes to widen in horror, but for some reason she suddenly dropped her gaze to the bag lying on the street.

Staring at it in a trance, she felt her racing heart suddenly steady. Warmth radiated out from her chest all through her body, and she let out a slow breath, still hearing the screams and gunshots but not affected at all.

Her fingers twitched, and she turned her head as she felt drawn to go down the hall. Every bit of fear and sadness that had been tearing her apart vanished as the urge to be something greater settled in her mind.

She stopped thinking about how bad her life had been—how horrible her relationship was with Jason, how much she feared failing her children—and a new thought consumed her: what if I don't fail?

A confident and powerful feeling surged through her. She turned and walked away from the window, and only when she had a window from one of their back bedrooms pushed open, did she realize she was leaving her house.

As awareness touched her mind, she easily shrugged away the fear and climbed out the window, falling to the grass more gracefully than she normally would have thought possible. She looked around and shut the window before walking away.

Once she neared the edge of the house, she heard Jason whispering for her to get back. She glanced over her shoulder and didn't feel an ounce of emotion as she stared into his brown eyes. Nothing. She turned forward again and rounded corner of the house.

The bag on the street came to mind, and she nodded to herself: get the bag. She didn't know what was in it, but she knew she had to get it.

Peeking out behind a trash can, Jane watched the attack taking place. This was the second time she'd seen an infected crowd this size. There were too many to count, and they were busy gorging themselves on the fallen soldier's remains.

The soldier, originally unconscious, lifted his head, snarling with the blood of his companion dripping down his face.

Jane didn't react to the gruesome scene and continued focusing on the bag. She stayed low, not paying attention to the other bodies or trash strewn across her yard and the street, and got behind a truck that was only ten feet from the bag she needed.

The grunts, crunching of bone, and tearing of flesh did little to deter her from her task. She quickly ran out and knelt to look at the bag that had held all her attention.

It was partially zipped, but she could see weapons and ammunition inside. There was even an M-16 right beside it, which she only knew its name because of war movies she enjoyed watching, and she figured whoever had been carrying the bag, had dropped everything.

She wasted no time hoisting all of it onto her shoulder. A handgun on the ground caught her attention as she adjusted her hold, and she grabbed that one, too.

The hungry groans grew louder as their meal disappeared into their stomachs, and Jane knew time had run out.

Glancing up, she realized she'd been discovered. The infected people snarled and stumbled toward her. Returning home was out of the question now. So, she turned and sprinted in the opposite direction.

They followed.

Jane wasn't in great shape, but she ran fast without looking back. She would have kept going, but a groan made her look around for the source. There, about a hundred yards ahead of her, she spotted the soldier who'd been bitten in the neck. He was lying on the ground but still alive, though the amount of blood pooled around him said he wouldn't be much longer. He'd be one of them soon. A zombie.

She came to a stop beside him and finally looked behind her. The horde was getting closer, but she turned back to the soldier.

Blood seeped from his mouth and the gaping hole that had torn his neck open. His eyes, wide in fear, locked onto hers, and his gasps for breath increased.

Jane held his teary-eyed stare while he struggled to form words and tilted her head, not filled with any concern over his fate.

"Kill me," he said. She stared at him silently, turning once again to the ever closer mob of infected people. "Please," he begged as tears fell from his brown eyes. "Don't let them eat me." The whites had already started to turn red.

Jane lifted the gun. The brave soldier gave a slight nod as a single tear rolled down her cheek, and she squeezed the trigger.

The shot rang out louder than any of the previous shots she had heard since the beginning of the outbreak, but she lowered her arm and continued her jog down the deserted street.

After covering one more block, she knew she'd finally lost the crowd and doubled back toward her home. She stopped by the neighbor's fence to ensure the coast was clear before she made the final run to safety.

When she looked down at her feet, it was immediately clear she was standing above Max, her neighbor's dog. He was dead; the lower half of his body was missing, leaving nothing but dried up blood and bits of flesh covered in flies and maggots. She scrunched up her nose in disgust and proceeded across the yard to the bedroom window she had crawled out of earlier and tapped it lightly.

Jason must've been waiting because the window opened immediately.

After she managed to squeeze through, she shoved the bag at him. "There are your necessary items."

Jason took it but looked at her with a confused and angry expression, but Jane was too full of her adrenalin rush to care about his irritation with her, so she took the bag from his hands and brushed past him.

She stopped by the living room and stared at her children who still slept soundly. Her gaze lingered on the dinosaur toy in Nathan's hand, and she smiled as a proud feeling filled her.

"Jane." Jason grabbed her forearm roughly, spinning her around to face him. "Are you crazy?"

"You already know I am." She smirked and watched his eyes widen. "You remind me every time you look at me."

He let her arm go, and she walked to the kitchen.

She heard him following her, but she was ready for a fight. She looked forward to it.

"What are you talking about?" He stood on the opposite side of the table as she placed the bag down and opened it up.

She pulled out a few clips, a knife of some sort, a med-kit, and started to organize the rest of her haul. "What do you mean?" she asked, holding up another gun. "Do you want this one? It's an M9."

He stared at her before snatching it out of her hand. "How do you know what this is called? And answer my fucking question—what do you mean I remind you you're crazy?"

Jane kept going through the bag. "I recognize them from the movies." She slid the one she used to kill the soldier with into the waist of her jeans. "And I meant what I said—you look at me like I'm crazy and pathetic. It's fine. At least you feel something when you look at me."

"I do not look at you like that," he retorted defensively. "You're acting crazy now, though. Don't pull this shit again. And quit talking like this. I don't need to deal with your dramatics."

She calmly lifted her gaze to meet his. "My dramatics?"

"Yes." He jabbed his finger at a boarded up window. "I told you to pack survival items, and you get your feelings hurt and go run off. You're not a soldier, Jane. You could have gotten killed, or worse, made them come in here to get the kids."

"I ran away from the house so they would go away because I wanted the bag."

"You wanted the bag?" He let out a bitter laugh. "What the hell has gotten into you? Do you even care what happens to you?"

"No," she said and returned to looking at everything, then added, "But I knew I would be fine."

"What?" He took the knife out of her hand and tossed it on the table. "You knew you'd be fine?"

She nodded. "I can't explain it. I just knew I needed to get the bag."

Jason shook his head in disbelief. "You just had to get the bag?"

"Yes."

He glared at her. "Don't do it again."

"What? Why?"

"Just don't do it again. We need to stay together. I can't have you running off so you can pretend you're a warrior and getting hurt. This isn't like the movies or games you always want to fight in. When are you going to grow up and be responsible? This isn't some game! You can die and put our children in danger."

Her mouth fell open, but she quickly snapped it shut. "Don't tell me what to do. You wanted me to pack stuff that would keep us alive. Well, I got them. We're safer now. We can protect the kids because I ran out there like a warrior and got weapons. Take what you want, but I'm keeping the rifle and M9."

Jason sighed. "Did you take your medicine?"

Jane tensed and stared at him for a good thirty seconds. "Yes, I took my pills."

"Are you sure? You're acting like you used to. One moment you're crying and staring off at nothing, the next you have no fear and act like you don't have a care in the world. Why can't you just be—" He shook his head.

"Normal?" She supplied for him. "I'm not normal, Jason. I can't be better just because you want me to be."

He looked her in the eye. "I just want you to be level headed and not always jumping from one extreme to the next. I can't deal with you when I have to worry about everything else. I have to keep the kids safe. Just get it together. Get over your problems for once, but don't be stupid. You seemed to be doing better. I just don't get it."

"I'm never better," she said, feeling her eyes prick as the adrenaline pumping through her veins faded. "But for a tiny moment, I believed I wouldn't fail." She rubbed her tears when she realized she was crying but continued staring at him. His brown eyes suddenly reminded her of the soldier she killed, and she felt terrible. She hadn't failed, but she no longer felt great about succeeding. She had killed a man and felt nothing.

Jason was right. She was one extreme or another. She was either an emotional mess or a monster.

"Just make sure you take your pills," he said, looking back on the table. "And no more believing you're a soldier when we both know you're not. You're a mother, act like it. Now, go so I can figure out how to keep the kids from getting hurt with all this."

Jane turned away but snatched the M16 and ignored him as he told her to bring it back.

Her eyes and throat burned as she went back into the living room. Jason always managed to make her feel so bad about herself, but he was always right, and that's what killed her. She wasn't a warrior or anything special. She was a woman who had to take pills to control her moods. She had so many more they'd given her for other things, but she had stopped taking those because they made her feel how she felt right now: out of control. Like she was suffocating as the world fell to ruins around her.

She stood there, staring at nothing as Jason's words, all his words throughout the years, kept bombarding her mind. She kept seeing that look from him. It was the look she'd seen from others, too, but having him do it to her–

"Mommy?" Natalie's soft voice called.

Jane snapped out of her daze and put her weapons down on the floor. She crawled on the bed next to her daughter. "Go back to sleep."

"Where did those come from?" Natalie pointed to the guns. "Are those toys?"

"They're not toys. Don't touch them. But I found them so we can be safe from the sick people."

Natalie looked at the guns before smiling. "Good job, Mommy."

Jane smiled softly and wrapped her arms around her. "Thanks, baby. Go to sleep now."

Natalie rolled on her side as Jane struggled to accept her daughter's praise before crying herself to sleep.

Despite Jason's words getting to her, for the first time in years, she didn't have a single nightmare. There were no monsters, or fear of failing as she fell into a deeper sleep. That night she dreamt of a dark figure holding her. Then the mysterious being wiped her tears and placed a kiss on her lips. The dark figure, who she knew was male, didn't speak, but if he had, she somehow knew what he would say: *Sweet dreams . . . Sweet Jane.*

CHAPTER 5

BITTERSWEET

David awoke with a start. He sat up, scanning the C-17 plane he was aboard before glancing at his chest. There wasn't anything visible, but he felt a definite tug, as if an invisible rope had knotted around his heart and urged him to come to . . . something.

It did not frighten him, but it certainly had his complete attention. He brushed his fingers across his chest as if something would fall away, but there was nothing there. There was no pain either, but it made him restless, antsy. He was so absorbed in this foreign sensation, he didn't even take notice Gawain had taken a seat next to him.

"You feel it as well?" Gawain asked, staring at his own chest.

"What is it?" he asked, rubbing at the center of the pulling sensation. The more time passed, the more restless he felt.

"I do not know," Gawain muttered. "It doesn't hurt?"

"No, you?"

Gawain shook his head. "Just anxious. It looks like we are not the only ones." He nodded toward their waking comrades.

They wore confused expressions as many inspected their chests.

Arthur stood and walked toward where David and Gawain sat. "When did it start?"

Gawain answered. "Ten minutes ago. I only woke because David was tossing in his sleep. That's when I felt it in my chest."

Arthur nodded. "Was anyone else restless?"

"No," said Gawain. "Only David."

They all turned to David, and Arthur studied him before he turned to the others. "Knights," he said. "We are nearing Austin, Texas, where the concentration of the infected humans is significantly higher. We have no clue as to why, but it increases daily.

"In one hour, we jump. We will clear a perimeter before setting up base. David, Gawain, Gareth: you will scout ahead to locate any abnormalities."

David and Gawain exchanged a look, both understanding this meant locate the source of the disturbance, and either destroy or protect it.

"Tristan, Geraint, and Bors," Arthur said, "will go north after them and obtain a landing zone for Lucan and Dagonet to bring in supplies and set up camp."

Tristan nodded and left with his team.

Arthur continued issuing orders. "Lamorak, you will take Percivale, Gaheris, and Galahad to clear the power and water facilities. Lucan has a map for you. Bed, Kay, and I will do a perimeter sweep before making our way to camp.

"Stay sharp. I do not know what is going on down there, but we could be up against something we haven't come across yet. I don't want any of you brushing this off. Watch each other's backs. We are approaching midnight, so prepare yourselves. I want base set up before dawn."

Arthur dismissed the others before he approached David. He lowered his voice enough that even with their heightened sense of hearing the others wouldn't make out anything more than murmuring. "What do you think?"

"I'm not sure," David said. "I do not believe it's bad, though. It seems to be calling to me."

"I know what you mean." Arthur placed his hand on David's shoulder. "Just don't get your hopes up, all right?"

"Of course."

"Good, be careful now." Arthur smiled and began to walk away, adding over his shoulder, "Gwen will have my ass if something happens to you."

David felt Gawain's gaze. He knew why his friend was worried. No one wanted him to be disappointed that yet again he would not find her, but David would never lose faith in finding his love. The wait was agonizing, but that didn't matter. He would find her, and she would be everything. She already was.

There were so many times that he realized he was in love with a woman he had yet to meet. David smiled to himself as he imagined the eyes he often dreamt of. They were never perfectly clear, but he knew he'd recognize them the moment he saw them.

"All right," said Arthur. "We are dropping on the northern edge of the city. Once we've established a base camp, we will work our way out. The way things are looking, we may not have to move out far; the infected are all moving in this direction."

The cargo doors opened slowly, causing the violent winds to whip around them. The midnight Texas sky, free of clouds, greeted them. The lack of city lights left a blanket of sparkling stars scattered across its dark canvas. The silver moon was nearly full, providing a clear view of the streets below them. It was a breathtaking sight for any who could view the heavens. Unfortunately, the horror on the ground removed any wonderment.

"Tristan, your team is up," said Arthur.

Tristan's team stepped up, securing their swords and MK12 rifles. They adjusted their black masks, which left only their glowing eyes visible, and with only a nod from Tristan, they jumped from the open cargo door.

No parachutes were needed as they executed a drop from over five-hundred feet. They were certainly able to receive injuries, but this was a skill they had all perfected. Besides, their abilities mitigated any injuries they might receive from the fall.

David walked forward with Gawain and Gareth. He took one last look at Arthur and then jumped with his team.

✦✦✦

A cat cried out from behind a stalled car in the middle of the unlit street. The light breeze made the humidity more tolerable, but the deserted road was far too dark and eerie for anyone to enjoy the slight coolness that darkness brought with it.

Vehicles had been abandoned in and around the road, some still stuck in the collisions that had forced their occupants to abandon them. Sadly, some of those vehicles contained their rotting passengers, or what was left of them.

With no warning, three thunderous cracks echoed through the block, and Tristan's team, all dressed in black, rose quickly from their crouched positions, aiming their rifles outward, sweeping left and right for any threats.

One hundred yards behind them, three more claps of thunder greeted the quiet streets.

David rose and took in his surroundings as Tristan signaled the all-clear. David's team continued their sweep and, once satisfied, nodded to him. He pointed north where he felt most drawn to go.

Gawain and Gareth didn't question him and passed Tristan's team without a word. They proceeded swiftly across the streets, finding nothing but emptiness. There were no visible signs of life. Lights were off, cars were still. Only the insects called out, oblivious to the horror around them.

Though they all had enhanced senses, they couldn't hear *everything*. Still, a human's heartbeat rarely failed to elude them.

David listened to the steady beating of a few hearts as he ran. There weren't many, but none of them interested him. He only wanted to find whatever, or whoever, was calling to him.

The distinct snarls of infected humans had David coming to an abrupt halt. Gawain and Gareth stopped with him and searched their surroundings for signs of a threat, and that's when he saw them.

Two hundred yards ahead, there were at least fifty decaying, infected humans surrounding a small SUV. They grunted, growing impatient as their meal waited inside, weeping for her life. Growls and the sounds of cracking glass hinted that they wouldn't have to wait much longer.

David nodded to Gawain.

Gawain lifted his hand to his earpiece. "Arthur, we are one mile north of the LZ and will engage a mass with a count of fifty."

"Proceed. Notify me when you are ready to move on," was Arthur's brief reply.

"Let's keep it quiet," said David. "I don't want to alert any more inf—"

"Zombies," said Gawain, chuckling. "Just call them zombies, David."

David ignored him. "I want to keep moving. The source of the pull is close."

Gawain nodded. "Next time you will call them zombies."

Gareth chuckled and armed himself with his sword.

David put his rifle away and exchanged it for his sword, as well. "Try to keep your speed under control. The mortal does not need to be more frightened than she is now."

They nodded and approached the vehicle.

The smell of rotting flesh hit his nostrils, but he was used to it. The plague had been going for three months now, and most of the animated corpses were falling apart.

David struck first and left three headless bodies in his wake before moving on. His movements were swift and precise—only dismembering, fatal strikes were given. He had killed so many infected humans over the past three months; there was hardly anything enjoyable about the nonexistent fight.

A young teen grabbed hold of his free arm while he was preoccupied with beheading two others. When he looked down at the creature clawing his arm, he noticed it was a boy, maybe around the age of fifteen. He was missing part of his left arm and had a sizable chunk of flesh removed from his shoulder.

David released himself from the boy's grip and grabbed him by the throat. Rearing back with his right hand, holding his sword, he punched the boy's face, instantly caving in his skull and nearly decapitating him in the process.

He let go of the boy's body and let it fall to the ground. The boy was wearing a football jersey. The front read Panthers, and as the boy was knocked aside by another man, David noticed the name *Gonzalez* emblazoned on the back. It was a brief reminder to him that these were once people. They'd gone to school and had friends, but none of that mattered anymore. They were monsters now, just like him.

David continued without giving any further thought to the lives these creatures had once had. His haste was not a result of his lack of sport in this battle. It was from the pull in his chest growing more intense. Like a powerful magnet in the distance, it demanded he come to it. There was no choice for him but to obey.

Gawain matched his kills as the bodies dropped to the cooling pavement, but it was Gareth who made it to the vehicle first. Once he got there, the undead's interest was clear: a young girl, no older than thirteen, was huddled on the floor of the back seat with her hands pressed firmly to her ears as she cried.

Gareth turned his attention to their targets and proceeded to remove limb after limb as they reached out toward him. He was far too quick—not a single finger was laid on him. Whereas the others only took killing blows, he seemed to enjoy creating a mess out of them. His clothing was decorated in bits of bloody gore that ranged from fresh and healthy muscle to foul, rotting flesh.

David shook his head as Gawain approached his younger brother.

Gawain pointed his sword at Gareth's head in a casual manner, and his eyes twinkled with amusement as he shook the blood and guts off his sword—right onto his brother's face. "Can't you be a little more mature?"

"And you say I am the immature one," Gareth said, flicking the rotting meat from his mask.

David grew impatient with them. "Check on the girl and let's go." The tugging sensation seemed to be frantically pulling at him now.

"All right, I'm going." Gareth approached the SUV and ripped the door from its hinges.

Her ear-splitting scream rang out, and Gareth quickly clapped his hand over the young girl's mouth. Her strawberry-blonde hair was greasy and tangled. Dried blood stained her hair and face.

"Dammit, Gareth," Gawain hissed.

"Sweetheart, we are not going to hurt you," Gareth told the girl. "I need you to be quiet. Can you do that for me?"

David glanced around before turning back to see Gareth's eyes swirling as he used his extra abilities to hypnotize her.

She nodded.

"Good girl. Now do you have somewhere to go?" His tone was soothing, and his presence clearly comforted the once hysterical teen. She still appeared incapable of forming words, though.

Growing frustrated with how long this was taking, David was about to cut in, but he stayed quiet as he watched Gareth's eyes swirl into a misty jade color.

The girl nodded.

"Is it close?" Gareth asked. "Can you get there quickly?"

Gareth removed his hand from her mouth and let his eyes return to their normal, forest-green color.

"Y-yes," she stuttered. "I was trying to go across the street. My uncle lives there." She pointed to a two-story house.

David listened carefully and heard two healthy heartbeats coming from within the house.

Gareth released her. "I will walk you to your uncle. Let's hurry." He helped her out of the destroyed vehicle and led her to the house.

"It's stronger," Gawain told David.

"I know," David said, scanning the street as he listened to a man thanking Gareth. "It feels stressed. It's moving, I think."

Gawain nodded and they both looked in the same direction. "Yes, it's definitely on the move."

Gareth ran back. "It's moving."

"We know," David said with his gaze aimed down the street.

Gawain smacked Gareth across the back of his head once he was close enough. "Try to be more cautious. You cannot just go ripping doors off cars and not expect to frighten a mortal. We might as well have shown her your fangs!"

"Gawain, enough." David said roughly. "Let's go."

With a roll of his eyes, Gawain shoved his brother, who was rubbing the back of his head.

David ignored their playful behavior and began to run at a slower pace. He felt a protective urge encouraging him to hurry, but it still moved, making him unsure which path he should take.

"We're moving on, Arthur," Gawain muttered into his earpiece. "The source of the anomaly is on the move."

"Affirmative," Arthur's voice came through his communication piece. "David?"

"It's not threatening," he replied. "We'll report when we find it."

"Affirmative."

David tuned out the others and concentrated on the force calling to him. He took a right, noting this neighborhood had more bodies than any of the other streets they'd traveled on.

A house was still smoldering, leaving only bits of the frame and fireplace. Clothing and other personal belongings were scattered throughout yards, along with decaying and bloated bodies that the Texas sun had caused to swell. Some remained more intact than others, enough to the point you could at least identify whether they had been male or female. Dozens of vacant cars lined the streets, most painted in blood with shattered windows, which left no doubt as to what had happened to their occupants.

Rapid footsteps suddenly broke the silence. The abrupt sign of life had him coming to a halt.

Gawain and Gareth stopped, flanking him, as all of them raised their rifles. David grew so antsy with anticipation; he could hardly keep himself stationary.

The runner was small, as evident by their light footfalls, but the all too familiar stumbling and scraping sounds that followed behind had him wary.

They prepared to open fire, but a shot rang out. It was followed by four more rounds, none of which belonged to any of them, but they didn't have to wait long to discover who they did belong to.

Rounding the corner and bursting through twenty infected humans, a petite female emerged.

David fired at the undead closest to her first, Gawain and Gareth taking aim at the others. The sounds of flesh smacked the concrete. They only stopped when the last body fell.

Hazel. David lowered his weapon in a daze as he stared into the enchanting hazel eyes looking back at him. He knew those eyes.

She was his angel, and his heart was no longer his own.

The woman suddenly raised her gun and aimed at him. They were so stunned, none of them reacted as she squeezed the trigger.

A grunt and the sound of a body smacking the concrete immediately followed her shot.

David turned his head and found her victim on the ground. She hadn't been aiming at him. In fact, she was *saving* him from an infected human. There, face down on the cement, was an overweight male whose skin had a slimy, gray pallor. She'd delivered a perfect kill shot, right between his eyes.

The incessant tugging in his heart grew stronger than ever, and David tore his shocked gaze from the disgusting blob that had once been a man and found the woman disappearing into the darkness.

His enhanced eyesight enabled him to still see her clearly, so he admired her petite but curvy frame as she ran back the way she'd come. Her long, dark hair blew in the wind, and he sniffed, picking up her sweet scent.

"David," Gawain whispered.

He turned from the wonderful view ahead of him and responded. "What?" His voice sounded strange to him. This had to be a dream.

"Congratulations." Gawain's eyes shone and crinkled as he smiled, happy for David, who realized he was smiling like a fool. "Shall we go see where she lives?" Gawain suggested and took off after the mystery girl.

David shook himself out of his daze and turned to Gareth. "What?"

"Oh, nothing." Gareth laughed before taking off as well.

✦✦✦

They caught up to Gawain in a matter of minutes since David no longer cared to keep up their human façade if that meant taking longer to find her. As he and Gareth approached Gawain, they realized he was gazing at a single-story house.

David noticed a small sandbox that held some battered toys as well as a tricycle on its side in the driveway. The yard was littered with corpses, more than any of the other homes around it.

Gawain pointed to a large house across the street from the home that held their attention, and David hesitantly followed his second in command. Hearing no signs of life, living or otherwise, they entered and made their way to the second floor.

Gawain walked up to the window that overlooked the street. David came up beside him and scanned the house. He shifted his gaze from one boarded window to the next, hoping to get a glimpse inside, but saw nothing.

"David, a man greeted her when she knocked at the back window." Gawain's voice was soft, and any normal human being would have struggled to understand, but David heard clearly and his heart clenched as he waited for him to continue. "There were also two small children. She's a mother, and I believe the man was her husband."

David closed his eyes, lowering his head as he steadied himself against the wall. He felt sick to his stomach.

Gawain grabbed his arm and pulled him away from the view that had held so much promise while Gareth sighed and went to the window to keep watch over the home.

David let himself get led to a neatly made bed. He sat, his mind racing and his heart torn open.

Gawain placed his hand on his shoulder and bent to meet his gaze, but David couldn't look at him. He could only stare at the window. Never did it cross his mind that the woman he'd been searching for would be married or have children. Of course she would be married, though; she was beautiful. Still, he didn't understand. She was supposed to be his.

"David, we will watch over her," Gawain said. "We will keep her safe. We'll keep all of them safe. I'm sorry, brother. Perhaps—"

David held up his hand. He didn't want his pity. He needed to be alone. No one would be able to give him peace besides the woman who was across the street—with her family.

This wasn't fair. He'd spent centuries waiting for this very moment. Immeasurable love and happiness had been promised. She was supposed to complete his immortal soul and hold his heart for all eternity.

David refocused on his friend, though, and nodded. He was a soldier—a captain. He needed to keep that attitude. "I'll take first watch," he said, walking to the door. "Check the perimeter and inform Arthur of our location. Tell him we have located the target." He paused at the door and sighed before looking up at the ceiling. "Tell him to have the others come set up post here. I will not leave her in danger."

With that, he left the bedroom. He couldn't stay there and feel sorry for himself. He had a job to do, and this woman and her family were now his top priority.

No matter how much suffering he might endure, he would not leave her. He would keep them safe because he was completely in love with a girl that he had yet to speak to. He didn't even know her name, but she already held his heart.

Quickly exiting the house, David ran over to the house neighboring hers and scaled a tree until he was on the roof. He searched the area briefly before finding a spot to sit.

He stared at one of the windows and noticed a faint light between the cracks of the wood. He closed his eyes as he heard a delicate sigh from inside. Somehow he knew it was her, and he listened to the four heartbeats, instantly feeling drawn to the one beating faster than the other three. *Hers*. It had to be hers because it was the only sound he wanted to hear.

Arthur was right, he should not have gotten his hopes up.

David opened his eyes and gazed down at the house again, realizing despite all his pain and disappointment, this was still the best moment of his life. Bittersweet, but still the best night of his life. He had found her, and she was everything he had dreamed of.

He smiled, remembering her lovely, hazel eyes. They were not a new sight to him; they had haunted his dreams for centuries. Now they were perfectly clear in his mind, and he had the most beautiful face to go with them.

Her flowery scent still lingered in the air. He inhaled and let it fill him with peace. When the sweet scent of blood hit his nose, he let out a breath and shook his head. There wasn't time to weaken to his thirst.

A low groan sounded to his left. He turned and saw a corpse, crawling across her front yard. It seemed he couldn't even have a few moments to ponder her face anymore. He lifted his rifle and fired.

They wouldn't touch her.

CHAPTER 6
RED

Exhausted, Jane pulled herself through the window and into her home. She took the water Jason offered her with a shaky hand and held it as tightly as she could. Her muscles shook from fatigue, but she lifted the bottle to her lips and greedily drank.

"Are you okay?" Jason asked.

Sweat dripped down her neck. "I'm fine." She took another sip of water before wiping her forehead.

"Mommy!"

Jane smiled and squatted down to hug her children. "Hi, babies." It was such a relief for her to see them safe. This was why she took the risks she did. She squeezed them a little more to reassure herself that they were really there. "Were you two good?"

With a big smile, Natalie answered. "I helped Daddy find Nathan's dinosaur toy, and he stopped crying."

"You did?" she asked.

"Yep," Natalie replied, bouncing in place.

Jane kissed her head then Nathan's. "That's my big girl. Go and lie back down. It's not time to get up yet."

Jane led her back to the makeshift bed, then picked up Nathan and placed him down next to Natalie. She gave them one final kiss goodnight and returned to the couch.

Jason sat beside her and offered her more water, tucking a strand of hair behind her ear. "You were gone a while this time. I got worried."

She was slightly stunned by his concern and affectionate gesture. For the past three months, they had continued down their spiral of separation, and while she hoped they'd become stronger, it hadn't seemed likely. Too much damage had been done, and both had changed in ways that neither could accept. She was risking her life to keep them safe, and Jason was doing what he'd always done: making her feel like she was the craziest person in the world.

Yet, the soft expression he was giving her made her wonder if she had been wrong. He was staring at her like he had early on in their relationship. Maybe they would make it through everything together.

Despite being so detached from each other, she desired a life with him. He was her husband, after all. Yet, when she looked into Jason's brown eyes, she couldn't help but suddenly wish they were blue.

The image of those sapphire eyes peering out from under the black mask wouldn't leave her mind. They had brought her a sense of peace for some reason. It was ridiculous, but she wanted nothing more than to look at them every day for the rest of her life. One word had formed in her thoughts when the mysterious soldier, dressed in black from head to toe, gazed at her: home.

Jane shook her head to free her mind of her savior and focused on Jason. She couldn't believe she was thinking about some guy she knew nothing about while her husband sat there. As poor as their relationship was, she was still Jason's wife. "Don't worry. I'm fine."

"I know." Jason sighed. "I just wish you wouldn't go out there. It should be me saving us. I shouldn't have to sit here and watch you offer yourself up as live bait."

Jane leaned back against the couch. "We've had this conversation already. I can't carry the kids if something happens. They'll die. You can protect them better than I can, and they would be better off anyway. I'll sacrifice myself if I have to."

"I'm trying to be nice. You know the kids need you. I don't know why you act like this. It's like you want to die. Just like you never want to get better."

She sighed. He always said stuff like this. He thought it was so easy to be "better". He didn't even care that his words hurt her so much. Her only defense was to give him attitude. It was better that than do the things she really wanted to do to him.

"Well, did you run into any extra trouble?" he asked, snapping her out of her sudden darker thought. "You look really out of it."

Barely stopping herself from rolling her eyes, she nodded. It was like he didn't care she was willing to die for all of them. "Yeah, a little. I guess I was more tired than I thought. I wasn't paying attention to where I was going."

"What do you mean? What happened?"

"Well, I was leading them away like I have been doing, just jogging down a few streets before speeding up to lose them. But I ended up running into more of them, and I panicked. They surrounded me—one even grabbed me, so I just started shooting until I got free."

Jason's eyes were wide as he looked her over, checking her for injuries.

She thought about those blue eyes again and wished she'd seen his face. "I don't know what I would have done if he hadn't been there."

Jason looked up. "Who?"

"I don't know," she said, not looking at him and continued imagining the masked man and his shimmering sapphire eyes. The way they glowed under his mask wasn't natural, but she wasn't alarmed by them. "After I got away someone started firing at them and saved me. I think they were soldiers of some kind; they wore uniforms. But they looked like a special military team. There were three, and they were wearing black, even black masks."

"Did they say anything to you?"

"What?" She focused back on Jason. "Oh, no. They kind of just looked at me. Then a zombie came up behind one of them, and I killed it. I didn't stick around. When they turned to look, I ran." She shifted her gaze away from his questioning look to stare at her hands. She didn't know how to hide she was practically swooning over the blue-eyed one. Actually, she didn't look at the other two, but she knew there were three of them. But *he* was all she cared about, all she wanted to see.

Jason pinched the bridge of his nose. "You didn't think to see if they could help us? We haven't had any sign of help for three months, and you run away the first time someone comes to your aid?"

"What, Jason? I panicked!" She smacked her hand on the sofa. "You imagine being out there and see if you think to ask questions when a group of huge dudes wearing masks and holding rifles are just staring at you."

"I told you I'd go." He glared at her. "But you like to act like the hero. It's like you just don't think sometimes. They could have taken us with them or helped us gather more food. You don't think about what's going to help our family. You're more concerned with this little high you get from running out there than taking care of us."

She fought to keep herself from screaming at him. "Yep, I'm the one thinking about myself. You always think about me and the kids. We're the only thing that matters to you."

"What's that supposed to mean?"

"Nothing." She turned her head. If she had to look at him and have this conversation one more time—

Jason stood up and, surprising her, he held out his hand. "I don't want to fight. Just go get some sleep. We'll forget about this. And next time we see them, if there's a next time, we can ask for help."

Jane was too tired to argue and let him pull her up. He led her to the bed and even pulled the blankets back and covered her after she laid down.

"I'll keep an eye on things," he said before leaning down to place a soft kiss to her forehead.

She watched him leave as she blew out a breath. It bothered her he was kissing her—he hadn't kissed her in months. *He probably wants sex tonight.*

Jane sighed, not wanting to think about that. She didn't want to think about Jason at all because he was right. Those men had been the perfect opportunity to save them, but she didn't think about that when she saw them.

No, when she saw *him,* she wanted to run right into his arms like an idiot. That's why she ran. All he did was look at her, and she wanted to go with him. Everything else had slipped away from her mind, even her kids, and that was wrong. Jason was right, she was selfish.

Jane rubbed her face. She was tired and needed sleep, but she found herself trying to imagine what the man with glowing eyes looked like. He was probably gorgeous, and he saw her all sweaty and ugly. She even fired a gun in his direction like a crazy person. He was probably glad she had run off.

"Stop it, Jane," she whispered to herself. It was stupid to keep thinking about him; she would never see him again. Besides, it wasn't like she could really do more than fantasize about him. She was married, and although her relationship with Jason was practically nonexistent, she couldn't picture herself with anyone other than him.

Jane rolled on her side to try to get more comfortable and settle the chaotic thoughts. As much as she tried, though, she kept thinking about how stupid she was. Any time she felt a little bit proud, Jason knocked her down, and he always made her feel like a moron for the way she thought about things. He made her paranoid and turned every argument around so that she ended up hating herself even more—made her feel crazier than she normally felt. Made her feel sick when he . . .

A nauseating feeling stirred in her stomach and mouth. Blowing out a slow breath, she closed her eyes, ignoring the sudden sick feeling and tried to fall asleep.

Those blue eyes suddenly formed in her mind. Well, they made her feel better than the direction her previous thoughts were trying to head, so she gave up. The twinge in her stomach vanished, and she smiled with the image of her savior's gaze on her. The icy-blue color of his eyes swirled into the darkest ocean blue. There'd been so much emotion and passion in his stare. She couldn't recall Jason ever looking at her that way, and she basked in the brief attention the stranger had given her until, finally, the stormy-blue color lulled her into a deep sleep.

✦✦✦

David sat atop the roof of a large two-story house and took aim at the thirtieth walking corpse before firing.

"You know," Gawain said, taking a seat beside him, "it's not like it's the end of the world."

Glancing in his direction briefly, David lifted his rifle again and fired. *Thirty-one.* "What do you want?"

For the past five hours, the others had left him to his thoughts while he prevented any threats from coming within a hundred feet of her door. Knowing the undead couldn't touch her as long as he was there brought him some comfort.

"Jane," said Gawain.

David lowered his rifle and looked at him full on. "What?"

"Her name is Jane."

Returning his focus on her house, David remembered her soft face and how her hazel eyes sparkled in the moonlight along with the freckles sprinkled across her nose and cheeks. When Gawain chuckled, he realized he was smiling and stopped. She was already someone else's.

He had heard the man, her husband, asking her if she was all right, and David used every bit of skill he'd learned to block out their conversation. He didn't think he could handle hearing them together.

"Thank you," was all David could mutter.

Nodding, Gawain lifted his rifle and released a shot. Despite using silencers, the dead continued to come. "Sure. You know this isn't the end for you both."

"How is it not?" he asked, almost growling. "She's married and has two children. They are a family. I won't break that up. I could never do that to her."

"Maybe she's not happy." Gawain's response was too casual.

He glared at his friend. "What do you know?"

Gawain held his hand up in surrender. "Nothing. I am only suggesting that maybe you shouldn't give up."

"Arthur should stay out of people's heads and mind his own business," David said.

"He's only trying to help, and you are his business."

"It does not matter." David hated sounding defeated. "I will not be the cause of anything happening between them. She would only hate me if I tried to take her away."

"I didn't say that you needed to take her away. I'm merely pointing out that you are her soul mate just as much as she is yours. She stands to lose just as much."

David pondered over Gawain's words while he focused on the four heartbeats inside the house. Hers still stood out. He could even identify her soft breaths as she slept. No, he couldn't hurt her that way.

He wouldn't take her away from her family. His destiny would have to go unfulfilled. She hadn't even seen him completely anyway. It wouldn't be hard for her, like it was surely going to be for him.

Gawain interrupted his thoughts. "I know what you are thinking, and you're wrong. She didn't have to see your face to feel that you were more than a mere stranger to her. Even without Arthur reading her mind did I know that. It was obvious by the way she looked at you . . . She looked into your eyes, David. Her soul recognized yours."

David chuckled. "You really believe our eyes are the windows to our souls?"

Gawain grinned. "Didn't yours whisper to you: there she is."

He smiled but said nothing.

Gawain released another round, drawing David's view from the house. "They don't stop, do they? We have not had anything like this in all the cities we have come across."

"It's her," David said, looking down on the home again. Gawain looked there as well. "I think she's pulling them in—like she did us," he explained. "Let Arthur know we need to strengthen the perimeter around the house."

"She's a magnet?"

David shook his head. "I'm not sure, but it's definitely her."

Nodding, Gawain stood and stepped off the roof, landing lightly, and sped toward their base camp.

Dawn was approaching. David scanned the glowing horizon before looking back at her house. "Jane," he whispered, before he jumped down to the crispy brown grass.

Arthur's troubled voice rang out in his earpiece. "David, we have a situation. Get over here. Tristan and Bors are coming to guard her for you."

He looked up in time to see Tristan and Bors already approaching him. They cast worried glances at each other before Tristan greeted him. "It's not good, David. You had better hurry. We will keep her safe."

"I know you will," David said. "Thank you." He received a pat on the shoulder as he passed Tristan. If there was anyone he trusted more than Gawain or Arthur to watch her, it was Tristan. Not only was he a loyal friend, but he was also their third best fighter.

"Sure thing, brother," Tristan said.

✦✦✦

"What is it?" David asked when he arrived at the house he had been at earlier. It was their new camp, and he was glad that it was so close to Jane.

Arthur stared at him for a moment before finally speaking. "Are you all right?"

"Fine. Now what do we have?" David dismissed their concern. They wouldn't understand what he was going through—they all had their wives.

"Wolves," Gawain said, getting to the point.

David glanced at Gawain and then to those around him before focusing on Arthur.

Arthur ran his hand through his hair. "Kay, Bed, and I were out expanding the perimeter. Eight miles southeast, we found a family of five, completely slaughtered. We could still smell the wolves. They were heading north, but we lost the scent after two miles. It was as though they vanished."

Letting out a breath, David already knew what Arthur would tell him next.

"I need you to track them down, David," Arthur said. "You and Gawain are the best. They need to be eliminated to keep her safe anyway. I would not ask you to leave her if it wasn't important."

David looked up at the ceiling. He was torn over the decision to leave while such a dangerous threat was near.

"Gawain told me your theory about her being the cause of the increased activity," Arthur said. "I think you are right. For some reason, we are all drawn to her. We will leave her in good hands, though. Her safety is all the more reason to take care of the wolves quickly. Tristan and Bors will be within view of the house, and Geraint will be up top. If need be, we can come back."

David looked back at Arthur. He didn't have to voice his worry. He knew Arthur was reading every thought going through his mind. "Fine. But I want to get this done quickly." It took all his effort to walk out and away from her, but he had a job to do.

Arthur nodded to the others. "Good, let's go. Lucan, Dagonet, keep guard and assist Tristan. Consider using the neighboring house as a separate post."

David looked at the two men. They were Arthur's most trusted guards, and he'd known Dagonet since he was a boy.

Dagonet smiled at him. "We will fight to the end for her, my prince."

Lucan nodded. "Be safe, Sir David. We will guard her well."

David nodded stiffly and walked away, praying he wasn't making a mistake. He had confidence in his comrades, and even Jane. She had, after all, kept herself and her family alive this long.

✦✦✦

Opening her eyes, Jane realized it must already be mid-afternoon. She rolled over and let out a painful groan. Everything hurt. Her entire body ached more than she had ever known it to. She shivered and goose bumps rose across her arms, but she didn't dwell on her discomfort when she heard Nathan giggling in the distance.

If he was happy, she could suck up the pain.

Jane sat up, gasping as pain shot throughout her body. Her arms burned and shook from the effort she'd used to push herself up, but she toughed it out and made her way to her bathroom.

She didn't bother going to the sink to wash her face and went straight for the shower in hopes that the hot water would relieve her aching muscles.

As the scalding water beat down across her neck and back, she shivered again. Her teeth chattered, and she clamped her mouth shut to keep from making the irritating sound. She was so tired. The simple act of washing her body was draining her, and she was starting to feel lightheaded.

Jane decided to give up on the warm shower, turned off the water and got out. She wrapped a towel around herself to dry off before stepping out into the chilled bathroom. As bad as she was feeling, she knew she must look awful and didn't even want to see her reflection. So, she grabbed her tooth brush without glancing in the mirror and entered the attached walk-in closet.

Getting dressed was even worse than bathing. Her muscles trembled like she'd just had the workout of her life, but she finished, and quickly spit her toothpaste into the sink on her way back out. All she wanted to do was get back to bed and sleep off whatever was wrong with her.

Jane stepped out of the bathroom and found Jason changing. He was midway through pulling his shirt down when he glanced up at her. She was all set to walk past him, but she stopped as the color drained from his face, and he stumbled back, grabbing the small hatchet he'd gotten in the habit of keeping on himself.

Confused by the fearful look on his face, Jane gave him a "*what the hell is wrong with you*" look, but he continued to stare at her with his hand clenched tightly around his hatchet.

"What?" she asked.

Jason shook his head back and forth as though trying to make sense of what he was seeing. "Your eyes," he said in a shaken voice.

She had no idea what he was talking about, but she reentered the bathroom and walked to stand in front of the mirror. What she saw had her frozen.

Red.

The bottom half of her left eye was a mixture of pink and blood-red busted blood vessels. She looked at her right eye and was terrified to see more than half of it was red, too. Tears blurred her vision. She raised her hands to touch her face, earning a fiery shot of excruciating pain up her arm.

Jane turned back to Jason's horrified expression. "I wasn't bitten. I swear! I don't understand." Her hands shook as tears fell to the carpet, and she frantically looked over herself. She needed to prove that this wasn't happening.

Jason gasped. "Your arm."

Turning her left arm every which way, she finally saw the small scratches along her forearm. Red lines were faintly visible beneath her pale ivory skin, but they were there, spread all the way up her arm.

Jane whipped her head back and forth, whimpering as Jason fell back against the wall.

"No," she finally sobbed, and fell to her knees as she buried her face in her hands.

"Mommy?" It was Nathan on the other side of the closed door.

Jane snapped her head first to the door and then to her husband as she bit her trembling lip to hold her cry from spilling out.

Jason jumped to his feet, the hatchet still in his hand. He turned to look at her before cracking the door open. "Mommy's not feeling good right now, buddy." He took a calming breath and continued. "Go into the living room. I'll be there in a minute."

Nathan disappeared down the hall before Jason shut the door.

A tear rolled down his cheek as he turned back to Jane. "You can't die." He crossed the room and fell to his knees in front of her before wrapping his arms around her.

Jane began to cry with him but found herself caressing his hair. "*Shh*, it's going to be okay." He shook his head. Jane leaned back, holding his face between her hands and told him, "I'm going to go and get as far away as I can. Y'all won't have to hear it."

"No," he said quickly, placing his hands over hers.

"It's the only way." She smiled as best she could. "I won't let myself turn into one of those things, and I won't let them hear me go."

Letting out an anguished groan, he finally nodded. He pulled her hands from his face and held them, fingering her wedding band. He looked back up at her, his gaze moving all over her face.

He placed his cold hands on her cheeks and leaned forward. Kissing her forehead, he whispered, "I'm so sorry for everything." He placed another kiss there. "I never meant to hurt you." She sobbed now, but he continued, "You are the best thing to ever happen to me. I love you so much." He finished by placing kisses across her face and hair, avoiding touching her mouth.

When his last words sunk in, she broke down again and wailed, "I love you, too. I'm so sorry." It had been so long since he had told her he loved her.

She didn't know how long they sat there, but she finally leaned back. "I'm ready." Giving him the best smile she could manage, she stood to her feet as Jason did the same. Neither moved to leave the room, and they simply faced each other before he pulled her against his chest.

"I love you," she mumbled against his chest.

"I love you, too."

He stepped back and took her hand. He hardly ever took her hand anymore, but he was taking it now so she could leave them.

She started to panic as she realized what she was about to do and tried to pull away, but Jason stopped her by giving her hand a gentle squeeze. It was a simple gesture she had wanted from him and now she finally had it. Only at the end.

CHAPTER 7

NOT COMING BACK

When Jane stopped after taking only a few steps from the hallway, Jason halted and glanced over his shoulder. She felt him looking at her, but she could only stare into the living room where their children played quietly on the floor.

Natalie lined up her dolls in a row while Nathan drew a picture, neither aware of the sorrow their parents were suffering. Jane whimpered. This would be the last moment she would ever watch them do something so simple as playing—the last time she would see her babies.

Jason wrapped his arms around her trembling figure and whispered in her ear, "Stay here." He left her there, but she didn't look away from her son and daughter.

Memories flashed before her eyes of happier times: learning of her pregnancy and how scared but excited she was. The ultrasound that showed they were having not one but two babies. Then the excruciating delivery that resulted in two perfect bundles they would cherish for all time. Every birthday, every trip to the zoo, every cold, nightmare, cry, laugh, and kiss. The first time Nathan had finally called her mommy.

At the sudden caress from Jason's hands on her cheeks, her memories shattered. She looked at Jason as he wiped her tears.

"Everything will be okay. We need to be strong for them, all right?" His raspy voice showed how much he was struggling.

She nodded repeatedly, knowing he needed her to be strong, too.

"Put these on." He handed her a pair of her favorite sunglasses.

She had forgotten about how her eyes looked, and she was thankful he'd taken the initiative for once. It gave her hope that their kids would be all right because he was thinking about them by preventing their last memory from being one where they'd see her as a real monster.

With a sad smile, she roughly wiped her tears and took the glasses from him so she could hide what she was becoming.

Jason smoothed back her still slightly damp hair as a shaky smile formed on his lips. She wished they had more time, but Jason took her hand and pulled her into the room.

She trembled with heartache as she sat on the sofa next to Jason. Neither of the two children even bothered looking away from their activities, and she and Jason sat there for an extra moment to watch them.

Finally, Jason cleared his throat. "Guys." Nathan and Natalie looked up and between their parents with confused expressions. "We need to talk to you both." His voice was stronger than before.

"Mommy?" Nathan asked with sad eyes.

Jane nodded yes, and Jason squeezed her hand. She'd never hear him call her that again.

"Baby, Mommy is very sick." Jane's voice cracked, and she stopped to take a deep breath as Nathan's eyes widened.

"Like the people outside?" Natalie asked, darting her gaze between each family member.

Even though they were young, and Nathan had autism, both children were quite perceptive. They'd seen her mourn her best friend's illness and death. She knew they understood the meaning of serious disease and what it could bring.

This time, Jason answered. "Yes. Like the sick people outside."

"Are you gonna die?" Natalie cried out.

Nathan's mouth dropped open. Natalie's lip began to tremble as tears pricked at her brown eyes.

"Mommy is going to leave to go get medicine for it," Jane said. "But I can't stay with you, or else you will get sick too. Mommy doesn't want you to get sick."

She hated lying to them, but there was no way she could tell them she was going to die. Relief shone in their eyes, but worry still overshadowed any comfort her words might have brought them.

"Are you coming back?" Natalie croaked.

Jane shook her head. "No, baby." Her eyes started to burn with the effort she was making to contain her tears. "I'm not coming back."

"Mommy, stay." Nathan's cry tore out her heart. Tears rolled down his chubby cheeks as Natalie's began to fall. He knew. She knew he could tell what was wrong. He always seemed to gravitate toward her when she was falling apart, and he knew. The image of his little face popped in her head of him panicking when she would not be there anymore.

Unable to answer, Jane turned to Jason for help.

"Buddy, she just can't," he said. "The people that have the medicine won't let her because she could still make you sick."

His lie sounded believable. Jane tightened her grip around his hand, and she slid down to her knees on the floor. She held out her arms, and they both jumped into her embrace. Her muscles screamed, but it was nothing compared to the agony her heart felt.

Jason knelt behind them and took them all into his arms while they listened to their babies crying.

"No matter what, Mommy will always be with you," she cooed, stroking their hair. "You have to be strong for Daddy and take care of him for me, okay?"

"'Kay," they croaked back in unison.

"Mommy loves you both so very much," she continued. "Never forget that. I love you, always." She kissed the tops of their heads. "You're the best thing to have ever happened to me."

They cried together. "Love you, Mama."

They held each other tightly, but Jane started to feel a painful pressure in her chest. Breathing was already becoming difficult. Panicked, she leaned back to look Jason in the eye.

He nodded and pulled them all into a big hug. "Guys, Mommy has to go now."

They sat there for a few seconds before Jason released his hold and stood.

Jane squeezed them again and leaned back on her knees. "I have to go. Be good for Daddy and take care of each other." She couldn't stop her tears. "I love you both so much."

Her heart was dying. More tears fell, and she gasped out painfully before giving them another quick hug. She kissed both of their foreheads and breathed in their baby smell.

She couldn't believe that this was it. Out of all the times that she had never wanted to exist, she was finally getting her wish, and it was the most horrible thing in the world.

She sobbed again and stood, covering her mouth. Jason quickly pulled her to him and hugged her, kissing her hair over and over.

She felt her body shaking and struggled not to scream against his chest. She didn't want to go, but she had to. It was the only way to keep them safe.

Even though she had every feature of her children memorized, she turned to take in their adorable faces one more time. She'd seen them cry so many times but never had she seen them so devastated. Their tear-stained faces were the last images of them she would ever see, and she couldn't take it anymore, so she blew them a kiss and walked away.

Her hands shook as she climbed out the window. Whether it was from the virus or sorrow, she didn't know, and it hardly mattered.

Once she was outside, she turned to Jason as he pressed her gun into her hand. It seemed as though he couldn't talk anymore, and he simply nodded to her as a tear slid down his cheek.

"Take care of them, Jason." Her lips trembled when his face crumbled. "Tell them I love them. Don't let them forget me."

"Mommy, don't go!" Nathan cried.

She choked on a cry and nodded to him as new tears rushed down her face. She knew Jason had forced himself to close the window and felt her heart break when the latch clicked.

Sobbing uncontrollably now, she turned away and ran. It was over. Her life was over.

✦✦✦

The eerie stillness surrounding Jane's home seemed to unsettle Tristan. He glanced around the perimeter, meeting Bors' gaze for a moment before continuing his survey. Geraint's figure was standing on top of a tall house fifty yards away, but he nodded when Tristan looked his way.

Bors' voice interrupted the silence. "I cannot believe this happened to David."

Though they were about two hundred feet apart, his voice was easily heard by both men.

Geraint joined the conversation. "Do you think he is mistaken? About it being her, I mean. All our wives came to us quickly."

"No," said Tristan. "David has not once looked upon another. If he says she is the one, she is. And it's not like she knew he was looking for her."

"Perhaps there's still—" Bors was cut off by a series of groans.

"Dammit!" Geraint's curse rang out. "There's activity. Northeast."

"Take them out quickly," Tristan ordered.

Their attention was drawn to the home when the children's cries sounded.

"What do you think is going on?" Bors asked.

The weeping continued, and they caught the parts of the conversation and lots of crying taking place inside: *I love you . . . Goodbye . . . Mommy, don't go.*

"What the hell is going on?" Bors exclaimed.

Geraint alerted them. "She's on the move. She went out the back window."

"I got her," Tristan called out, "Fuck! Notify David."

Geraint spoke again before they could send the alert. "Tristan, we have more coming from the west. Fuck and the south—they're heading straight for her."

"Bors, let's go, we need to keep them away," Tristan commanded. "Geraint, stay on her. Do not let her out of your sight. Lucan and Dagonet, I need you to stay with the family."

They took off at lightning speed to get ahead of her already swift pace. Geraint leapt from rooftop to rooftop, never losing sight of her, and only paused to take shots at the advancing swarm.

Geraint called out. "Tristan, something's wrong with her. Do you hear her heart and breathing?"

Tristan paused taking several shots. "Yes, it's fast, and her breathing is labored." He grunted and took another shot. "Why are there so many?"

"I think she's infected," said Geraint.

"Get David and the others here now," Tristan yelled.

"David, we have a problem," Bors said into his comm-unit. "It's the woman—she's on the move." He spoke quickly, then added, "David, we think she's infected."

"What?" David shouted, his voice roaring through each of their earpieces. "Where is she?"

"We're two miles directly north of her house. Several large masses are surrounding us. We need everyone. Now," Tristan yelled while taking more shots.

He and Bors kept close to her slowing silhouette, mowing down the growing crowd in the process. Geraint was still on the rooftops, shooting every few seconds.

"We're on our way, nearly eight miles south of you." Arthur was the one to reply. "Keep them back."

Though the small team dispatched the undead one after another, it seemed they weren't making much of a dent in the mob. Tristan and Bors closed in tighter around Jane.

Jane's own shots began to ring out, but she finally stumbled and fell to the pavement.

Tristan watched Jane from the corner of his eye as she smacked the ground with her hand and cried out in defeat.

She stayed on all fours, then, and didn't seem to realize the hail of gunfire they were unleashing around her. She continued to wheeze and let out sobs of hopelessness between each frantic gulp for air.

Tristan turned away from her, and focused on the battle.

✦✦✦

David raced forward with the others right behind him. Without warning, they came upon the horde of undead. Tristan's team laid down a continuous hail of gunfire, but the mob was massive. He hadn't seen one this size in months.

It didn't stop David. He cut through the mob, unleashing destruction in his wake. When he broke free of the wall of bodies, he spotted Tristan and Bors guarding a sobbing figure who looked oblivious to the carnage taking place around her.

Hearing her struggling efforts to breathe and feeling the anguish seeping out of her, time seemed to stop.

The others were quick to take positions around her and began their slaughter, but David could no longer see the world around him.

He only saw Jane. His Jane.

She screamed and lifted a gun to her temple.

"No!" David's desperate yell rang out as she squeezed the trigger.

CHAPTER 8
HEAVEN

Click . . .

Never had the sound of an empty chamber sounded so wonderful to David.

"Why?" she cried, looking down at where her useless weapon lay.

Although he was relieved the gun didn't fire, he couldn't stand to see the misery she was in. So lost and defeated.

He snapped out of his panicked state and rushed to her as soon as she began to fall forward.

Wrapping his arms around her, his heart pounded, feeling her go completely limp. Carefully but quickly, he turned her around, watching in fear as her head rolled to the side. She was barely hanging on, and David's heart ached as he tried positioning her head in the crook of his arm.

"I've got you," he whispered. It felt so strange to hold her. He never thought he'd get this close.

Her eyes remained closed, and she continued gasping for air. David heard the wild pounding of her weakening heart, but it meant she was alive.

Still, his heart tore at the sight of her. Her skin was pale and clammy. Tangled brown hair stuck to her face, and her blue lips were parted as she tried to suck in precious oxygen. She definitely looked on the verge of death, but to him, she was beautiful.

He smoothed the hair off her face, and whispered again, "I've got you."

She seemed to hear him this time. Her eyelids fluttered for a moment, before finally opening to reveal two crimson orbs. David sucked in a breath but made no other outward sign of distress. Inside he was dying, though. She was infected and turning into one of the very monsters he destroyed without a second thought. He wanted to yell. He wanted to kill something–but he could only stare at the girl who lay dying in his arms.

He didn't know what to do. She kept gasping for air and staring at him with those ruby eyes. Several blood vessels had burst, tainting the whites of her eyes with bright red and pink. Even the irises had been penetrated, but tiny specks of hazel still broke through the bloody color.

It made him smile even though he felt like he could almost cry. He had never shed a tear over someone before, but his eyes burned when he noticed the fear lingering in her delirious gaze.

David abruptly realized she was only able to see his eyes. He wanted her to see his face, so he removed his mask.

Her fearful gaze turned stunned for a moment, and despite the situation, he hoped she was pleased by what she saw.

David didn't notice the mayhem around him anymore. Nothing else mattered. Just her. The yells for him to get her to safety were not heard, nor the blasts of fiery slaughter and exploding gunfire. There was only Jane.

He smiled at her confused expression and caressed her cheek as he checked her over, absorbing every single detail of her face. The way her eyes widened made him wonder if she recognized him. He hoped she remembered him from their brief meeting before. It wasn't like they had talked, or she had even seen his face, but he wanted her to remember.

Jane let out a sudden gasp, and a few droplets of scarlet blood sprayed across her pale lips. She was trying to speak. He would give anything to have her talk to him, and so he waited while she opened and closed her mouth a few times. "Heaven," she whispered, lifting a shaking hand toward his face.

As soon as her cold hand touched his cheek, he felt complete.

With a contented sigh, he put his hand over hers and leaned into her palm. She was so soft and sweet-smelling. It didn't matter that she was covered in sweat and sickness; David held his angel for the moment.

He couldn't help but chuckle at what she said, and watched as her eyes widened. "Not yet, my love."

Arthur and his knights continued to dispose of the oncoming horde. They had created a strong perimeter and were holding them back.

The flashes of light from their rifles were endless and, for a few seconds, the roar of their massacre broke through David's daze.

"David, she's fading," Arthur yelled over the blasts from their guns. "You need to change her now."

Arthur's words yanked him out of his dreaming and back into a nightmare. He looked between her red eyes. Her panic from before was no longer present; she looked almost at peace. But she was dying.

Change her, Arthur's words repeated in his head.

He had promised he wouldn't take her from her family, but she'd already been forced to leave them. He still worried about how she'd react to being forced to leave them again.

"They would want her to have a second chance," Arthur yelled. "Your blood should destroy the virus. Change her before it's too late."

Gunfire resumed as the clanging of magazines were thrown to the concrete. Rotting, now inanimate corpses, polluted the ground beneath their feet as body after body collapsed on top of one another.

David stared down at the woman in his arms. Her disoriented eyes were locked onto his while she continued to take harsh breaths.

It didn't stop her from murmuring, "Beautiful," while he still held her weak hand to his cheek.

All second guessing went to hell for him. "I'm going to make it better, my love. I will make the pain go away." A peaceful look came over her, making him smile and continue with his decision.

Taking her hand from his face, he placed a small kiss to her palm and placed it against her chest before repositioning her so she sat on his lap. He lightly grabbed the back of her neck and didn't take his eyes from hers. "I'm going to make it all better."

She looked so trusting. He knew she thought she was dying, and probably didn't understand what he was telling her, but her comfort with his presence eased his heart. He was relieved she thought he was an angel. For so long he had considered himself a monster and worried about what the woman he was meant to love would think of him. It gave him a tiny bit of hope that she would understand and accept what he was. What he was going to do to her.

David took a deep breath and leaned down over her neck. His fangs elongated and sank into her delicate skin. She whined in pain, but he became too consumed with the sweet nectar pouring down his throat to think on it further. He could taste the infection, but that did not stop it from being the most delicious blood he'd ever sipped.

He moaned against her skin and continued to drink selfishly. His whole body thrummed with excitement, and he struggled to stop himself from becoming aroused. Everything about her—her soft skin and sweet taste—her beauty—it all sent a deep fire through him. He wanted to take her right then, and he nearly forgot she was dying.

These frenzied thoughts ceased, and he quickly regained his rational thinking. Now was not the time to think of such things. So, instead of imagining how it would feel to have her legs wrapped around his waist as her body arched into his, he concentrated on the fact this could be the first and last moments he'd ever have with her.

The painful realization brought him falling back to earth. Later, much later, they could consider an intimate relationship. He didn't even know if one was possible, but that could wait.

He had never changed a person, but as if already programmed, he knew he'd taken enough of her blood and stopped drinking. David withdrew his fangs and ran his tongue over her wounds before he pulled back.

Everything was automatic then. He placed her head back in the crook of his arm and bit down on his wrist, then lifted it to her lips. "Jane, I need you to drink." Greeted again with a ruby stare, David pressed his wrist to her mouth and ordered again, "Drink."

Those daunting eyes stayed fixed on his own, but she obeyed and opened her mouth. David secured his wrist to her mouth, and she began sucking, gradually increasing her pace and vigor the more she drank.

As her crimson eyes faded back to their hazel color, his body weakened. "That's enough," he said.

She released her hold and licked her lips. The wounds on his wrist healed within seconds, but he wasn't concerned for himself. A faint smile graced her face as David rubbed his thumb across her lips.

"Good girl." Again, his voice sounded foreign to him. He had never heard himself speak so tenderly to another person.

Everything about her was soft and fragile. Taking care of her was all that mattered. She was like a precious doll, but he knew she was a fighter, too.

"David, get her out of here," Gawain hollered.

"No, Gawain," said Arthur. "Take Gareth and go with David. He's too weak."

David was about to protest, but he was hit with a wave of dizziness when he stood. Shaking it off, he rearranged her to carry her in his arms. Even with their considerable size difference, they fit together perfectly.

Bracketed by Gawain and Gareth, he made for their camp.

He gazed down at the sleeping beauty and couldn't stop the smile that stretched across his face. She was here. She was alive in his arms where she belonged.

Tightening his hold, he pulled her closer and placed a small kiss on her forehead. She was warming up. He left his lips there and breathed in her flowery scent. When she sniffed his scent, he grinned, loving the effect he already had on her, and kissed her once more before picking up his pace.

✦✦✦

While Gareth stood guard outside, David followed Gawain upstairs to the master bedroom. He glanced around, pleased that the room was in good condition as he walked to the bed. As he lowered her down, she tightened her hold and whined. He stopped trying to put her down and held her closer as he shushed her. She instantly relaxed and curled into him, causing him to grow unsure of how to proceed with her.

He glanced at Gawain and found an amused grin stretched across his friend's face.

"It is best to hold on to her," Gawain said. "She will not wake for some time anyway. Here." He led David to a large chaise near a window.

David sat, pulling Jane's head to his chest as he did so, and he smiled when she quickly curled into him. She no longer struggled to breathe and was completely at ease in his arms.

"Do you think this is okay?" David asked, still a little worried about holding her like this.

Gawain laughed. "David, this is fine. It's better for her anyway. Your presence soothes her whether she is aware or not. I doubt she knows what she's even doing, but you are what her body and soul want. Enjoy it."

David focused back on Jane. She was safe. He never thought she'd be in his arms. Now that he had her, he never wanted to leave her side. Some might find it a bit extreme, but he had waited centuries for her to finally come across his path.

"I will get you something to drink," Gawain said, interrupting his thoughts of holding this girl for the rest of his life.

Stroking her hair, David breathed out and closed his eyes. As horrible as it had been leading up to now, he couldn't be happier. It nearly destroyed him when her finger squeezed the trigger. In his entire existence, David had never felt so helpless as he did then.

But he held her now, and all worries slipped away. Everything ahead of them could wait. He wanted to enjoy holding her and marvel at the fact his Other was so much smaller than him. Most women of his kind were tall and toned from years of fighting, and his fellow knights all had rather statuesque Others. Not her, and that was fine by him. She was petite. He'd guess she was a little over five-feet tall. She didn't have much muscle tone either, but that didn't bother him. He already loved the feel of her body against his.

Returning to the room, Gawain held out a large glass of blood for him.

David felt tired, and his thirst was more significant than usual, so he took the offered blood and started to drink quickly. He surprised himself when he gagged and nearly spit it all out.

Gawain snickered. "It will take some time for you to get comfortable with any blood other than hers now."

"Really?"

Gawain took a long drink from his own glass. "Yes. It will be the same for her, as well."

David looked back at him, horrified. He couldn't imagine her reaction if he asked to feed from her.

Gawain covered his laughter by coughing when Arthur and Tristan entered the room.

Arthur smacked the back of Gawain's head as he passed him. "Stop terrorizing your captain. I will never forget the day you changed Elle. Don't you remember, you tried to get me to lie to her by saying only her blood would keep you alive?"

Gawain moved to stand next to a chuckling Tristan.

Arthur crossed the room, grinning at him, then caressed Jane's cheek. "She's lovely, David. How are you both?"

David kept his eyes on Jane's face. "Good, I think. How long will she be out?"

Straightening, Arthur frowned. "I am not sure. With everyone else, it took a day. Besides you, no one else has been as close to death as she was."

David frowned as he realized there was no guarantee she would be okay. "So that could affect her change? Do you think she will suffer any side effects? Maybe we should find her medicine. What if I need to give her more blood?"

Arthur placed a hand on his shoulder. "Calm yourself. She will be fine. It may take a little longer for the transition, but you can see it happening already."

David looked at her and saw Arthur was right. Her once sickly, pale skin was gradually becoming more radiant and had a faint silver glow. Even though her hair was still tangled, the texture seemed softer and more luscious than it had been the first time he saw her.

He gazed at her pink lips and felt tempted to steal just one kiss from them. After feeding from her, he knew she tasted incredibly sweet, and her skin was so soft. It had been cold before, but now she was warm. He wanted nothing more than to feel every bit of her skin pressed against him. It was going to take all his control to keep him from doing anything of the sort. Even a simple kiss was out of the question. Hopefully, that would change in the future.

He sighed and looked away from the lips he wanted to suck and nip. Arthur smirked, and David knew his brother-in-law could hear every improper thought he was having. David shrugged, *she's beautiful.*

Chuckling, Arthur turned to Tristan. A serious look was on his face now. "What happened?"

"I'm not sure," Tristan answered. "We were positioned around the house and everything was calm. Then we heard the children crying inside and Jane telling them goodbye. At the same time, Geraint picked up movement and began taking out a small grouping of undead. Then she was out her window and running."

Panic filled David and he looked at Tristan. "Is her family all right?"

"Yes," Tristan said. "Dagonet refuses to leave his post. They had a little action but took them out without a problem. I think he is just shaken up about the children's cries for her."

Relief washed through David, but he was worried about how she would react after waking up. She ran away to save her family. To die. Now she would wake as a different kind of monster, and she'd still have to face never returning to them.

"I am sure she will appreciate what you have done for her," Arthur told David. "Clearly she is a strong woman. Not many of the infected are brave enough to take their lives. I'm sure the fact that she can continue to keep them safe will bring her comfort. And, of course, she'll have you now."

David nodded but remained uncertain. None of them had the opportunity to have children. To do so resulted in horrible consequences that none in their party were willing to take. He imagined, though, the bond between mother and child might be similar to the bond he felt growing with Jane. He now knew what it felt like to possibly lose her. For her to have that kind of pain worried him and saddened him at the thought of her children growing up without her. He hadn't met them, but he already felt connected to them. He wanted to protect them as much as he did her.

"It will work out," Gawain assured him.

David smiled at his friend's comforting words, hoping he was right. He wasn't used to feeling so vulnerable. Never had he considered what it would be like to have a weakness, and that's what he felt at this very moment, completely weak.

"You need to rest," Arthur told him. "She will be out for quite some time. You will need to be rejuvenated to help her along once she wakes. This will not be easy for her. Be prepared for the worst. A mother's bond with her child is unbreakable. When she cannot return, it's going to be hard on her. So, relax, but reflect on how you will help her cope."

David nodded. "I will."

Arthur smiled. "Congratulations, brother. Your sister will be happy for you. Call if you need anything."

David looked up, receiving grins from the others and a wink from Gawain. He smiled back as they left him to rest with his angel.

He leaned down and kissed her forehead. "My Jane."

CHAPTER 9

HUNGER

Jane teetered on the edge of consciousness, fidgeting a bit before relaxing again.

Wherever she'd chosen to rest was not soft. Its firm surface rose to meet her softer body at every curve, while a thick bar across her waist held her in place. It was heavy, but that did not disrupt her comfort.

The masculine scent which wrapped around her might have had something to do with her calmness. Although it smelled nothing like Jason, it overwhelmed her senses and begged her to come closer. Her semi-conscious state agreed and was more than happy to oblige her body's desire. She inhaled deeply, nuzzling her face against the source of heat and its delicious smell.

Her new *bed* pulled her closer, letting out a low rumble before relaxing again. Beds didn't move on their own, though.

Keeping her eyes closed, Jane used her senses to tell her where she was, and it wasn't long before she realized she was lying on someone. A male someone. A very large, intoxicating, and surprisingly cozy male, but he was still a man she was certain wasn't Jason.

She held her breath as her situation grew worse than she could have imagined. Not only was she asleep with a man she didn't know, but she was lying right on top of him. Her left arm was wrapped around his neck while her face was snuggled into the crook there. She felt her cheeks heat up. Before she got too embarrassed about her cuddling, she realized the steel bar holding her in place was, in fact, an arm, and his other arm was wrapped around her back where his hand nearly rested on her butt.

Her mind screamed to get away, but her body was another entity altogether. She pulled herself closer and ran the tip of her nose along his hot skin, breathing in more of his scent.

His hold tightened, and he let out a sigh. For a moment, she wanted to suck down his minty breath.

Finally, Jane's loss of sanity cleared, and she froze when her nose touched the stubble along his jaw. The man beneath her seemed to have woken as well, but neither of them moved. However, the rhythmic beating of his heart, which had no doubt kept her in her blissful slumber, began to pound in his powerfully built chest.

"She's awake." The voice didn't come from within the room she was in. Jane didn't know how she could come to that conclusion, but she knew it was well out of normal hearing range. She couldn't focus on her strange ability to hear so clearly; she had more important concerns to address.

As they both held their breath, Jane decided she would make the first move. She moved at a remarkable speed to cross the room and instantly met the concerned gaze of her captor as she turned around. All her confusion about her swiftness vanished along with the urge to scream for help.

Those eyes. She knew them immediately as her savior's—her mystery man in black. Just like before, the sight of them calmed her, and all hysterics she'd been prepared to unleash died on her lips.

Jane didn't know why she felt so relaxed under his gaze, and even though he was still a complete stranger, she continued to look over every inch of him. Luckily for her, he seemed to know she needed to assess him, and he kept quiet while she continued to look him over.

He's gorgeous, she thought a little too excitedly.

Blinking repeatedly, she couldn't quite believe what she was seeing. Gorgeous had never been a word she'd use to describe a man, but the man who sat on the bed was just that, gorgeous.

She quickly became aware of how much man he really was, too. She wanted to slap herself; she'd been all over him.

He wore the same black hi-tech military-style uniform she'd seen him in before. His muscles were fighting against his T-shirt, and Jane instantly fell in love with the veins running up and down his arms. The sudden urge to run her fingers up them shocked her, and she clenched her hands at her sides.

When she saw his gaze drop to her clenched fists, then back to her face with a smirk teasing his lips, she knew she'd been caught. He knew very well the effect he had on her, and he was enjoying it.

She was embarrassed and knew she should start asking questions, but she couldn't stop looking at him. Besides his tempting body, she found herself studying his face. Just as she had imagined when she ran into him before. Absolutely perfect. It wasn't fair to other men how attractive he was.

Jane took in his stubbled jaw, across the sharp angles of his cheekbones to his flawless lips. She wanted to slap herself for focusing on how soft they looked, but she couldn't help it. She wanted to feel them on hers.

Something was wrong with her. She shouldn't be thinking like this, yet she already knew before ever seeing him that she wanted him to touch her.

He suddenly smiled, and it nearly knocked her to the floor. She didn't fall, and she found her eyes drawn to his. Her memories didn't do them justice. They were beautiful and caring. Jane could only let them pull her into their blue depths. She didn't even remember what she was so startled over or dwell over how unworthy she considered herself to be in his presence. She was practically a drooling bimbo now, and she didn't care.

He slowly lifted his hands in surrender and began to stand.

That small action jolted her from admiring him, and she took a quick step back, prepared to flee or defend herself if needed. She didn't think he would hurt her, but she wasn't ready to let her guard down simply because he was the sexiest man she'd ever seen.

"I'm not going to hurt you," he said quickly.

The deep timbre of his voice sounded sexy as hell to her, but she still screeched, too panicked to swoon anymore. "Who are you? Where the hell am I?"

"*Shh*, it's okay," he said, keeping his voice low. "My name is David. You are in a house my team and I are using as a base camp."

"Camp?" She looked around as she tried to figure out where she might be. "Why am I here with you?"

The sight of the hurt look on his face made her chest ache. She didn't know why she would feel this way, but she knew she didn't want to see that look on his face again.

Jane softened her features, realizing he had saved her once before. He'd probably just done so again. "Why am I here?" she asked, calmer.

"What is the last thing you remember?"

Jane stood a little taller as she considered his question. At first, nothing seemed obvious, but as if a play button had been pressed, she was quickly bombarded with memories.

She had come home after her run-in with this man, then gone to sleep and woken up later than normal. She'd felt awful. Sick. All she'd wanted to do was go back to sleep. Jason. *My eyes!*

Her hand flew to her face in horror as she stared straight at David. She looked right at him, but she did not see him anymore. Her memories raced through her mind, blinding her from all that existed around her.

She had become infected. She'd left her babies! She'd left her home.

She whimpered and looked down at her hand as she remembered trying to shoot herself.

"I'm going to make it better, my love . . . I'll make the pain go away," David had said.

Jane looked back up to him. He had saved her. Why he had called her such a precious thing didn't register. Not even Jason had said such tender words to her. Instead of wondering about his tenderness, though, she remembered fangs.

He had fangs. He had bitten her. He'd sucked her blood. She touched her neck and felt the healed puncture wounds under her fingertips. Her mouth fell open as she remembered him drinking from her and then ordering her to suck the blood from his wrist.

Vampire.

✦✦✦

David watched her nervously. She was terrified, and he had no idea how to make it better for her. He realized she was too distracted to notice her quick movements.

He had heard the others become silent. They were waiting and listening as well.

She looked so beautiful. When he first saw her, she had already become the loveliest creature he would ever look upon, but now she was an angel. Her flawless, snowy skin radiated a faint silver glow in the dim room. The moon's light complemented her fair complexion and brought out the darkness of her long hair. It was still tangled, but the rich dark-brown color with hints of red mingling within the brown tones prevented him from finding her tangles unattractive. He wanted to run his fingers through her hair every day for the rest of his life.

During her transition, any time he had attempted to extract himself from her, she would cling to him tighter, preventing him from prying her off. She would press her face into the crook of his neck, and her hair would spill over his face, allowing him to breathe in more of her sweet smell.

He found it amusing that she was so clingy and grumpy while she slept, but he was only concerned with her waking and finding them in such a compromising position. Still, he would move from time to time, and she would hiss and dig her nails into him. It wasn't threatening to him, and he enjoyed the feel of her soft body squeezing his.

Every part of her beauty enchanted him, but it was her eyes which truly captivated him. They were unlike any immortals he'd ever seen.

He still recognized their beautiful green and brown hazel color, but now they were more vibrant. The green seemed to dance between dull olive tones to a fiery emerald color, while the brown almost turned a golden-amber color around her pupil. They mesmerized him with their constant shifting of color. It was as though they couldn't decide which color they wanted to be.

David wanted to stand there and watch her all day, but he had to help her through this. "Do you remember now?"

She gaped at him.

What he was had been dismissed as fantasy these days. If any sane person claimed vampires were real, they would be laughed at. Now the entire world was experiencing another outrageous monster, maybe learning other immortals existed wouldn't be so hard.

"I'm not dead?" she asked after a few minutes.

David shook his head. "No. You are not dead."

A small look of relief crossed her face. "You're the guy from the street when I was running?"

He nodded to her. "That is the first time I looked upon you, yes."

She stared at him for a few seconds. "I got infected. I left to keep them safe. I was going to kill—but you—"

David interrupted her. "Yes, you were infected. I do not know when you contracted the Zev virus, but I was informed when you fled your home. I came as fast as I could. I couldn't let you die."

He felt like a fool as he watched her head tilt to the side at his words. He shouldn't have said that.

He watched her confusion at his affectionate gaze. She seemed shocked to see him looking at her like he was. It might be odd for a stranger to appear so enamored with them, but her reaction confused him. It was as though she wasn't used to receiving such an adoring look.

David started to wonder over the idea that she wouldn't be used to being shown affection but stopped all musings when she looked at him in horror.

"What have you done to me?"

David's heart plummeted. This was what he had feared. "I made you what I am."

She scanned him again. "What are you?"

"I am called many things." He knew she'd figured it out. Clearly, she wasn't ignorant. A bit reckless with her safety, obviously, but he could tell she was a clever girl.

"Are you bad?" Surprisingly, she didn't sound so scared now.

"I'm not sure how to answer that," he said calmly. "Some say I am bad, but I promise I will never harm you."

A faint smile touched her lips as she nodded, appearing to accept that he wouldn't hurt her. "Am I bad?"

"No, my love," he said, too quickly to stop himself. "You could never be bad."

Her eyes widened at his words, but she quickly shook her head.

The dismissal of his softness toward her relieved him at the same time it caused a slight twinge of pain in his heart. David wasn't going to let it bother him, though. She didn't know who they were to each other anyway. He couldn't expect her to jump into his arms.

"Does my family know I'm here?" she asked, looking hopeful. "Can I go home now?"

His heart sank. "They are safe. Men from my party are keeping watch over them. I'm afraid, though, you cannot return to them."

Her lip trembled slightly. "Why?"

"Sweetheart, it's not safe. They will be in danger around you." He paused, trying to decide what to say. "Please do not be sad. We will keep them safe. I promise."

His attempt to comfort her was ignored, and anger overcame her sorrow. She probably wasn't even aware of it, but he saw a deadly girl clawing her way to the surface.

Her sweet face that was previously so sad and confused morphed into one of a dangerous predator. Her eyes slanted upward, reminding him of a cat preparing to attack, and the soft curves of her face became more defined while her new fangs revealed themselves. *Beautiful.*

Despite his attraction to the lethal female she was becoming, David shifted defensively. He would never hurt her, but he couldn't let her harm herself or anyone else. She was unstable right now, and he would have to watch her.

"I want to go home," she said, baring her fangs.

"I know you do, but it's not safe," he said. Such a threatening display from any other immortal would have earned his wrath instantly, but he couldn't be that way with her. He didn't want to be the normal, fierce warrior who others of his kind were accustomed to. No matter the fact she was eyeing him like he was her next victim, she would always be delicate and someone he would be soft with.

"No," she said sharply. "I don't know you. Thank you for helping me, but I'm going back to my family."

Her swirling hazel eyes suddenly fixed on a green so dark they almost passed for black. *Almost.*

She trembled with much in her rage that the ground beneath their feet began to vibrate. It was faint, but he could feel it due to his heightened senses, and it seemed to have worried the others.

Jane's furious gaze darted toward the door when their footsteps drew closer. David took advantage of the distraction and lunged for her before she could react. She screamed and thrashed in his hold just as the others burst into the room.

Arthur, followed by Gawain and Gareth, entered the room and looked on as David held her tightly against his chest. She was a lot stronger than he had expected, but not as strong as him.

"*Shh...* It's all right. You have to fight it," he said soothingly, eying her neck. He barely held back from kissing or biting her.

Her silver glow pulsed with every furious breath she took. Despite the illumination she emitted, the air felt heavy and dark. The faint vibration of the floor had spread to the surrounding walls and grew in strength. As he had expected after all these years, there was a lot more to his Other than the average immortal.

David held her tightly. "You will be able to see your family eventually. Calm yourself, sweetheart."

Temper tantrums from newly made immortals were to be expected. They were notorious for being the deadliest during the weeks, and sometimes months, after their change. It was part of the reason he had been created. David wouldn't treat her as he would any other immortal, but he had to calm her by any means necessary.

At the mention of seeing her family, she stilled. Gradually, the lovely hazel color returned to her eyes, and the trembling walls ceased. Whatever she had just done appeared to have exhausted her, and she slumped back in his embrace.

"There we go," he said. "Good girl."

When he turned her in his arms, she quickly crumpled against his chest. David lifted her and went to sit on the edge of the bed, not ready to let her out of his hold. He caressed her hair, gently rocking her as if he were soothing a baby. The repetitive action visibly relaxed her and drew a sigh from her lips.

"Jane, my name is Arthur." He stepped forward.

She seemed to show more ease and looked at his brother-in-law. David knew he was reading every thought she was having, and something she was thinking clearly amused Arthur because of the slight smile he wore. David wondered what she'd be thinking that was funny, but he trusted Arthur to tell him anything important.

"You need to relax," Arthur said. "David will not let any harm come to you, and we will keep your family safe. I give you my word that when it's safe, you will be able to watch over them yourself."

Jane nodded.

"I know you have an idea as to what we are now," Arthur said. "So do you understand the danger—why we must take these precautions with you?"

"You are vampires."

Arthur nodded. "Yes, that is one of the many titles we hold."

"So, I'm a vampire, too?"

"You are one of us now," Arthur confirmed.

"Do I have to kill people?" Her voice cracked, and David squeezed her, hating that she sounded fearful now.

"We are not like what you see in movies," Arthur said. "But we do need to drink blood."

At the mention of blood, her eyes glowed a bright shade of green before they quickly went back to their normal vibrancy. "Is that why I feel dizzy?" She sounded like a young child.

David had seen many new immortals, and her behavior was nothing new to him or the others. While most became volatile, many often became so overwhelmed with their new senses and intense emotions that they often reverted to child-like states of mind.

"It has been two days since you were turned," Arthur said. "Your body needs nourishment."

As she began to squirm again, David tightened his grip and looked to Arthur for guidance.

"Jane." Arthur drew her attention. She was behaving like a hungry toddler, and that's exactly how they'd have to treat her. "You will have to feed from David."

David waited anxiously, continuously darting his gaze between her and Arthur. From the side of her face, he saw her eyes flash to an icy-jade color, and he knew her hunger had won.

She quickly turned her head and focused on the pulse in his neck.

Fuck. He couldn't believe how much this turned him on. Knowing that she was thirsty for his blood had him ready to rip off her clothes. Her pink tongue wet her lips in anticipation while her fangs began to lengthen. Awareness of their audience slipped away from David and the need to have her consumed him.

Arthur stood, chuckling. "We will give you two some privacy."

David watched them leave as Gawain mouthed, "*Have fun,*" before he shut the door.

Returning his focus to the woman in his arms, he lifted her slightly to look into her glowing eyes. "It will come naturally, Jane."

She shivered when he spoke. The urge to flip her over onto the bed entered David's thoughts, but the instinct to feed her pushed the temptation away.

He placed his hand behind her head and guided her to him as her predatory instincts took over, and she sank her fangs into his neck.

She straddled him and her fingers tangled in his hair before he could react. He knew these were the results of her hunger; she was only securing his neck to her mouth—similar to a lion preventing their prey from fleeing.

Still, it was a very sexual position. He had to concentrate on not losing control, but he only pulled her closer. She felt so good in his arms. She was soft, and her sweet scent tore at his morality. He wanted to taste every inch of her—be inside her.

He couldn't do that to her or himself. David forced himself to stop pulling her closer and gripped her shoulders to prompt her to stop feeding.

A growling noise rumbled in her chest. It briefly made him think of a baby kitten, growling as it guarded its food. As cute as the thought was to him, his more dominant side took over. She was a predator. But so was he.

He let out his own growl to chastise her. The aggressive sound caused her to whimper, but he wasn't backing down. Squeezing her shoulders again, he finally felt her submit.

She abruptly stopped sucking and removed her fangs. The adorable stare she greeted him with as she licked her lips pushed back his need to dominate her. He reminded himself that she'd only just learned of what she was. Her entire life had been turned upside down in the small amount of time she'd been awake.

"I'm sorry," she said.

He nearly kissed her pouting lips as she tilted her head slightly. She was giving him puppy eyes. He'd seen several of the wives use it on his friends but never understood why they caved to their demands.

Well, he knew now. He wanted to give her the world, but he overcame her charm.

"It's all right. You did well." He rubbed the remaining droplets from the corner of her mouth with his thumb. She still gave him that look, but she seemed more innocent than the women he'd seen using this tactic.

She sighed with a sort of intoxicated gleam in her eyes. "I felt hungry." Her gaze locked with his, and she gave him a dreamy smile. "You growled at me."

Definitely innocent . . . and maybe a little drunk, he thought. Her innocence along with her reactions to him and his blood made her a more dangerous opponent.

"I did." He chuckled. "You need to focus now. We have a lot to talk about."

CHAPTER 10
TRUTH & LEGEND

Jane was drowning in the dark blue pools of David's eyes and right now, she didn't care about her doomed fate. She'd heard him say they had to talk, but she just wanted to touch him.

She moved her hand from his neck to the side of his face. He reacted by shutting his eyes and tilting his face toward her palm. He smiled again, and she couldn't stop herself from smiling back. Everything felt perfect until she suddenly thought of Jason. With the picture of her husband's face looking back at her, the veil of ecstasy lifted.

Jane quickly took in her current situation, noting the pair of strong arms holding her. Arms that belonged to David. It felt right to have him hold her so close to him. She wanted to wrap herself around him. Even their current embrace, straddling him, wasn't enough.

Oh, God, I'm straddling him, she truly realized. She was betraying Jason.

She jumped off his lap and backed up, holding her arms out to keep him away.

"Sweetheart," David said softly, "please stay calm. I will explain everything to you."

"Don't talk to me," she shrieked, panicking because everything inside her said to go back to him. "I'm not your sweetheart."

It hurt her heart to see his devastated expression, but this wasn't right. This wasn't her. She wouldn't cheat on Jason. She wasn't even mad that he called her sweetheart. In fact, she liked it. And that was wrong.

"Fine, I will try not to call you that, but you need to give me a chance to explain."

His pleading made her resolve weaken. If he came closer, she didn't think she could stop herself from touching him or begging him to call her something sweet again. She wanted to be all over him.

"Just leave me alone," she said, holding her head. "I don't want to talk about it right now. Oh, God . . . Jason's going to hate me so much."

David's shoulders dropped, and she hated how it looked to see him that way. Everything about David told her to trust him. A part of her whispered he was truth and safety, but her logical side disagreed. She had just met this guy. He was a vampire, and he'd changed her into a blood-sucking monster.

Jane squeezed her head with both hands. She couldn't stop thinking. Her mind was total chaos. Two sides screamed at her: one told her to just jump into his arms while the other insulted her for even looking at him.

Jane pulled her hands down and stared at his eyes as her heart begged her to give him a chance. She rarely let her heart have what it wanted, though. She didn't want to—she wanted the opposite—but she closed her heart up tight in a box.

"David," said a man as three knocks sounded from the door. "Arthur needs to see you."

The door opened to reveal a man she briefly remembered seeing earlier.

"I'm a bit preoccupied," David told him.

The man gave David a knowing look. "He needs to speak with you. I will keep her company while you are gone."

Jane was relieved at the request, but at the same time, panic coursed through her at the thought of David leaving.

She pushed through her fear and kept her eyes on this newcomer. She could feel David staring but refused to look at him. If she did, his deep blue eyes would paralyze her, and she'd beg him to stay.

"Fine," David relented with a harshness she didn't expect from him, but when he turned to her again, his tone was even. "Jane, this is my friend and comrade, Gawain. Will you be all right with him while I go speak with Arthur?"

"Yes," she said, lowering her gaze.

David did not immediately leave, but after a few seconds, he let out a frustrated breath and exited the room.

Tears pricked at her eyes, but she was accustomed to pushing them back. It made them burn more, and caused a deep ache in her throat.

Even closed away, her heart felt his withdrawal and cried for him to come back. It was hard to process such a strong attachment to a stranger, and even though she had denied her heart many relationships, this new feeling of loss was destroying her. This was why she never let anyone in.

"Like he said, my name is Gawain." He reached out for her hand.

She looked up and held out her hand. "I'm Jane."

He surprised her by lifting her hand and placing a kiss on the back of it. "It is a pleasure to meet you, Jane. Why don't we sit and chat a bit? David will be a little while." He led her to the chaise by the window.

Hearing David's name caused her to flush with heat. Part of her felt embarrassed for how she had been all over him and the other part was saddened that she'd pushed him away. She tried to hide her reaction from his friend. Her eyes burned from the aching in her chest, but she was more embarrassed by her teenage reaction. She was a grown woman for God's sake, but just hearing his name had her blushing?

A finger under her chin forced her to look at the grinning man next to her. "Don't be embarrassed, love. Your reaction to him is normal. Let me explain everything, all right?"

"What about David?" She didn't know why she even asked.

"Don't worry. He will be back, but I think it's best that you hear this from someone else."

"Okay."

Gawain smiled. "I know you must have a thousand questions, so I shall go far back. I am sure that you have heard of the fallen angel, Lucifer?" She nodded, and he went on. "Well, when he fell from Heaven, he wasn't alone. Although Lucifer did not have any part in the creation of the first Earthly immortals, he is important to the story.

"Now there were other angels who wanted revenge against God. Since they cannot reach him, they chose to target the human race.

"You see, angels and demons do not have the ability to directly harm a human. Every human, even immortal, can be influenced to do good or bad, but the fallen and demons wanted to inflict physical pain. They found a way by creating the first of Earth's immortals. They gave their new creations great strength and immortality. This was not meant to happen in the world we live in. They were created out of hate. These new immortals were ruthless and life was chaos for mankind. Villages were destroyed, lives were lost–it was complete hysteria, which was their aim. God was heartbroken for what was happening to humans, but the laws were set. He would not allow His angels to stop these earthly demons because they were once human. His angels could fight Fallen and creatures from Hell, whom created these monsters, but they were difficult to catch. Most were once angels themselves, so it was easy for the Fallen to hide from Heaven's warriors.

"As time went on, Heaven and Hell grew more hostile with each other. Just as God loves us, so did the angels who remained in Heaven. While many of Heaven's angels located and destroyed the fallen and demons responsible for these monsters, more immortals were created on Earth. With God's law, the angels had no way to stop these monsters. The human race stood on the brink of destruction.

"After some time passed, Lucifer suggested an idea that would bring order. Even though he is Lucifer, he was angry that not even he could control these beasts who ran free over the world. He suggested Heaven create its own protectors."

Jane sat wide-eyed, listening to this great tale. "But he's Lucifer. Why would he want to help humans?"

"Because there is no evil without good. No Heaven without Hell. Balance is necessary, and Lucifer knew that. God agreed that only Heaven's own immortals could bring balance but warned Lucifer to not create his own immortals. Lucifer agreed, and so a group of angels selected humans to gift with immortality.

"I am sure you have heard myths of different gods: Greek, Roman, Norse, and so forth?" He went on when she nodded. "Well, they were the first of Heaven's immortals. They had great strength, speed, and, of course, they were immortal. The Titans and other monsters from mythology were the creations of fallen angels and demons.

"To maintain that immortality, they needed to feed on the blood of humans. The earlier immortals had already instilled beliefs of human sacrifice among humans, but Heaven's immortals knew that their purpose was to protect us, so they were more careful with their feedings. Food of the gods is what they used to say. Humans believed it was some magical substance and didn't realize the *gods* were simply feeding on human blood."

"Why did the new immortals have to feed from humans?" Jane asked. "Why not just make them strong and immortal?"

Gawain smiled. "Power changes a person, Jane. They needed a reason to protect mortals. Same as a shepherd who guards his flock.

"Now, in the beginning, Heaven's immortals were successful. They defeated much of the evils that plagued our world. An example would be the Olympian gods defeating Titans. They did a tremendous job, but after a while, they grew bored of their duty. The evil ones continued to populate the world by either creating or breeding, and Heaven's immortals began to want more for themselves. They began to create their own immortals to take over their duty.

"It was disastrous." He shook his head. "This is when newer stories of monsters like vampires, sirens, and many others started to spread. Heaven's immortals did not take responsibility when their creations ran wild. Many of these newer immortals were as terrible as those created by Hell and Fallen. This upset God. Not only did the original, evil immortals start to regrow their numbers, but these creations and offspring from Heaven's immortals were just as bad. He punished them all by cursing them to darkness."

"Like real vampires?"

"Exactly," he said, clearly happy she was taking this all in so easily. "Humans assumed these were new monsters, but they were the same. Some were simply more monstrous than others. Don't get me wrong, some were physically different than what you might think of a classic vampire to be, but they were basically the same. Just more diluted and more crazed than the originals. It gets very complicated but focus on the fact we are all a result of either demons, Fallen, or Heavenly angels. Those immortal creations made via the same process that David made you. They also bred with other immortals or sometimes their creators."

"But they're all cursed?"

He nodded. "They are cursed to darkness. If they sinned or created more immortals by breeding or turning, they would damn themselves to Hell. This is what Lucifer desired all along. He must have known they'd fall to temptation. His collection of immortal prisoners still grows to this day.

"Wow. So they're all cursed, but not all are damned to Hell?"

He chuckled, his eyes flashing brightly. "Right. We label them all Cursed, and those sentenced to Hell, you will often hear them referred to as Damned. Now, let me get back to the story. Since Earth had even more monsters roaming the lands, God chose one of his archangels to create a new protector. The archangel Gabriel was chosen. He had to select mankind's most noble man and gift him with not only immortality but also the combative skill of his creator. Gabriel chose Arthur.

"Arthur was meant to destroy Hell's immortals and maintain order over all immortals. Just as there are good and bad people, there were good and bad cursed immortals. Some wanted to earn God's forgiveness; they work for Arthur to earn it.

"Anyway, Gabriel is said to be very wise. He proposed the idea that Arthur be allowed immortal companionship. God agreed to his proposal and Arthur was instructed to choose and create eleven companions to aid him as well as a personal companion—a wife. Each of these selected would not suffer from the curse.

"The eleven would be allowed to create an *Other* to remain their companion, as well. Had only Arthur been allowed a wife, there would be little doubt that the rest of us would succumb to the same lure evil had to offer. If we followed the rules given to us, we would remain in God's good graces and free of the curse or damnation.

"Since Arthur was considered most noble, he was given greater power than the rest of us. Arthur had to be able to take us out should we fall. Our Others, which are our wives, were not cursed, but to keep a rein on them, they must also stay out of the sunlight or else they feel very weak."

"When you say, they're cursed to darkness, that's where the vampire part comes in?"

"Yes. They are prevented from entering sunlight. God's light. If they do, they suffer severe damage or death. We are the exception. Our wives will not die, but they feel lethargic. Now, back to Arthur. He was changed and given the task to select eleven men. They are myself, my younger brothers Gareth and Gaheris. Then there is Tristan, Bedivere, Kay, Bors, Geraint, Lamorak, Percivale, and Galahad."

Jane knew those names from somewhere. When she realized why they sounded familiar, she smiled brightly. "Knights! King Arthur and the Knights of the Round Table!"

Gawain laughed. "Yes, the very same."

"I don't believe it," she whispered. "I always loved those stories. You guys were my favorite legends besides Greek myths." She squeezed his arm, which made him laugh. "This is crazy. I feel like I'm meeting a superhero. Wait." She looked back up. "You didn't say David's name."

His expression dropped. "No, David is not one of the eleven. He is the younger brother of Guinevere, Arthur's wife. He was the most skilled and bravest soldier in the kingdom when Arthur wed Guinevere—even we were no match for him. But Arthur was instructed not to choose him. He was also instructed not to choose Lancelot, Arthur's close friend at the time.

"Arthur learned of Lance's infatuation with Gwen, but he never believed it was possible for Lancelot to betray him so greatly.

"Guinevere had already been granted immortality, but she was no match for Lancelot when he went to her chambers and forced himself on her. Luckily, David had been coming to visit her, and he stopped Lancelot from doing anything more to her. They fought, but they both received fatal wounds during their fight."

Her heart pounded a little harder and her eyes burned. Gawain squeezed her hand. She knew he didn't understand what bothered her, and she would not tell him. She sucked in a fresh breath and looked back up.

Don't think of it, she thought quickly.

Gawain studied her face for a moment and finally smiled. "Gwen held David and prayed for help. When Arthur and I arrived, we knew there was little to be done; he was dying.

"Now," he said solemnly, "Arthur and I were not as close to David as we are now, but he was still Arthur's brother-in-law. He could not bear to watch his wife suffer the loss of her brother, so he called out to Gabriel, begging the angel to appear and save him.

"Gabriel heard the call and appeared before us, but he explained he could not help David. However, when it seemed David's final moments were near, another appeared. This angel was Michael.

"He knelt and began speaking to David. He told David he was being blessed by God. Michael said his skill in battle would be added to David's already impressive fighting abilities.

"David already surpassed us, so now he would exceed all made immortals. There would be a great sacrifice for all of this, though.

"Just as we were granted the right to immortalize our companions, David was told he would have the same. Only, he would not come across her until it was time for her on Earth. Michael said he was not given knowledge of when this person would cross David's path, but he implied David was in for a significant wait.

"David asked how he would know, and Michael promised him that his heart would tell him." A soft look overcame his face. "He also said she would have abilities unlike any other immortal, and with them, she would be able to save the world from darkness. But until she crossed his path, David would have to remain alone. He has been without a companion until now."

"But he changed me," she said quickly. "What about the woman he's been waiting for all this time? Isn't she like his soul mate?"

Gawain took her hands in both of his. "Love, he's been waiting for you."

CHAPTER 11
THE BLACK-EYED MONSTER

Scowling as he passed Arthur, David shoved open the back door and exited the house.

"Calm down," Arthur said. "It's better this way. She is too emotional right now to hear this from you."

David paced the yard, baring his fangs when the sound of her sweet laughter reached his ears. "Can you hear that? He's laughing with her. It should be me she's comfortable with. Not him." He was nearly yelling as he jabbed his finger toward the window of the room she was in.

"Everybody is comfortable with Gawain," Arthur said with a chuckle. "He's an idiot."

"Arthur," David said, annoyed with Arthur's attempt to calm him down.

His brother-in-law sighed. "Everything is hitting her and then you're there, stirring emotions she hasn't felt before. She's attracted to you, and to her, that makes her an awful person. You must remember she is dealing with losing her family all over again while trying to accept she's become one of us. That's all before you come into the situation."

David stopped his pacing before looking up at the sky. "I did not think of it that way."

"I know, and that's not your fault." Arthur gave him that almost fatherly look he would wear sometimes. "You have been the most patient man I have ever known. Unfortunately, you must continue to show patience. If you push her, you run the risk of losing her forever." Arthur sighed, adding, "She has had a painful life, brother."

David darted his gaze to Arthur. "What do you mean?"

"It is probably better if she opens up to you in her own time," Arthur said. "I will say, though, the abuse she's suffered has left her damaged. She's hiding a lot from me; I do not think I can fathom all that she's suppressing, but it's taking a toll on her. She's been doing it for a very long time.

"If you force her to return your feelings before she is ready, I don't think she can balance everything out. We all saw she has power we do not. If she can't figure out a way to harness it, and that pain inside her breaks free, she could be lost to darkness."

He wanted to demand Arthur tell him what she'd suffered through. If Arthur was unwilling to divulge anything further, he knew it had to be terrible. He sensed she was sad, but who wouldn't be under these conditions? "Do you think she has been this way for long?"

Arthur nodded. "Like I said, she's suppressing a lot. It's almost as if she does not know all that she has hidden."

David frowned. "How is that possible?"

"I don't know," Arthur said. "She's thinking a hundred different things every minute, but some of her memories are sealed away. She's very open with certain thoughts, though. For example, her giddiness over how attractive we are."

He glared at him. "Be serious, Arthur."

Arthur laughed softly. "I am. Despite her sadness and knowledge from the experiences she's lived through, she is very silly. She has an innocence about her I have not experienced in some time. I think the playful personality she has hidden away will suit your serious nature."

David sighed, wondering how Arthur could say she is silly. "She does not seem playful, brother, and she is terrified of me."

"She thinks you're sexy," Arthur said, smiling. "She thought I was handsome as well, but nowhere close to how sexy she thinks you are."

David fought the urge to smile. "Stop trying to distract me from what you refuse to say."

Arthur ran his hand through his hair. "Fine. While she slept, she had very vivid nightmares. I think your presence helped her from becoming too frightened by them, but she still dreamt awful things. It took me a while to realize they were more than her imagination. They were memories."

"Memories," David echoed, his stomach beginning to cramp as all sorts of dark thoughts appeared.

"A few moments ago," Arthur said gently, his tone full of pity, "Gawain told her something and it triggered an onslaught of memories in her mind. When she was asleep, I had sensed something dark, but it was hidden. She does this so she can function, but at triggers can cause her to relive painful events in her past. The pain and amount of trauma she relived for those few seconds"—he shook his head—"nearly knocked me to the ground."

David's heart was pounding. "Is she all right?"

Arthur held up a hand before he ran upstairs. "She was able to suppress it. This is normal for her. I believe she suffers from Post-Traumatic Stress Disorder. Among other things, brother."

"What was the memory?" David began pacing again. "What happened to her?"

"Let her open up to you," Arthur said, his eyes trailing David. "I feel sick for accidentally obtaining those memories without her permission. She's very ashamed. She hates nearly everything about herself. If you barge in there knowing what she finds disgusting about herself, she will break down. Do not expect the perfect woman you have imagined."

"She is perfect." David groaned and looked up at the moon. "She hates herself?"

"I didn't mean she would not be perfect for you. I am merely warning you she is not like any woman you have met. Be patient. Despite her method of avoiding or hiding painful memories, she's very honest and good. Like I said, she has a very innocent, playful mind, but she has been by herself in all of this."

David's mind was racing. "Why would she be alone?"

Arthur gave him a sad smile. "She does not trust easily, and she refuses to burden others with how she hurts inside."

"She wouldn't be burdening me," David snapped.

"I know." Arthur held a hand up, hushing him. "But she will not see it that way. It's been a long time since she's had someone there for her. Once she sees you are honest and trustworthy, I think she'll open up quickly. She craves friendship, but she's afraid. Gawain and Gareth will be good for her."

David focused on the window again, ignoring how comfortable she was with his friend and not him. "It's that bad?" He prayed it wasn't what he was already fearing.

"Yes."

He took a deep breath, closing his eyes for a moment. "What should I do?"

"I don't know," Arthur admitted. "I would give her time to come to terms with your bond. Her marriage wasn't perfect, but she's loyal. It's eating her up that she's so attracted to you. I've quickly gathered she avoids thinking about him because she feels guilty for thinking about you. Neither of you are really at fault for that."

"I cannot bear the thought of her hurting because of something I am responsible for." This wasn't how David envisioned his life after finding his Other. He would do whatever he had to and still wouldn't trade her for anything, but it didn't make it easy. *Maybe I did something wrong?*

"You have done nothing wrong," Arthur said, reading his thoughts. "I have faith everything will fall into place as it is meant to. She already has feelings for you. Let her accept them when she's ready. The girl only woke up an hour ago. She figured out we are knights. We are her favorite legends, apparently." Arthur laughed. "She's amusing, but I think she's focusing on her excitement to hide what's scaring her, and her guilt for wanting to be near you. That's why she ran, the first time she saw you. At least you know that she does desire you."

David ran a hand through his hair and sighed. "I won't let her hate herself for being attracted to me. I will distance myself until she is more stable. Since she likes Gawain, he can befriend her."

"David, you do not need to push her away."

"I do, though," he said, growing angry with his decision. "All I want is be close to her, but to see her regret accepting my affection . . . it feels like a knife is in my heart."

"I am sorry, brother."

"Save your pity. I only meant that perhaps she hurts as well. She keeps tearing up whenever she looks at me. I do not think she realizes how much I can read from her expressions." He nodded to himself. "This is the right choice. She will not feel guilty and it will keep her from hurting. I won't be far."

"As you wish," Arthur relented. "I'll be mindful of her thoughts. If I feel this is causing her harm, I will tell you."

"As soon as she feels bad, tell me. Now, how is her family?"

Arthur's face dropped. "They miss her, of course. The children, especially. Her husband remains strong, but he grieves. Her son is struggling most. He has autism, did you know?"

David shook his head. "He has been quiet, but I did not realize there was a reason for it."

"It's not severe," Arthur said, nodding. "But it makes it more difficult for him to cope with her absence; I worry for him. I believe Jane was his main support, but her husband is trying his best. It seems like he doesn't know him as well as Jane did. They are also running low on food and water."

He'd never interacted with anyone who had autism, and even knowing he would never meet him, he was terrified about the idea of Jane never being there for her son. "What about her daughter?"

"She's hurting more than she lets on. I think she tries to be strong for her father and brother." Arthur smiled sadly. "She's like her mother, more than even Jane realizes."

David tilted his head back and stared at the moon again. No matter how much it pleased him to have Jane, he never wanted to cause her family pain by taking her away.

Arthur responded to his thought. "You did not take her away from them. We will find a way to make sure they are cared for."

"How?" he asked because that simple question had no real answer that would make Jane happy. "We will have to leave eventually, and if Jane goes to them, she will want to stay. You know she cannot. She'll kill them."

"We will let her know what we are going to do," Arthur said. "It will relieve her to know we are caring for them. I'll make sure she understands that she cannot return. Just like you are sacrificing for her, she will sacrifice for them."

David focused on the window. "She's powerful," he said quietly. "More powerful than any of you."

Arthur looked over at it too. "We knew she would be different."

"She can't go near them, Arthur." His unease with Jane so close to her home was increasing. "Not anytime soon, at least."

Arthur patted his shoulder. "We will help her understand the danger. Come. If you are distancing yourself, we might as well make a round together. She feels perfectly content with Gawain."

✦✦✦

"Is this a joke?" Jane asked, staring at Gawain. "There's no way I'm his soul mate—or any type of savior of mankind."

"It's not a joke." A knowing look crossed his face. "You can feel the connection between the two of you. I saw it from the very moment you two laid eyes on one another."

"But I'm married," she whispered. There was no use denying she felt a connection with David. Just thinking of him made her insides turn to mush and looking into his eyes made her feel at home. "He's waited so long for—"

"—you." Gawain finished. "He would wait until the end of the world."

"Which is now," she whined. This was so wrong.

Gawain chuckled. "Oh, a few zombies are nothing for us."

She appreciated his attempt to lighten things up, but it was too much. "I'm not the girl for him, Gawain."

He scoffed. "Nonsense. You are perfect for each other. I'm his best friend—I know these things."

As sweet as that was, as warm as the thought made her, she had to put a stop to whatever they might be thinking would happen now. "Even if I was good enough for him, I'm married."

"He knows that," Gawain said with a nod. "Don't worry, love. No one is pushing you into anything, and David will always do what he thinks is best for you. And I'll be here to help you. Think of me as a big brother. We'll rub it in Gareth and Gaheris's faces that I'm your favorite knight."

Help her. She hadn't had help in so long. She hadn't had anyone wanting her. Jason. She held her breath as her heartbeat sped up. Thinking of him was out of the question. She'd just fed off a vampire for God's sake. No, she would accept Gawain's help. At least until she could figure out how to fix things. "Well, I lost my family a long time ago," she told him. It was true, and she hadn't realized how much it still affected her until saying it just now.

He pulled her into a brotherly hug. "There, there. How about you go freshen up? Afterwards, I'll introduce you to the others. They're all eager to meet you."

Jane pulled away and looked down at herself. She was filthy. "Oh, God."

"I did not take you for one to get upset over a little blood and dirt." He stood, still holding her hand, and led her to the door nearby. "Don't be embarrassed. Look, we already gathered some clothes for you."

She walked inside and saw three stacks of folded clothes on the counter. There were black pants, tan pants, and jeans. She looked at the sizes and quickly looked up at Gawain. He was blushing. She grabbed the panties and bras, checking the sizes on each one. "How'd you know my size?"

He scratched the back of his head, wincing. "Arthur suggested we start gathering items for you, but none of us attend to our wives' garments. We did not know how to guess."

"Gawain," she said sharply.

He cringed. "David checked your tags. He looked at nothing else, love. I swear. I was there to supervise."

She was about to pass out. "He checked my panties and bra that I'm wearing?"

"He was very respectful, Jane," Gawain tried to reassure her, though his panicky hand movements suggested it had been the most awkward moment of his life. "He did not want to, but he wanted you comfortable when you woke. He didn't let anyone else in. I stood across the room."

"Okay." She said it, but the wasn't okay. "Can I be alone now?"

Relief flooded his face. "Yes. Call if you need anything." Then he was out the door in a flash.

"Why, God?" She turned to lock the door and stared at it for a second. "Like that's going to keep out a vampire." She shook her head but as soon as she spotted the toilet, the only thing she could think about was the need to pee.

She'd never pulled her pants down so fast in her life. As she sat there relieving herself, the loudness of it shocked her. It's not like she'd never peed loud before; she'd been pregnant with twins after all. It was just this sounded more like a roaring waterfall. "Oh, no." She squeezed her eyes shut and tried to clench to no avail. She had to go.

David's voice sounded, but she could tell he was moving away.

"Great. He just heard me pee like a race horse." Jane finished and looked around the bathroom. It had a style like hers, which meant . . .

She spotted a small window over the toilet. Lowering the lid, she stood on top and peeked out. First, she spotted David standing with Arthur across the street. They were talking to two other men she hadn't seen before. Only a few words were exchanged before David and Arthur headed down the street. That's when she recognized the house they passed.

"My house," she whispered, touching the glass. "Natalie, Nathan." She covered her mouth and cried. She needed to see them.

Jane rubbed the tears from her face and looked for the latch on the window. In her mind, all she could see were their faces, them crying for her. *Nathan. He's probably been so devastated.*

She sobbed and pushed the window open, only now realizing it was too narrow for her to fit through. "Shit."

She looked at her home and imagined herself holding her children again. She could almost hear their voices, their laughter, sniffing their baby smell that never really went away . . . *tasting their blood.*

Jane was at the door, wrapping her hand around the doorknob before any other thoughts passed her mind.

She only stopped, hissing, when she locked eyes with a black pair across from her.

She watched the monster hiss at the same time a deadly sound rushed past her lips. It tilted its head and bared its fangs just as she moved.

"Oh, God." Jane covered her mouth. The monster copied her. She blinked and the black from the monster's eyes turned to hazel. It was her reflection.

She shook her head back and forth, realizing what she'd nearly done. All she had wanted was blood. Their blood. She had wanted their necks snapped and their bodies broken.

Jane fell to her knees. She couldn't go home.

I'm a monster.

"Are you all right, Jane?" Gawain called from the other side of the door.

"I'm fine." She sniffed and slid to sit on the floor.

"Are you decent?"

She chuckled and wiped her tears. "I'm fine, Gawain. Just a lot to process."

"You're sure?"

Jane stood up. "Yeah. I'm going to shower now." She quickly turned the water on and turned back to stare at her reflection. Her eyes were hazel, glowing, but hazel. Not black.

"All right, love. The lads are making you something to eat. But take your time."

"Thank you." She kept staring at her reflection, knowing a monster was hidden there. "I'll be out in a few minutes."

She listened to his retreating footsteps, still staring at her reflection, waiting for the monster to show herself. When nothing happened, her thoughts went back to her family and almost instantly a pair of black eyes were glaring back at her.

Jane gasped and closed her eyes, clearing all thoughts of her family. *Don't let me hurt them*, she thought over and over. A tingling sensation spread out from her temple, and she sighed as it relaxed her.

"I have to stay away from them," she whispered, opening her eyes. Hazel. "I can't even think of them." She nodded to her pitiful reflection and took off her clothes.

Silently crying, she entered the shower and leaned back to let the water wash away her tears. "Don't let me hurt them."

The tingle warmed as it slid around her body, quieting her cries along with the snarling, black-eyed monster.

CHAPTER 12

THE KNIGHTS

"Ah, there she is," a male voice rang out.

Jane looked over to see a young man—well, vampire—approaching as she came downstairs with Gawain.

"Gareth, you were supposed to be making her meal," Gawain said.

Gareth shoved him aside and stepped in front of her. "Already done." He smiled, looking her over and held out his hand. "I'm Gareth, Gawain's younger and more handsome brother."

Jane took Gareth's hand. "I'm Jane."

Just as Gawain did, Gareth winked and placed a kiss on her hand. "Pleasure to meet you, Jane."

Gawain shoved him. "Leave her alone."

"Afraid I cannot," Gareth said. "We are up for watch after she has something to eat. The boys are waiting to meet her; she's joining us."

Gawain shifted his eyes between Jane and Gareth. "Is David coming?"

Gareth's smile dropped. "He went with Arthur."

"He left me here?" She didn't even know she'd spoken aloud until Gareth responded.

"Don't worry, darling. He won't let us keep you from him for too long." He slung his arm over her shoulder and led her through the halls. "You are a tiny thing," he said, chuckling at her frown. "Don't be upset—it's a good thing. Gives you an extra advantage among your bigger opponents. You'll be quick and hard to hit."

"She's going to kick your ass," said Gawain.

"I can take her." Gareth glared at his brother.

Gawain laughed loudly. "I'm sure David is going to take that well."

Gareth grinned down at her. "Aw, she blushes when she hears his name."

"Gareth," Gawain snapped.

Jane looked down. She should not be acting this way about David.

"Lighten up, brother. There's nothing wrong with either of their reactions about each other." Gareth squeezed her shoulder. "Darling, never let your feelings for him bring you down. You were destined to come into his life. Whatever, and whenever, things happen between you, they are meant to."

Gawain sighed. "I cannot believe I am saying this, but he's right, Jane."

Gareth smacked Gawain's chest. Hard. "Of course I'm right."

Jane chuckled, seeing Gawain glare at his brother. They both looked down at her and smiled. "I know you're trying to help, but I just can't think about him that way. I'm married. I'm a mom." She winced and closed her eyes before she could say more.

"Jane?" Gareth called softly.

She stopped walking and squeezed her eyes tighter, clearing all thoughts of her family.

"You all right, love?" Gawain asked.

She looked up at the two brothers' worried expressions. They shouldn't worry over her. She did not want them to look at her like she was a ticking time-bomb.

Smiling probably too brightly, she nodded. "I was just imagining how it's going to be fighting zombies as a vampire." They frowned and glanced at each other. "Can we fly or turn into bats?"

Gareth laughed and started pulling her along again. "I can feel the power inside you, but I do not think you can fly or turn into a bat. Come on. Let's go meet the boys and get you suited up."

"I get a suit?" Yes, this was much better. Anything but turning into the monster in the mirror.

"Yes, love, you get a suit," Gawain said, chuckling. "And a sword."

"A sword?" Right, they were knights.

"It'll come to you," said Gawain easily. "And you have me to train you."

Gareth shook his head. "You'll make a fool of yourself if you follow his instruction. Let me train you."

"Not once have you beaten me in a fight, little brother." Gawain laughed. "Did you hit your head on the jump? Shall I call Bed to check you over?"

Jane ignored their banter and looked in the kitchen as they rounded the corner. Three men—vampires—were eating at the table. *Eating.*

One set down his fork and stood. "Finally," he said, holding out his hand. "I was wondering when we would get to see your lovely face again. I am Tristan."

She wanted to scream from excitement. He was one of her favorite knights of the Arthurian legend. "I'm Jane," she said, feeling her cheeks heating up, "it's a pleasure to meet you."

She felt like a silly girl, but how could she not? These men had stepped out of her favorite legends, and they were smiling and joking with her, not to mention kissing her hand as if she were a maiden back in medieval times.

"We're her favorite legends," Gawain gloated.

Tristan's dazzling blue eyes sparkled with amusement. "You have terrific taste in 'myths', then. Let me introduce you to my team. We will be accompanying you for your first watch. This is Bors." He pointed to a rugged looking man with a shaved head.

Bors smiled at her, and she was instantly jealous of his forest-green eyes. "Pleasure to finally meet you." His serious voice would've had her on guard, but his smiling face eased her worry, and she nodded back politely.

"And this is Geraint," Tristan continued, pointing to a shorter man with black hair and green eyes.

"Hello, Jane," said Geraint. "I am glad you are doing much better. We were worried about you."

"Thank you," she said, sort of awed that they had all been waiting to know if she was okay. "I'm feeling much better now."

He smiled at her and returned to his meal. They were eating food.

Gawain snickered as he pulled her to the table. "We eat food as well, Jane. How do you think I keep all this muscle?" He flexed his arm, making the others laugh.

She didn't like feeling stupid, but she knew vampires drank blood. "How was I supposed to know this?"

"Well, are you not hungry?" Gawain asked.

"Ignore them," Tristan offered her a plate of pancakes and eggs. "You really must throw out your ideas of myths if you want to understand your new world. We eat food. A lot, actually. The more we eat, the less blood we tend to require. We, including you, are a bit of an exception among other immortals when it comes to blood consumption. You will need it but once you adjust, you shouldn't need it to the point you are crazed over it. But that will take you some time. It takes strong will and practice to control your thirst, especially in the beginning. But you'll have David."

She looked down at her plate. Did they really think it was so simple? She had David?

Gawain cleared his throat, and a moment of silence passed before Tristan continued. "You will see how there are differences and truths to the myths once you come across Cursed and Damned."

Jane looked up, relieved for the change. "All others are cursed, right?"

"Yes." Tristan grinned over at Gawain, who was shoveling food in his mouth. "I take it Gawain gave you a crash course on your immortality?"

Gawain glared at him. "I am an excellent tutor. She understood fine. Isn't that right, Jane?"

"For the most part," she said. It was an information overload, but she appreciated it.

Tristan chuckled. "She must be a genius." The others laughed at Gawain's frown. "Every immortal, besides ourselves, is cursed to darkness. There are two categories they fall into. Cursed is the general term for all immortals made or birthed on Earth—besides us, that is. Then there are Damned. They have either broken God's law or they were created after God cursed all immortals. Some are not so bad, though."

This was the one part she was confused about, so she asked, "How can you tell if one is considered Damned?"

"Their eyes," Tristan said. "They're black as the darkest pits in Hell."

Jane swallowed as her blood ran cold. "No one else has black eyes?"

He frowned and looked around at the others. "Demons and Fallen?"

The group nodded.

"But some of them have red eyes, too. I don't know why," said Gareth.

Gawain pointed his fork at her. "She has lovely eyes, doesn't she?"

Jane blinked, thinking for a quick second they were black.

"They are lovely," said Tristan. "I have never seen an immortal with hazel eyes."

"Does that mean something's wrong with me?" She was too afraid to tell them her eyes had turned black.

They all shook their heads as Gareth answered. "Not at all, darling. You are just unique."

Jane pushed her eggs around with her fork. "Does our eye color ever change?"

Tristan nodded. "Our emotions tend to cause the color to lighten or darken, but never black. It will take time to learn how to control your emotions. Until then, you want to avoid humans. We look human, for the most part, but glowing eyes and fangs are kind of a giveaway. Your fangs are easier to hide than your eyes. You will likely only bare them during a fight or if you need to feed."

"I see."

"You will learn," Tristan said. "We slip up, too. For example, we have all adjusted our accents and learn to speak in the same manner as the current generations do. But if we are really angry or emotional, you may hear our natural tongue slip out. It's not a big deal. Unless someone finds an immortal feeding, they sort of dismiss when their conscience tells them to be cautious."

"Oh, that's interesting," she said. "I did notice y'all sound more formal than people around here." When they grinned at her, she asked, "What?"

Gareth chuckled. "She said y'all. Oh, I have missed interaction with Texans."

She blushed. "I think other states say y'all."

"They do," Gareth said quickly. "But Texans are my favorite southern state. We think it's hilarious that other states believe you all ride horses and carry pistols."

Jane laughed. "They do! I never understood that either." Feeling more at ease, she began eating. "What else should I know?"

It wasn't until perhaps her fourth bite that she registered their silence. She looked up to see their mouths all hanging open. She paused and then swallowed. "Dudes, I've hardly been eating for three months. And I just slept for two days, I think. I'm hungry." *And David's not around to see me eat like a pig*, she added silently.

"Did you just call us dudes?" Gawain asked as a few of them laughed.

Tristan began speaking before she could say anything else. "Well, let's see. Your light is different from ours."

"I noticed," she said, looking at the faint glow from her arms. "Are we like vampires in movies?"

Gawain laughed loudly as the other men chuckled. "We are not like any movie vampire. The glow we emit is very faint. It comes from the angels. We see it clearly because of our eyesight, but humans will only think you have flawless, radiant skin, which you do. Most immortals have a golden glow, but you are the first we've seen with a more silver shimmer. It's quite lovely. It makes the gold color in your eyes stand out."

She smiled, flattered by his compliment but worried upon hearing she was different again. "Thank you, but what does it mean?"

Tristan shrugged. "I don't know. I am sure it's nothing to worry over. It probably has something to do with David or Michael. You and David are the only immortals to come from Michael's bloodline. It's an envied honor."

The others nodded in agreement.

"What else?" Her excitement grew as the worry faded.

"You are obviously noticing your heightened senses," said Tristan. "Your hearing, sight, strength, and speed are all incredible. It will take time before you can control your speed and strength, but we are sturdy enough to handle your slip ups. A mortal would not be able to, though.

"And never forget you can sustain injury. Your speed and strength greatly reduce the chances of someone getting a hit in, but you can die if you lose enough blood or are dismembered.

"We heal very quickly, but we need blood to aid the process, especially for severe injuries. Your Other's blood is the best if the injury is severe. Silver is always a worry, as well. It doesn't restrain us unless it is in our system, but the reaction to it is significant. Should it enter your body, it would slow your ability to heal. The same goes for werewolves."

Werewolves? They were probably the scariest of monsters to Jane. She wasn't ready to find out more about them yet. She'd been fighting zombies for months. She didn't want to imagine fighting a huge wolf.

"What about my heartbeat?" she asked. "I thought we were supposed to be dead or something."

Tristan shook his head. "Well, *you* are not dead. Neither are we. That is why we have heartbeats. The stories you have heard about vampires being undead are true, but that only pertains to specific, Damned—it's very complicated. However, to give you a simple explanation, there are some of us who have never died, and some who were changed as their heart stopped beating. When that happened, they truly lost their humanity. You will understand it more easily as time passes."

Gawain waved his hand. "That's not true. Dagonet, for example, died during his change."

"Dagonet is a good soul," Gareth chimed in. "His change was tragic, too."

"And he had David to help him," Gawain added.

Tristan looked her in the eye. "I am mistaken. There are some without heartbeats who are good. They are few in numbers, though. Most do not have the will to remain good."

"How are they not more like zombies?"

"Their soul remains," Gawain answered. "Their hearts are gone, but their soul remains. Stronger the soul, stronger the will to stay away from evil."

"We're not sure how these zombies came to exist," Tristan added. "The virus kills the person, but their body continues to function. Unlike vampires, their souls have moved on."

"And blood?" she asked. "How do we get it? I don't think I can feed on a person." She shook her head to push away thoughts of her children's blood.

"There are many mortals loyal to Arthur. They act as blood donors for us. Before blood could be stored, we did have to feed on humans, but we"—Tristan gestured to the men—"have not killed during our feedings. We either persuaded them to allow us to feed or we used our talents to subdue them."

"You mean hypnotize them?"

Gareth laughed. "I can hypnotize another being. Some others can, as well. He means they seduced their victims to give without realizing they were being fed on."

Jane looked at them, noticing them all avoiding eye contact with her. "Oh." She didn't want to imagine David seducing anyone to feed on.

Gawain coughed. "Donor blood is preferred now, but many prefer feeding from a live person. In our case, we mostly feed from our wives and feed them in return. An outside source is still necessary, though, so we take turns on who drinks donor blood and who gets fed. For those who still like to feed on a living host, humans volunteer."

"*Hm.*" Again, she found herself wondering who David fed from, but her empty plate got her sudden attention.

"It's just your speed," Gareth said, nodding toward her plate. "You'll get used to it."

She smiled, thankful that he didn't think she was a pig. The others finished as well and started to rise.

Tristan took her empty plate. "I think it's time for you to go with Gawain. You need to get geared up so you can begin training."

"Training?" She darted her eyes to Gawain.

"Of course," said Gawain. "We are all eager to see what you are capable of. You've handled yourself well already. With David's blood, you should be remarkable."

He stood and took her hand before leading her to the garage where they had an arsenal. Two huge black crates were open, revealing a wide range of weapons and ammunition. Most of them she recognized from movies, but it was still an awe-inspiring sight.

Gawain took her to a table where a black vest and combat boots lay. "Here." He handed her the boots and vest.

She took them and sat down on a nearby chair to put on her boots.

"We heard she was awake," said another man's voice.

Jane looked up as four men walked into the garage. They were all wearing black, dressed just as David had been the first time she saw him. Now, she noticed they also wore metal accents as shoulder pieces, much like a knight's armor.

Gawain motioned for her to come. "Jane, this is Lamorak and his brother Percivale. Then you have my brother Gaheris and lastly, this is Galahad." He pointed to each one.

She was practically bouncing on her feet. She still couldn't believe these were the knights from the legends she adored.

Lamorak stepped forward. "It's wonderful to meet you, Jane. We are extremely happy to have you be a part of the Table." He grabbed her hand and kissed it.

"Table?" She looked at them confused.

Lamorak grinned. "King Arthur's Round Table, of course. Some of your legends got it right. Once we return home, Arthur will knight you."

Her eyes went wide. "What?"

Gawain pulled her from Lamorak and led her to one of the tables. "Don't you worry your pretty little head about that right now. Arthur will explain more to you later. Right now, let's get you ready." He strapped a belt and holster to her waist and tightened it. Jane shook her head and focused on what he was doing—there was no way she could think about being knighted.

Gawain turned, picking up the M9 and put it in the holster. "You already know this one." He grinned at her before turning back to the table to pick up a large sword. She stared at it in amazement. "Your sword." He moved around her to sheath it. "Normally, these are worn at the waist, but we've altered them slightly. We run too fast for them to swing about. Since we are mainly doing long-distance combat, you will use your rifle. But with close range, your sword is your baby." He then handed her an MK12.

Gareth moved to stand beside Gawain. "Let's go see what you can do."

✦✦✦

David and Arthur walked through the bloody hallways until they found Kay and Bedivere standing in a living room.

"It is a few hours old," Bedivere told them. "They were attacked, and this one lost a limb." He gestured to a deformed hand lying in a puddle of black blood.

"Someone fought them," Arthur commented, receiving a nod from both Bedivere and Kay.

"Someone skilled," said Bedivere. "There are too many scents for the number of bodies. Some must have fled before he could finish them all."

"This person was alone, Arthur," Kay said. "He's a wolf."

"Who?" Arthur asked.

Bedivere hesitated. "We think it's Lance."

David paced the scene. "Impossible. He wouldn't destroy his own. He has no need; they obey his every order. It had to be another wolf."

"Take in the scent, David," Kay said.

David felt foolish for not picking up on Lance's scent sooner. He took a deeper breath. "There is something else. Some of the other scents—they are tainted with death." He looked to Arthur.

"They are infected," Arthur guessed. "How many?"

"Only two. The others, maybe a dozen or so, are fine."

Bedivere lifted something. "We found harnesses. I'm not sure what to make of all this."

Arthur took the muzzle and harness into his hands, turning them over with a frown on his face as he inspected it.

David tensed. "Jane . . . Do you think Lance knows about her? He was the only one who might have overheard Michael."

David knew the others were in the dark about his and Jane's predestined union, but he didn't care what they learned now.

"I don't think he knows about her," said Arthur. "But they may feel the same pull toward her that we do. We need to get back."

David did not have to be told twice. He was rushing to their camp, and it didn't take him long to get there. He rounded a corner on the final street and came to a halt.

All his panic faded away. Jane was outside with the others, and she was laughing. No, she was giggling as though she was having fun with a group of friends and not standing in the middle of an apocalyptic setting with immortal knights.

She was watching his two immature friends as they wrestled each other on the ground. He didn't care what they were fighting about—they were making her laugh. He was also thankful they had at least taken her down the street, away from her house.

He stopped thinking about her family and watched her throw her head back and laugh. She was breathtaking with her face all lit up and happy. He always wanted to see her this way.

Gawain succeeded in getting Gareth in a headlock and ordered his brother to surrender.

"Fine, I give," Gareth yelled in defeat. "You can show her how to shoot."

Gawain released Gareth, grinning back at Jane. She beamed at his closest friend as if she'd known him her whole life.

"You'll never beat me, little brother." Gawain picked up Jane's rifle and handed it to her. "I do not know why you insist on challenging me."

David was so entranced by her smiling face that he couldn't look away. She had showered and changed. He hoped Gawain didn't tell her he checked her sizes. He'd kept the fact she has one dimple at the top of her cute ass to himself.

As if sensing his gaze, she turned her twinkling eyes to him and gasped. Gawain chuckled and tossed her a wink, which only caused her to blush.

As adorable as the sight was, there wasn't time to stand there and admire her or ponder the fact his friends could be so relaxed with her. He needed to remember he shouldn't let her get attached to him. He meant it when he said he'd push her away, but the danger Lance posed left him no choice but to remain close for now.

David approached but kept his focus on Gawain rather than her. Though a sudden breeze blew her sweet smell directly at him, making his efforts to ignore her more difficult. "Gawain," he said, keeping his voice tight and serious. "We have a problem. The wolves we were looking for are nearby, but there are also some that harbor the infection. I don't know how that happened, but I smelled death in them.

"We also picked up Lance's scent. It appears that he fought against them; I'm just not sure why he would attack his own, but that's how it looked." He wanted to groan because he could feel her staring at him. She was like a magnet—he needed to touch her.

"Well, that's new," said Gawain. "What will we do?"

"We have no choice but to hunt them. I don't know what Lance has to do with this, but him being here isn't good." David finally lost his internal battle with himself and exhaled before turning to look at her.

He smiled as she straightened up. "Jane, you will need to come as well. It's not safe for you to be alone. I want you to stay with me or Gawain always. Do you understand?"

"Of course," she said quickly, but looked down, her posture tensing suddenly as she pressed her lips together and closed her eyes.

"Jane?" David scanned her face once she finally opened her eyes. The colors rapidly shifted between shades of green and brown. "Is something wrong?"

"It's nothing," she said. "Well, actually," she continued nervously, "I was wondering how my family will be kept safe?"

He wanted to hug her. The pain in her eyes broke him, but he knew showing any lack of confidence would stress her out. "Yes," he told her. "Dagonet and Lucan are already guarding your home. I'll have Gareth stay with them, too. They will keep them safe for you."

She stared up at him and had that slightly dazed look that amused him. He was glad he wasn't the only one in awe.

David lifted his hand to push her hair back but stopped once he realized he had moved so close to her, and he stepped back.

"Thank you," she said, frowning.

Arthur approached with Kay and Bed at his side. "Hello, Jane," said Arthur. "You look terrific. I realize you must be overwhelmed with information and meeting everyone, but I'd like to introduce you to my personal team. They'll be coming with us." He turned and pointed to each male as he said their names. "This is Bedivere and my brother, Kay."

She exchanged hellos with them before Arthur spoke again. "I'm afraid that we have to cut Jane's training short. I trust that David has informed you all of the new situation." Everyone gave a quick nod back. "Good, we need to head out immediately."

Arthur addressed one of the knights. "Galahad, should it come to it, are you prepared to fight against him?"

David listened to Gawain whispering in Jane's ear, "Lancelot is his father."

Her mouth fell open as Galahad answered. "Yes, I will be fine."

Arthur nodded back. "All right, gather your things. We leave in five minutes."

The others all took off in different directions, but David stood there watching her turn to his friends. She looked so at ease with them.

"You will keep them safe?" Jane asked Gareth.

Gareth grinned. "Of course, darling. You needn't worry. Just take care of my brother."

She handed Gawain the rifle with a grateful smile on her face before his friend grabbed her hand to lead her away. "He says that as though I did not just best him."

He couldn't let her get too far, so David stepped forward, grabbing her free hand.

Gawain let her go with a faint smirk and walked away.

"Jane," David said, turning her palm up. He noticed her knees wobble but pretended he didn't. "I want to give you something." Keeping her hand in his, he removed a dagger that was attached to his waist and placed it in her hand. "It's tipped in silver." He took the holster from his belt and attached it to hers. "If anything gets too close to you, do not hesitate to stab this through their heart. I plan to keep anyone from getting within reach of you, but I do not know for sure what we are about to face."

Well, that was partly true. He'd just never gone into battle with his Other at his side, and it terrified him. "Werewolves are vicious and a lot quicker than you might think," he told her. "Not to mention, they are incredibly strong. If there are many, it will be very dangerous. Please stay close. Do not let yourself become separated."

Unable to fight the urge to be close to her, he moved closer, lifting his hand to hold the back of her neck. He closed his eyes, hoping this would calm him down. All he wanted to do was kiss her and take her somewhere where nothing could hurt her.

She grasped his wrist, and he sighed. She was so warm and soft.

David bent low and pressed his forehead against hers. "I can't lose you."

She squeezed his wrist as if comforting him. "You won't."

His heart pounded. He knew she didn't mean anything more, but hearing her say that made him almost believe she was accepting him. He shouldn't have, but he lightly kissed her forehead before stepping back.

A conflicted look crossed her face, and he knew it was time to put his walls back up. She wasn't ready to deal with more from him yet.

So, he forced himself to send her a final smile and turned away, not looking back as he entered the house.

As soon as he was inside, the situation sunk in for him.

I'm taking her to hunt werewolves.

CHAPTER 13

TRUE MONSTERS

An eerie silence blanketed the deserted streets as Jane ran with the knights. The horror of what her world had become hardly registered when she'd gone outside by herself. Now that she wasn't running for her life, she could take in the devastation. The world was dying.

Bodies in various states of decay lay all around her. She wanted to cry for them, but the nauseating scent of death poisoned her lungs and distracted her from her sorrow.

Jane frequently encountered horrible smells. She especially grew accustomed to the scent of blood, feces, and urine. It wasn't something she was going to brag about, but when most people ran away from awful stenches, Jane rolled up her sleeves and cleaned it. Still, the smell of a rotting human corpse hit her newly sensitive nose and made her stomach turn. It wasn't something she could get used to.

She didn't want to whine, though. The knights had seen and smelled it all, no doubt, and she didn't want to hold them back by whining. They didn't know she was a crier, so she was going to try her best to impress them and herself.

So, she tried to quietly breathe without gagging, though a sudden thumping caught her attention. Humans. There were humans hiding, and their heartbeats were calling to her.

Her stomach tensed from hunger, but she forced herself to acknowledge these were people. People she could easily hurt or kill now. She squeezed her eyes shut but kept running, not even surprised that she could still follow the others with the aid of her other senses now.

Her stomach ached, and she licked her lips from thirst.

They're people, she repeatedly chanted in her head. *They're people.* It helped that she hadn't seen another person in so long, which was strange and worried her that she could imagine the worst on the little people who did.

Not letting her mind drift that way again, she began counting in her head. By the time she reached sixty, the pang in her stomach eased, and she opened her eyes. Perhaps having David nearby helped, or maybe the sizable meal had something to do with her relief. She didn't feel as out of control as she'd been earlier, but she wasn't ready to put confidence in her ability to overrule the craving.

Jane glanced at David. Everything about him helped distract her from wanting to do something horrible, and his strong pulse tempted her more than any of the numerous beating hearts around her. He tasted so sweet . . .

She jerked her eyes away from David and scanned her other companions. It was still hard to believe King Arthur and the Knights of the Round Table were her saviors. What they *were* was even more incredible. They were immortals—vampires—and now she was one of them. Well, she was going to try to be.

They seemed so unreal, though. They were swift—alert. Their predatory gazes continuously scanned their surroundings while they communicated with each other in hushed whispers. They weren't wearing the masks she'd first encountered them in. It seemed they weren't going to bother hiding their identities while they hunted. *Hunted Werewolves.*

It was insane to think about what she was actually doing, yet Jane found her body humming with anticipation. A pungent scent blew their way, and it drew her attention as well as the others. They turned their heads in the same direction before changing their course. They were running toward it.

The knights kept closing in around her when the smell grew more intense and then they'd spread out as soon as it dissipated. Their protective behavior should've relieved her, but it only stole every ounce of anticipation she'd fulfill a fantasy about fighting alongside the Knights of the Round Table.

What was she thinking? She wasn't a warrior.

Jane pressed her lips together as she tried to relax. Surely they'd have left her behind if they thought she'd be hurt.

As she watched David, she noticed he often tilted his head to the side to keep her in view. Arthur was doing the same as he and David led the team.

Well, so much for them feeling at ease with her being there. Though she tried her best to put faith in them and herself. They were Heaven's chosen warriors to fight against these monsters, and she had fared well by herself. The werewolves should be a piece of cake.

After all, David was with her. He'd been created by Michael, the most famous powerful angel of all time.

Something stirred in her chest as the thought of Michael being the greatest warrior angel flitted through her mind. It was as if a part of her subconscious yelled: *FALSE.* Whatever it was, an abyss opened in the deep recesses of her mind. She almost felt something had been hidden from her.

"Jane?" David called.

"*Hm?*" She broke out of her musings and glanced at him.

"Do you know how we were able to find you?" he asked.

Jane continued to run but didn't respond. No one had told her anything about that. She'd assumed they'd stumbled across her by accident.

"No, Jane," said Arthur. "We felt you before we even landed. David felt drawn to you most, but that is why we found you."

"Drawn to me?" She glanced between them.

David answered. "When we were still on the plane arriving in Texas, we felt what I'd describe as a tug at our chests. I was affected more than the others, but I did not know what it was. Still, we searched for you. The night we first came across you was the night we landed. My team immediately sought out the source of the pull we felt. It led us straight to you."

"Oh," she murmured, unsure what to make of this information.

"The area surrounding your home seems to have a significant amount of activity compared to other sites," David added. "Do you have any idea why?"

She thought over the past three months. It wasn't like she had anything other than movies to compare her experience to, but she knew they had never stopped coming. No matter how many times she ran out to draw them away, the undead returned.

"How many times did you run out there?" Arthur asked.

Jane stared at Arthur and struggled to answer as she quickly realized something: He could read her mind. His kind smile and nod made that knowledge comforting instead of frightening. The only thing was she desperately hoped David didn't have this ability.

"Y-yes," she said, stuttering. David gave her a concerned look, so she tried to shake away her shock. "Several times, actually. I don't know where I got the guts to do it, but a couple days after the plague broke, I took the chance to get some weapons. I couldn't let them get in my home. But no matter how many times I lured them away—or how many I destroyed—they always came back."

David let out an angry growl, but he didn't say a word.

Gawain spoke up. "Where did you learn to shoot, Jane? That was quite a shot you took before."

"I don't know," she admitted, relaxing under Gawain's grin. "The first time I went out was because I'd seen a military truck under attack. One of the soldiers had dropped a bag, and I knew I needed to get it. When I picked up the first gun, shooting just came easy to me."

She shrugged quickly, not understanding her ability to handle a gun. "It's funny because I've never been able to play video games where you have to shoot, but, apparently, I can do the real thing." She giggled at the end as she suddenly remembered her attempts to play video games with Jason. Somehow her man on screen always ended up staring at the ceiling, spinning in circles as Jason barked out instructions that she couldn't follow to save the virtual life of her poor character.

Oh, Jason, she thought. It was dangerous to think of him, but she couldn't stop herself. She missed him and worried about him and their children.

Thankfully, Gawain's laugh yanked her thoughts from drifting to her family. "I will teach you how to play. We play a lot of video games when we are home. Except David, of course—he's no fun. He's far too serious."

"I do not waste my time," David muttered.

Gawain rolled his eyes. "I promise we'll play one day, Jane, but I think we should make sure you know how to shoot your rifle."

The others all came to a sudden halt, and David made a frustrated sound as he turned away from her.

Jane watched Arthur place a hand on David's shoulder as he whispered something to him. Whatever they were saying, they spoke low enough so she couldn't make it out, but it was clear David was angry.

He nodded to Arthur as he let out a breath, but his jaw was tight as he turned to face her. "I'm sorry, Jane." He stepped closer, and his expression relaxed. "I should have made sure you knew how to use your weapons before we left. I hope you can forgive my carelessness." He smiled, and she almost swooned.

"Don't worry." She knew she was blushing and felt embarrassed when his gaze moved to her cheeks before returning to her eyes. "If you would just show me how to unlock the safety, I think I can figure it out."

David's lip twitched as he looked at her cheeks again, but he quickly went about showing her how to hold her rifle.

He placed his hands over hers and guided them as he slid her fingers to flick the safety off. "You will get a six-hundred-yard range." He positioned her grip which sent her body into flames. "Each magazine holds thirty rounds. There's a silencer to keep from drawing unwanted attention, but you will still hear the shot. Silencers only dampen the sound but don't kill the noise. For us, it will appear louder because of our heightened senses."

She nodded and forced herself to stare down at her rifle while he carried on.

"If you run out of magazines," he said, "call one of us. We carry a lot. While you wait, do not hesitate to pull your M9. I believe you require no instruction for that one." He wore a proud smile that made her whole body heat up even more.

"No," she said probably too dreamily. "I think I've got that one covered."

"There are around thirty zombies ahead," Tristan said as he jogged over. "Want some practice, Jane?"

His excitement over her chance to show them what she could do caused adrenaline to rush through her veins, and once again she felt the urge to fight rise.

She beamed at him in response.

Arthur chuckled and motioned for Tristan to lead the way. "Let's see what you can do, Jane."

✦✦✦

The sight in front of Jane had her grimacing. Tristan had taken them on a short detour a few blocks from where they'd been, and he was right, there were roughly thirty zombies huddled together, completely unaware of them.

She thought that was a bit unfair. They always noticed her when she was alone, but the time she has the ultimate killers around her, they stumble around oblivious. *Figures.* Jane shook her head. These monsters had ruined the world. They'd taken too many lives to count, including hers. Because they didn't have to succeed in killing her; they still stole her life from her.

Pursing her lips, she recalled her encounters with people infected with the Zev virus. Up until her last run in with them, the time David's team saved her, she'd been able to get away from them. She'd shot at several but not like the knights. She'd not been able to stand relaxed and destroy them without the risk of being harmed. Her gaze hardened, and she tightened her grip on her rifle. They would pay from now on.

A sudden change in wind direction hit her hard. She held her breath and cursed her heightened senses as she fought the urge to throw up.

She'd been so absorbed in watching the unaware group of zombies and trying not to puke, that she didn't notice David had come closer.

He lifted his hand to her cheek. "I know it smells awful." It took a tremendous effort on her part not to lean into his hand, and she sighed as she stared up at him.

A faint smile touched his mouth as his thumb caressed her cheek. "You will get used to the stronger smells," he said gently. "Continue breathing out of your mouth—that should help you from feeling too sick."

Unable to respond, she nodded and wondered how he knew what was bothering her. David smiled before his gaze fell to her lips, and she couldn't stop herself from looking at his mouth. Before she could scold herself for being so tempted to close the gap between them, he had lowered his hand and stepped back.

Gawain pulled her to his side. "We'll let you have at them, Jane."

She gave herself a mental shake and focused on the disgusting scene in front of her. The others flanked her position while David and Arthur stood behind her.

"Start when you are ready," Gawain said. "They'll notice our presence rather quickly, but keep shooting. We will be right here, should you require our assistance."

Jane tuned everyone out and selected her first target. The woman had obviously been dead for quite some time. Her wild black hair stuck up in every direction, and her graying skin stretched tight over her bones. A wicked skeletal smile was visible where her lips had once pressed together, but the skin was completely gone on one side of her mouth now. Not that that stopped a guttural groan from leaving her.

The sound would have previously made Jane shake, but not anymore. She raised the rifle and aimed.

It was different from using her M9, which she had grown comfortable with, but even without ever using such a weapon, she felt confident when she found her mark. She squeezed the trigger, hitting her target exactly where she'd expected to, and without pausing to even watch the body collapse, she moved on to the next, placing precise kill shots until her magazine was spent.

Finally, her presence was acknowledged. Her victims turned, snarling and letting out raspy groans of hunger. They started toward her, but Jane was in a trance. She changed out cartridges as if she'd been performing the exchange every day of her life. The zombies fell one after another until no more posed a threat.

Lowering her weapon, a satisfied smile spread across her lips. She took in her slaughter, noting the efficiency of her assault. The bodies lay in almost a neat pile. Not one single corpse had come closer than her first kill.

She felt a bubble of happiness at her success and turned to look behind her. Immediately, her eyes met David's. "How did I do?"

He chuckled and smiled. "Perfect, sweetheart."

"Perfect?" Gawain shouted. "That was awesome!"

"Thanks." She grinned, proud of herself and giddy from their praise.

A sound in the streets grabbed their attention, abruptly ending her moment of triumph.

David snatched her elbow and pulled her to his side. "Stay close."

She nodded back to him as Arthur came to stand next to her, and Gawain positioned himself behind her.

Snarls and growls had her tensing as she searched for the source. She looked around, desperate to locate the oncoming threat. They knew it was coming, but still none of them had laid eyes on their targets.

The sight of Tristan, Bedivere, and Kay running toward them from the south end of the street, and the worried expressions they all had etched across their handsome faces, increased the quickening beat of her heart.

The team moved their positions closer to her. They no longer looked like the carefree men she had been introduced to. These soldiers were frightening monsters. Pale glares had replaced their beautiful gem-colored eyes. They stared down the road, their rifles raised, ready to destroy.

The noise increased and the sound heavy footfalls and scrapes brushing against the pavement. She still couldn't make out what was coming but was relieved when Tristan stopped in front of Arthur.

"Wolves," Tristan said. "More than we thought."

Jane sucked in a breath.

David reached down and grabbed her hand. "It's all right." His strength calmed her fears, but only slightly. This was what they'd been going after, but now it was real.

Tristan briefly glanced at their joined hands. "It's more than a dozen, David. I counted twenty-five. There could be more."

David bared his fangs. "We'll be fine."

Jane squeezed his hand, and David darted an agitated glare to her, but softened his look quickly.

"I'll be okay," she told him. "Don't worry."

"She'll be fine, David," said Arthur. "Tristan, get back in formation."

David looked at her. "Remember what I said?"

"I remember," she promised. She hoped her terror wasn't showing. The growls were closer now. She was afraid to look but it was too late to run.

He glanced between her eyes, then nodded to her side. "You have your dagger. Use it if they get to you."

She nodded repeatedly, scared out of her mind now. "I'll use it." Her voice cracked, and so did his hard expression.

"Be brave, Jane. I need you to be brave."

"Here they come," Tristan hollered.

She broke eye contact with David and wished she hadn't.

If she'd thought of the knights and herself as monsters, these beasts were nightmares.

They were much more gruesome than those she'd seen in movies. Most ran upright, reminding her of what she'd thought of as Lycans, while others came at them on all fours, more like a cross between wolves and apes.

It didn't seem to matter how they ran, their speed made them scarier, and she was frozen in place.

These were true monsters. Their muscles rippled under patches of dark fur. Nothing like beautiful wolves in the wilderness.

Globs of thick saliva dripped from their razor-sharp teeth. Their soulless, black eyes were all fixed on her. She didn't need to wonder what they might be thinking; the crazed gleam in their black eyes said it all. They wanted to rip her flesh with their bearlike claws and bathe in her blood as they feasted on what was left of her.

Painful goosebumps erupted across her arms and neck as she began to shake.

Her heart threatened to burst from her chest, and she began to panic more when she looked off in the distance. There were four larger creatures jerking against harnesses held by a more humanoid figure.

She darted her eyes between the man and the four monsters. While he appeared to be a man, the other four were definitely werewolves. But they were not the same as the group running at them. They had clumps of hair clinging to bits of decomposing muscle while ghastly white eyes replaced the onyx pairs the others had.

Her mouth fell open. *They're zombies.*

David's hand closed painfully around hers when she started to hyperventilate. "Now," he roared and then let go of her.

Then—chaos.

CHAPTER 14

SOMETHING ELSE

Monstrous growls and gunfire bounced off the surrounding structures. Everything was louder and more violent than any war movie Jane had ever watched. It occurred to her only a few of them had silencers, as most of the knights' rifles and handguns fired with loud bangs.

They'd unleashed a hail of gunfire in one direction, but they were now shooting all around them. These new monsters moved at alarming speed, and her group was surrounded in no time. David had told her they were fast, but she wasn't prepared for this. Her previous targets had moved lazily which made them fairly easy to dispatch as long as you could keep your distance. This was an entirely different ballgame, one she didn't think she should've been brought along to.

Yet, underneath all the panic, a desire to destroy begged her to let it loose.

With her heart pounding, she lifted her rifle, aimed, and she didn't stop shooting. The sound of her own chaotic pulse in her ears muffled the roaring gunfire and snarls, but she didn't let go of her focus on the fast-moving targets.

Unfortunately, her shots didn't seem to be effective. She was hitting her marks, but wolves wouldn't go down. As soon as she'd hit one, it quickly changed direction, leaving no choice but to switch from one target to another.

Orders were shouted out, but Jane couldn't understand them. The only thoughts in her head were to shoot and stay with David. She hoped that was all she had to do.

Finally, two wolves fell and remained motionless. Their bodies were littered with shots, revealing the immense resilience these monsters had. There were visible signs of healing, but the blood loss had been too significant for them to recover. Seeing they were indeed inflicting damage on these beasts spurred her thirst for their death.

Out of the corner of her eye, she saw a strong concentration of wolves had broken through the knights' line. She also noticed Tristan and Bors had exchanged their rifles for the swords. Blade against flesh proved much more effective.

The knights were powerful and efficient. They were cutting down the wolves quickly now. But her group was still outnumbered.

More knights abandoned their rifles for steel. They were all keeping her at the center of their fight, but one-by-one they were being pulled farther away from her.

The need to stay by David's side became more evident now. Even though he focused on his targets, he was being mindful of her location the entire time. She didn't know how she'd made that conclusion, but it seemed something spoke in her mind, a connection of sorts that linked her with everything and everyone around her.

Arthur moved away, which left only Gawain in their company. The count of bodies littered the street, and it seemed they would finish this battle without incident.

Foolish to ever think such a thing.

As if her name had been called, Jane turned her head and saw a figure standing at the end of the street. It was the *man* she had seen holding the four mutated wolves earlier. He still held the wicked creatures on their leads as they snapped and thrashed in their harnesses, but he remained in complete control.

His dark eyes moved between her and David, and he smirked, catching David's attention.

Her skin crawled when he focused on her again. There was an evilness in him she'd encountered before, and dread consumed her heart when his haunting eyes roamed over her face and body before he gave David a knowing look.

David's posture changed, and his movements became more violent.

He knows him, she thought, and she gasped as a second thought manifested. *This is Lancelot.*

David started to take aim at him, but a high-pitched whistle rang out and suddenly they were flanked on both sides by more wolves than she could count. "Shit."

Jane's confidence faded as the air shifted. It as if Doom had thrown itself over them. She pressed her trembling body against David's.

"Keep shooting, Jane," David said. "We're still okay."

They weren't okay, though. He was only saying what he had to.

David aimed his rifle at Lancelot and fired a single shot. Lancelot ducked it and let out a sadistic laugh before releasing the four beasts in his grasp.

They had already struck terror into her heart, and now they charged right at her. She could hardly breathe as their pale, corpse-like eyes settled solely on her.

David turned his entire attack on them. If the original werewolves had been difficult to destroy, these mutations would be near impossible to bring down.

The others were already heavily engaged, and many were taking on two or more at a time. So far, the knights didn't appear to have serious injuries, though you could see rips in clothing and taste their blood in the air. The battle was too close now; hand to hand was inevitable.

Her sharp breaths started to burn her lungs when Gawain left her side, and she pressed herself against David's back even more. She was absolutely scared to death. If being eaten by zombies wasn't scary enough, now she had to add infected werewolves to her nightmares.

"Jane," David hollered. "Aim for the infected wolves. Don't stop shooting."

She was shaking. "I am."

"Just keep shooting," he said. "We'll make it."

"I'm running out of ammo," she told him, terrified. The wolves were so big compared to her—compared to all of them. What would she do if they got too close? Would the werewolves eat her alive? Would she be strong enough to fight them off for a little bit?

The others received slashes from the huge claws of the wolves. If they were receiving wounds, she stood no chance.

David pulled the last magazine from his belt and slid it inside her waistband. "This is the last one I have," he said quickly. "As soon as I'm out, I have to use my sword. Switch to your gun as soon as you're out. When that's out, be ready with your sword but stay close to me. Whatever happens, do not go after them."

Listening to his instructions, she pulled the last magazine for her rifle. *Just thirty rounds*. The fight was so scattered now; there was no way for her to isolate anyone. Her knights were overwhelmed, particularly Tristan, who was taking on an infected wolf as well as two others. Jane wasn't sure which opponent was worse, but Tristan was doing very well on his own. He was nearly as good as Arthur.

He seemed to be the busiest knight at the moment, so she concentrated on that particular, infected wolf with the last of her ammo. Hitting her mark seemed pointless. The monster just wouldn't fall.

Seemingly out of nowhere, a flame ignited around Tristan. The immense heat could be felt all the way across the field where they fought. The wolves in front of Tristan caught fire before she could blink, and her mouth dropped open in amazement; the flame had come from Tristan's free hand. He still swung his blade to deliver the final blows with a frightening roar over his victory. Mangled bodies fell in a charred heap by his feet. The smell of burning fur and flesh reached her quickly, but she held back a gag and swallowed the bile trying to rise in her throat.

A loud yell of pain had Jane turning. She knew the voice belonged to Gawain. He was limping, but it wasn't slowing him down. With perfect timing, he side-stepped the wolf he had been fighting, and swinging his sword, he removed the monster's massive head from its body.

She smiled, proud of her new friend, but her smile fell when she felt David move away.

"Stay close, Jane," David said, pulling his sword.

She nodded, panicking now as she put the last clip into her M9 and began shooting. David was moving farther away. She followed but pulled back when the swarm began closing around him.

He battled ferociously. His violent gaze darted in her direction often, but he didn't slow his fight. He was a ruthless warrior, and had she not known his tenderness, she would have feared him.

Jane didn't understand why the wolves surrounded him so quickly. It was as if they had been ordered to focus solely on him. Like they wanted him away from everyone else–away from her.

She breathed faster when Lancelot entered the pack around David. Her anxiety calmed a little when he didn't immediately attack, but she was still worried. Although Lancelot appeared human, he was an immortal.

A sinister smile stretched over his lips, and his dark eyes gleamed wickedly under the moonlight. She might have considered him handsome, but there was an undeniable vindictiveness in him when he looked David in the eye. He wanted her vampire to suffer.

Lancelot said something to David suddenly, and the vampire roared, shouting words she couldn't understand. Then they fought.

Their battle was fierce. Lancelot was skilled, but David was better. Yes, her handsome vampire was stronger, faster and more controlled with each attack he delivered or deflected. He was violently beautiful. She could watch him all day, but her brief admiration of her maker ceased quicker than it started.

In horrifying unison, the werewolves' heads turned in her direction.

"Shit," she screeched, firing until her last round was spent.

Gawain and Arthur started coming to her aid, but the wolves were already isolating her. She had to fight.

Without thinking, she pulled her sword. The cold steel felt pleasant against her fingers. She squeezed her grip, and a strange familiarity touched her mind. It was as though she'd been reunited with an old friend. She didn't let her fascination sidetrack her. A part of her awareness switched off, and she just acted.

Her attacks were swift and accurate. The power behind each swing was unimaginable. Jane was angry, though, and her strikes became wild. Still, she hit her targets with devastating force. She was keeping them at bay for now. If she could just hold her ground, the knights would soon join her.

Gawain made it close enough to touch her, but he was tackled from the side and dragged off.

"No," she screamed and realized she could no longer see him.

The wolves were keeping her knights away from her.

Her anger increased. The sounds of blades cutting into flesh and bone, along with an occasional grunt from her companions, filled the gaps between growls. All of it, especially David's yells for her pushed her emotions into overload.

Tears blurred her vision, but strangely, she wasn't scared for herself anymore. David, the knights, and her family were the only ones she worried about.

"Jane," David shouted.

A sharp sting shot through her free arm, and she screamed. Blood quickly soaked through her sleeve from the large gash running down her arm. It hurt a lot, but she let out a fierce snarl and cut into the beast that had scratched her.

She cut off its hand and then ran her sword through its throat. Black blood dripped on her hand where she gripped her sword. She yanked free and watched it drop to the ground with a sickening smack.

The wolves were dwindling, but another infected wolf was already attacking her, while the rest continued to hold off her knights.

Jane panted; her energy seemed to drain with every beat of her heart. The wound on her arm was much more severe than she'd expected. It was only a scratch, but it was deep. She had not been hurt as an immortal yet, but the others appeared to be healing from their injuries. She wasn't.

The monster growled, and a feral hiss escaped her lips in response. Her vision tunneled, focusing on the creature she'd been terrified of earlier. She was her own monster now. She wanted destruction.

She sliced across its chest, excited to see the muscle tear. But the wolf took her by surprise and hit her across the face with its clawed hand. The blow stunned her, and her face throbbed badly.

She turned to swing again, but the beast knocked her sword from her grasp, then grabbed her by the throat. It lifted her right off the ground and pulled her close to its horrifying jaws.

Thrashing in its hold, she delivered punch after punch to its massive head until it finally dropped her to the ground. She grabbed her throat, coughing painfully and went to stand so she could ready herself for the next attack. She just had to keep him off long enough for the others to reach her.

As she began to straighten, a powerful blow to her chest forced all the air from her lungs. A silent cry formed in her throat as tears burned her already watery eyes. She tried to breathe, but she couldn't.

The wolf snapped its jaws in her face. Somehow, Jane didn't flinch. She grabbed and held the wolf's wrist to hold it in place as it began to pull away.

Fury pulsed through her body and her mind gave over to something *else . . .*

With her free hand, she pulled the knife David had given her earlier. Finally, she let out the loudest roar she'd ever heard. Everything blurred between black and white, but she continued to yell and plunged the dagger straight into the monster's heart.

Fire rose inside her, and she impaled the infected werewolf into the tree behind him.

✦✦✦

At the sound of a loud roar, David watched an enormous wave of silvery blue energy shoot toward him. It hit him like a speeding car, knocking him onto his back. Nothing was safe. It exploded in all directions, sending everyone to the ground. The force of the blast bent trees; some even snapped in half while buildings rattled and windows shattered. Even the small house nearest them blew apart completely.

Everyone looked around in shock before they pulled themselves up to resume battle.

David immediately searched for Jane in the chaos.

Movement caught his eye, and he turned to see Lancelot scramble to his feet and retreat. *Always the coward.*

David growled but kept searching for Jane again while his brothers reentered battle with the confused wolves. It didn't take long to find her.

Pride filled him as he watched her stagger backward. Her back was to him, but he was so relieved to see her standing.

When she moved aside, he saw an impaled wolf that had been blown to pieces. Nearly all the skin was peeled away. Nothing but muscle and bone remained.

David stood up, but his smile fell as soon as Jane turned in his direction.

Her pained and confused expression didn't make sense until she removed her hand from her chest and looked down. Dark, red blood filled a gaping hole in her chest.

He looked back up to her face in complete terror.

Crying, she looked like she was trying to speak, but instead, she coughed, spilling far too much blood from her mouth before collapsing to her knees.

"Jane!" David ran to her as she slumped to the ground. He reached her side and turned over her broken body.

"No, no, no," he said at the sight of a gruesome hole in her chest. Blood pumped out of the wound and poured down the sides of her body. He put his hands over it to stop the bleeding, but it was too wide for him to cover.

"David," she whimpered.

"Hang on, Jane," he said. She cried out when he pressed down on the bloody wound. "I know, baby. I'm sorry." Tears stung his eyes when she screamed for him to stop. "Arthur! Bed!"

He was completely oblivious to the others while they finished off the last of the wolves. All he could do was stare into Jane's frightened eyes as she continued to cry, their beautiful hazel color quickly swirled from one shade to the next.

"Dear, God." Arthur dropped to his side. "David, let me see."

David shook his head no. "It's too deep. Why isn't she healing?"

Arthur looked at the mangled body nailed to the tree and found a blood-soaked silver hand hanging at its side.

"It's silver," Arthur said in complete fear. "She probably has pieces lodged inside her."

David's heart stopped for a moment while Arthur looked around franticly. Never had he known Arthur to lose his composure, but David was witnessing a scared king. It shattered his hope that she would be okay.

Gawain fell to his knees on her other side and lifted her limp hand. "I'm sorry," he said, his voice cracking as she sobbed louder.

David's heart was being crushed. The others gathered around them. "No," he roared when someone tried to pull him away.

They all had cuts and bruises that were slow to heal. Obviously, Jane's wolf wasn't the only monster that wore a poisonous contraption.

Jane's cries quieted, and her eyelids began to shut.

"No, Jane. Stay awake," David begged, darting his panicked eyes between hers. "Here, take my blood." He offered her his wrist, but she barely opened her mouth. He raised his arm and bit, then held his bleeding wrist over her lips. "Drink!"

A few small gulps took all her strength, but it was no use. She was already choking on her own blood.

Arthur yelled orders out, but David didn't listen. He only looked away when Bedivere arrived and pushed his hands away to begin working on her wound.

Jane's eyelids closed again and his blood began spilling out of her mouth.

"No, Jane." David gently shook her. "Stay with me. Please don't leave me."

Her eyes fluttered open again and locked onto his. He'd never felt so much pain in all his life.

"Don't leave me—please, Jane," he whispered, caressing her hair with his bloody hand. "I can't lose you."

Arthur sent Tristan and Bors to their camp so they could prepare for Jane. Kay and Lamorak's teams were to stay and clean up, and the rest would help transport Jane.

Arthur squeezed his shoulder. "David, we need to move her back to camp. The silver needs to be removed for her to stand any chance of surviving."

David didn't respond and kept his gaze on Jane.

Arthur sighed and told the others, "Get ready to move her."

David didn't look away from her face. He hoped she at least knew he was there. He didn't know if she could tell what was happening anymore. All she did was blink her watery eyes every few seconds.

"Please, my love," he whispered. "I only just found you."

She was fading quickly. He knew she couldn't hear him anymore, but he said the words he had wanted to say the first moment he held her. "I love you, Jane."

Her eyes shut.

Arthur leaned down and said, "She heard you."

CHAPTER 15
THE UNSEEN

A whole new kind of chaos began once they reached the house.

With Bedivere still applying pressure on Jane's wound, they made their way to the bedroom where Tristan and Bors had placed a table, waiting with several bags of blood to be administered intravenously. Emergency medical supplies were lined up on a separate table they had dragged in, creating a makeshift emergency room.

David laid her down, staring at her pale face until Bedivere pushed him out of the way. His friend went to work immediately, tending the gaping hole in the center of her chest.

Tristan inserted a catheter into her arm, and after he was done, Bors hooked up the line to start the transfusion.

David didn't know what to do. He didn't even realize he was only standing there until Arthur was pulling him to a chaise and lifting his legs. "Gawain, let's draw his blood."

Gawain was there within seconds, handing Arthur a 16-gauge needle and tourniquet. Arthur inserted the needle in the vein near the elbow while Gawain attached the flexible bag to hold the blood.

"Raise your arm," Arthur said.

David followed instruction and the bag started filling immediately.

Bors placed an oxygen mask on Jane and wiped the blood from her face while Tristan prepared sedatives to keep her out so they could work. They didn't have the equipment to put her under anesthesia, like she should be, so they improvised.

"Silver fragments are lodged in her chest," Bedivere commented. "Her sternum is fractured and some ribs are broken. Somehow he missed her heart, but she has a lacerated lung. I need to put a chest tube in to drain the blood and air. That should stabilize her long enough for me to remove the silver fragments. Her spleen is ruptured, too. It should start to repair after I get the silver out." He let out a frustrated breath. "She's just lost so much blood. It might not be eno–"

He stopped talking and set to work, with Bors and Tristan elevating her and maneuvering her arm behind her head. Bedivere put on gloves while Geraint assembled the drainage system. After Bedivere was ready, he identified the incision line with a marker. Tristan then handed him a needle, and Bedivere injected the local anesthetic solution for the initial incision. She had already passed out from pain, but they all knew she could wake at any moment.

Getting a longer needle, Bedivere delivered the anesthetic to a wide area. Blood and fluid aspirated into the syringe. "Ten-blade," he said.

Tristan handed it to him, and Bedivere made a small incision along her rib.

"Kelly clamp." Bedivere took the clamp and used it to dissect a tract in her tissue and then stuck his finger in the incision before adding more local anesthetic. He then used a clamp to pass through the muscles, twisting it with force that made David's stomach turn.

Bedivere opened the clamp and pulled it out. It was a gruesome process, but he couldn't look away.

When David tried to stand, Arthur pushed him down. "Just wait. Let them finish and then you can go to her."

David nodded as Bedivere inserted a tube through the incision. After he finished, Geraint attached the tube to the drainage device. Bedivere then sutured the tube in place, and they finished by taping gauze to support it.

Bedivere finished his work on the tube, and Bors lowered her back onto the table. He arranged a cloth over her exposed breasts but left the massive wound accessible.

Arthur helped David to his feet and led him to a chair near Jane's head. He sat, then Arthur went to help Bors lift a drape, blocking his view of her wound.

Gawain handed the first bag of David's blood to Geraint to hook up to Jane's IV line.

"Should I start another bag?" Gawain asked.

"No, let him recover before he gives more," Bedivere answered without looking up.

At first, David was hesitant to touch her, but he finally reached up and brushed back the bloody hair from her forehead. Most of her face was hidden under the oxygen mask, but he still saw his Jane. There weren't enough words to express how sorry he felt for not protecting her or how much he loved her, so he kept smoothing her bloodied hair back and tried his hardest to ignore the sounds around him. Her shattered ribs grinding against each other as she struggled to breathe made that impossible, though.

Arthur pulled her limp hand out from under the drape and put it in his. "She can feel you," he murmured before leaving the room.

David caressed the back of her clammy hand with his thumb and lifted it to his lips, placing a kiss there. He was barely aware of what the others were doing to her. He heard Bedivere muttering a few words every now and then, but the actual words didn't make any sense.

When a sucking noise sounded, he looked over to see Tristan suctioning blood from her chest wall. The sight of how much blood she was losing made his eyes burn. He didn't know how she was still alive.

He opened his mouth to ask Bedivere if he really thought she'd make it, but a small groan made them all freeze.

"She's waking up," said Bors.

"Give her morphine," Bedivere instructed him. Bors nodded and injected it through her IV.

David felt her fingers moving in his hand and looked down to see her eyes fluttering open as another groan became muffled under her oxygen mask.

He leaned over her, placing his hand on the side of her face. "Jane, it's all right. We're giving you something for the pain. Bedivere is fixing you up." He stroked her hair, and she moaned out again. "I know it hurts." He kissed her forehead. "Just hold on. You're doing great."

She focused on him for a few seconds; then her eyes rolled back as her body began to convulse. He panicked, watching her muscles spasm for a few more seconds before stopping completely.

"Jane?" he whispered.

Her head rolled to the side.

"Relax." Bedivere stepped closer and checked her pulse. "It's all right. She just passed out from the pain."

"I thought you gave her something," David snapped, carefully positioning her head again.

"She has a hole in her chest, David," Bedivere said matter-of-factly as he went back to work on Jane's wound. "She's in shock—morphine is only going to do so much. I think she will stay out this time. We can search the hospitals for more drugs if we must, but I have got the fragments out now."

Bedivere worked for a while longer, occasionally giving instructions to the others, but he finally seemed satisfied he'd gotten every piece of silver. "I'm going to close her up and dress her wound. David, get more blood in you so we can draw again for her. She's not out of the dark yet."

Arthur returned to the room when they were wrapping her wound. "How did it go?"

Bedivere turned to look at Arthur. "As well as it could, given the conditions. This is the most severe injury I have ever attempted to treat. I don't have the equipment I would like, but this is the best I can do. I am going to keep her sedated and give her morphine while she heals. I'm still worried about her breathing. I know the rules change with donated blood from Others, but she already has a lung injury—they may still react to the blood transfusion and shut down. Plus, she's in shock, and the silver was in her long enough to slow her healing completely. We need to put her on the bed and get her warm. Even with the silver out, she's going to have to fight as though she was still mortal."

Arthur patted Bedivere on the shoulder. "You did well." He walked toward David and handed him a glass. "Start drinking." He was about to refuse, but Arthur spoke again. "She needs you to be strong. Drink."

Arthur was right. He could not afford to fall apart. David took the glass offered and drank.

He glanced over at his best friend. Gawain was wiping the blood from her face with a wet cloth. In a way, David was angry that Gawain left Jane in the battle, but he couldn't blame his friend. She was his Other, not Gawain's.

David had promised to keep her safe, and he'd let her down at the first chance he had to show her how great he was. At least Gawain had tried to get to her. Unlike him who wouldn't leave the fight with Lance.

I'm the worst fucking soul mate to ever exist, David thought, not caring his brother-in-law was nearby and no doubt reading his thoughts.

Tristan and Bors removed the tarp that had been blocking the wound from his sight. He saw her bandages and the chest tube sticking out of her right side below her armpit. Swelling and bruising were visible along the edges of the bandages. The pink tinge appearing on the white cloth and tape hinted at the damage that lay beneath it.

Tristan covered her with a blanket. "Let's move her to the bed."

David didn't want them to hurt her, but he didn't want her on a hard table. He stood as the others took positions around her, grabbing the sheet under her.

"Lift," said Bedivere.

David kept her head and arm still as they carefully carried her to the bed. After they had her where Bedivere instructed her, they pulled out the bloody sheet they'd used to carry her.

"She's lost too much," said Gawain, staring at the bloody towels and blankets covering the table and floor. "How much blood did she lose, Bed?"

"At least forty percent of her blood volume, probably more."

"She's not going to make it," Gawain said. "She's going to d—"

"Shut the fuck up," David yelled, his body shaking. "She's not going to die!"

Gawain roughly shoved the table out of his way. "We shouldn't have brought her. Look what they did to her! Lancelot made zombie werewolves. She wasn't ready for that."

"If you are only going to cry"—David snarled and bared his fangs—"get the fuck out of here."

Arthur gestured for Tristan to take Gawain out of the room, and Geraint started to clean up the mess while Bors and Bedivere fixed several blankets around Jane, adding heated packs to help warm her.

Arthur stared at him for a few moments. "You need to rest and calm yourself."

David watched Gawain leave the room, then looked back to Jane. "I will not go rest. If something happens, I want to be with her."

"He didn't mean what he said," said Arthur. "He's worried."

"What if he's right?" David asked. "I should have taken her away. Lance built an army greater than we could have imagined. He led us into a fucking trap. Once he saw her, he knew she was my—"

"David, calm down," Bedivere said. "There is nowhere she could have gone, and she would have fought you every step of the way if you tried to take her far from her children."

Arthur nodded. "He's right. We know for some reason the dead are drawn to her. Since we are too, it's safe to assume that Lance is as well. He would have followed her. She's been fighting by herself for months. She has always been destined to battle beside you."

David growled and turned to Arthur. "But we all know newly made immortals get ripped apart if they face a pack. We should have scouted longer—been more certain of their numbers."

Arthur laughed. "Do you think she would have been thrilled to wait until a pack that size came close to her family?"

David looked back to Jane.

"You are looking for what-ifs," Arthur continued. "What happened, happened. Yes, she's lost half the blood in her body, but she's one of us. She has the advantage of us adding your blood, and with the silver out, she's healing."

"Slowly," David said. "You know her healing abilities will not return until her body has enough blood. She's practically human."

Bedivere sighed as he checked the monitors. "She's as stable as I am going to get her. The morphine seems to be keeping her comfortable. We will all be downstairs. And Arthur is right, if you want to help her, you need to rest. I will be drawing more blood in two hours for her. You should keep donating until she's conscious and able to feed from you."

"I understand I need to rest, but I am not leaving this room. I'll rest in the chair."

"Fine," Arthur relented. "After I debrief with the others and clean up, I will come sit with her so you can shower. And before you argue that you cannot shower until she does, think of how ridiculous that sounds. There's no reason for you to remain in this state." He gestured to his bloody and torn clothes. "I'll be back." Arthur followed Bedivere out and closed the door.

David brought her cold hand to his cheek. "I'm so sorry." He kissed her hand. "Please keep fighting. I'll be right here, but you have to fight."

He heard the others talking about Jane and the wolves downstairs, as well as the blast she'd emitted. He had no idea what to make of that yet. It had come from her, though.

"The Zev virus," Bedivere was telling the others. "It was named after the first victim of the virus: Zev Knight. I just remembered Zev is a variant for Zeev, the Hebrew name for Wolf."

David's eyes widened as he listened to Arthur voice the conclusion he was coming to.

"Wolf Knight," Arthur muttered.

"Lancelot was sending us a message with the first victim of the plague," Bedivere said. "Somehow he made a weapon, and he wanted us to know it was him."

David was shaking. He took his Jane to a fight with monsters he'd never faced before, monsters he should have seen coming if he paid attention to the news reports. It made sense Lancelot would look for a way to even the odds, but he never would have thought him capable of orchestrating a worldwide epidemic.

As they continued to discuss theories, David forced himself to tune them out and let the hissing sound of the oxygen mask lull him into a relaxed state. He was exhausted from the fight and the blood they'd taken. He didn't want to sleep, but he didn't want to think about his mistakes right then.

✦✦✦

The unseen presence stood against the wall, watching David and Jane. He had been there during the entire procedure, but none had noticed the powerful being. The man–being–knew Jane all too well, and a smile formed on his lips as a plan formed in his clever mind.

Moving closer to Jane's vacant side, he observed the curves of her pale face and her matted, bloody hair without showing any expression. His emerald colored eyes drifted over her body, halting briefly at the wound that lay hidden there before returning to her face.

Staring at her for a short time, he returned his attention to David. He knew who the knight was. Although they had never properly met, he knew David would recognize him and smiled when the famed knight's posture tensed.

The concealed individual watched David look around the room, amused at the unease his presence produced.

"Sleep," he said in a voice so smooth, any who heard it would know either peace or doom awaited them.

David's head dropped to the bed next to Jane's hand.

A smirk teased the man's full lips as his aura shimmered green then black. Now visible, should anyone look in his direction, he extended a tanned hand and caressed Jane's forehead before sliding his fingertips down her jaw.

She did not move, but her heart rate increased and her skin erupted with goosebumps. He eyed her prickled skin, then returned his gaze to her face and smiled.

With a sudden flick of his wrist, the machines monitoring Jane's vitals were silenced. He then slid the oxygen mask off her face. The numbers and lights on the monitors flashed rapidly, yet he showed no concern. Instead of aiding her like most would in this situation, he lowered his face.

Hovering his perfectly shaped lips only an inch over hers, he slowly began to close the small space between them.

Two flashes of brilliant-white light filled the room, halting him, though.

The green-eyed man smiled, almost allowing his lips to touch hers as he spoke. "I wondered when you two would show up." He straightened himself and turned, smirking at the two arrivals, however, his attention was drawn to the corner of the room. His eyes suddenly flashed with emerald fire. "But I didn't expect you."

A white light shone briefly, and a fourth man, wearing a white suit, stepped forward. He lifted a hand, fixing his neatly combed, pale-blond hair as his gray eyes slid from one man to the next until his gaze settled on the green-eyed man. "Hello, Death."

CHAPTER 16

THE KISS OF DEATH

Death calmly eyed the three individuals. He was outnumbered, but that mattered little to him. He always had the upper hand in a fight.

He ran his hand through his jet-black hair, smirking as the two men in black suits eyed his attire and scoffed. He chuckled, amused by their dislike for his preference of this time period's designer jeans and white T-shirt look.

Death looked at the fourth man, the man in white, and smirked as he watched him tug the cuff of his white sleeve. "Still ashamed to be in their presence, Luc?" He nodded to the two men wearing all black. "We all know what you try to hide."

Lucifer lowered his hands to his sides. "I have places to be, little brother. Shall we get to business?"

"You have no business here, Lucifer," said the male with dirty blond hair.

Death chuckled and addressed the seething angel. "Nor do you, Michael." He glanced at the brown-haired male next to Michael. "Nor you, Gabriel. The girl is my concern."

Gabriel sighed. "You know she is no mere girl."

Death glanced at Jane and shrugged. "That may be, but she still is no concern to any of you."

Michael scoffed. "She is David's mate; she is my concern."

"Ah, yes. The golden boy." Death glanced at David's unconscious form and laughed. "Some mate he turned out to be. I hear he is admired by all females in his presence, but I am certain this girl would find herself incapable of taking her lovely hazel eyes off me."

Lucifer scoffed. "Father made you most beautiful for his precious humans, not because he preferred you."

"Still gets under your pale skin, doesn't it, Luc?" Death chuckled.

"Do not address me so casually," said Luc. "We are not friends."

"Your pride and jealousy know no bounds," Death said, smirking. "I wonder what makes you more jealous. Is it the fact Father made me his most beautiful creation, or that he made me this way for the human race?"

"Enough of this," said Gabriel, turning to look at Death. "The girl is important. Father wishes she stay on Earth to aid the knights."

"Does Father?" Death pulled off his leather jacket and tossed it on the bed, over Jane's legs. "If that is Father's wish, why does he simply not make it so?"

Gabriel sighed. "He gave you that power. He will not take it from you."

"Yet he asks specific souls be spared." He nodded toward Jane. "This girl, for example—"

Michael interrupted him. "She has been destined to fight beside the knights."

"You think that matters to me?" Death asked. "None of you matter."

"Then why are we discussing whether the girl lives or dies?" A hellish smile formed on Lucifer's face. "We are all here because you want her for yourself."

"Always the clever one, Luc," Death said. "Though I am no fool; do not pretend you have no interest in her. You want her as well."

"Neither of you will have her," Michael yelled. Gabriel placed a hand on Michael's shoulder.

Death didn't acknowledge the archangel, keeping his eyes locked on Lucifer, waiting for his reply.

"She is powerful," Lucifer finally said. "She will make a fine queen with the power she has surging through her. She happens to come in a nice little package—what a pleasant bonus." He looked back at Death. "What do you want with her?"

"My existence is lonely." Death looked back at Jane. "She intrigues me—and as you pointed out, she is lovely. Care to make a deal?"

Michael surged forward. "There will be no deals."

"Calm, brother," Gabriel told him, pulling him back.

Death turned to the two archangels. "The way I see it, your hands are tied. If I take her life now, she will go directly to Father. That does not help any of us though, does it? She would enter Paradise, and I would still be alone. If she dies, your knights fail. You lose, I lose, and not that any of us care, but Luc loses too." He chuckled. "Though as powerful as I am, I cannot keep her for myself in her current state. Her soul shines too brightly." He smiled slyly at Lucifer. "I require a neutral soul."

Lucifer chuckled "You want me to introduce her to my darkness?"

"You wouldn't dare," Michael roared. "Do not even think of entering this deal, Lucifer."

A menacing glare contorted Lucifer's features. "As Death has so cleverly pointed out, our hands are tied. Do not threaten me, Michael. If it were not for me, your precious knights would never have been created, and this woman's life would mean nothing to you."

"It is your fault she is dying now," Michael said. "You should never have given Lancelot immortality."

"And Father should never have let you create David," Lucifer snapped.

"That is what this has always been about." Michael scoffed. "Your jealousy blinds you. What do you want with her anyway? Immortal or not, we all know you despise humanity."

"She's a tortured soul," Lucifer said calmly, "a perfect vessel to corrupt. I can already envision the wicked smile she will wear as she destroys those who oppose me."

Michael seethed, ready to attack.

"Enough," Gabriel said. "Death has given us no choice, brother. We shall simply have to pray and hope her pure heart holds against our fallen brother's darkness."

Michael glared at Death and yanked himself free of Gabriel's grasp.

Death looked at Lucifer. "Give her your blood. If David keeps her pure, nothing changes, and Father gets his wish. However, if her soul is rendered neutral, I claim her for all eternity."

Lucifer smiled. "And if she loses to darkness?"

Death smirked. "I am confident her heart and soul will withstand darkness. I am more concerned with the knight's influence on her."

A silver glint sparked in Lucifer's eyes. "You doubt my abilities to lure a soul to the dark?"

"No," Death said. "In fact, I am counting on your talent in the matter."

Lucifer glanced at Jane, then to a fuming Michael and an indifferent Gabriel. "You two will not interfere with our deal."

Gabriel pulled Michael back and glanced at Death.

"If Heaven interferes, she dies," Death told him calmly. "You already have Heaven's greatest hero to fight for her." He inclined his head in David's direction.

"You would kill her yourself?" Lucifer asked.

"I am the only one who can," he said, glancing at Jane briefly. "She lives on borrowed time anyway. Do we have a deal?"

"Almost." Lucifer glanced at Gabriel. "She has no guardian."

"There is no record of her ever having one," said Gabriel without any indication of his feelings on the matter.

"And I thought I was cruel." Lucifer chuckled, then looked back at Death. "I take it you will step in if her life is in danger?"

"If she is in danger, I will keep her safe."

"Do you take me for a fool, Death?" Lucifer asked.

Death's eyes flashed. "Always clever. Only if her life is in threat of ending, will I come for her. I will remain until the threat is clear, but I will not interfere with your methods of persuasion."

"Deadline?" Lucifer asked.

Death looked at Jane, his gaze drifting over her battered body. "One month. If she has not fallen to darkness by then, you will leave her be, and I will cease my attempts to neutralize and claim her as mine." He eyed Michael. "If we do not, Michael shall deliver Father's wrath."

Lucifer approached Jane's side and looked back toward the other two, a smirk teasing his lips. "We have a deal."

Gabriel put a restraining hand on Michael's shoulder again. Death knew they had not planned on this happening.

Lucifer reached out with his hand and gently caressed the side of her pale face with his fingertips. She shivered and, for a brief moment, the Prince of Darkness's hellish features softened.

Michael and Gabriel exchanged a look, and Death realized his plan would not go as easily as he had anticipated.

Lucifer bit down on his wrist, letting his blood free as he lowered his wrist to Jane's mouth.

Surprisingly, she sighed and closed her lips around Lucifer's wound, sucking down the offering eagerly.

"Feeling confident still?" Lucifer asked him, not looking away from Jane sucking his blood so greedily. After a few more sips, the fallen angel removed his wrist and rubbed his thumb over her blood-stained lips. He studied her face again, then leaned down to place a kiss on the corner of her mouth and whispered, "Be great, Jane."

Lucifer stood and stepped back, and Death took his place.

Death leaned down and murmured his words over her soft lips. "Live, Sweet Jane." He then kissed her lips, sealing both Heaven and Hell inside her, and initiating his wager with Lucifer.

Moving his face back, Death smirked at the flush on her cheeks. "I think she likes me." He straightened and placed her mask back over her nose and mouth, then held his palm over her chest. A green glow cast from his hand, and he looked at Lucifer. "I healed her spleen and lacerated lung. She still has bone fractures and needs blood to heal. She'll stay asleep for a couple more days, but our game begins now."

Death lifted his jacket off her legs, chuckling when Jane noticeably inhaled his scent. "And she likes leather. Good girl."

"You will suffer for this, Death," Michael said.

Death glanced at David. "Do you have such little faith in your charge?"

Michael shook his head. "You do not know love, Death. I assure you David's love for her is greater than you can fathom, and it will roar louder than any temptation Lucifer offers."

"*Hm*," was Death's only reply.

Gabriel and Michael looked at Jane and David once more before two brilliant beams of white light took their place and shot upward.

Lucifer and Death set their gazes back on Jane; her color was already returning.

"You just cost this sweet girl her soul, Death." Lucifer's steely gaze focused on him. Death didn't reply, and Lucifer chuckled, vanishing in a flash of white light.

Death watched as a beam of sunlight slid across Jane's face. "Good morning, Sweet Jane," he said, sliding his fingers over her forehead.

Then he was gone.

CHAPTER 17
NEVER FORGETTING

"She will be all right," Gareth said as he stepped over an open suitcase on the sidewalk.

Gawain sighed and glanced at his younger brother. "You know there's a chance she won't make it. You did not see her wound—she lost too much blood. That mutation put a fucking hole in her chest."

Gareth let out a strained breath and pushed open the door to the house neighboring Jane's home. "Don't think like this. They started her transfusion quickly. David will give as much blood as his body can withstand. He is the strongest and her Other—that has to make a difference."

Gawain turned to shut the door, barely glancing at the bullet holes littering the doorframe. "I don't want to see her family. I will not be able to see her daughter or son and pretend all is well. You know she misses them; I see through her brave front. She's trying not to think of them. It is unfair that we see them when she cannot."

"Knock it off," Gareth said. Gawain glared at his brother, and Gareth returned the severe look. "I know you are upset, but she would not want us to stop caring for them. She did what she had to do to keep them safe—we will do the same. Stop behaving like a child."

Gareth pushed open the bedroom door, and both knights immediately caught sight of the guard they'd set out to meet.

"How is Jane?" Dagonet asked, not looking away from the view outside the balcony window.

"She is stable, according to Bedivere," Gareth told him. "But her injuries are severe. She's suffered significant blood loss after an infected wolf, wearing a silver contraption of some sort, impaled her chest. She couldn't heal because of the fragments embedded in her wound. Though, from what I've heard, even with our abilities, she should be dead."

"How is David?" Dagonet asked.

"I did not see him." Gareth answered. "He refuses to leave her side. I told Arthur her family needs supplies—and he agreed to let you and Gawain approach them. We will keep our identity secret. If they do ask about Jane, we are to inform them that we came across her, and she asked us to aid them. Nothing else."

"Are you sure he wants *me* to go?" Dagonet asked.

Gareth chuckled. "I am sure. Do not look so shocked, Dagonet. We all know you care for this family, and you have been more than honorable in your duty toward them. Despite the fact Jane has yet to meet you herself, I am confident she'd be grateful for your aid to her family."

"Thank you," Dagonet said, taking the bags of supplies Gareth carried.

"Of course," Gareth said. "Why don't you go collect yourself for a few minutes? I want to speak to Gawain about the developments around the perimeter. Get a drink before you meet them."

Dagonet, still looking shocked, nodded and left the room.

"He will be fine, Gareth," Gawain said.

"Maybe," Gareth said. "But we can never be too cautious. Jane is their biggest threat, and if we are keeping her away, we should still remain alert with Dagonet as well."

✦✦✦

Jason sighed as he looked around his empty bedroom. Jane's scent had already begun to fade. Every single cherished item of hers still sat in the space she had made for it. She only kept random trinkets like movie stubs to her favorite movies and little things the kids had made, nothing valuable.

His gaze landed on a picture of Jane with the kids. She was smiling. He loved seeing her smile; it was rare, almost non-existent. It should have made him feel happy, but guilt caused him to see everything negatively.

The picture wasn't too old, it had been taken just before her friend's death over a year ago. She'd taken Wendy's illness hard. He knew she was Jane's only friend and had seen how devastated she was when it became clear Wendy wouldn't make it. He'd understood her sadness but hated how she'd let herself slip away from him.

He'd resented her for getting so depressed when Wendy got sick. He'd already dealt with Jane's other problems, and it frustrated him when she'd let other people's problems affect her so much.

He realized now the way he'd behaved was wrong. He had put his needs as a man above those of his grieving wife. He had expected her to stop being so sad when she came home. He wanted her to treat their life as though nothing was wrong—as though she hadn't just spent hours with her dying friend.

Jason let out a low breath. He didn't want to think about these things. He didn't want the bad memories. But it seemed like that's all he could think of now that she was gone. It had been six nights since she had left their home. He still couldn't believe she was dead or that this plague was real—that it had taken her from him. He had always assumed she'd be there.

From the beginning, he'd known Jane was different from most girls. That was what had drawn him to her. The pull toward her had bothered him because he wasn't interested in having a girlfriend, but the urge to be close to her was hard to fight. Of course, he always thought she was pretty;

attractive girls were normal for Jason, but something about Jane possessed him.

There were rumors about her, but for some reason he didn't believe them. He had told her he'd listen, and he had. Part of him wished she hadn't told him, though. Once he knew the reasons behind her guarded behavior, his rage knew no restraint. His teenage mind couldn't deal with the weight of her problems. It baffled him that those who should have cherished her had chosen to hurt her in such sick and brutal ways, not to mention, those she loved had been taken away from her so painfully and abruptly.

Jane had never been in Jason's plans. He had no desire to get tied up in a serious relationship, but he couldn't walk away. She consumed him, and he needed to protect her, take her pain away—save her. But he wanted her to be normal, too.

She looked every bit normal. She would smile and laugh, but when you really observed her or noticed how she never looked you in the eye, you knew something was up. Jason had wanted the girl hidden inside.

At first, he expected her to get better; most people got better after time passed. She had the potential to be an amazing person, and he thought once he came into the picture, she'd snap out of the sadness that had resulted from her cruel treatment. She didn't.

No, even if she seemed happy, there was a sadness that lingered with her. Instead of moving on, she held on to pain. Instead of being the great girlfriend that he could show off to his friends and family, she'd panic, and he'd be forced to leave her behind.

He hated her for that, especially since she didn't turn everyone away. She seemed to connect strongly with strangers and people who were outcasts or thugs. He didn't understand it. She said they shared things in common, but they weren't the people who'd put up with her through all her problems like he had. She should've connected with him—confided in him. Not these people he didn't care for.

Now he wondered if that had been a mistake. Perhaps he should have allowed her the chance to bond with people who shared a similar pain. But he'd taken that from her. He'd made her choose because he was jealous of the attention she'd given these people. She came alive around them, and he hadn't liked it. He also hadn't liked that many of these *friends* were men. Some had even lived wilder lifestyles than he would have expected her to approve of. But she accepted them. He hated that she let them off so easily for their wrongdoings.

There's no way he'd let another man have her company. He wasn't stupid—he'd seen the way they looked at her—she was beautiful. She'd always been gorgeous, though he never remembered telling her that. It was a given, wasn't it?

Well, it didn't matter now. She was gone, and those men would never get a chance to take her from him. If she hadn't known he thought she was beautiful, that wasn't his fault, and he wasn't going to let some other man come and tell her what she should have known.

She never let on that she would stray, but he knew if a man had been smart, he would've told her things that would turn her against him. They'd sympathize with her pain. She'd feel like they cared instead of him.

It wasn't like he didn't care. He just didn't want to put up with her crying and her depressive episodes. She should've been over her pain by now. She should've forgiven him for the things he'd done; they weren't as serious as she made them out to be. After all, she forgave others so easily and understood their bad choices, why couldn't she forget about his mistakes with her?

She shouldn't have had such high expectations of him. He was human. Everyone made mistakes. But she remembered everything! There was no way one person could remember so much, so clearly. Jason had convinced himself it was a grudge she'd developed.

He admitted that he did wrong. It should have been forgotten. That's what he was trying to do. Forget and move on.

But she wouldn't forget.

She'd say she had forgiven him but still end up crying. There was no way to catch a break with her. It wasn't like he had meant to hurt her.

Jason let out an angry breath and gazed at her side of the bed.

She had always curled up so far away from him. He loved having her soft body against him. All he'd wanted was to take her every second, but she never seemed to enjoy his touch. Well, not after he'd told her she was just his wife and pointed out his disgust over the stretch marks she'd gotten from her pregnancy—when he'd admitted he wasn't in love with her.

Why did being *"in love"* with her matter so much? He loved her. Why did she have to make it so complicated? Life wasn't like the fairy tales she'd always talked about. She needed to grow up. He loved her, let her stay home to be a housewife—paid the bills and dealt with her issues. That should have been enough to show he cared. Those weren't excuses to deprive him of his needs. Husbands had sex with their wives—she should have understood that.

He looked away. This was only making him angrier. He kept telling himself not to think of these things, but he couldn't stop. It was almost like she was still there, throwing his mistakes in his face.

Jason noticed her medications. Stupid pills—they'd only made her worse. He roughly tossed them in the trash. He'd never got over how horrible she looked on them, like a zombie. His heart pounded at that thought. "She's gone," he whispered. "She didn't turn."

He threw the last of her pills away. She'd only kept them because she said it wasn't safe to throw them out. What did he care if some druggie got them? It wasn't like there were drug addicts to worry about now.

He stood up, considering if he should throw out or pack up the rest of her belongings. *No, not yet.*

He was about to leave when he glanced at their laptop. "I'm such an asshole," he muttered to himself before he groaned and ran his hand through his hair, refusing to acknowledge why she'd looked so broken. So worthless. "Stop thinking. Please, God, let me forget."

Maybe this was punishment. Punishment for all his sins—all his lies to her. God, how she hated lies, even small ones. They were only little lies, but he'd known what he was doing. At first, he'd only wanted to keep her from being upset. However, if he were honest, that wasn't the only reason. He was ashamed that he'd disappoint her, and instead of owning up to his shame, he'd made her feel crazy for her accurate accusations.

He hadn't understood how perceptive she could be. It was almost as if she could sense a person's genuineness or their malicious intentions. She'd seen through him, and instead of mending their failing relationship, he pushed her away and began to drink away his stress. Jane hated alcohol of any kind; it brought back horrible memories for her. Even when she asked him to stop, he brushed her off. He could do what he wanted.

"Fuck," he yelled, kicking aside a toy he'd stepped on. This had to be punishment, and it would never stop because he couldn't make up for it.

"I'm sorry, Jane," he whispered before leaving his room and heading to the kitchen.

His home was slowly turning into a trash dump. Jason leaned down to pick up an empty water bottle to refill. Luckily, the water still ran, and the electricity hadn't gone out, but he knew it would go off one day. He needed to start boiling water to make sure it was still clean.

They had fewer supplies now. He wasn't sure how he would ensure their survival with Jane gone. He couldn't leave the kids alone, and he understood Jane's risk-taking now. She'd kept their chances of survival up.

A faint knock at the window nearly caused him to drop the bottle. He tensed and stayed completely silent.

"Mr. Winters," a deep voice called.

Jason didn't know if he should respond, so he waited.

The man spoke again. "Mr. Winters, we are soldiers who want to help you and your family. We've brought you some supplies."

"How do you know who I am?" Jason asked, keeping his voice low as he walked closer. It could be someone trying to take his stuff. He grabbed his bat.

"Sir, we met your wife—Jane." Jason held his breath. "She told us where we could find you and asked us to aid you. We mean you no harm. Let us help you and your children."

Jason debated whether he could trust this person. There was really no choice, and if Jane told someone where to find their house, she had trusted them.

"All right," he said. "Let me clear this stuff away."

Jason began shifting around the barricaded hall.

Finally, he had made way and lifted the window that revealed two men in black uniforms. Jane had been right, they were soldiers. They gave him genuine smiles, but Jason was unsettled by the vibrancy of the first man's eyes. It didn't look natural. He didn't look natural. The second man disturbed Jason even more because his eyes were black.

Jason's instincts told him to be fearful, but Jane had trusted them. He had to have faith that this was her final blessing. He felt awful now for putting her down because she didn't get help from them the first time. "Please come in."

"Thank you," they said.

The man with bright eyes climbed through first, and turned to take the bags from the black-eyed man. After him, the black-eyed man entered.

They glanced around the room and their expressions fell when they took in the disorder that had overtaken his home.

Jason looked around, embarrassed. "I know it's a mess, but I can't do much about it now."

"Not at all," the first man said, dismissing his apology. "Let us introduce ourselves. I am Gawain, and this is Dagonet."

Jason shook their hands. They were strong. He almost winced but kept from showing his discomfort. He had a feeling they were restraining themselves already. They did not look like simple soldiers. "Nice to meet you. I'm Jason Winters."

"The pleasure is ours," said Dagonet. "We brought a good supply of drinks and food, along with some personal hygiene items. If there is anything else you might require, let us know. We are willing to search for it."

"I don't know how to thank you," Jason whispered, looking at the bags of food in shock. "I was beginning to lose hope. I knew I wouldn't be able to get more for us." He cleared his throat from the sudden hoarseness that escaped. "She got infected and decided to leave. When did you see her?"

"We came to her aid a week ago and then again shortly after," said Gawain. "We wanted to help her and this is a way we can. It's not much, but we hope it makes matters easier on your family. We know you are all suffering right now, and we offer our deepest sympathies."

"Thank you," he whispered, feeling that terrible pain in his chest again. "Were you with her when–"

Gawain gave him a tight smile. "We did what we could to help her."

Jason nodded and was about to speak again when Nathan and Natalie stumbled into the kitchen.

"Daddy," Natalie whispered, glancing cautiously between the two men. Nathan was right behind her, peeking around but avoiding eye contact with anyone.

Jason stared at his children, still a little worried, but when he looked back at the two men, he was surprised to see Gawain's face had lit up upon settling on Natalie.

Dagonet also looked at them fondly. It was a bit strange to see them reacting so strongly toward a little boy and girl they didn't even know, but Jason figured it would be a blessing to find children safe at all now.

Gawain knelt on one knee in front of Natalie. "Hello, sweetheart. My name is Gawain, and this is Dagonet." He pointed behind him.

"I'm Natalie, and this is Nathan," she said. "What are you doing here?"

Gawain smiled at her. "We brought you supplies, and Dagonet has something special for you."

Instantly, both children looked to Jason for approval. They had not looked so hopeful in the past week. He couldn't help but smile at their small joy and nodded when the other two men chuckled.

Hesitantly, Dagonet stepped forward and held out a doll. "I hope you like princesses."

Natalie nodded eagerly, not taking her eyes off the toy. She didn't hesitate to snatch it up and hug it to her chest.

"What do you say, Natalie?" Jason prompted her.

"Thank you," she mumbled into the doll's hair.

"You are very welcome. This is for you, Nathan." He reached back into the bag and pulled out a T-Rex plush.

Surprisingly, a smile formed on Nathan's lips, and without showing any nervousness, he walked up to Dagonet. He wrapped his hand around the dinosaur's arm and then threw his arms around Dagonet's neck.

"Dragony," Nathan said, completely mispronouncing the man's name.

Jason was speechless. Nathan loved dinosaurs, of course, but he never hugged people. Except Jane.

Slowly, with a strange sadness to his smile, Dagonet hugged Nathan back. "You're welcome, Nathan."

Jason shook his head as he watched Nathan and Natalie drag Dagonet to the living room. They were all smiles as Nathan pulled the man toward his pile of toys.

Jason looked back at Gawain. "Thank you again. They haven't been this happy in a long time. It has been very difficult for them since Jane left."

Gawain shifted awkwardly. "I'm glad we could make them happy for the moment. Is there anything else we can get you?"

Jason picked up on his sudden discomfort but chose not to voice his curiosity. "No. Thank you. You have done more than enough."

"No need to thank us. We will be close by, and I will make sure we check on you again. I think we'd best be off now. Dagonet."

They entered the living room together and found Dagonet holding a dinosaur, roaring at the kids as they giggled.

Gawain let out a light laugh before squatting down next to them. "I am afraid that Dagonet and I must leave now. But I promise we will return to check on you."

Both children frowned, but Natalie nodded and stepped up to Gawain before wrapping her arms around him. "Thank you."

"You're welcome, sweetheart," he replied, suddenly looking like he didn't want to let go of her. "We will see you again."

Jason led them back to the window. He almost regretted that they had to leave. It had been so long since he had seen anyone besides Jane and the kids. It made him wonder how she dealt with never talking to anyone but him.

"Take care, Mr. Winters," said Dagonet.

Jason nodded and shook his hand before he watched him ease back out the window. "Please call me Jason." They nodded with smiles while Gawain shook his hand. "And thanks again."

"It was our pleasure," said Gawain.

Both men gave one last glance at the children before leaving Jason alone with his thoughts once again.

CHAPTER 18

A BEAST INSIDE

Sore didn't come close to describing what Jane felt. She opened her eyes and blinked several times as her senses came alive.

The beeping monitors and hissing sound from the oxygen mask made her head throb, but she quickly gathered she wasn't dead. Death probably felt wonderful compared to the pain she was in.

The blurry images of a ceiling let her know she was back at the base house. Jane glanced at her chest to see the damage. She remembered the werewolves, the mutated werewolves, Lancelot, and the blow she'd taken. It still hurt. She felt like she was being squeezed but at the same time, ripped wide open.

The oxygen mask obstructed her view, but she saw someone had bandaged her up. There was a tube sticking out of her side. She also had two intravenous catheters with fluids running through her left arm. One obviously delivering blood, and she assumed the other bag to be standard fluids. Besides all the pain, a noticeable pressure between her legs caught her attention.

At first she panicked, thinking the worst, but it soon made sense what she was feeling. *A urinary catheter is in me.* That would mean she'd been there for a while. While it shouldn't matter, she couldn't help but wonder who had put it in, and she prayed it wasn't David.

Poor, David. He'd been there with her, tears in his eyes as she tried to stay awake.

As soon as she wondered where he was, her side warmed, and there, her gaze fell to the vampire in her thoughts.

He was slumped in a chair with his head resting near her hand. Asleep, he looked a lot younger, but she noticed straight away how pale he was, as well as the dark circles under his eyes. *He must need blood.*

Still, he was absolutely perfect, and she hated that she'd caused him to suffer. He'd saved her twice now, and his whole life had been ruined because he believed she was his soul mate.

He deserves better, she thought, hopeful he would see that and move on from her. Though, as she thought of him finding someone else, she hated and pitied herself.

Some hair fallen over his forehead, and the urge to move it filled her. She weakly managed to raise her hand enough to do so, and almost immediately, he awoke.

Without warning, his eyes opened. Her hand stilled in his hair, and they stared at one another. It was like couldn't believe what he was seeing, but he finally smiled.

David put his hand over hers and held it to his cheek. Her oxygen mask hid her smile, but she couldn't hide her sigh when he turned his face toward her palm and kissed it, then each of her fingers.

She melted. She'd never been treated like this. The noisy monitor made her reactions to him more obvious, and she thanked God the mask hid her flushed face.

"I did not think you would wake." His voice was a scratchy, but it still made her skin sizzle.

"Can I take this off?" she asked, motioning to the mask. Her voice was hoarse and muffled, but it seemed he had no problem understanding.

He nodded and slid the mask down before grabbing a glass of water. She eagerly accepted his help to pour some much-needed liquid down her dry throat. She took small sips and gave a nod that she was done.

"Thank you," she said and cleared her throat. "How long have I been out?"

David put her drink down. "Three days. We feared we had lost you for good this time."

She couldn't believe that she had been unconscious for so long, and she had a feeling he'd stayed with her the entire time.

Tugging on his hand, she said, "Come here." When he didn't move, she pulled harder. "It's okay."

He appeared nervous about getting close with all the medical equipment still hooked up to her, but he finally moved to sit beside her.

"It looks like someone fixed me up," she said, unsure what to say now that she had him there. Honestly, she felt dumb for it now. Why was she asking him to get in bed with her?

He watched her carefully as he asked, "Do you remember what happened?"

She almost laughed. "Yeah. I got my ass kicked by a werewolf."

His lip twitched, but he looked sad.

"I think I prefer the kind of werewolves in new movies and books," she told him. "You, know, the kind that are just big wolves."

The corners of his eyes creased as he hid a smile from her. "There are different kinds of immortal wolves. I have heard the overgrown versions of natural wolves are popular in fiction. Shifter-romance, yes?"

She nodded and stared into his worried eyes. "Yeah, I'm a silly girl, I guess. These ones were scary. Like old school movie werewolves. I wasn't expecting them to be like that."

"It's my fault–I should have prepared you. We should have been more prepared."

"It's not your fau—" a sudden pain exploded throughout her chest. Her eyes watered. "Oh, Jesus."

"Lie still." David gently pushed her back down. "Are you all right?" He pushed some hair behind her ear as she nodded. "You need to relax," he said. "And of course it was my fault; I should never have let you get away from me. I'm so sorry, Jane."

It wasn't his fault, though. She remembered most of the fight and how scared she'd been. David had stayed with her as much as he could. If he hadn't joined the fight, she probably would have died. How he could blame himself? She could see how much he cared for her. She remembered dreaming of him telling her how much he loved her. Too bad it had only been a dream.

David frowned. "Why are you smiling?"

She chuckled, embarrassed because she didn't know she was. "It's nothing. And don't blame yourself. There is no way you could have kept them all away. I don't think any of you were expecting that to happen. I'm just glad you were there with me."

He sighed and closed his eyes. "But I've almost lost you twice now. I never wanted to see you so close to death again. This was so much worse than the first time, if that is even possible."

"Stop," she told him quickly. When he opened his eyes, she added, "I'm all right. Look, even the pain just now is going away."

He grinned. "That is because you are tougher than any person I have ever met."

Her, tough? She almost laughed. "I doubt that. So, who fixed me?"

He sighed, leaned back, and brought her up to date, and after telling her everything, he said, "Bed has kept you sedated, but I've been afraid you would not wake up."

"Why do you look like this?" She reached up to touch the circles under his eyes. "Have you been sleeping?"

"I've been worried about you," he said, not seeming at all ashamed to admit so. "And I am fine. They're just drawing my blood as often as possible to administer to you. It's only a little more than I would normally feed you."

"David," she murmured. "I don't want you to hurt because of me."

He caressed the side of her face. "Sweetheart, the only way you could hurt me is if I were to lose you." He smiled, and she knew her watery eyes didn't go unnoticed. "Why don't I have Bed come check you out? Then maybe you can get cleaned up. I think you should get some food in you, too. Do you think you can handle that?"

Unable to talk, she simply nodded.

"Good," he said, leaning down and kissing her forehead. He left his lips on her skin while he spoke. "I will go get him and tell the others you are awake."

Jane closed her eyes to savor his presence. He always made her feel so warm and safe. But he was gone before she could truly enjoy it. Part of her was grateful he kept doing that, but the pathetic girl inside her who couldn't remember being precious to someone craved every bit of affection he offered her.

What she was going to do now? It was wrong, but he was already claiming a place in her heart.

No matter that she told herself he deserved better, she didn't think she could handle him leaving her all the time now.

✦✦✦

"Well, everything is healing nicely," Bedivere said as he finished wrapping her fresh bandages. "You can eat, unless you'd like to freshen up first."

"Yeah. I feel gross, and I smell worse." She looked at her binding. "How do I shower like this?"

He chuckled. "My dear, you smell fine. We are used to blood and dirt. And David has been doing a terrific job cleansing you where I instructed him to." Her face burned, and he laughed as he said, "Forgive me. I only meant that he's been wiping your arms and face. I thought he could use a task to feel useful."

"He wasn't the one who put the catheter in, was he?"

His eyes twinkled. "Goodness, no. He was more embarrassed than you. Anyway, he's been afraid to move you too much; he stuck to your arms and face."

"Great," she said just as her stomach rumbled. It was honestly the loudest stomach growl she'd ever heard before. "Oh, my gosh."

Kind Bedivere didn't laugh, but he smiled, amused. "I believe the beast inside you is ready to be fed. Let's get you in the shower. Do you think you can stand and walk to the bathroom?"

"Yeah." Jane slid her legs over the side of the bed.

Bedivere helped her stand, but he moved back after she was up.

Jane pressed her lips together and took a step. "Ow." All the air came rushing out of her mouth as she almost collapsed from the excruciating pain that ripped through her body.

Bedivere rushed back to her and lifted her up. "I think you can worry about walking after you eat." He carried her toward the bathroom as she struggled to catch her breath.

She felt silly for being carried, but she was thankful for his help.

Bedivere set her down on the counter, checking her bandage "Are you all right?"

"Yeah," she said, trying to steady her breath. "Thank you."

He smiled. "It's going to be very painful for a few days. Relax for a moment while I get something to cover the bandages."

He left and was back with a roll of plastic wrap before she could count to ten. Their speed amazed her.

"I know it hurts," he said, "but raise your arms for me."

Jane gritted her teeth together and complied. Thankfully, Bedivere worked quickly, and he was done in no time.

"Good job," he said as there was a knock on the door.

Jane swore she could sense David on the other side.

"Here, cover yourself." Bedivere handed her a towel and waited until she was covered before he opened the door.

It was her vampire, and he was holding a folding chair. Bedivere moved back for him, and she smiled shyly when David briefly made eye contact with her.

She thought his cheeks turned pink, but he looked away so quickly she wasn't positive. Bedivere shook his head, smiling as they watched David position the chair inside the shower. He even stepped back, snatching a hand towel off a shelf before placing it on the seat of the chair.

Jane pressed her lips together to keep herself from awing. He was too cute.

As he turned around, she realized he hadn't meant for them to watch him as he shifted his stance nervously all while he avoided looking at her exposed skin.

"Uh—" he said, shaking his head, still not looking at her. "I will just wait in the room if you need anything." He didn't wait for either of them to respond and moved for the door but still glared at Bedivere who was barely hiding his laughter.

"Wait," Jane said, smiling when he came to an abrupt halt. "Could you find me some clothes to change into when I'm done?"

Bedivere chuckled at the blank look on David's face now.

"Yes, of-of course," David said, stammering a bit over his words. "I will be right back. I'll give them to Bed." He was out the door in a flash.

Bedivere laughed now. "I have not seen him so flustered before. All right, let me help you get into the shower."

He sat her down on the chair, turned on the water and made sure that she could reach everything before he stepped back. "I will put your clothes on the counter, and you can call for David if you need anything. You are free to pull the wrap off or wait until I return. I need to leave with Arthur, but I can be back if there are any problems. I think you will be okay, though. Just get back in bed after you are finished."

"Okay. Thank you for everything."

"You are very welcome." He smiled and gently caressed her head. "You should have David make you some breakfast when you're done—he's a terrific cook."

Gosh, the man could cook? All she could say was, "Okay."

"Good. I will see you later, Jane."

After Bedivere left her alone, she heard him speaking quietly to David. She didn't know what he was telling him, but it didn't last very long because a few seconds later, the bedroom door shut.

She sighed and removed the now wet towel to begin her seated shower. It wasn't an easy task. The bandages were tight and made it hard to move. The slightest movements seemed to hurt the most. There was no getting out of this, though. She wasn't going to spend another hour covered in old blood and whatever else stuck to her skin.

She held her breath as she bathed, swallowing her painful cries. Now, all she had left to do was rinsing the conditioner out. But she wanted to cry. Every movement, every second was hurting more and more.

"Ow." Jane began panting as the stabbing sensation in her chest grew more intense.

"Jane, are you all right?" David called from the room.

"It hurts, but I'm all right," she answered him quickly.

"Sweetheart, I think you need to get back in bed now."

Her eyes went wide because she realized he wasn't just outside the door—he was in the bathroom.

"My hair still has soap in it," she blurted without thinking.

He was quiet for a few seconds before he spoke again. "Do you have something to cover yourself with?"

Jane glanced at the wet towel hanging on the rail and answered. "Yes."

"Cover yourself, and I will help rinse your hair."

Jane knew she had to listen or she could wind up sprawled on the shower floor. She pulled the towel over her lap, holding it up was out of the question because of the pain was too great. At least she was already covered around her chest. "I'm ready."

David opened the shower door slowly. He gave her a tight smile and immediately reached for her hair.

She stiffened at first, but his touch felt so good that she quickly closed her eyes and relaxed while he massaged her scalp.

"What happened?" he asked, still working the soap out of her hair.

His touch had soothed her so much, she almost didn't respond. "Oh, I think it's just going to be sore for a while. I feel really tired."

She quickly opened her eyes when his hands disappeared and watched him shut off the water. Without him touching her, she could think clearly again. It also meant that her pain was the main focus.

Her breath came out fast, and David's attention instantly returned to her.

"What is it?" He looked her over carefully.

"It just hurts. Do you think you can get me a dry towel and help me get out?"

David nodded and handed her the clean towel he grabbed from the counter. Without another word, he turned around and closed his eyes. Despite the agony she was in, she grinned at his thoughtfulness and removed the wet towel to wrap herself in the dry one. "I'm ready."

David turned back to her and put his arm around her to lift her up. She nearly swooned but hid her face so he wouldn't see her dreamy look.

"Don't move," he said as he gently placed her on the bed. "I will get your clothes." He went back into the bathroom and returned in no time with her clothes and an extra towel. "I'll wait in the hall. Call me when you are dressed, and I will help you back in bed."

Before she could reply, he was out the door. Again with the swift retreats. She was afraid he was going to bolt as soon as someone else came along to help her.

She looked at what he'd given her to wear. There was a pair of white cotton panties, a man's T-shirt, and sweat pants. She grabbed the panties and awkwardly slid them on. It felt like she had run a marathon by the time she had them on properly; she was almost sweating. She let out a breath after adjusting them.

The pain just wouldn't go away now. It seemed David's presence provided her pain relief, or at least distracted her enough that her brain couldn't help but to turn to mush when he was close.

Jane sighed, put her feet through her pants, and pulled them up. Now the shirt. It was a plain gray tee; an extra-large, and David's scent was all over it. *Is this his?* She put it to her nose and inhaled deeply. *It's his!*

It was stupid, but she felt giddy that he'd given it to her. He smelled so good. It was a bit creepy of her, but she wanted to roll in his scent. She held the shirt and tried lifting her arms over her head. The movement made her eyes water, and she whimpered.

David called from the closed door. "Do you need help?"

Briefly, she debated on letting him help her. It would be stupid not to just take the help again. He'd already seen her in less.

"Yes, I need help."

The door opened, and he peeked his head in before entering. He looked at her chest but remained a gentleman by not ogling her. "Do you need me to take off the plastic?"

"Please," she said, relieved he knew what was wrong. "And help me put my shirt on. It feels like my chest is going to explode whenever I move my arms."

David quickly kneeled and began removing the wrap. His brows furrowed while he concentrated on not tugging her too roughly.

Jane found herself staring at his face and then down toward his powerful chest. Entranced, she then admired his muscular arms and the way they flexed with each movement his hands made.

She felt strange. Burning.

She started panting. *It's so hot . . .*

David removed the last piece of plastic and looked up. His eyes drifted over her face, but Jane could only stare at his lips.

He swallowed and didn't look away from her face as he reached for the shirt.

Jane saw him move, but it seemed like she was looking at him through a very small window. She tried to focus on his face. He moved slowly, as if he were keeping himself from making sudden movements—like he was encountering a wild animal.

He raised the shirt over her head, and for a second, she felt tightness around her entire body.

David paused. She thought she heard something fall, but he was moving again, although now he looked far away. Almost like she was glancing through a peephole of a door. Something blocked her vision, and the constricting feeling around her body let up.

David came back into view, and she realized he'd slid the shirt over her head.

She didn't understand what had happened, and David seemed to want to say something as he kept searching her eyes for something. But he shook his head and carefully pulled her arms through the shirt.

"Is that better?" he asked.

At first, she didn't know what he meant and wondered if she'd almost blacked out. By the way he continuously searched every part of her face, she could tell something worried him.

"Yes," she said. "Thank you."

David didn't look satisfied by her response, but he stayed quiet and lifted her into his arms again.

This time, she sighed and rested her head against his shoulder. She swore he nuzzled her.

Their closeness ended all too soon though when David placed her down on the bed. His fingers seemed to linger for a bit longer against her arm as he pulled the blankets up over her, and she briefly wished she could find some excuse for him to keep touching her.

"I changed the sheets while you were showering." He pulled his hand away. "I need to make your meal. I want you to rest until I get back."

She nodded eagerly at hearing that she was finally getting fed.

David chuckled and quickly placed a kiss on the top of her head. "I'll be right back. Call if you need anything. After you eat, I will give you more pain medicine." He moved back and exited the room without another word.

Jane stared after him for a bit before closing her eyes and relaxing into the pillows. The pain was still present, but it was tolerable now that she wasn't moving.

She tried to process everything, but she was still too consumed with David to care. She let go of her worries and inhaled his scent that lingered on his shirt. Instantly, images flashed in her mind of her naked and in David's arms.

His lips and tongue tasted her skin while an animal like growl rumbled within his chest. He roughly pulled her against his perfect body and nudged her legs apart with his knee.

A startled gasp left her lips, and she opened her eyes. Her breaths were ragged as she looked around to make sure she was still alone. Jane shook her head; she should not be thinking that way. Something was wrong with her if she was imagining that at a time like this.

Tears stung her eyes as she mentally berated herself for thinking about him like this. She was married. She was an awful person.

An intense fatigue swept over her before she could get carried away with internal hate. In fact, her mind numbed completely, she heard a man chuckle. For a moment, she considered David had returned, but she knew he hadn't. Perhaps the medications still lingering were causing her to hallucinate.

Satisfied with her resolution, she sighed and fell asleep.

CHAPTER 19
A TRAGIC TALE

Thirty minutes after David had left Jane, he quietly reentered the room. He'd been listening to her vitals since he left and knew, by the steady rhythm of her heartbeat and her even breathing, she had fallen asleep almost shortly after he'd gone downstairs.

David smiled as he took in how comfortable she looked sleeping now. It had been hard to watch her in pain. He knew she didn't want to ask for help, but Bedivere had told him she was struggling with simply moving her arms.

While he wanted to respect her privacy, he would have walked into the shower to get her if he needed to. Hopefully, she'd let him take care of her because it would still take a while for her to gain strength back, and healing would take most of her energy during this process.

David walked toward the dresser with the tray of food but before he placed it down, he noticed the items there had fallen over, and many had moved significantly in Jane's direction.

He glanced over his shoulder and sighed when he saw her still sleeping. She looked like an angel. Nothing looked out of place with her. There were no warning flags telling him she was a threat—but she was.

When he'd been helping her dress, he'd seen a beast trying to surface. She wasn't an ordinary immortal, and he didn't know what to think of her differences yet. Arthur hadn't been there to discuss what he'd seen. Her eyes had turned black. Even the whites of her eyes had been drowned in darkness. Damned immortals didn't even have eyes like hers.

The shock of her eye color wasn't the only thing worrying his heart. The sudden pressure that had surrounded his body while he watched her look more demon than angel had been so powerful he nearly collapsed under it. Only when the furniture shifted in her direction had it let up, and Jane seemed to come out of whatever trance she'd been in. Still, it proved to him she was more powerful than he initially believed.

He let out a breath. This was too much for him to contemplate right now. All that mattered to him was that she was awake and mending. She was still his Jane. No matter what was different about her, he loved her.

As he continued to watch her, stress over their no doubt complicated future melted away. He grinned when she suddenly sniffed the air. He knew she liked the way he smelled, she'd taken his scent countless times already without even realizing it. Maybe it comforted her. That was why he'd given her his shirt to wear. Plus, he enjoyed having his scent all over her.

Even if she wasn't his all the way, he wanted others to know he was there. It was also a welcome sight to see her in his clothes. It was a display of how feminine she was, and though she could fight with the best of them, he hoped she would eventually see him as a man who was big and strong for her.

Jane let out a sigh and shifted. He didn't want to disturb her while she was so relaxed, but he did want her to eat. She had been very hungry, so he didn't feel too bad about walking over and taking a seat next to her.

"Jane, it's time to eat."

She didn't stir in the slightest. In fact, she smiled and looked more at ease than before. He leaned over her and placed his hand on her other side by her waist. As he stared down at her face, he wondered if he would ever be able to wake her up with a kiss. He shouldn't be thinking about kissing her; it only made their situation harder to bear, but he could dream.

Jane's eyes suddenly opened, and she beamed up at him.

He chuckled and watched her shiver. He knew she had been trying to hide her reactions to him, but he'd seen the way she would bite her lip and how her skin would flush or prickle whenever he spoke or, especially, when he laughed.

"I guess I dozed off there for a bit," she said with a slightly dazed expression.

"That's good," he said, wanting so badly to lean down and kiss her. "But you need to eat now; I made us breakfast. Sit up. I don't want you getting out of bed yet."

She took his hand as he held it out for her, though she pouted her lips and said, "I don't have to eat in bed."

He chuckled but continued helping her get situated. Her personality was showing more now, and it was clear she wasn't used to someone taking care of her. *Too bad, sweetheart.* "I know you do not have to eat in bed. I just thought we could have breakfast privately, so we can get to know more about each other."

"Oh, yes. I'd like that." She smiled, blushing as his hand grazed her side.

"Perfect." David fetched the tray of food.

"You made this?" she asked, looking at the plates in his hands.

He nodded and handed her the one he'd made for her. It contained Belgian waffles, eggs, bacon and orange juice; Gareth had told him she ate well with them, so he hoped she'd eat his food.

"Where did you get all of this?" She moaned but quickly quieted herself with an embarrassed smile. "Sorry. It's just really good."

He chuckled before answering. "I am glad you like it. To answer your question, we came with a large supply of food and receive air drops with new rations every two weeks. Gawain had waffle mix stashed for himself, but I don't think he'll mind sharing with you—you need something filling."

She only nodded, and although she glanced up somewhat embarrassed a few times, she ate energetically. He didn't know why she was embarrassed about eating; a good appetite meant she was feeling better.

He cleared his throat. "So tell me something about yourself."

"What do you want to know?"

"Anything," he said before making a suggestion. "Perhaps we can start off with simple facts like your birthday, favorite color, or your family?" Her eyes grew fearful when he said the word family, so he added, "Or something else."

"No, it's fine," she said, but her gaze darting around the room as if she were looking for a way to escape. Surprisingly, though, she took a big breath and answered one of his questions. "My birthday is December nineth. When's yours?"

"December twenty-third," he answered.

"We're Christmas babies." She smiled. "Okay. Oh, my favorite color is green. And I guess you already know I'm married. His name is Jason."

She looked up at him, a worried frown forming on her mouth. It was the most difficult reality David had to accept about her, but he would deal with anything when it came to Jane.

David gave her a small smile. "Yes. I know you are married."

She didn't stop frowning but carried on. "We met my junior year of high school. He's a year older than me, but we stayed together even after he graduated. I didn't have that many friends. He was kinda all I really had besides my best friend, Wendy."

She looked sad, and he wondered why she didn't have friends or why she rushed out her friend's name, but she was speaking again before he could think on it further.

"After I graduated, I moved in with Jason at the apartment he shared with a few guys from college. I didn't like being around them, but he didn't want me staying at my house anymore." Jane fidgeted and kept her eyes down.

"Why would he not want that?" he asked.

Jane shook her head. "I'll tell you that in a minute. Anyway, we were growing apart. He wanted to go out all the time, and I didn't like to. I didn't like being around all the drinking, and that's all his friends ever did." She shrugged. "I thought it would be better if we broke up since he seemed to want that kind of lifestyle. He'd get in arguments with his friends whenever they'd talk to me for too long. There were a few that I sort of bonded with, but Jason said they just wanted to get in my pants. I just liked talking to a few of them. One guy had some issues I could relate with, but Jason hated him. He made me choose between him and his friend. I chose Jason."

"That's not fair," he said, annoyed. "I understand his fears about another man, but he shouldn't have made you choose."

"I know," she murmured. "But I didn't want to hurt him. Everything was good with us after that, but he eventually went back to staying out all night and coming home drunk. He'd say he only had one beer, and I was paranoid. I started thinking I must be holding him back from fun because he would stay with me sometimes—then I'd see him with his friends when they'd tell him about all the crazy stuff that happened, and I could see he wished he'd gone with them."

She sighed and covered her face. "I don't know why I told you all this. I'm sorry."

Even he was surprised she'd reveal such things, but he was glad she trusted him to be open. "There's no reason to be sorry," he told her. "I want to know whatever you want to tell me."

"I haven't had anyone to talk to in a while," she admitted, an embarrassed grimace flitting across her face. "I guess I got carried away. You can tell me about you if you want. I really don't have an exciting life or anything special to say. I just haven't had anyone. I guess I miss it."

He smiled sadly. "You can talk to me, sweetheart. I want to know you."

"Really?"

David wanted to hug her, she looked so nervous and surprised. "I am positive."

"Okay. But tell me if I'm boring you—I don't mind." She eyed him for a second before she took a deep breath. "Okay, so Jason and I—I think things would have ended between us eventually, but I got pregnant. He wasn't thrilled, but he was supportive and we got married."

David's heart felt pained, but he kept his face relaxed as she kept talking.

"We moved out and three months into the pregnancy, we found out we were having fraternal twins, a boy and a girl. I was actually excited even though I was terrified I'd be a horrible mom. They came out healthy, though.

"Well, Nathan has autism," she said, watching him for a reaction before she continued. "But he's perfect to me. He's just different. He loves to learn about animals, dinosaurs, and movie monsters. I don't know much about dinosaurs, but I love animals and nature, so I like to help nurture his interest in them."

David grinned at finally hearing her speak passionately. Her eyes had lit up, and despite a continuous flicker of fear in them, she smiled.

"Natalie is a funny little girl," she said. "I never really baby-talked either of them, so I think that's why she's like a little grown-up when she addresses people. Everyone says she looks just like me, but I see Jason whenever I look at her. She's a lot like him, too—very carefree and social. She cares for her brother a lot; I adore that about her. I don't think Nathan would be as able and high functioning as he is now, if it weren't for her."

"They sound perfect," David said. "I wish I could meet them."

"I wish you could meet them, too." She looked like she meant it. "I think they'd like you."

"They are doing okay, you know," he said. Jane looked at him, confused, so he explained what he meant. "Two of our men have kept a constant watch over your house. Dagonet, one of the guards, refuses to leave his post next door, even during daylight when he is susceptible to damage. When you were hurt, Arthur sent him along with Gawain to your house with supplies."

She gaped at him. David took her hand in his. "They're all right, Jane. Dagonet picked up that they were looking for toys and went to find a toy for each of them. He really likes them."

"Thank you so much," she said, nearly sobbing. "Nathan probably can't find his dinosaurs."

David smiled sadly. "I believe it was a dinosaur toy Dagonet found for him. We will always be there for them." David was nervous talking about her children. He had noticed she'd been avoiding bringing them up as much as possible, but he could tell this news brought her relief.

To keep their conversation going, he asked another question that had been plaguing him. "What about your parents? Are they close by? Perhaps we can send for them."

Her posture tensed. Arthur had told him her past was unpleasant, but he didn't think it would have anything to do with her family.

"My parents?" She fidgeted again, not looking at him.

Whatever her past involved must have been more traumatic than he had imagined. David removed the tray from her lap and put it back on the dresser. He was back at her side the moment a tear fell to her lap.

He cupped her face between his hands to make her look at him. What he saw there made his heart ache. So much pain. So much sorrow.

"*Sh*, sweetheart," he said, wiping her tears. "It's all right. We don't have to talk about it."

"No, it's okay." She sniffed. "I just haven't talked about them in a long time. You deserve to know." She broke eye contact with him. "You should know what I am."

David frowned. *What does she mean by that?* "You don't have to tell me if it hurts to speak about it."

Jane smiled sadly. "I know, but it's okay."

He smoothed her hair away from her face, then leaned back. Before he could move all the way, she grabbed his hand. He caressed the back of her hand with his thumb, happy that she was at least seeking him out for comfort on her own.

"My mom's name was Sarah," she said softly, and David's heart already hurt for her. *Was.*

Jane carried on without pausing. "She met my dad, Eric, in college. They got married when they were both twenty and had me five months later. They had my little brother Jack when I was two. We were the kind of family you'd see on TV shows or something. Perfect. I loved my baby brother so much. I liked to pretend I was his mom." She shut her eyes tight, trembling.

David shifted so that he sat with his back against the headboard, then easily lifted her so she was sideways on his lap. Since she didn't protest, he wrapped his arms around her. She leaned her head against his shoulder.

Though he was thinking out his actions, he could tell she wasn't. Not once had she looked to him.

"We were on our way to my ballet practice," she said in an empty tone. "I really don't know much about how it happened, but we were spinning suddenly. My mom was screaming for my dad and then it was all a blur, and green. I remember green. There wasn't anything after that. I woke up alone in a hospital. They were gone, all of them. I was only five and no one was there with me. It was the doctor who told me. He told me they died on impact, and that they hadn't felt any pain.

"He said my aunt would be there soon to take me with her. I didn't know her, really. When she got there, I had to go with her. She said something about how the money better be worth putting up with me. I didn't understand at the time what she meant, but I realized as I got older, she only took me in because of some stipulation in my parents' will about receiving personal funds to care for me."

David rubbed his hand up and down her arm. It hurt him to know she had lost a family that clearly adored her, and she had to go with a greedy family member, but as awful as that was, he could tell she had a lot more to say.

"Aunt Katherine was my mom's older sister. They were ten years apart, I think. I realized quite early on the reason why I didn't know her: she hated my mom. She made sure I knew it, too. She made sure I understood that I wasn't wanted in her home."

She moved a little on him, so he squeezed and tried to let her feel that he was still there.

She started up again. "Anyway, I went home with her after the funeral and met Uncle Stephen and my cousins. Stephen Jr. was three years older than me, and Adam was four years older." Her voice had an edge to it upon uttering Stephen's name.

"I kinda liked the idea of having older brothers. I just wanted someone to care for me, and my aunt clearly didn't.

"Everything was fine in the beginning. I missed my family, obviously, but Stephen and I got close. He always tried to take my mind off things. My aunt and uncle completely ignored me, but I was fine with it. Adam was nice, but he wasn't around much. I figured I'd be okay as long as I had Stephen.

"But after maybe two years of living there, Stephen changed. He was still nice, but something seemed off with him. I was little, but I remember thinking this. I've remembered everything since my parents died." Her head tilted to the side at the last part she mentioned.

He thought it was strange, too. Some head injuries caused people to lose memories, not gain the ability to retain everything.

Jane spoke again. "I thought he was being overly protective. Kinda like how a big brother on TV is mean to boys around his sister. But I was wrong.

"He started coming into my room at night. I didn't worry too much when he did this. He was only sleeping in bed with me. I thought maybe he had bad dreams like I did. I used to sleep next to Jack or climb in bed with my parents, so that's what I thought. But Stephen wasn't having nightmares."

David stiffened, but she continued speaking, her voice still void of emotion, like she wasn't really aware she was telling him at all.

"A couple of months of just sleeping in my bed, he started touching me under my nightgown. He said that was normal, that I'd get used to it. He said we'd get in trouble if we told others about our game, so I stayed quiet.

"Adam had come into my room one time and asked Stephen why he was in there, but Stephen told him I was sad about my parents. Adam didn't check to see that Stephen had both of our pants off, and I started to feel more worried about our game. If we couldn't tell Adam, it must be a bad game.

"Stephen had never hurt me. He told me things, gross things he'd seen in videos. He laughed about some of them, so I decided what we were doing must not be so bad. If other people did it on videos for fun, it should be okay."

David felt sick and furious. He didn't know where he'd find this cousin, but he'd seek him out very soon.

"One day, though," Jane said in that empty way but also a little lost now, "a little girl in class told me the boy next to me had his hands down my pants during nap time. I thought she was going to get me in trouble and begged her not to tell on me. She said her mommy said no one is supposed to touch her there, and she's not supposed to either."

Her tone softened, almost childlike, though she still acted as if she wasn't really telling him, just speaking. "The next day I pretended I was asleep, and the boy stuck his hands down my pants. For the first time, I felt ashamed. I kicked him as hard as I could, but my teacher saw. She yelled at me and put me in time-out while everyone laughed at me. I tried to tell her what happened, but she said we don't hit no matter what and for me to be quiet."

David was shaking, but he couldn't speak to tell her to stop.

"I told my aunt about Stephen. She just stared at me for a minute, then told me I just dreamt it up. She told me not to talk about it again and said people would get upset, and she'd be angry. I tried to tell her I wasn't lying, and she slapped me. So I stopped saying anything about it.

"When Stephen came, I let him do whatever he wanted. I kept telling myself it didn't hurt like a slap or punch, so it wasn't so bad. And he'd always seemed happy. He'd ask me if I liked certain things."

She sucked in a breath and shook her head. "One time, he had some friends over. I had gone to the bathroom, and one boy followed me while Stephen played a game with the others. The boy told me to use the bathroom, and he'd wait in there with me so I wouldn't get scared. I didn't know what to do, so I peed. He watched me and when I got up, he told me to lie on the ground. He got on me, and I let him." Her voice cracked.

"Jane, please—" He couldn't hear anymore, but she just kept talking like she couldn't stop or even hear him.

"I didn't tell anyone," she said in a hushed whisper. "Not even Stephen. Not Jason. No one. The boy was bigger, and his—you know—was bigger, harder. He told me he knew what I did with Stephen. I didn't know what it was at the time, Stephen had never done it like this boy—it felt different. He was rougher and faster. He was pushing me so hard into the floor, I held on to him because I didn't know what to do and it was hurting. He liked that I did that."

Father, help her, David thought, already knowing she couldn't be saved. The monster had already gotten her.

"When he finally stopped," she said as a tremor rolled through her body, "he told me to stay still. I just laid there, and he pushed his shorts down and showed me himself. He put my hand on him and asked me if I'd seen come before. I shook my head, and he laughed, calling Stephen a pussy. Then he pulled my pants down and touched me. He said I had liked it because I was wet down there. He rubbed me in ways Stephen hadn't and when I made a noise, he laughed. He said I was a dirty little girl for liking it, then pulled my pants back up. He kissed me and reminded me not to tell anyone, then left."

David had never felt such rage. His body was shaking as his mind raced with terrible images. Yet, Jane didn't seem to notice his distress; she talked as though no one was there, though he could see now she was trapped in her memories.

"I didn't tell anyone," she said, ashamed. "He'd come by sometimes, but he'd just smile at me. Stephen hung out with him a lot and didn't come in so much. Still, every once in a while, Stephen would come in my room and do things he'd said he heard about.

"I started considering telling someone at school, but one day, a boy and girl in my class got in trouble. Cops came and everything. I asked one of my classmates what happened, and they said a boy and girl were touching each other's privates. I thought I'd go to jail because of what I'd done, so I kept my mouth shut again."

David wanted to hit something. She wanted someone to help her, and she didn't know where to go. She had no one to trust or protect her.

"Time went by," she said, though calmer now. "There'd be periods of peace and then he'd come back. Stephen had gone off to some private school for the beginning of his senior year. It was nice without him, but when I found out he was coming back, I don't know what happened, I went about my normal routine–went to school, smiled, did my assignments, but when I came home, I took every pill in the house."

David tensed, his mind flashing with the image of what was to come.

"When I took those pills," she said, her voice dead as she had clearly tried to make herself, "I stared at myself in the mirror and saw what was really there–I was so ugly. I didn't think about what I was doing. I just kept staring at myself and swallowing pills with a glass of water. I had never thought about killing myself before, but I knew what would happen. I didn't care. I just kept taking medicine; the pills went down so easily.

"After I'd taken everything, I got in bed and fell asleep, but an hour later, I woke up. I wasn't afraid. My body was weak, but I stumbled through the house until I got to my aunt's room. I found more medicine and took all of it."

David squeezed his eyes shut. Arthur had said she would open up to him, but he wasn't prepared for this.

"I made it back to my room. I remember leaning on the walls for support, but I made it. I think I fell on the floor, and that's where Stephen found me. He was the one who called an ambulance."

She blinked, her heartbeat speeding up. "It was like a weird dream. There were moments of awareness and then nothing. I remember throwing up a lot, but nothing hurt–not even the needles they kept sticking in to draw blood.

"My aunt and uncle had been furious. They said I'd traumatized Stephen; he was hysterical, apparently. My aunt said I would be put in jail or a mental hospital if I told lies. I knew she meant about Stephen. So, when the psychiatrist came to talk, I said I did it because I missed my parents and brother. The hospital let me go after almost a week."

David pressed his lips to her hair. It was common for survivors of sexual abuse to lie, but he was always sickened that family members who were aware would protect the abusers. They were sometimes more responsible than the monster hurting the victim.

"Stephen seemed different when I saw him again," she said. "He left me alone for a while. I think Adam had figured out what was happening. He'd watch Stephen all the time. I didn't dare tell him, though. I wasn't afraid of death, but I didn't want to be put in a mental hospital. Aunt Kathrine said worse things would happen to me there."

He knew the woman wasn't lying, but it gutted him that Jane was saying she'd continue receiving abuse just to avoid the chance of another type. That her aunt had her believing it would be her fault if she went off to be abused elsewhere, essentially telling her there was no point getting help.

"Adam had been living on campus," Jane said, "but he moved back home shortly after I went back to school. He tried to make sure he was home when I was. Eventually, he got caught up in school and Stephen started up with me again. Adam hadn't caught us, and Stephen made me skip school so he could have time with me, and I was blamed for Stephen's absences. I didn't even try to argue that he was making me. I figured this would last until he left for college. I had dealt with it so long; I could last a little longer. But Adam finally caught us."

David wanted to kiss her and tell her to stop, but he couldn't say anything.

"Adam yanked Stephen off me. As he tried to drag me away, Stephen lost it. They were both the same height, but Adam was stronger, more built. When they started fighting, Adam beat him badly."

Good, David thought, but he didn't celebrate because now Jane was weeping.

"Stephen had lost consciousness, but Adam didn't stop. There'd been so much blood. I knew he was going to kill him, but I just stood there. My uncle finally burst into the room, got Adam off Stephen's lifeless body, and called an ambulance. Adam pulled me onto his lap and cried."

Her tormented voice broke his heart.

"After they took Stephen to the hospital, my uncle turned to us and called me a whore. He said I'd seduced his sons and made them do this to each other. Adam tried to defend me, but the police arrived and arrested him.

"Stephen went into a coma and never woke up; my Aunt refused to take him off life support, and Adam has been in prison ever since." Her face scrunched up. "My uncle started drinking a lot. He'd yell at me whenever I came home or come up to my room and stare at me. He'd say it was my fault his sons were gone—none of this would have happened if it weren't for me. He said I ruined all their lives, and I should have died with my parents."

Christ, David thought. It was no wonder she was suffering with the disorders Arthur had told him about. It was no wonder she was blocking certain things out.

"I tried to tell him what had been going on and that Aunt Katherine knew," she said. "I told him everything, and he asked me if I would let him do the same thing, then. I was terrified, but I said no. I thought he was going to force himself on me, but he said if I didn't want it happening, I would have told someone. So, I must have encouraged it."

Bastard, David nearly snarled, but he hugged her instead of spewing his thoughts.

"I tried to make him understand, but he only yelled louder and said if I wasn't so pretty, they'd have left me alone. It was my fault everyone was gone."

"Jane." He was in agony. "No, baby, it wasn't your fault."

She continued as if he was not even speaking. "Everyone at school made fun of me. The girls already hated me for some reason, but now they didn't care if I heard them whispering mean things. They ganged up on me, circled me as they made fun of me and called me names. No one helped.

"There was a time I thought they'd changed. A girl said I should come with them when they went out; I thought they were finally being nice, but then I heard her telling the other girls if I went, all the hot guys would come talk to us. And since my family was all gone, I wouldn't be interested which would leave the hot guys for them."

David saw red.

"When I met Jason, I trusted him. I don't know why—it was just a gut feeling to let him in. I told him some of the things that happened to me. He showed up at my house one time because I'd been crying over fighting with my uncle that morning. He threatened my uncle and told him if he didn't leave me in peace, he would kill him and Stephen."

David hadn't expected that after everything she'd said about her husband, but it relieved him that she'd finally found someone to take her side.

"Jason's not a violent person," she said, "but he looked terrifying that day. My uncle backed off. After that, when I came home, my uncle would leave or go in his room. I never liked Jason more than a friend before but when he did that, I felt drawn to him. He'd have other moments where he'd yell at someone whispering I should just kill myself, and I started seeing him as more than a friend.

"We became a couple after a while, and when I was a senior, I made a new friend, Wendy. We became best friends. She never judged me, but I didn't tell her everything. She was understanding when I'd turn down going places, but she still asked. She never gave up on me. But I lost her a year ago."

David heard a greater sadness from her leak out with those words. Out of all the unspeakable horror she'd just revealed, the death of her only friend is what hurt most.

"She was diagnosed with cancer," she croaked. "She's dead. She was my only friend. I have no one now. Not even Jason. He just says I should let go of the past, but I can't." She jerked, panicked now. "I can't get better. I'm a horrible mom. They're going to turn out like me."

David hugged her as she sobbed. Fire rushed through his veins, and he wanted the blood of every person who had hurt her. Right now, though, he had to calm her down. "Sweetheart, I'm here now. I'll help you through it all, okay? I will never leave you."

She nodded but continued to weep. Her body temperature felt high. She kept holding her breath and tensing up for several seconds at a time before gasping for air. Eventually, though, her cries died down, her breathing evened out, and she fell asleep.

It was almost like she hadn't been the one to tell him everything, and he wondered if he had pushed her to talk too soon.

His misery was worsened at the knowledge that he was the most powerful immortal to ever be made. He had so much strength, and he'd been alive while she suffered repeated horror, and yet she was abused again and again. Why? That's all he could ask God. Why give him so much power, if he couldn't save her? If he couldn't find her until her death was ready to claim her?

The sound of Gawain muttering out curses reached David's ears, and he panicked; they'd heard her confession. Gareth was trying to calm Gawain. Thankfully, David surmised it was only two of them in the house. He didn't think Jane would be comfortable with too many people knowing what she'd shared.

He rolled onto his side and tried lowering her to the pillow, but just as she'd done during her transition, she dug her fingernails into him, refusing to let go.

So with a sad smile, he pulled her close and silently prayed for a way to bring her peace.

CHAPTER 20

WHERE DEMONS HIDE

David had dozed off, but he was roused from a dreamless sleep when Jane's breathing changed. She whined and kept panting like she was terrified. Her face covered with tears and sweat as it contorted with pain.

David pulled himself out from under her and leaned over her, gripping her shoulders. "Jane, wake up." He shook her by the shoulders and raised his voice. "Wake up!"

The most heartbreaking scream tore out of her lips, and her eyes flew open, wide and confused. "David," she choked out, reaching out to hold his face.

"I'm here." He tried to soothe her. "It was only a dream. I'm here."

Her hands shook as she caressed the sides of his face and hair. "I thought he killed you."

David shook his head. "No. It was only a dream. We're both fine. We're still here in the house."

Relief washed over her, but she kept stroking his cheek while her eyes still searched his face. It looked like she was only confirming he was truly okay, but her eyes devoured more of him. She slid her hands over his shoulders and down his biceps.

"Jane," he said, warning her to stop.

She ignored him and explored his chest. David squeezed his eyes shut and gathered the mental strength to push her away. Her fingers splayed out across his chest and up around his neck where they played with his hair.

"Jane, you need to stop."

She disregarded his order and locked her hands behind his neck and pulled.

David opened his eyes. "Enough."

An unseen force suddenly yanked him toward her and furniture in the room shifted toward them. He braced himself from falling on her and looked back to her eyes.

Black. None of her lovely hazel color was present.

Then, as if he were watching a horror movie, a wicked smile stretched across her beautiful face. He went to stand again but only received a more powerful tug while at the same time several items in the room jolted in their direction.

"Please, Jane," he said, straining against the force pulling him down to her. "You need to stop this."

"I want you, David," she said, and her siren voice weakened him. Her leg curled around his waist and pulled him against her.

She felt good. Too good.

She moaned, rolling her hips up, and he couldn't stop himself from getting aroused. This wasn't right, and he tried to ignore her movements and pulled against the force to keep himself from collapsing on her. But she wouldn't let go.

"Shit," he said as she pressed hot, needy kisses along his neck all the way to his jaw.

Her lips brushed his ear. "Don't you love me, David?"

"Yes, I love you, Jane," he said, his arms shaking under the pressure. "But this isn't you. We can't do this."

"Don't you want me, David?" Her voice didn't sound at all like her usual sweet voice, and he suddenly wondered if she had a multiple personality disorder that Arthur had missed.

She slid her tongue along his neck.

"Not like this," he told her. "Please stop this. Snap out of it."

The whole time he pulled against the unseen force keeping him close to her. The muscles in his arms began to spasm, and his dick was throbbing. He could feel her heat as she used him to get herself off. His eyes went wide as she moaned, climaxing.

He shook his head, trying to get her lips off of him. This was wrong.

"Get inside me," she panted, reaching down, moaning when she grabbed his erection through his pants.

"Fuck. Stop!" David's arms shook. She let go of him and went to slide her hand inside his pants. He dropped his weight to one forearm and grabbed her hand, stopping her, then forced it over her head.

She grinned up at him and moved her hips again. He tried to pull away, but he wasn't getting anywhere. If anything, he was only pressing against her more.

He finally stopped fighting her then lowered his mouth, dodging her lips and kissed her cheek. "Remember Jason," he said against her skin. She stilled her movements, and he continued. "Remember Nathan and Natalie." He lifted his face but placed another kiss on her forehead. "I love you, Jane. I love you so much. That's why I will not let us do this." He moved back to look at her face.

The blackness faded from her eyes, and a fearful, hazel pair stared back at him. The force broke, and the furniture crashed to the floor.

David smiled sadly at her confused expression as tears filled her eyes.

"I'm sorry," she said, crying.

David sat up and lifted her into his arms. "It's all right. I'm not mad." She cried harder. "Oh, baby," he said, hugging her.

"I didn't mean to." She touched between her legs and whined. "Oh, God. I-I–"

"*Shh.*" He rocked her, kissing her hair. "It's okay."

"I don't remember doing it. But I can feel it. I can feel you."

He sighed, unsure what to tell her and desperately hoping she didn't think he'd done it on purpose. "I know. I'm sorry I could not keep myself from reacting to you. Are you hurt? Did I hurt you?"

"It's my fault," she shouted.

"No, Jane." He kissed her hair again. "That wasn't your fault."

He had to talk to Arthur. Something was wrong, and they needed to find out before she lost control again.

✦✦✦

"That was hot," Death said, not looking away from the scene in front of him, but he knew he'd startled Lucifer, and that the fallen angel was glaring at him.

Death leaned against the wall, his arms crossed, mimicking Lucifer's position on the other side of the bedroom. He finally looked away from Jane and David and smirked at his older *brother*.

Lucifer scowled at him before turning back to watch the couple.

Death let out a deep chuckle. "Why the long face, Luc? Are you unhappy with your minions' handiwork? I cannot look into her eyes and see her past as you can, but her story seemed to contain an awful lot of darkness for one soul to suffer. How long have you been fucking with her?"

"What do you want, Death?" Lucifer asked, turning his attention to him.

Death shrugged, unconcerned with the glare Lucifer was giving him. "Did you order her attacks?"

Lucifer sighed. "Are you going to bother me until you find out what you want?"

"I only gain their memories when they die," he told him. "She makes it like I have a Christmas present all wrapped up, but I can't open it until Daddy says. Do you want me to open her early?"

"Child," Lucifer muttered. "Fine. I have had no knowledge regarding her past. Something is wrong with her memories, but I only came to her when I felt her power surge during her fight with Lancelot's wolves. I cannot tell who is responsible for her torment, but I assure you it was not me. Then, at least. Now tell me what you are doing here. I have no desire to be in your company."

"We're on a deadline, Luc. I was curious about how things were progressing." He watched Lucifer carefully, noting his rising anger. "It bothers you to not know who harmed her, doesn't it?"

"I prefer to have background on any pawn I seek to acquire or destroy."

"I see," Death said. "You look uncertain of your plan now. If you want her, you should up your game."

Lucifer shot him an annoyed look. "Why would I listen to anything you have to say? You are out to acquire her yourself."

"I am," Death admitted. "But if you plan to use David, you will fail. If you fail, I stand no chance. He was chosen for a reason, Luc. He's too good. Do you think he would wait all this time only to hurt her?"

Lucifer gazed at the couple in question. David was rocking Jane as she cried. A brief lapse in the fallen angel's controlled features allowed Death to witness the twinge of guilt that flashed through Lucifer's gray eyes.

Jane whimpered, and Death turned to look at her tear-stained face. She looked pitiful, but he showed no reaction to her sorrow. "Not feeling guilty, are you?"

Lucifer scoffed. "You are very aware I feel no guilt over tampering with her mind. Besides, I only seduced the lust she already has for the knight. Her emotions make her unstable."

"*Hm* . . . I believe there's more to it. Have you developed a soft spot for the girl?"

"I have work to do," Lucifer said, ignoring his question. "I would imagine you do as well." He sent a sinister glance at Death before disappearing.

Death glanced back as David lifted Jane into his arms. He let out a tired breath as he watched them leave the room, and only then did he vanish.

✦✦✦

Jane caught sight of Gawain sitting on a sofa as David carried her into the living area.

Gawain jumped up, and she hid her face in the crook of David's neck. "What's happened?" Gawain asked David. "Is she all right?"

"I have to go see Arthur," David told him. "I thought she could stay with you while I am gone."

Gawain nodded. "Of course."

David pulled Jane close and whispered in her ear. "Sweetheart, I want you to stay with Gawain. I need to speak with Arthur so we can figure this out. I'll get updated on everything that has happened and bring him back."

She whimpered and squeezed her arms around his neck. As much as she was ashamed of herself for whatever she'd done to him, she didn't want him to leave her again.

David shushed her before he turned his back to Gawain. "I will be back. I promise. Gawain will keep you company."

She shook her head in protest and held him tighter. "Don't leave. I don't know what's wrong with me."

He turned his face toward hers and kissed her cheek. "I know you're scared right now." His lips did not even leave her skin. They burned her in the most pleasant way. "That is why I must go speak with Arthur. I need to find out how to help you. I swear I will return."

She bobbed her head and received another kiss to her cheek. All that she'd done wasn't clear to her, but she knew enough, and she knew he was afraid.

Loosening her grip on him, she tried her best to smile. David looked between her eyes. His worry over leaving her was obvious, but he quickly placed another kiss on her forehead and carried her back to Gawain.

Gawain held out his arms, and David passed Jane to him. "Hi, Gawain," she said, not caring about the cheerful knight's presence.

"Hi, love. I'm so glad you are healing."

She nodded and turned to David as he placed his palm against her cheek.

"I will be back," he promised. "Gawain, why don't you tell her about your visit to see Nathan and Natalie."

Jane remembered what David had told her they'd done for her family. It would help keep her distracted until David got back.

"I will see you two later," David said, giving her a final glance before he left the house.

Gawain smiled and carried her out to the backyard. It seemed silly to be carried, but she didn't have it in her to be rude.

After he sat them down on a bench, he gave her a gentle hug. "I'm so happy you are going to be all right. I felt terrible for letting you get hurt."

"I could never blame you or anyone for what happened," she said quietly. "I didn't know what to expect, but me getting hurt definitely wasn't yours or David's fault. If you guys hadn't fought as well as you had, I'm sure I would've died."

Gawain smiled. "It wasn't us that saved you. You saved yourself."

That wasn't what she expected to hear.

"Do you remember what happened?" he asked.

"I remember the attack and receiving my injury, then everything is hazy until David came."

Now he appeared confused. "You don't remember the blast you created?"

"No. David hasn't said anything about a blast."

"Well, none of us actually saw how you did it, but you threw out some sort of energy blast. It completely destroyed the wolf that hurt you. None of us are sure what to make of it yet, but it was really impressive."

He had a proud smile on his face, but Jane was horrified.

Gawain's smile dropped off his face once he realized she was upset. "It's all right, Jane. You did nothing wrong. We will learn the extent of your power and help you harness it."

Jane's eyes watered. "No. You don't understand. I did do something horrible."

"What do you mean?"

"It's just like the blast or whatever—I don't remember what I did, but I used some sort of power." She looked away, her heart racing as she feared there might have been more instances she wasn't aware of. "I attacked David."

He was quiet for a moment. "Is that why you were crying?" She nodded. "What happened with him?"

Gosh, she couldn't tell him. "I'm too ashamed to say."

He turned her head to look her in the eye. "Love, I won't judge you. There is something unstable about your power, but that is not surprising. I have seen many immortals with great power; it takes time to learn proper control."

"I don't think that's the same as what happened."

"Explain it, then," he said easily. "I will do my best to offer help."

She sighed and debated whether or not to tell him anything. She still didn't know all that happened, but she decided to confide in him. "There are times when I feel overly attracted to David. I mean, I'm always attracted to him; I'm not blind, he's hot. But I can ignore it, you know? I'm married, and that's not me. But there are times when it feels out of control.

"I feel like I'm not completely there, like I'm someone else. I sort of know what's happening, but it's confusing. It's like I'm looking in from the outside, but I'm obviously right there. I feel hot and like everything is happening really fast but at the same time, in slow motion. I feel everything around me, too. Then it's like I wake up or I'm allowed to see. I don't know what's real. But I can feel what's happened to my body."

She breathed out and told him the rest. "I told David about my past. I haven't had anyone to talk to in so long. When I've gone to psychiatrists, they were cold; I didn't want to talk. Jason used to listen, and Wendy was willing to, but I don't know, I just couldn't stop telling him."

"That's called trust, love. Your heart trusts in him."

She shrugged. "Did you hear?"

He clenched his hand into a fist. "I did, but I do not want you to recount it so soon. I'm here to listen if you wish to let it out, though. It's good to talk to someone."

"Thank you," she said. "Well, after I told David everything, I guess I cried myself to sleep. I had a nightmare that Lancelot killed him right in front of me. It felt so real. But David woke me up. I thought he was the dream."

She almost sobbed and rushed the next parts, "I was touching his face, trying to make sure he was really there with me when I started to have that out of control feeling again. I wanted to touch more of him. I heard him telling me to stop. His voice was muffled like I was under water. When I looked at him, it was like looking through a tunnel or a small window. I didn't feel like I was the one he was talking to, but I knew he was. I knew I needed to stop, but I didn't. It got darker, I could barely see him, but I *felt* him."

Gawain rubbed her arm. "What do you mean? Like you couldn't see but feel?"

"Yes and no. I felt like I couldn't move, but I was. I could feel his body heat, then it was like I could touch everything around me, but I wasn't touching anything but him. I knew I needed to let go, but I didn't.

"He kept telling me to stop and when he tried to move away, somehow, I kept him there. I could feel him struggling against me, but I was able to hold him there." She looked up at him, worried. "Gawain, I wasn't holding him there with my hands—I was using my mind. Only it felt like there were two sides to my thoughts."

His forehead crinkled up as he frowned. "You used your mind to hold him?"

"Yes. I don't know how, but I did it." Jane paused, breathing in deeply. "I could taste him and feel him. I was turned on, but it was so dark around me. I kept hearing my voice, but I didn't know what I was telling him. I heard David, but he was still muffled. He sounded stressed, though. And it's like all I wanted was for him to make the ache go away. I've never—" She looked down, ashamed and embarrassed.

"I'm sure David understands you are under a lot of stress right now," he soothed. "It is not that bad, Jane."

She shook her head repeatedly and whined. "I think I had an orgasm."

He cleared his throat, uncomfortably. "Love, there's nothing wrong with that. Well, there is, but it's not unexpected. You two have a connection and are more stimulated by each other than most."

"I've never had one," she admitted even more humiliated. "I don't even know if that's what really happened, but I felt him."

Gawain sighed. "Not that it's okay, but David is going to have a hard time not reacting to you. If you are touching him, especially in a sexual way, his control is going to be tested." Then he looked angry, his eyes darkening. "Did he penetrate—"

"No," she cut him off. "It was over our clothes. But it's not his fault. It's always my fault." She wiped her face, realizing she was crying. "I anticipated him giving into me, and I was excited. He stopped me. I felt him kiss my cheek. He looked blurry, but I felt him closer than before, and his voice was clear. He reminded me about my family. I felt hate—hate against them. Intense hate. Then it all snapped. I could see, and the hate against my family went away. He was so worried, and I felt what I'd done. My body, you know? I still feel him. What if Jason finds out?"

Gawain rocked her. "Your husband will not know. I don't judge you, and David still loves you."

"He said that," she said, holding onto that memory. "It's the first thing I heard when I snapped out of it."

"That's not the first time he has told you." Gawain gave her a little squeeze. "When you got hurt, he told you more than once."

"I thought that was a dream," she said, unsure how she felt about it, other than it made her feel warm all over.

He grinned and placed a kiss on her forehead. "No, it wasn't a dream. He loves you more than anything in the whole world." He tucked her head under his chin before adding, "Don't worry. We will figure this out."

She nodded and looked out toward the yard. "What happened with my family?"

"Oh, right. It went well. We took them a good amount of food and drinks, along with some toiletry items. We told them we would check on them again."

"Are they all right?"

"Yes, love, they're fine. Your little Natalie is adorable, by the way. They both are."

She smiled, relieved but filled with loss. "Thank you."

"No problem. It was nice to meet them. We all want to make sure they are safe. Dagonet, especially, has grown protective over them."

Jane pulled back from his hold to look at him. "Who is he?"

"You will like him," he said with a fond smile. "He is one of our guards, but we consider him a knight. He was attacked and changed by a cursed immortal close to the time most of us were. Do not worry, he is completely loyal to Arthur and David."

"He won't hurt my family?"

He shook his head and assured her. "I think he would lay down his life for them without hesitation. He and Nathan took quite a liking to one another."

Jane grinned. Her little boy hardly liked anyone new.

They sat in silence for a while before a thought occurred to her. "Gawain, how is there still electricity? In the movies, everything always goes out."

He chuckled. "We have been working our way down from Canada since the plague broke out. We only move on once the remaining authorities can resume their duties. Obviously, we do not make contact with them, but there are still humans putting up a good fight. At least, here, that is. I am not sure about the rest of the world.

"When we go to a new area, we start our attack at the energy and water supplies. I suppose it is dark because people have their lights off to keep from giving away their location. Some cities are truly blacked out, but we have cleared most power plants that can explode without operators. Lamorak's team specializes in repairing and operating city energy systems. While we clear, they do what they can to stabilize things. Oftentimes, there are humans around, and we do make contact. We do not reveal what we are, but I'm sure they are suspicious. We usually bring them supplies or locate their loved ones if we can.

"There are two teams who do reconnaissance missions to scout every nuclear reactor in North America. They check other nearby power plants and inform us of where we need to go. We make those towns priorities. The facilities in Texas have been reported operational, but we still planned to eliminate as much of the plague threat as possible. Our reports said Austin had a high concentration of undead. That is why we chose to drop here."

"Oh, that makes sense, I guess."

They sat in silence after that. Jane pondered a million things, and it wasn't long before she was completely lost to the world around her. She barely even registered him speaking to her again.

"Jane, I think we should get you something to drink," he said.

Yes, she thought but did not speak. It felt as though her body was moving, but she didn't understand why or where she was going.

"Gareth," Gawain called.

Jane blinked away the darkness that had surrounded her vision and noticed they were back inside the house.

"What's the matter?" Gareth asked, coming around the corner. He paused as soon as he made eye contact with her.

"Get her blood. Fast," Gawain ordered as he sat her on the counter. She felt his hands on her face and saw his bright eyes, but her vision grew dark. "Jane, you need to focus. Stay with me."

Gawain seemed so far away.

She felt her lips curve up as Gareth came closer and offered her a glass. "You need to drink this."

She looked to it and grinned before taking it from him. She did not hesitate to bring the glass to her lips, but she kept this new knight in her sights.

Disgusting. She smashed the glass onto the floor and glared at him.

Gawain backed away but stopped his retreat when she turned her head in his direction. "Jane," he said, "we'll get David for you. I know it does not taste as good. Let us get him for you."

She tilted her head. "David?"

"Yes, darling," Gareth said. "David. I will bring him. He will take care of you."

She glanced at him from the corner of her eye before turning to face him. Her gaze dropped to his rapidly beating pulse at his neck.

Everything went dark.

✦✦✦

David arrived at the small house where he knew Arthur to be. He walked around and found Kay and Bedivere waiting with Arthur.

They all looked at him as Arthur spoke. "How is Jane?"

David was thinking over the past several hours when Bedivere suddenly said, "We are sorry, David."

David looked at their worried faces before looking at Arthur. "They know?" he asked, referring to Jane's past.

Arthur nodded. "I told them."

He sighed and looked down, his shoulders dropping in defeat as he finally let his devastation show.

Kay put a comforting hand on his shoulder. "I know this is difficult to take. Do not lose hope. You will get her through this."

David's chest ached, and he felt sick to his stomach. The awful things she had told him hurt just as much as it had when he thought she was dying, perhaps even worse. He shook his head to rid himself of those memories. He was strong enough for this. He needed to take care of her. "Have you come across Lance?" he asked them.

"Not yet," Kay answered. "There are traces, but he is constantly on the move. We'll find him. We have reduced the plague's numbers considerably here, so we will be able to focus on finding him now. Did you hear our theory about him and the Zev virus?"

"Yes." David glared at Arthur. "Do you think it's truly possible he could create something like this?"

Arthur shrugged. "It's possible, I suppose. It seems too great a coincidence the first victim would basically have the name Wolf Knight while Lance just happens to have infected wolves. We will only find out if we can capture him. The good news is he seems in control of them. Or he is disposing of those he loses control over judging by the attack we found before."

David nodded as his mind wandered to what had happened with him and Jane. He could barely concentrate on Lancelot's association with the plague after everything he'd just gone through with Jane.

Arthur obviously picked up on the frantic thoughts racing through his mind. "What did she do?"

He breathed out. "She has been acting strange. There have been moments where she does not seem to be herself. I've seen her eyes change. I thought I imagined it at first, but I wasn't mistaken. They turn black, even the whites of her eyes.

"The first time, she seemed aroused but quickly snapped out of it. Her normal eye color returned, and she looked confused. I did not want to alarm her, so I didn't say anything. But she had a bigger episode. Whatever is happening to her is wrong. She doesn't seem aware of her actions. It's like a total personality switch. She's aggressive and has no problem expressing her sexual desires."

Arthur frowned and looked at the others. They only shook their heads, unsure of what to make of it.

"She was able to overpower me," David added, mentally recalling everything she'd done to him.

Arthur chuckled. "I bet that was exciting."

David scowled while the others raised eyebrows trying to understand. "Can we get back to the problem here?"

"Yes," Arthur said. "Now, you say she overpowered you, what did it feel like?"

"Like a force was pulling me to her. It was all around me. Her eyes went black again, and her face—" He sighed, remembering her beautiful face wearing such an evil smile. "It wasn't her. I tried to make her stop, but she would not. No matter how hard I tried to pull away from her, it only pulled me harder. Everything in the room was being pulled in, as well. When I mentioned her family, it was like she woke up. She was devastated and scared. She seemed to know what physically happened between us but only because she could feel it." He felt sick that he'd done that to her.

"I'm sure she doesn't see it that way," Arthur quickly assured him. "The power she used seems like some form of telekinesis, but that doesn't explain her behavior. This could also be why so much is drawn to her."

"What about her eyes turning black? I know that's not normal." David was desperate for some helpful news.

"I'm not sure," Arthur said. "It may be that someone dark has attached themselves to her."

David looked at Arthur, horrified. "What do you mean?"

Arthur gave him a sympathetic look as he explained. "What you are describing is similar to someone under the influence or possession of a demon. However, Jane is more powerful than a normal human or immortal; the result is going to be more severe. I have been thinking about it since first meeting her. She's had so many awful things happening to her. But she was always being attacked. Now it's as though she's being used as a vessel. I fear, if my suspicions are correct, something or *someone* powerful is behind this."

David was devastated; he couldn't even respond.

"What should he do, Arthur?" Kay asked.

"We all need to be careful, but David, you need to be cautious. I think she would be better controlled if you keep her satisfied all the time. If she wants something, give it to her before she gets upset or wants more."

"I am not going to take advantage of her," he said. "She's clearly not thinking properly when this is happening. I will not let her be unfaithful to her husband."

An angry look crossed Arthur's face at the mention of Jane's husband, but it quickly faded. "Calm down," Arthur said. "I only meant that you should give enough attention to keep her from becoming upset. If she's upset, there is a higher chance that whatever has a hold over her will come forward. If she becomes too angry, she could be completely taken over by it. Think about it, she displayed this power under stressed conditions.

"She's powerful. When someone has this kind of power, it can easily take over, and instead of using her abilities for good, they shift and become dark. So be careful. Make sure she is fed and continue showing your love for her; it soothes her. She still needs to learn how to control her hunger as well. With everything that's been happening, she hasn't had to consciously deal with it."

An awful feeling of dread came over David.

Bedivere sighed. "You haven't fed her, have you?"

David was about to respond when suddenly Gawain's voice roared for help through Arthur's communication piece.

"Dammit, David," Arthur snapped, but he was already rushing back to camp.

CHAPTER 21

SWEET JANE

Nearly ripping the back door off its hinges, David rushed toward the kitchen where Gawain was yelling. The others were right behind David, but they all came to an abrupt stop once they finally caught sight of Gawain's distress.

His best friend was punching an invisible barrier between him and, Jane and Gareth. Gawain was panicked, desperate to save his brother as he yelled for her to stop. She didn't acknowledge him in the slightest. Her back was to all of them, but he could see Gareth's frightened eyes peering over her shoulder. She was feeding on him, and David knew his comrade was losing too much blood. She was killing him, and she didn't care at all.

Arthur stood beside him and held his hand up to the faintly shimmering wall that Gawain continued to beat at. "It's a force field," Arthur whispered. "David, you need to stop her or she's going to kill him. Do whatever you have to."

David walked up to the wall and called out to her. "Jane?" She tensed but did not turn. He tried again. "Jane, my love, please look at me."

Without removing her mouth, she slowly turned in his direction and looked into David's eyes. The others all gasped at the wild sight of her, and even though her black eyes seemed to glint with a devilish hate for him, David remained calm.

He didn't react to Gareth's blood dripping down her chin and onto their shirts. "Sweetheart, come to me. I will give you what you want. Just come here." His plea was a broken one. This was not the woman he loved.

To all their relief, she removed her mouth from Gareth and looked back at him. David almost didn't believe he'd seen the change when her eyes returned to their hazel color, but he knew it happened because of the frightened expression she suddenly wore.

"David," Jane cried.

"I'm here, baby."

Tears rolled down her face, and she sobbed, "Help me." But blackness filled her eyes again, and she dropped Gareth to the ground with a sickening thud.

Gareth didn't move, and blood continued to slowly seep from the vicious wounds she'd left behind. She had not been gentle, and it was unclear if she had ripped his friend's jugular. David could only hope Gareth's healing abilities would save him.

The sudden loss of the force field almost made him fall forward.

Gawain hesitated but rushed to Gareth's side, and thankfully, Jane ignored him, still making her way toward David as Arthur and the others stood by silent.

When she stood in front of him, she reached up to touch the side of his face and smeared it with his friend's precious blood. She stood on her the tips of her toes and placed a kiss on his cheek with her ruby-stained lips. "David," she said with a sickly, sweet voice against his cheek. "We've missed you."

He shut his eyes as his fears were confirmed. This was not his Jane.

She slid her arms around the back of his neck as she trailed her nose along his skin. "You smell delicious," she said before placing a kiss to his jaw. "Do you want me now?"

David opened his eyes and stared into her onyx pair before he glanced at Arthur who nodded. He knew what that meant: do what you must. His gaze slid over to where Gareth still lay unconscious, and he took in how badly she had hurt him. She was too powerful. If he fought her, she'd win.

He let out a defeated breath and slowly wrapped his arms around her back. The evil creature grinned up at him, and he hated that he could not find her any less beautiful than his Jane. "Yes, Jane. I want you now. Come on, sweetheart—let's finish your feeding."

She smiled excitedly and jumped into his arms. Without hesitating, she wrapped her legs around his waist. He caught her with one hand under her butt while the other held the small of her back.

David looked to Arthur one last time. His brother-in-law had been staring at the ground, and David wished Arthur could tell him there was another way. There wasn't, and he knew Arthur could not find a solution when he turned away from him.

"Don't keep me waiting," she whispered, tracing his earlobe with her tongue.

David didn't respond to her and quickly took her upstairs, away from the others. When he arrived at the bedroom, he hesitated, hovering his hand over the doorknob while she licked the blood she'd smeared along his neck and jaw from kissing him downstairs. He squeezed his eyes shut, trying not to lose himself to lust and opened the door.

The soft click of him shutting the door gained her attention. She pulled away and looked around the room before turning back to him. The sticky blood had begun to dry on her snowy skin. It made her silver glow more bewitching to watch as it flickered, lighting up the room.

"I'm still hungry," she said.

Nodding, he carried her to the bed. He took a deep breath and sat down with her straddling him since she had already wrapped herself around him.

She leaned down to his ear and whispered, "You have no idea how much she wants you."

An explosion of sadness and rage consumed him, and the creature leaned back laughing.

He grabbed the back of her neck. "Drink."

She had no fear of his wrath and merely pouted her lips before leaning down to sink her fangs into his neck. Her moan of ecstasy as his blood poured down her throat stirred all the desire he had for Jane. He knew this was not really her, but she felt and smelled like the woman he loved.

David clenched his jaw to contain the groan wanting to come out of his mouth. The pleasure he felt made him hate himself. He never wanted to be with Jane like this. No matter how long or how badly he desired her, this was not what he wanted. This wasn't *his* Jane. Still, he could not stop the thought of flipping her over and ripping off her clothes.

He fisted his hand in her hair while she continued to drink from him. Her moaning increased, and she began to roll her hips against him. With all his pent up desire, he could not stop himself from growing hard and knew she felt it. He remembered how distraught Jane was at realizing she'd had an orgasm before, and he didn't want to hurt her again. No matter how good it felt for her, he needed to make her stop.

He squeezed her waist to keep her still and growled. It angered him to have his body react to her so easily. Beads of sweat formed on his forehead. It took all his control to keep himself from taking her. Jane withdrew her fangs and slid her tongue over the small trail of blood that was left on his neck.

She tugged at his hair and whispered, "*Mmm* . . . Thank you, David." She then began kissing along his jaw toward his chin, nipping his skin there before inching her lips closer to his.

With a force he would not normally expend on Jane, he grabbed the sides of her face and looked into her dark eyes.

She was not at all concerned with his roughness. "Take me, David."

He shook his head, gripping her face harder. "Come back to me, Jane. Please, you need to fight it."

A hateful glare formed on her face. "She's weak. She's nothing without me."

"She's not weak," he snapped. "Whoever the fuck you are—let her go."

Shaking her head, she leaned back and laughed. "You'll never get to have her without me, Sir Knight. No matter how badly she wants you, she's too pathetic to take what she wants. She's more likely to let that wife-beater of a husband fuck her again, than ever kiss you."

His glare dropped as he tried to process her words.

She smiled at his confusion. "She didn't tell you?" She tilted her head. "Aw, don't worry. He only gave her a little smack. It was only once—just a slip of the hand, really. I guarantee she doesn't even think of it." She grinned evilly. "The weakling forgave him quickly." She giggled, but it was a wicked sound. "I promise she's had far worse. She'd take a thousand hits over the memories she can't seem to forget. Poor thing panics now whenever he touches her, and the dumb bastard never realized she's been reliving the nasty things those boys did to her when he's on top of her."

David's chest hurt. "You're lying."

"Am I? I know her better than you. She's a broken girl. She gave up trying to be happy all because he told her he wasn't in love with her." She cackled, and his heart ached. "How pathetic. It's really all her fault–she should have already known she wouldn't be good enough. She's just a real-life fuck-doll. She should be put out of her misery. You know what she wishes for at night?"

"Shut up!"

She ignored him, grinning more madly. "She wishes she never existed. All her happy memories with him–all her pictures of them smiling–she thought she'd been a great mom and wife. She thought she was happy. She'd given Jason everything she could, but she wasn't enough. All she sees when she looks at those pictures now, is the day he said, "*I'm not in love with you. You're just my wife,*" and she realizes all her happiness was a lie. She thinks peace will be found with her death." She lowered her voice to a whisper. "If only she knew what the devil would do with her." She laughed again and played with his hair, smiling at the heartbreak in his eyes.

Fury and sorrow. He didn't know which emotion to focus on. This possessed Jane might not have been telling the truth, but his instincts told him she was; his baby was dying inside.

He was pulled out of his growing rage when she reached for the hem of her shirt. She lifted it, but David quickly grabbed her wrist to stop her from pulling it all the way off. It didn't restrain her for long, though, as an unseen force pinned his arms to his sides.

She waved her finger at him. "Now, David, you said you wanted me."

"I said I wanted Jane." He glared with hate he never thought possible. "And you're not her. You have had your fun. Let her come back."

She ignored him and pulled off the shirt but the bandages were still in place. She frowned at the binding for a moment before looking back at him. "Why would you want to hurt her?"

"What?"

"Touch her. Take her."

David watched as the bandages covering her chest disintegrated. His eyes widened farther at the sight of her bare breasts.

"This won't do." She snapped her fingers, and the wounds there healed before his eyes.

She was far too powerful.

Her sadistic laugh pulled his attention away from her naked body, and despite the realization he was outmatched, he refused her demand. "No."

She grinned back at him. "No?"

"Bring her back. I'm tired of your games."

"I am her, though. The better Jane."

He snarled. "You're not my Jane."

"Be careful, David," she warned. "I can break her mind to the point you won't even recognize her anymore." David tensed, and she added in a deadly voice, "Or I can bury her so deep down that none of you will ever see her again. But she will. I'll let her see every cruel act I carry out while she cries inside me. She will never be more powerful than me. I will destroy her. The question is, do you want any part of your precious Jane to exist?"

He felt hopeless and his anger turned to fear. "Please don't hurt her. I will give you anything you want."

"That's a good boy," she whispered and kissed his cheek. Leaning back, her victorious smile stomped on his heart. "Don't worry." She grabbed his hands, sliding them up her sides. "I'll use her voice when you make me come. I'll be nice and even let her feel you inside us."

"Please stop," he said. "I can't do this to her."

"*Shh* . . . You'll enjoy this and forget all about her. Now fuck me, and I promise I'll keep her safe and clueless in the dark."

"Forgive me, Jane," he whispered, closing his eyes just as his hands cupped her breasts.

"ENOUGH," boomed a deep voice.

David's eyes flew open, and he yanked his hands out of Jane's as they both looked in the direction of the voice.

A dark figure suddenly appeared, and David pulled Jane to him, momentarily forgetting she was half naked and completely evil at the moment.

"I'm not going to hurt her," the figure promised.

Jane shivered and peered over her shoulder to get a look at the intruder. The man stayed in the shadows, but David knew it was a male, and this male outmatched him in both power and physical strength.

There was something about this shadowed person that seemed familiar, too. David tried to make out the man's face, but all he could see was a pair of glowing green eyes.

Those eyes slowly drifted over to Jane. If the stranger was surprised to see her dark eyes, he didn't react to them.

David looked at Jane and watched with fire burning through his veins as an impure quirk of her lips caused the mysterious man to smirk. He had to tighten his grip on her when she tried to turn toward the intruder. "Stop, Jane." David turned his focus to the unknown man. "Who are you?"

The green-eyed man's gaze narrowed at David. "I think David is done playing with you, beautiful." He glanced back at her. "Why don't you come play with me?"

She immediately began to pull herself from him.

David tightened his hold. "No, Jane."

The glare she shot him should have burned him alive. She ripped herself from his hold and opened her mouth, but the man interrupted her before she could spew any harsh words at him.

"Jane," the man said, a firmness that could not go ignored. She closed her mouth and looked back at him. The smoothness returned to his voice now. "Come here, beautiful girl."

The wrathful look fell from her face, and she smiled at the green-eyed man as David sat speechless.

Still half naked, she stood and walked up to the newcomer. David tried to stand. He had not made a sound, but she still sent him an angry hiss, and without seeing anything, a force knocked him on the bed, pinning him down.

David looked at the stranger, wondering how he was going to get out of this. Even possessed, or whatever was wrong with Jane, he didn't want her taken or harmed.

The man did not react to David's glare and looked away to watch Jane approach.

David could see more of the man's face now, but his expression gave nothing away as he held his hand out for Jane.

She took it without any hesitation and allowed the man to pull her close to him. She ran her hand up his stomach to his chest, smiling wickedly as she pressed her naked breasts against the man's body.

The stranger let out a hiss as her hands slid under his shirt.

"She knows you," she murmured, still in the alluring voice that dominated the real Jane's sweetness. She peered up into the emerald eyes that watched her and added, "She is blocking her memories from me. She is not stronger than me, so how is she doing it?"

The green-eyed man smirked and trailed his fingers up her side as his other hand moved to tuck a strand of hair behind her ear. "I wouldn't worry about that."

She lowered her hand and palmed the man through his pants, moaning as she began stroking the man's erection.

Sighing, the bastard grabbed the back of her neck and pulled her even closer, tilting her head upward in the process. He cast a quick glance at David, then returned his focus to Jane. His green eyes never left Jane as his lips covered her mouth.

She, however, closed her eyes and slid her hands around his neck and into his hair. Her gasp broke David's heart as she eagerly opened her mouth.

Immediately, the man deepened the kiss, thrusting his tongue into her mouth and finally closed his eyes. They moaned together and, growling, the stranger lifted her off her feet. She wrapped her legs around the man's waist just as easily as she'd done with him.

David was devastated. He was angry and panicked. He tried to get up again but stopped when the man's eyes suddenly opened.

Confused and unable to break free anyway, David had no choice but to watch as they continued their rough kiss.

The mysterious male's eyes intensified into an electric-green color, and he squeezed Jane's waist tightly as their kiss grew more urgent.

Then, suddenly, Jane's arms fell limp at her sides.

The man broke their kiss and watched her head roll to the side; then he calmly repositioned her so she was cradled in his arms.

David was worried but confused more than anything by the way this man now looked so adoringly down at her.

"There you are," the man said in a completely different tone than he had spoken in before. It was loving. "Wake, Sweet Jane."

David saw her weak smile from where he still lay and stayed silent as Jane reached up to touch the stranger's face.

The man smiled tenderly and turned his face against her palm.

"I knew you were real," she said, breathless. "They weren't dreams."

"It was real—I never left you." He lowered his face to softly kiss her swollen lips. "Do you remember now?"

"I remember." She whimpered, nodding as she hugged him. "Thank you, Death."

CHAPTER 22
DEATH

Never taking his eyes off the two people across the room, David slowly sat up. The entire situation with a possessed Jane had overwhelmed him. He was worried, angry, and sad that she was going through so much. Worse, he hadn't been able to save her. Again. All his great strength had been utterly useless. He'd been defeated, and she didn't even have to lift a finger to do it.

The woman he'd waited centuries for had been trapped; she'd begged him to help her, and he couldn't. His only hope to keep Jane safe had been to give that thing what it wanted. She had enough power to destroy them all, and he stood no chance in defeating her. But this stranger did.

David studied the man who held Jane. *No, he's not a man,* David reminded himself. He was Death. The Angel of Death held Jane as if she were his most treasured possession, all while she looked back at Death with equal adoration. So much tenderness, awe, longing, and devotion passed between them. They did not need to say a word—they loved each other.

Finally, Death replied to Jane. "You're welcome, Sweet Jane."

David stood and walked closer, and Death suddenly looked away from Jane to meet his gaze. All the tenderness Death had looked upon Jane with was nowhere in sight. Now the deadliest of all immortal beings stared David down with a glare so terrifying, it should have sent him running.

David would do no such thing. He wanted to fight the bastard, but something told him to back off. To wait. So he did.

It wasn't that he feared fighting something that no one could, but more that he felt Jane needed the being holding her. David felt a warmth radiating from her he'd never experienced before. Her eyes shone brighter, and despite the sorrow still visible in her smile, she looked at peace.

Death pulled Jane's naked chest flush against his, hiding what both men had already seen. She glanced down briefly before quickly looking back to Death with an embarrassed grin. Again, they gazed at each other, and Death's threatening look was gone.

David cleared his throat when Death smiled at her again. He might have felt the need to hold back, but he wasn't going to be able to watch their loving exchange much longer.

Jane turned toward David. He could still see her sadness and fear, but Death had given her something he didn't think he ever could. He saw it clearly. She was relieved and happy to be united, or reunited, it seemed, with Death. She really knew the Angel of Death, and David realized she'd lied to him about her past.

"David, I'm so sorry," she cried. "I didn't mean to hurt anyone."

Angry or not, he couldn't stop his tender reaction upon seeing her cry. "*Shh* . . . No, sweetheart. It's all right. I know that wasn't you."

His efforts to soothe her failed. She shook her head back and forth, unleashing more tears as shame and guilt rolled off her in waves.

"No. Please don't be sad," David was cut off when Death let out a threatening hissing sound.

After glaring at David, Death turned his attention back to her. "Jane, my sweet, no one is angry with you."

She looked back up at Death. "What about Gareth?"

"He'll be fine," Death told her.

"Are you sure?" Her tears ceased.

Death nodded. "I promise, baby girl."

Just like that, she calmed down. "Okay."

David didn't know how he felt. Apparently, all she needed was a few simple words from Death and she was fine. This was all wrong. She was meant to be with him. He'd known it would take time for her to grieve the loss of her family, but he believed Jane would eventually accept him. Now it seemed someone *else* had already claimed her.

"Jane," David said, trying his best to not let out his frustration on her.

She tore her eyes from Death to look at him but quickly lowered her gaze. David's heart cracked. She was ashamed, but he'd seen the flicker of guilt she was overwhelmed with. He wasn't sure if she felt guilty for what her evil counterpart had done or because she had clearly lied to him about her past.

David wanted to be furious with her. He wanted answers. If they were destined, he wanted to know why it seemed every obstacle possible was coming between them. He watched her expression as she tried not to break down. She refused to meet his gaze, but he could see her struggle with sorrow. When she silently cried with only Death there to comfort her, the fire building inside David burned out.

He sighed. "Are you all right, Jane? Do you hurt anywhere?"

Finally, she looked up, and he was so relieved at the sight of her hazel eyes. "I'm not hurt—my wound is gone. I only feel tired and weak."

David nodded but continued to check her for any injuries. Once he was satisfied she showed no outward sign of pain, he turned to Death. The fire reignited inside him. "What did you do to her?"

Death's face contorted with rage as his green eyes illuminated, casting a glow over Jane. "What you could not, Knight!"

"I doubt kissing her like that is what she needed," David said, his blood pumping fast now.

"It worked, didn't it?" came Death's quick retort. "I did what needed to be done. I'll do it again when she needs me to."

David opened his mouth ready to voice his own promises of what would pass if such an event took place again, but Jane's sniffling made both men look away from each other.

"Please don't fight," she whispered.

Death threw a final glare at David before pulling her closer. "We're sorry. We will not fight anymore. I promise." He kissed her forehead sweetly, but his eyes gleamed with mischief as he made her this vow and eyed David's balled fists with a cruel smirk. "David, will you make yourself useful and get her a new shirt?"

Before David could tell him to go fuck himself, Death carried Jane away.

David wanted to kill something, but he needed to calm down. So, he closed his eyes and breathed in deeply. Her smile formed in his mind, steadying his pounding heart. Jane came first, and as he opened his eyes, he pushed down the rage he so badly wanted to unleash.

He went to the dresser and quickly snatched up a shirt. *My shirt.* He'd make sure that bastard saw whose shirt she wore.

When he turned, Death was sitting on the bed with Jane across his lap. The angel had pulled a sheet up to cover her and was brushing his fingers under her eyes to wipe away her tears.

More of David's anger dissipated. Though it had already been clear that Jane adored Death, and had somehow known him, she wasn't jumping for joy. She was still sad and scared, but Death was helping her. He had saved her.

Death looked away from Jane and held out his hand.

David knew he was asking for the shirt. He had been ready to politely hand it to him, but when he looked at Jane, and she avoided him by hiding her face in Death's chest, his anger spiked again.

That might've been easy to tolerate, but not when the angel kept his eyes on David and grinned before placing a kiss on her head.

Unable to fight stooping to Death's immature level, David roughly threw the shirt at the angel's face.

Chuckling, Death caught it before it hit. "Thank you, David."

David grabbed a nearby chair. He needed to find out what was going on. At the moment, other than being a potential rival for Jane's heart, Death didn't appear to be a threat to him. He could at least find out how the hell he stopped the thing controlling Jane.

Death leaned back and grabbed Jane's chin, forcing her to look at him. She sighed as Death slid the shirt over her head, and the angel showed no hesitation when he reached through the arm holes for her hands, nor did he display any unease upon hearing her gasp.

The sheet she had been holding tightly fell to her waist, and David wanted to punch the satisfied look on Death's face as he pulled her hands through the shirt. An awareness of some sort flickered in Jane's eyes, and a pink blush spread over her cheeks while Death smirked, a similar recollection dancing in his gaze.

David reached his limit. He could not sit there and watch her being pulled under Death's seductive spell. He loudly cleared his throat.

Jane quickly tore her eyes away from Death and stared at David with worried eyes. He smiled, trying to show that she did not have to fear his wrath. Unfortunately, it didn't produce the desired reaction from her. Her features scrunched up in sadness, and like earlier, Death was the man who soothed her.

David sighed and folded his arms across his chest. "Can the others hear us?"

"No one will hear us unless I wish them to," said Death.

David figured as much. "Explain what you did to her."

Death continued running his hand up Jane's arm. For a moment, David's eyes darted there and Death smirked before saying, "I absorbed her energy. Well, enough to let Jane take control again."

Jane closed her eyes, appearing sad but so tired she might fall asleep as well, but she suddenly took several panicked breaths.

"*Shh . . .*" Death pulled her head to his chest again. "Rest, Jane."

She nodded and took a slow breath while relaxing against him.

David was at a loss on how to feel about their affection. "You took her energy?"

Death looked up. "Yes. I could not let it hurt her anymore." His face saddened as he glanced back to Jane, but the emotion vanished when he looked back at David. "Though, I realize you felt you had no choice, I would not stand by so she could be raped."

"I didn't want it to destroy her," David said softly.

"Neither did I," Death said. "So I stepped in."

"What is it?" David asked, letting go of a bit of his hatred toward the angel.

Death shrugged. "I am not sure. I never caught it before. It was hidden deep inside her."

"Before when?" David snapped.

Death grinned and stared David in the eye. "Jane and I met a long time ago. That's all you need to know."

"Fine." David wasn't going to argue like a child with him. "What do you know about it?"

All the playfulness vanished when Death spoke. "It's a part of her. I cannot take it away without killing her, too."

"Do you know how to keep it from taking over again?"

"No," Death said. "From my observations, her emotional state and need for blood made it easier for it to come forward. If Jane is relaxed and fed, she stands a better chance at keeping it confined. It would also benefit her to train in combat and learn how to use her abilities. If she masters them, she may be able to overthrow the entity when it harms others. The entity doesn't need Jane's knowledge to wield her power—it is the source of her power."

David shook his head. This didn't make any sense to him. She was supposed to save them, not destroy them.

Death went on. "If we can help strengthen her mind, there is a better chance she will be able to stay in control." Death paused and looked down at Jane. "Until we are confident in her ability to control this, we will have to give her whatever she wants."

This is what Arthur had told him, but hearing Death say it didn't sit well with him.

"Of course"—Death smirked—"if it comes back, I can drain her again."

"I am sure you would enjoy that," he said as Death chuckled. "How do we call you?" It was hard to admit, but Death had been able to help her when he could not.

"I'll know if she needs me," Death answered.

Jane gripped Death and stared at the angel with panic. "Don't leave me again. Please don't leave me."

With adoring eyes that he seemed to only have for her, Death whispered, "I'll never leave you."

David felt torn. Death had succeeded where he had failed. In fact, since finding her, David realized he had done nothing but fail and bring her pain.

Death looked David in the eye. "I need to speak with her privately."

David wanted to argue, but it was clear Jane wanted Death. There was a possessiveness in her desperate hold on the angel.

"Yes," he said. "I will go and check to see if everything is all right. Jane?" She finally lifted her sad eyes. "Call if you need me, okay?"

She nodded. David wanted to touch her, but when he reached out to caress her face, she whined and turned toward Death. David's face fell.

Surprisingly, Death gave him a sympathetic smile. "I will take care of her, Knight."

David nodded to him before giving Jane one last look; then he left the room—leaving Jane with *her Death.*

✦✦✦

Jane peeked over her shoulder as the door shut. Her heart wrenched, and she cried. She was in agony over everything she'd done. The darkness she'd always felt inside herself had finally been unleashed. She had hurt Gareth, and worst of all, she hurt David.

Death held her close to him and caressed her hair. "If it hurts so much to push him away, why are you doing it?"

She cried harder. "I have to. I was horrible. I hurt him. I can't face him again."

"No," he said, kissing her hair. "He understands. That wasn't your fault."

"I couldn't stop it." She pressed her face against his chest more. "I tried, but she wouldn't let me. She was laughing at me, letting me see what she was forcing him to do. She told him things I didn't want him to know." She sobbed, squeezing Death's shoulder as she screamed her heartache into his chest.

"*Shh* . . ." Death rocked her. "He knows that wasn't really you. Just like I did, he saw you being held down inside her."

"I tried," she cried.

"I know you tried. I'm proud of you. You kept it hidden even from me. That shows how strong you really are."

"I'm not strong. I'm nothing but a tool. Just like she said, I'm a flesh and blood fuck-doll."

"Jane," he chided lovingly, "do not speak that way about yourself. You are nothing of the sort. Were you aware of everything?"

"No. It was mostly dark. There were moments where I could see shapes and hear muffled conversation, but she controlled what I could see and hear. I saw her face—my face—in my mind. She wanted to see my reactions." She looked off to the side as a hollow feeling spread through her chest. "How long have you been here? Did you know that wasn't me?"

He sighed. "I've been here most of the time. I did not know what it was. I saw fragments of it recently, but I did nothing because I did not know what I was facing. I needed to get information to keep from harming you. It was just luck that draining you of energy allowed you to come back. I wasn't going to sit back and watch you basically get raped."

"He didn't want to," she whispered, her eyes watering at the thought of David taking her that way. "I think it would be her raping him."

"Well, I wasn't going to watch it happen and do nothing. Not anymore."

She whined. "She said she wasn't going to let me witness him take her, but she'd show me later how much she satisfied him. Do you know what she is?"

"No. She was already there." He muttered something in a language she didn't recognize. "I didn't know—"

Jane didn't like how upset he sounded with himself. "What if she comes back?"

"I will be with you," he promised. "But you will need David, Jane. I don't like him, but he will help you keep her back."

She sniffed and roughly wiped the tears from her face. "I can't have him with me right now—it's too confusing. And I hurt him too badly. I could see it on his face. He thinks I lied."

"About?"

"Us," she said. "I could see he felt betrayed."

"You didn't lie, though. You didn't remember me until I lifted the block when I kissed you."

"He saw us kiss." She was only commenting this, further realizing the pain she'd inflicted. What would she have done if David had kissed another?

Death chuckled. "Good thing he doesn't know that's not our first kiss." Tears slid down her cheeks. She didn't know how to feel. "I'm sorry, Sweet Jane. I do not mean to hurt you like this. It has been hard to see you in his arms."

"I'm sorry." She felt like she was betraying them: Death, David, and Jason.

"Don't be," he said. "You didn't remember me when Jason asked you to start a relationship with him. I made the choice to remove myself from your memories, not you."

It wasn't something she wanted to focus on right now. "I still feel awful," she told him. "I feel like I betrayed you with Jason, then I was betraying Jason with David and then there's you. I feel like I'm betraying both of them because it's like I never stopped loving you."

"You still love me?"

She looked up and met his intense gaze. Those green eyes that always seemed to linger in the back of her mind were staring at her now. She'd craved them even when she didn't know who they belonged to. "I still love you, Death."

He smiled and slid his fingers down the path of her tears. The tingling sensation made her weep harder. He'd been there every time she cried. "Don't worry over us."

"What do you think he's thinking about us?" she asked, fearful of his answer.

Death sighed. "If I were him, I'd assume you had a relationship with me before and kept it secret. Considering Arthur can read minds; David will probably demand to know why he wasn't told about me."

"Could Arthur see you in my mind?"

"No." Death shook his head. "Just like you, he hit my walls every time he searched."

She nodded, relieved that at least Arthur could vouch for her. If David ever looked at her the way others did, she'd break. "What does this mean for us? I don't know what's right."

"It's up to you," he said.

She touched his cheek, smiling sadly as the beautiful tingling sensation danced from his skin to hers. "I don't know what to do. But I won't give you up."

He grinned and turned his face to kiss her fingers. "You don't have to, Sweet Jane. I'm yours to keep."

CHAPTER 23

JANE & DEATH

"I can't believe it's been almost ten years since we've been like this," Jane murmured, nuzzling Death's chest. She was struggling to process the onslaught of memories from her past with him. The life she thought she'd known now clashed with the one she had, pushing her mind so far to the brink, she physically clutched Death, afraid he might not really be there.

Death chuckled and slid his hand along her arm. "I've been with you like this. You just didn't know I was there."

"The tingles?"

"You know I never liked when you said that about my touch. You are closer to my physical age—at least use a mature word to describe our contact."

She smiled, loosening her grip on him. "I love the tingles." He sighed, and the tightness in her chest eased. They had always been so comfortable with each other. Playful. "Was that really you?"

He kissed her forehead. "Yes. I wanted to do more, but I tried to be there as often as I could. I held you when you cried in bed, whispered in your ear when I knew you needed to hear my voice, and I kissed you when I couldn't stop myself—when I could not stand the sight of your sadness."

A tear quickly fell from her eye. It was hard to grasp he'd never left. It broke her heart as much as it filled it with peace. "Sometimes I thought someone was speaking to me in my dreams."

"It is easier for you to hear me when you're asleep," he said softly. "I cannot read your mind or speak telepathically with you, but I'd kneel beside you and talk to you. When your emotions consumed you, you would lose the rational side of your mind, and there was nothing to tell you I wasn't real."

"I felt crazy, though."

"I know. I wanted to reveal myself, but I thought I was doing the right thing." He nuzzled the top of her head. "You are all I feel. I ached every time I had to leave you, but I had to keep you secret. If others had found out I'd formed some sort of relationship with anyone, they would have harmed you more than they already were. Even now, I risk losing you. My veil is powerful, but we will be found out in time."

"I won't give you up again," she said fiercely. "If I lose you, I lose me."

"So would I."

She pressed her ear to his heart, smiling because she'd done the same thing when she was a child. "Do you remember when we first met?"

Death kissed her hair. "Of course. I'll never forget."

Five-year-old Jane had whimpered as she opened her watery eyes. Every part of her body had hurt while her head throbbed. Nothing made sense. Screaming. That had been the last thing she remembered.

Her panicked breaths were the only noise filling the dead air. She looked around the smoke and twisted metal surrounding her, until she spotted her little brother. "Jack?" He did not stir.

Stinging tears blurred her sight and eventually soaked her cheeks. Jack was still strapped in his booster seat. Blood dripped down his cute face and seeped through his shirt, but she hoped he was only asleep. She stretched and touched his lifeless little hand. "Jack?" she cried. "Wake up, Jack." Still, he didn't move. Even his chest was still. It didn't look right. "Mommy! Daddy!"

No one responded.

It became harder to breathe, and she felt so sleepy. She'd cried and cried, but now, she only wanted to sleep.

Just as she felt herself drifting away, a green flash lit the demolished car. She turned her head and fought closing her eyes as a figure inside the green light came closer. A man.

Finally, he was close enough that she could see his face. She stared at his green eyes, then the rest of his face. He was pretty–so pretty. She wanted to go with him and stay with him always.

He smiled, and his eyes glowed brighter. The pain she'd felt went away, and her chest warmed. For a moment, he simply watched her–studied her face until he reached out and pushed the hair away from her forehead. As soon as they touched, a tingling sensation spread throughout her body. She never wanted it to go away.

The man pulled his hand back, looked at his fingertips before he placed them on her forehead again. "Shh . . . it's all right, little one." His voice made her want to smile.

"I'm scared," she told him.

"Don't be afraid. I will not harm you."

"It won't hurt?"

He tilted his head. "What won't hurt, baby girl?"

"When you take me with you. When I die."

He said nothing for what seemed like a long time and kept staring at her. His gaze continuously swept over her face and every time his eyes met hers, they'd burn brightly. "You're not going to die," he finally said.

"I'm not?"

"No. I am going to make the pain go away, and you will go to sleep for a while."

"Will you come see me again?" Her eyelids felt so heavy. She didn't want him to leave. She had wanted to go with him.

He smiled, the most beautiful smile she would ever see. "I will come see you again." Death had lowered his face to hers and an inch from her lips, he had murmured, "Now sleep, Sweet Jane."

The distant memory slipped away from Jane, and she smiled. "You were my first kiss."

He chuckled. "I suppose I was."

"It's hard to process that you came back after my family died. You had come every night for almost a year and held me until I fell asleep."

"You were sad," he said, resting his cheek on the top of her head. "I'd never felt anything before—then this little girl had me wrapped around her finger, begging me to tell her stories until she was dreaming of dragons and knights. I told you Arthur's knights were real."

She did remember his stories of battles and myths. "You always made me happy. I wish you could have stayed."

"I had to leave." He breathed her in. "I have a duty to fulfill. It was never right for me to be with you; you were human. No matter how much I wanted to take care of you, it was wrong."

She shook her head and pulled herself closer to him. "It wasn't wrong. When you left me, it all fell apart. I needed you. I didn't understand why you'd left. They told me you were an imaginary friend I'd created to help me mourn my family's death."

Death wrapped his arms around her and kissed her head. "I'm sorry. When I kept you alive, I was afraid to let anyone find out about you. I shielded you with my veil. My own reapers could not locate me because I refused to give you away. I didn't understand leaving you to grow up would turn out so disastrously. I always meant to come back, but there were many responsibilities I had to attend to. I'd never felt panic and pain before, but finding you barely conscious with empty bottles on your dresser—I lost my mind."

"I saw you when you came that time. It's so strange to realize you'd been there. It feels like I have two lives now."

Fourteen-year-old Jane had weakly turned her head toward the green glow that had illuminated her room. She hadn't been able to see him, but she'd felt his presence and smiled. It had been so long, but he'd finally come to take her. He hadn't been a figment of her imagination after all.

Only the outline of Death's figure was visible as he stood over her. She wanted to touch his face—to hear his voice. It hadn't been her intention to kill herself, but now that it was done, the medicine mixed with her blood, she was ready to follow him.

But he didn't take her.

Through the broken images of the paramedics working and speaking to her cousin, she faintly caught a glimpse of two separate flashes of white light before Death growled and turned away.

After that, there were only flickers of what happened: the white lights of the ceiling passing overhead as they wheeled her on the bed down the hospital halls, and the strangers looming over her as they asked questions she did not care to answer. She just wanted to be with him now. But they wouldn't leave her be.

"Don't spit it out, sweetie," someone said. "You need to relax. This will absorb what's left in your stomach."

She didn't like it. The needles didn't sting, and the nurses pulling off her clothes didn't embarrass her, but she didn't like this sensation of having a tube shoved down her throat.

"No, sweetie. Let us help you."

She tried to shake her head as they pulled away the cloth they'd wiped her mouth with. Black liquid soaked the towel, and she realized that was what seeped down the side of her mouth.

"ENOUGH, JANE." Death's voice seemed to be everywhere but nowhere at the same time.

"How much did they say she took? And when?" someone asked.

Jane knew the answer, but she could not talk. The medic still assisting the doctors supplied the answer, though.

Death's voice came back as the medic informed the doctors and nurses. "Why, baby girl? How could you do this?" She wanted to tell him what had happened since he'd left, but she didn't know how.

"Jesus. She's so young," said one of the nurses.

"Jane, sweetie." A different nurse leaned over her face. "You need to keep this down. I know you don't like how it feels, but this is going to help you." The nurse shook her head at someone. "She's still not swallowing."

Tingles, she'd thought she'd dreamed up as a little girl slid back and forth over her forehead. "Stop fighting them." Even though she could no longer feel her body, his voice kissed her skin in a way only he could. "You will not die–I won't allow it. But if you do not do as they say, you will suffer more." For a tiny moment, she saw his face. So terrifying. So beautiful. He smiled. "That's my girl."

The nurse praised her as she swallowed the activated charcoal being pumped into her stomach.

After a while, she only woke to turn her head and throw up a black substance or when a nurse would draw more vials of blood. And every time, he was there. Watching.

"Sleep, Sweet Jane. I will be here when you wake."

Five days of hospitalization seemed to last forever. His presence remained the entire time, though.

When a male nurse walked up to her side, she sleepily turned to look at his eyes. Their unusual shade of emerald reminded her of Death, and so did his smile. "Hey, baby girl."

"Hi," she whispered, unable to look away from his gaze. "Do I know you?"

He didn't answer, but he caressed the side of her cheek. Tingles.

"Death," she said.

"Shh . . . They are watching us."

"Who?"

He had looked up at the ceiling but did not answer her question. "Do not speak of me to anyone. Do not call for me. I am already here."

"They're sending me home tomorrow."

Death had nodded and rubbed her cheek. "The demon who attached himself to your cousin has fled. I'm so sorry, Sweet Jane. I did not know. I will hunt him down and slay him. I promise you it will not hurt you again."

"Do you still believe it was only a demon in Stephen that made him do everything to me?" Jane asked, opening her eyes, no longer seeing the hospital she'd been in as a teenager and, instead, she was back in the bedroom.

"Anyone is capable of doing evil, Jane. It is difficult to say how long your cousin was under the influence of a demon. I do not know if he would have been different had he not been persuaded by darkness. Still, *he* made the choice to hurt you."

"What happened when you left to hunt it?"

He let out a hissing sound and squeezed her. "It was more than one. The one I finally managed to capture and torture was the one who had been with Stephen during your overdose. He held out long enough for another to seduce Stephen, and by the time I realized that, it was too late. You'd already been abused again, and Adam had fought Stephen."

"Did you keep Stephen from dying?"

He chuckled. "No. You are the only being I have spared. Others may have escaped by prolonging their time on Earth with immortality, but I wait for them. You, however, are someone I will not part with."

"Is he dead now?" she asked.

"Yes, angel. All but Adam are dead. I might have woken Stephen long enough for him to experience his end."

She nodded, not sure how she felt about her abuser being dead or that Death had made him suffer before he died. Her heart pounded as she considered asking him about their relationship.

"I know you want to ask about what happened between us," he said, twirling a lock of her hair before letting it slide between his fingers. "Ask."

"You made sure you came every night after the boys went away. I was young, I know, but I thought you cared about me more than just a young girl."

"You have always been more than a girl to me, Jane, but you were a child. You certainly were more mature, in your own way. Apart from when I came to you at night, and you would try to scare me." He chuckled, kissing her head. "Still, you were a human child."

"You could have pretended to be scared at least once," she said lamely.

Death sighed and took her hand, playing with her fingers. "I have the most powerful veil in all realms. I could have hidden you somewhere, but I would not have been able to be there all the time. I'd still leave to carry out my duty, and I could not see you living that life."

"I would have followed you."

"I know," he said softly. "But I wanted you to be happy. I saw nothing for us."

"Even on my birthday? When we—"

"When you asked me to kiss you?" He lifted her hand to his lips and kissed her fingers. "You were only seventeen."

Jane teared up and looked across the wall as she remembered that night.

He'd been late. Death had been punctual and consistent in his visits since her cousins were taken away. Every night he had come and either told her stories or simply held her to push away the bad memories.

"Happy Birthday, Sweet Jane," he whispered in her ear.

She whirled around, smiling as she lunged forward to hug him. "I thought you forgot!"

He grinned and hugged her. "Never. Did you have a good day?"

Jane shrugged. "That Jason boy asked me to go to the movies with him, and Wendy bought me a cupcake."

He nodded and held her away, looking her over. "You still look the same."

She glared at him. "I saw you last night."

He chuckled. "Are you going to go out with that boy?"

"No," she said quickly. "Why would I?"

"Is that not what humans do?"

"If they are friends or dating, yes," she said. "I think he wants to be more than my friend."

He smiled, but it wasn't his usual smile that made her heart flutter. "Do you want a boyfriend?"

She blushed and nodded. "I like someone."

"You do?"

"I love him, actually. I'm in love with him."

He tilted his head. "How do you know?"

She frowned. "That I'm in love with him?" When he nodded, she said, "I don't know. I think I loved him before I even met him."

"So why not go on this date?"

"It's not Jason that I love," she whispered quickly. Death was quiet as he watched her. She didn't know if he could see she had realized her true feelings, and she feared he would deny her. She'd felt this way for as long as she could remember but only recently begun to realize what it meant. "Death, I'd like a present from you."

He seemed unsure but smiled. "What would you like?"

"A kiss."

Immediately, he shook his head and reached out to hold her face in his hands. "No. I'll give you anything else."

Pain tore at her chest and tears welled up in her eyes as her heart broke. This wasn't something she had ever wanted to feel because of him. She thought he must have loved her as well.

He held her, keeping her from pulling away. "Don't cry." He wiped her tears.

She tried to hide her broken heart with a smile, but she couldn't. "It's you I love, and you don't want me. I'm too ugly!"

Death chuckled. "You are not ugly. You are the most beautiful girl I have ever seen."

"Then why won't you kiss me? Do you not love me like I love you?"

He sighed and did not answer her question as he stared down at her. However, her heart felt like it might explode as he caressed her cheek, then slid his hand behind her neck. "Just this once, Sweet Jane."

She nodded quickly and held her breath as he lowered his face to hers. His lips touched hers, lightly at first, and she closed her eyes as an explosion of tingles spread across her lips. Something powerful stirred deep inside her; she needed more of him.

It felt right for his lips to be against hers. Any fear she'd had over rejection faded from her mind and with complete love and trust, she pressed her lips against his.

He kissed back.

It was sweet. He held her close, one hand on the back of her neck while his other hand found its place at the small of her back, but she needed more.

She slid her hands up and gripped his strong shoulders in fear that he'd end their kiss too soon. Then she took the bold leap and licked his lips.

He hesitated but suddenly tilted her head back and pushed her mouth open with his. He met her tongue with his, quickly leading her in the most incredible kiss she'd ever dreamed of.

She sighed and wrapped her hands around his neck, lightly caressing his hair. All that mattered now was him. Them. She needed more and, thrilling her, he seemed to need her just as much.

A possessive rumble sounded from his throat and without warning, he lifted her up, guiding her legs around his waist as he squeezed her thigh while his other hand slid down her spine.

She clung to him, not willing to part. They had to be closer. The constant yearning for more of him took over her actions as he carried her to the bed.

He sat down with her straddling him and groaned when she rolled her hips. A throbbing sensation between her legs became too much for her. She'd never felt such a need before. Instinct made her move to relieve the beautiful ache at her center. She knew they were meant to be together this way. There would be no convincing her otherwise.

Jane gasped for air, but Death didn't move away. He turned his assault to her neck. His lips left shocks across her skin. She felt like she was vibrating from the tingles as they went everywhere. They seeped into her pores, and she still couldn't get enough.

Death slid his tongue up her neck, sucking hard below her jaw before he worked his way back down. He squeezed her waist while he held her neck to keep her where he wanted her. She felt how much he wanted her now. She'd felt a boy between her legs before, but Death was different. She needed to give him all of her. She wanted to give him everything.

Rolling her hips, she moaned. She didn't want him to deny her; she wanted him to take her. She wanted to be his in every way.

She didn't mean to say it out loud, but she did. "I love you, Death."

He stopped his kisses and pulled back. His expression was peaceful as he stared into her eyes, and he smiled.

She began to smile back, but his smile fell, and he pulled her arms off his neck. She didn't know what to say and sat quietly as he held her face between his hands. He kissed her sweetly and sighed, leaving his lips touching hers for a few seconds before moving back.

The most affectionate look was on his face. "My beautiful, Sweet Jane, you mean so much to me. I want you to know that I will always do everything in my power to protect you."

She had nodded and smiled. "I know you will."

He wore a strained smile as the green in his eyes dulled slightly. "I want you to be happy. I cannot give you a happy life. I am Death–I can only bring you sorrow.

So, from this point on, you will forget me. You will go on with your life and find love."

She had frantically tried to shake his hands off her face, but he was too strong.

"I'll never be far," he had said. She had wanted to scream and cry. "Live, Sweet Jane." He then placed a final kiss to her lips and removed her memory of him.

"Even though you hid yourself from me, I don't think I really forgot you." She pulled her head back from his shoulder to look at him.

Death smiled. "I guess I lost my touch, then."

She touched the side of his face. *So beautiful.* "No, you didn't lose your touch. I don't think we were meant to part. I loved you then, and I love you now."

A torn smile formed on Death's lips, and he gently pulled her closer. He kissed her softly, and when he pulled back, he pressed his forehead to hers. "And I love you, Sweet Jane."

She closed her eyes and smiled. What she felt to finally hear him say those words could not be expressed in even the most beautiful of words.

"I don't deserve your love, though," he added. "I have done something terrible."

She opened her eyes. "I will always love you."

He kissed her nose and pulled back. "It's my fault this entity inside you came forward. I had already been with you most of the time. When the plague spread here, I came to check on you. It had already arrived on your street, so I pushed worry into your thoughts to get you inside your home. I urged you to get the bag from the soldiers, gave you the push to be the person I knew you always wanted to be. My little warrior."

She smiled softly, but anxiety had her breathing faster.

"I wanted to stay with you," he said, "but I left to get news I'd been waiting on. Then I realized you'd been infected and returned. I was shocked to see the knights already guarding your home, so I waited to see their intentions. That's when I realized David had recognized you as his Other.

"I had intended on finding a way to keep the infection from spreading too far until I could have you cured, because I could not cure you myself. But I knew the immortal's blood would neutralize the infection, so I stepped back and let David change you.

"I missed you. Whispering to you and letting you feel my presence is nothing compared to truly holding you in my arms. So, when I saw the chance that you would be immortal, I let it happen. I knew your transition would take time, so I left to figure out why the plague kept coming closer to you. I knew David would guard you with his life, but I didn't expect that he'd take you to hunt werewolves."

"I was supposed to die again," she said, touching her chest.

"You are on borrowed time," he told her as if it was the worst truth of his existence. "I felt the injury you received as if it were my own. When I wiped your memory, I bonded with you. I should have done it much sooner—it would have prevented so much of your pain, but I did not think it was right or necessary. When you received the injury from the infected wolf, I had to think fast. I knew now it was no coincidence that we met when you were younger. If you were fated to be David's mate, you had an important role to play on Earth."

"What did you do, Death?"

"Don't hate me." He kissed her forehead. "I came up with a plan to make you mine. I did not think about how much it would hurt you or any other consequences—I only wanted you back." Death caressed her jaw with his thumb. "I could not take you with me as you were, though. Your soul was still too innocent. I needed some way to balance you between light and dark."

"So what was your plan?"

"When you had fallen in battle, I arrived the same moment Lucifer had. I assumed he was merely there because of Lancelot, but he could not take his eyes off you. I saw him as my opportunity to introduce darkness into your soul.

"I proposed that for me to let you live, they allow Lucifer to give you his blood. I knew he would want something in return, and I made a wager that if you became neutral, I would claim you. If you fell to darkness, you'd follow Lucifer. If your soul and heart stayed pure, we would leave you be. I assumed because you were so good, it would balance you between good and evil, and I could quickly claim you for all time after I returned your memories."

She stared at him in shock. "You had me drink Lucifer's blood?"

He stared at her, defeated. "I did not think he had a chance. If Lucifer saw that you meant something to me, he would become more obsessed with you. If I spared you without Michael and Gabriel stepping in, it would have given me away. Even if rumor spreads in Heaven, Luc will hear of it. He has always had a strong dislike for me. If he saw I had a weakness, he'd destroy it.

"So, I did what I thought gave you the best chance. I didn't realize there was already something dark inside you. Lucifer's blood set it free from the cage you'd trapped it in."

She couldn't process everything, but she understood his panic and desire. "You bet my soul with Lucifer?"

"I never meant to hurt you. I only wanted you back." His tormented voice broke her heart. He was the first man she had ever loved, the only person who continuously comforted and protected her—no matter how many times he'd left, he always returned.

"What happens if I don't become neutral?"

"If you stay in the light, David technically wins, and we leave you alone." He scowled, which made her smile for a moment. He nuzzled her cheek. "If you fall to darkness, you would be so evil that you would follow Lucifer without question. He won't win. Even if I have to lose to David, I will. If Luc manages to take you, I will destroy every world and being in existence until I have you back."

"Oh, Death." She held his face and pressed a kiss to his lips, loving so much that he allowed her such intimacy. "You always became so volatile when it came to something happening to me."

His lips turned up against hers. "You're all I have, Sweet Jane."

She wrapped her arms around his neck and mumbled against his skin. "I know I should be angry with you, but I forgive you. I think I'm incapable of being upset with you, actually. Besides, we'll figure this out, and I know you will do everything you can to keep me safe. Whatever happens though, please, don't make me forget you."

"I will never do that to you again." Death held her back by the shoulders as his gaze drifted over her face. She smiled sleepily, and he rewarded her with a chuckle. "You're tired, Jane. I took a lot of energy from you. I'm surprised you're still awake."

"I'm not ready to go to sleep," she said, pouting her lips.

He laughed softly and lifted her up before he moved toward the headboard.

This made her drowsiness vanish. "What are you doing? Are you leaving?"

"No," he said quickly. "I just want you to rest. It will help you remain in control of your emotions. I realize you nearly bled Gareth dry, but I did take most of your energy."

Jane relaxed and let him lay her down on the bed. Before he could pull away, though, she pulled his hand and scooted to the center of the bed. She tugged on his hand and gave him her best puppy dog eyes. "Please sleep with me. You can't remind me I nearly killed my friend and walk away."

He grinned and sat next to her. "He's a tough boy. He'll gloat about it for years."

"Shut up." She smiled and helped him remove his jacket before tossing it to the edge of the bed. She grinned, excited for them to do such a normal thing, and pushed him down on the pillows. Within seconds, she was snuggled against his side with her head on his chest.

His arm that was behind her head, pulled her closer. "You haven't changed at all." He chuckled and caressed her arm with his fingertips.

Tingles.

She sighed and soaked up the comfort he offered, but a sad thought came over her. "Do you remember Wendy?"

He continued caressing her arm. "Yes."

She hesitated, but this was eating at her. "You took her?"

"Yes, I took her," he said without hesitating. "I came for her myself."

"She was my only friend." Her throat ached.

"I know. Everyone has their time, though—and that was hers."

"Couldn't you have waited? She didn't want to die."

"Jane, my sweet, beautiful girl," he said with nothing but love in his tone. "I want nothing more than to see you happy, but humans must pass from this world to the next. That is why your lives are so precious."

She swallowed nervously before asking a question she feared but needed an answer to. "Do you know where she is?"

Death pulled her a little closer and placed a kiss on her head. "She waits in Neverland, Jane."

Any attempt to hold herself together failed. Her face scrunched up, and she sobbed. She realized where Death would have pulled those words from. He really had been there all along. She'd told Wendy she believed people came from stardust, and they returned to the stars when they die. They went to Neverland.

"I do not mean to change the subject from myself," Death said, making her laugh out the last of her cries. He chuckled and tilted her face up. "But you're going to have to feed soon. As much as I hate to say it, you must go to David for that."

"Can't I feed from you?" She looked at him, hopeful. "I don't think I can face him anytime soon. He's too good. Everything is overwhelming with him, but I know I don't want to hurt him. He's probably so mad at me anyway. I won't be able to take him looking at me like I'm evil." Her heart throbbed, but she nodded to herself. "Yes, I'd much rather feed from you. It'll be better for everyone."

"I don't drink blood," he said like it should be obvious that she couldn't feed from him. "I'm not human or a vampire. I can transfer energy to you, but you need blood and real food. You cannot feed from me."

"What do you eat?"

Chuckling, he asked, "What do you think? I'm Death."

"You feed on souls?"

"Of course." He grinned, laughing. "A soul gives me energy. The things I do—just like you—require energy. A soul is the ultimate energy drink." She crinkled her nose up, and he smiled as he spoke again. "Don't make that face. You're the one who drinks blood."

"It's not like I want to." Though as she thought of David's blood, her stomach squeezed with hunger. "Do souls taste good?" she asked to distract herself. "Are bad people gross?"

"I wouldn't really call it a taste, like you would. More like a drug, if anything. There are bitter and sweet souls. Some are very weak, and some surge through my system for days. The wicked are most addicting." He smirked. "You taste the best, though. Sweet. Mouthwatering. I will never kick my Jane Addiction." He chuckled and pulled her face to his and kissed her cheek which was incredibly hot. "I'm teasing you. But you do taste good—perfect amount of sweetness. I could spend every single minute with your taste on my tongue."

Her face was still red, and he chuckled as he pulled her head back to his chest. Jane blew out a deep breath to rid herself of embarrassment and giddiness. She wiggled a bit as she hitched her leg over Death's waist. His hand went to her thigh immediately and began to lightly rub it, relaxing her.

"I know we've always cuddled, but do you think it's wrong?" she asked him.

"It's not wrong. Most likely our bond urges you to be close to me."

"I don't think that's it," she said. "I've always been comfortable with you. It's like you're supposed to be with me. Like we are supposed to touch. Do you feel the same?"

"Yes. I have always felt the urge to be physically connected with you in some way." His hand flexed around her thigh. "More than physically, actually—but touching you helps calm my need. Obviously, when you were a child, it wasn't sexual, but I was confused by my desire to be so close to you. We had not even bonded then, so you might be right; perhaps it is something else."

"Is it different for you now? How you want to be close to me?"

Tingles erupted from his touch when he answered her. "Definitely. You're a woman now. I want to feel and taste every inch of you."

Her heart beat fast. "I really meant what I said. If you hadn't left, I wouldn't be with anyone else. But now I'm so confused."

"I know." He sighed, soothingly caressing her leg. "I can almost hear your thoughts. You're ashamed and sad for David and Jason."

"But you're back," she said.

"I never left, babe. But, yes, I'm back. Still, I must accept the fact that David and Jason were possible because I stood back and did nothing when you needed me."

"You did what you thought was best for me."

He nodded. "With Jason, yes. I wanted you to live a normal life and did not accept what I felt for you. That wasn't the case with David. With him, I saw an opportunity to gain what I wanted."

"I don't want to talk about this anymore," she quickly whispered. It hurt her to compare Death, David, and Jason while worrying over Death's bet with Lucifer. She also refused to paint Death as the bad guy.

"Nor do I," he said.

She sighed and tried to think of something to change their mood. "I still can't believe I did all that to David. And you were there. I'm so horrible—a freaking hoe."

Death laughed loudly. "You are not a hoe, Jane." He laughed again. "A sexy tease, definitely. But not a hoe. And I don't think horribly of you," he added. "It was sexy as hell. Got me hard and everything. And now I have two memories of hot make-out sessions with you. One wasn't the real you, but still—it was hot. Makes me wish I had one of those mobile phones to record it."

All she could imagine was Death posting them kissing on social media. She wondered if he ever got embarrassed and decided to tease him for once. "You know, Death," she said in the most seductive tone she could manage and looked up at him. "When I said that you were in my dreams—" His eyes burned while he stared down at her. She had to wet her lips to make sure she could form words again. "Our make-out sessions were a lot more intense than that. There was always less clothing, too. Well, you made sure I was in as little as possible, but I never put up a fight. There's just something about the way you'd rip off my bra and panties that had me—"

He groaned and spanked her butt. "Knock it off, Jane. You're killing me."

She laughed and kissed his chest. "I'm pretty sure you're the only one who can kill the Angel of Death."

"I'm sure you could find a way," he mused. "Your tits pressing against me almost had me falling to my knees."

She laughed with him until she finally took a deep breath and calmed down. "I love you."

"And I love you," he said, softly. "Now go to sleep. When you get up, you're getting fed."

She nodded and closed her eyes. Her dreams became her memories once again. Only this time, the dark figure beside her had a face, and he smiled in a way she knew was only for her. He was Death, and she was his Sweet Jane.

CHAPTER 24
BITTER KNIGHTS

The stair railing creaked before splintering under David's hands. He loosened his grip but kept his eyes closed. Since he'd left that room, he'd been trying to listen in. He needed answers, and he hoped something would slip through the sound barrier Death created. But there was nothing. As soon as he'd shut the door, Jane's cries sounded for only a second before there was absolute silence.

For five minutes, David had stood there. He didn't know what he was waiting for; clearly, Jane didn't want or need him anymore. His heart felt like it had been ripped right out of his chest.

"David," Arthur called from the main floor of the house.

David straightened and went downstairs. He knew Arthur was reading his thoughts, and he didn't care to hide them. He doubted they made sense anyway; there were so many.

Passing Arthur, David entered the living room where Gawain sat with Gareth.

His injured comrade was on the sofa with his eyes closed, looking like hell. David paused and met Gawain's worried gaze before glancing at the empty glass next to Gareth's hand. He sighed and shook his head. So much had happened, he'd nearly forgotten Gareth nearly died because of Jane.

David sat in a chair next to them, leaned back, and tilted his head to stare at the ceiling. His mind wouldn't rest. Jane was in love with Death. She didn't even have to say the words. The way she looked at the angel said enough.

"David, is Jane all right?" Arthur asked.

He didn't respond right away and continued to stare up at the ceiling. His thoughts were bitter as he pondered the simple question. She was more than all right. She was being pampered by the Angel of Death.

"David, how is she?" Gawain asked this time.

They moved to the edge of their seats. Perhaps readying themselves to run upstairs, but David finally responded. "She's fine. She is with Death."

"Dear God, David," Arthur whispered. "Did you kill her?"

David immediately shook his head back and forth. "No, I did not kill her." *I couldn't even if I tried,* he thought. "She's not dead. Death is simply with her."

"You're not making sense," said Arthur. "Why can't I hear her thoughts or even her heartbeat?"

He looked Arthur in the eye. "I mean, she is with Death, the angel. I do not know what he is, exactly, but she's not dead. The bastard is creating a sound barrier so we cannot hear them because she wants to be alone with him. Apparently, they know each other. She didn't want me with her anymore."

Arthur leaned back in his chair while Gawain stared at David like he'd lost his mind.

"David, are you sure?" Gawain asked. "Is there really someone in the room with her?"

"Yes, I'm sure," he said, harsher than he should've, but he didn't care anymore. He was furious and hurt. "I sat there while some entity inside Jane took over and fed from me," he said even angrier. "I sat there while she took off her shirt and healed her wounds right before my fucking eyes! I fucking sat there while she ordered me to fuck her and then threatened that if I didn't, I'd never see *my* Jane again.

"Then, out of nowhere, this bastard appears and tells Jane to come to him. I had to sit there and watch him shove his tongue down her throat while she held me down with an invisible force." He was yelling and breathing heavily now. It took several, controlled, even breaths to calm himself down. He kept trying to picture Jane's face, how he'd seen her in his dreams. It morphed now with her more sinister version, but he was able to focus on the smile he had caught glimpses of and calmed his anger.

David let out a breath. "He did something to her when he kissed her. It drained all the power away from it. He brought *Jane* back. He was saving the real her, and she knows him."

Gareth had woken up during David's rant, and they all watched him in silence.

After a few minutes of just staring, Arthur finally spoke. "David, I'm sorry."

"Save it." David balled his fist, wanting to fight someone.

"Brother, I know that's not the right thing to say, but I am." Arthur looked up at the ceiling. "Is she safe with him?"

David nodded. His gut told him that Death wasn't there to harm her.

"You said Death." Arthur looked back at him. "Do you mean the angel Azrael?"

David shrugged. "I didn't ask him his name. She just called him Death. His power is immeasurable. He would not tell me how they knew one another, only that they met a long time ago." He glared at Arthur. "Did you not see him in her past? Did she ever think of him?"

Arthur shook his head vehemently. "I would have told you if there was someone like him in her mind. She is very open with her thoughts, so I don't know how she could have hidden something like that. Though, there were many times I hit areas of her mind that I could not enter."

David sighed. "Do you think she was keeping him from us? It's not like I would think she was insane for saying she knew an angel. Surely she would realize we accept their existence. Why lie?"

"Jane's not the type to lie," said Gawain.

They glared at one another for a moment before David looked away and nodded. He knew Gawain felt a brotherly attachment to Jane. No matter what sort of evil she performed, Gawain would defend her.

David didn't see his Jane as evil either; he loved her with or without the darkness. "I know that she does not like to lie," he said, looking back to Arthur after Gawain relaxed. "You are certain you never saw him? She looked at him with so much trust and the tender way he talked to her—" David groaned. "They act like they're a couple. He called her Sweet Jane, and she practically melted in his arms. Why the fuck does this shit keep happening?"

"Calm down," Arthur warned. "We understand this is very hard for you, but let's talk about this. If she called him Death, I think we are dealing with *The Death*. We all know she has nearly died several times throughout her life. For some reason, he must have spared her. He must have returned when she was injured. Are you sure he won't hurt her, brother?"

David closed his eyes and nodded. "No matter how much I would like to rip him apart for what he did with her, I am certain he will not harm her. He was completely devoted to her; they were devoted to each other."

Arthur turned to Gareth. "How are you feeling?"

Gareth gave Arthur a thumbs up. "She got me good, but I'll be fine." He then smiled at David. "Chin up, brother. She definitely wanted your blood over mine."

David smiled a little, but his heart was aching. If she wanted him, she would have at least let him hold her. Anything but brush him off.

Gawain rested his elbows on his knees. "Did he say anything else?"

"Yes," David said. "He said whatever that was, it is a part of her. It has always been there, apparently, and cannot be removed without killing her. He can only drain her energy, but I believe he needs to get close enough to touch her. I have a feeling he is uncertain of her power over him.

"The abilities she displayed are controlled completely by the entity. From what I understood, *it* is the source of her power, not Jane. He suggested keeping her happy and fed. He thought training her to harness her abilities might help if the entity comes forward again."

Gawain looked away from David and asked Arthur, "What do we do now?"

Arthur leaned back in his chair. "All we can do is wait. We'll figure out how to train her and keep her fed." Arthur paused and looked back at him. "David, why do you think she does not want you?"

David cut his gaze over to him. "I tried talking to her and comforting her, but she would only cry and cling onto him. She begged him not to leave her, and any attempt I made to speak to her, she would look away.

"I get that she is ashamed of what she did, and I tried to tell her I wasn't mad—that no one was mad, but she only wanted him. Maybe she's upset that I was willing to give that thing what it wanted. Maybe she's afraid of me. All I've done is fail her so far, maybe she sees that he's more capable of keeping her safe."

Arthur sighed. "I'm sure she still wants you, but there is obviously more to their history than we can imagine. I think she also knows you would do anything for her. I know what you were willing to do, and I understand where you were coming from. It was a difficult decision I wish you never had to face, but I do not see how you had any other option. She would have killed you and we might never have seen Jane again. She was too strong."

"I don't understand why I was paired with her if I cannot even protect her," David said. "How can she want me after this?"

"She was trapped by that thing," Arthur told him seriously. "I heard her during that tiny moment she begged you to help; she was terrified, but she knew you'd do anything you could.

"As far as their relationship, I can only speculate from what you've told me. Death is an extremely powerful being. Out of all the realms, none are said to be more powerful than him. You should not be ashamed because you could not match his strength. No one can beat Death. Even we immortals will fall to him when it is our time. So don't compare your strength or abilities to his. And I do not think she knowingly hid their relationship from us. You are her soul mate, David. Nothing can change that."

Arthur's comforting tone did little for David.

He let out a bitter laugh. "Wait until you see them. They are completely in love with each other. She nearly glowed in his presence."

Arthur shook his head, ignoring his bitterness. "Give her time—she'll come back to you. She's going through more than any of us have ever had to consider. She deserves a chance to come to terms with her new life. Whatever it is that she has with Death is not up to any of us to judge.

"Put yourself in her shoes for one minute. Everyone she has ever loved has either hurt or left her in some way. If they truly know each other from long ago, imagine how this must feel for her to be reunited with him. Would you blame her for wanting to hold on to him when she suddenly has him back? She lost everything, David. It must feel like a piece of her has returned."

David sighed and ran his hand through his hair. "She has me. I've waited for her, too."

"You are not the one who lost everything you ever loved," Arthur told him. "She has reunited with someone she likely needed for a very long time—perhaps it is the same for him. Do not let bitterness overcome you."

✦✦✦

Tristan let out a slow breath and gazed down at the brunette woman curled up on the dirty ground. The bloody tinge in her eyes was an all too common sight now.

"Please find them," she whispered.

Tristan knelt beside the woman. "Find who?" he asked, wiping his blood-soaked hand on his pants before taking the woman's trembling hand in his. Her dirty, brown hair and soiled, ripped clothing proved she had been through hell.

"My daughter and son," she said, crying.

"*Shh* . . ." Tristan caressed her hand. "Tell me your name."

Bors had a sad look on his face when Geraint pulled open the shed door so Percivale, Lamorak, Gaheris, and Galahad could enter.

When they took in the battered woman, they all stopped in their tracks. Her arms had bite marks and ripped flesh across them. Her pants were covered in dirt and shredded from the nails of the undead trying to rip into her.

Tristan looked down at the woman and pulled off his mask. She let out a small gasp, but he hushed her again and stroked her hair in a comforting manner.

"My name's Kristi. Please." She whimpered. "My babies. Her name is Chloe. My little girl—her name is Chloe."

"Okay," Tristan said.

She shook her head. "And Brian, my baby boy. They might have gone to find my brother."

Tristan nodded as Bors held up a torn bag of canned goods, no doubt the precious food she'd sacrificed her life for to feed her children.

"We will find them," Tristan promised. "Do not worry now. It is almost over."

"Are you angels?" She broke into a coughing fit after her question.

Tristan helped her roll on her side to spit out bloody mucus.

Lamorak pulled out a bottle of water and squatted next to him. "Drink this, sweetheart." He held the bottle to her chapped but bloody lips. Her mouth opened, but she could only take a small amount.

"Your angels will come for you soon," Tristan said, wiping a droplet of infected blood from her lips. "And I believe our comrade, Gareth, came across your daughter. He took her to her uncle. I think they said his name was Mark." The way relief filled her gaze suggested they possibly had the right family. "We supplied them with rations a few days ago. A little boy was with them. They are safe."

She sobbed, nodding her thanks while her tears continued to slide down her cheeks and settle in her hair. Eventually, her breaths became more frantic. Tristan held her hand the entire time, staring down into her frightened brown eyes until she started to convulse from her fever.

Lamorak and Bors helped him hold her steady so she wouldn't bash herself up too badly, then finally, she stopped. Everything stopped.

Lamorak and the others sighed before some of them started to exit the decrepit shack she'd taken shelter inside.

Bors pulled out his knife, but Tristan reached up for it. "Are you sure?" Bors asked.

Tristan nodded, receiving a pat on his shoulder from Lamorak.

"Sweet dreams, Kristi." Tristan stabbed her through the temple so that her body would not reanimate. Pulling the knife free, he handed it back to Bors.

"We received word that Gareth is awake," Lamorak told him as Geraint started to cover Kristi's body. "He is doing well."

"Good," Tristan said as he stood. He took the small bag containing canned beans and spam. "I think we should take this to her children."

"Is Jane okay?" asked Bors.

Lamorak looked over at him and shrugged. "She's alive. David is a mess."

They all started to make their way out of the vomit filled room and out into the open yard, littered with more than fifty infected, lifeless humans.

"Don't burn them with her," Tristan ordered, looking at Gaheris.

"We were not planning on it," Gaheris said. "We will burn her alone."

Tristan nodded, handing the bag back to Bors and addressed Lamorak again. "Do you know what happened?"

Percivale was the one to answer. "We heard David yelling with Arthur about Jane having an entity inside her."

Gaheris snorted. "Well, that was obvious. She practically ripped my brother's fucking throat out while creating a force field. None of our kind can do that sort of thing. I knew something wasn't right with her."

Tristan shook his head. "Let's not judge her. We know very little about her, only that she is David's mate. I think we all expected her to be different. Let's not jump to conclusions and turn our backs on her before she's even had the chance to explain."

"An angel came to her," Percivale added.

"Which one?" asked Tristan.

"All I heard was that Jane had called him Death, and she apparently already knew him."

"What?" They all asked.

Lamorak nodded. "The Angel of Death is at our camp. We don't believe he is any harm to Jane or the others right now. From what we heard, he was gentle with her. I don't think we need to rush over and aid them. Although, he is with David's Jane—I imagine that makes him a threat as far as David is concerned. We will just wait until they call for help."

"Shit." Tristan looked around the shed that they had exited and over to the pile of zombies they had slaughtered. He took a step, squishing a severed hand under his boot. "We need to do another round before we go back. I also want to drop these items off for that woman's children. I am almost certain she was speaking of the same home that Gareth took supplies to the other night."

"What are we going to do about David and Jane?" Lamorak asked.

"I think we should give David time to cool off," said Tristan. "I'm sure this is hard for him. He's not used to being helpless. The fact he probably was not able to help Jane himself is going to piss him off. We will help him with the angel if he needs us."

They all nodded and looked ahead to where he now focused. He held his hand out toward the pile of rotting corpses and soon produced a bright orange and red flame.

His eyes burned with just as much spark when he turned his hand to the broken shed door. In seconds, the entire building became engulfed in a raging inferno. The smell didn't seem to bother them, but the immense heat did cause the other knights to step back.

For a moment, they watched the fire grow and crack before Tristan turned his back on the collapsing framework of the shed. The others followed his lead, leaving another victim of the plague to pass onto the next world.

CHAPTER 25

HELLO, SORROW

Leather and the most intoxicating cologne Jane had ever smelled greeted her as she stirred awake. She knew Death was with her and kept her eyes closed, not ready for this moment to end.

All her happy memories of them together were there. She merely had to reach out to touch them, and they'd open to reveal the life she truly had.

She remembered how it had been without those memories; it'd been impossible to forget how alone she'd felt. Now, though, every smile, laugh, and sweet moment with him was there within her grasp. Every single second with him made the sorrow she'd always had more tolerable. All because he'd been by her side through it all.

Death's fingers slid up and down her arm, leaving a delightful trail of tingles in their wake. The feeling was both hot and cold. It would ripple beneath her skin before radiating through her entire body, drowning her in ecstasy. It was beautiful when she and Death touched. No one else could make her feel this. Only him.

Another *him* suddenly popped in her mind, though. David. His touch was beautiful, too. She knew it was a bad idea to think of the vampire again, but she couldn't help it. The image of his sad face was impossible to banish. She'd hurt him, and she knew he'd continue to suffer because of her. She didn't want that to happen. David deserved perfection, and she was nowhere close to perfect. She had to let him go.

But I don't want to.

Even with Death holding her, she wanted to crawl onto David's lap and hug him. She wanted to hear his voice, stare into his blue eyes, and most of all, see him smile at her.

Her lip trembled; she did not deserve his smile. She brought too much destruction, and she did not want to ruin David. That's what would happen to him. Either she'd lose herself to darkness and harm him, or she'd break him because of her relationship with Death. Both would devastate him.

She might not be able to control the evil part of herself, and she was aware she could choose David over Death, but she wasn't willing to part with her angel. Death was peace and beauty. They were in a constant dance, always pushing and pulling, but keeping each other balanced. She needed Death.

David didn't balance her. He sent her mind, body, and soul into a frenzied inferno of emotions. There were so many sensations and desires; she couldn't process them. So much warmth, and not like Death's warmth either. No, David burned in the most pleasant way. She never liked the heat, but somehow David had her craving to be engulfed by his fire. Simply having him in the same room had her body flushing and humming, eager to have him closer.

Jane sighed and thought about how David's strong body complimented her smaller, soft one so perfectly. Death was slightly taller than David, but she fit David better. That made sense if he was supposed to be her soul mate, she supposed. She still didn't know how to feel about that. How could someone like David, so perfect and good, be destined for a mess like her?

Why would she have this incredible love for Death if she was meant to complete David? Then she was married, so she shouldn't even be asking herself these questions.

Her marriage wasn't the happiest, but Jason was still her husband. She still loved him and had promised to spend the rest of her life with him. Well, technically, *Death* had parted them. Jane pursed her lips. Even with that technicality, the fact was she was very much alive. Her marriage should come first.

Yet, here she was, lying next to a man she loved while she thought about another who was supposed to be her soul mate.

Jane nuzzled her cheek against Death's chest. She didn't want to think anymore. She wanted the chaos inside her mind and heart to settle. She wanted to stop hating herself for at least a little while.

"I know you're awake." Death's deep voice rumbled beneath her ear. "What are you smiling about?"

She had not realized that she was smiling, but she grinned wider with her eyes still shut and let his magic push back her inner turmoil. "I was just remembering you telling me something."

His thumb massaged her thigh. "I know you are lying; something is bothering you, but I am intrigued by your diversion. What did I say?"

She smiled. He knew her so well. "You finally said you loved me."

Before she could wonder about his response, he rolled them so she was on her back. He grinned down at her startled expression and held his body over hers.

She gasped as he carefully put some of his weight on her and watched him smile wider. *So beautiful,* she thought as he let go of her leg and cupped her cheek.

"I do, Jane," he murmured. "I always knew you were important to me. You are all I feel, all I need and want. I have always felt this way, but I only recently accepted that it was love. No, it is more than love I feel for you." His thumb slid over her lips. "I cherish you. I need you. You are all I see. If you are not in my sight, I am a void. I am only Death.

"I am not the same as I was before we met. Even apart, I know you are there; I sense you, and I do not want to stay in that abyss alone. I desire the light and warmth you grant me. I crave the connection we share, but I am destruction without you to balance me. I do not expect you to stay with me, Sweet Jane. But I will not lie—I want to keep you."

"Death." Her heart pounded.

He shook his head. "Let me finish. You don't have to choose me. It is selfish of me to come and expect you to give yourself to me. But I am selfish when it comes to you; I cannot stop myself from wanting all of you. You were mine, and I let you go so you could live a normal life. When you were a girl, and you spoke of love, I did not know I already loved you. I never thought I could give you what you needed, so I stepped away."

Her lips trembled, and warm tears slid into her hair.

"I see how torn you are over what to do." He smiled as she shook her head. "I know you, Sweet Jane. You cannot stop thinking about your knight, and you feel guilty about your husband.

"I cannot ask you to choose me or anyone, but I will follow you wherever you go. Even if I have to watch you from afar, I will be with you, and I will come when you need me most. I am yours no matter who you choose." His gaze swept over her face, pausing at her lips before looking back at her eyes.

Jane held her breath as he lowered his face to hers. His glorious body pressed harder against her, and she sighed when his breath warmed her mouth. She knew this kiss would be different. It would mean something different. She wanted it.

His perfect lips barely touched hers. It wasn't quite a kiss, but she closed her eyes, coming alive as electricity hummed between them. Something deep inside her sparked and reached out to him. She wanted to be closer than she'd ever been before. More than anything, she wanted to lose herself to him, but as he brushed his smiling lips across hers, another smile formed in her mind. David's smile.

She froze and whatever force she might have felt between them weakened. "Death." A light inside her flickered and dimmed.

He sighed against her lips. "I know." Instead of moving back, he kissed her cheek. His soft lips moved back and forth, but he finally withdrew and laid his head on her chest.

She cried and pulled her hands free so she could run her fingers through his hair. She hugged him and wept. She wanted to be with him, wanted to make him happy, but her mind, heart, and soul were at war. "I love you."

He lifted his head. They made eye contact, and she watched the emerald color of his eyes swirl violently. He pulled his gaze from hers to watch her tears. "I know you do and that is enough." His fingers followed the path of her tears. "I will always be here, Jane. Whatever you need me to be—I will be." A small whimper escaped her. He shook his head at her and lifted himself. "Don't cry. You have cried enough. Let's go downstairs, get you fed, then I will train with you." Death grinned when she nodded and quickly stole a kiss before he pushed himself up.

She laughed at the mischievous look he gave her and took the hand he offered. He pulled her up and wrapped her in his arms. She sighed as he rested his forehead against hers. "I'm not going to stop myself from giving you a kiss every now and then. I think I have earned them. Do you agree?"

Jane smiled brightly at him. "I think you have." It really didn't feel wrong to give him her kiss. Despite her worry over betraying Jason and David, she could not hide her love for Death. She knew he needed her affection and it was his way of cheering her up. "Are you going to train me?"

"Of course." He smiled. "I can't let my girl go out and fight monsters unprepared. I can't wait to see you in action; you're going to look so hot. You've never seen my weapons, either. Those boys down there don't stand a chance against me."

"Behave." She laughed at his glare. Death didn't like being told to do something, especially to behave. "No one likes a show-off."

He smirked. "Oh, you like it, babe." He squeezed her and pressed a kiss to her cheek. Jane smiled, shaking her head at him. A thought seemed to occur to him, and he pulled back with a serious look. "Jane, I want you to be prepared when you see me with the others. They do not see me the same way you do, and their reactions might confuse or anger you. They will not understand your ability to be near me."

"Why?" She didn't want to blurt it out, but he was the most beautiful man she'd ever seen. "Because you're Death? They know about angels."

The corner of his mouth twitched. "They have never met an angel like me. They will dread my presence here with you."

"Well, I don't." She would always see him as perfection and didn't care what anyone else thought.

He chuckled and kissed her forehead. "Because you are special. Now change. Pick something sexy."

She poked her tongue out and walked over to the dresser. "Are you going to leave so I can dress?"

He sat down on a chair and stretched his legs out. "Why would I do that?"

Jane picked out a tank top and shorts and watched him grin. "Because I have to take my shirt off."

His eyes sparked. "And? I've already seen your tits."

She blushed. "I wasn't myself!"

"I wasn't talking about today."

She gaped at him, trying to figure out when she might have been undressed.

"Think about your tingles." He winked.

Her eyes went wide. "Death, you come in the shower with me?"

He laughed loudly. "Don't flatter yourself, babe. You're smoking hot, and I might be turned on, but you'll know if I come for you."

Jane covered her hot face. "Stop!"

"Why?" He chuckled. "We're grown-ups."

"I know we are." She pulled her hands down and stared at his grinning face. "I didn't mean *come*."

"Are you sure?" He smirked. "I know you can make me come for you."

She shook her head, smiling so hard it hurt her cheeks. "Why were you in the shower with me?"

The playful gleam in his eyes faded. "Besides the wonderful view, I was there because you let all your sadness destroy you in there."

He stood up and walked to her. "So much sorrow and pain—I could not stand to let you bear it alone. Not in there. Never in there." He moved behind her and brought his arms around her stomach, hugging her from behind. Tingles spread on the back of her neck when he leaned down and pressed his lips there. "It's all I could give you, Jane."

He slid his hand under her shirt and caressed her stomach. She sighed and leaned her head back as the beautiful warmth spread through her belly and up to her heart. "I promise I only held you. Don't be angry with me."

She reached under her shirt with one hand to cover his. He spread his fingers so she could slide hers between his. She'd felt this exact embrace many times while she'd broken down in the shower, but he was right, it did not compare to the real thing. "Thank you, Death."

He pressed his lips against her neck again, then stepped back. "Always, Sweet Jane."

✦✦✦

With Death by her side, his arm draped over her shoulders, Jane stared at the knights who'd been waiting downstairs. Her gaze settled on Arthur first. He was standing next to Gawain, Bedivere, and Kay. She could only meet his stern gaze for a few seconds before dropping it to the floor. He did not look happy. With Arthur, she constantly felt as though he expected her to behave properly. It reminded her of wanting to please her father, and she had been a very disappointing child.

Death rubbed her shoulder with his thumb as she leaned against him for support. She would need to soak up his touch to get her through this.

The silence made her anxious. She chanced looking up and was met with a wide range of expressions. No one looked angry with her, but they sure as hell looked unhappy with Death.

Jane noticed Arthur's serious expression hadn't changed, so she guessed he wasn't thrilled with Death's presence. Bedivere and Kay seemed more astounded than anything while Gawain openly glared at her protector. She had hoped if anyone accepted Death, it would be Gawain. Then she remembered she had attacked his brother. He probably had the same amount of hatred for her.

Thinking of Gareth, she found him next. He sat with Tristan and his team. They gaped, unblinking, as they shifted their gazes between her and Death.

She glanced at Death, immediately catching a glimpse of his mischievous smirk as he stared at the knights. She didn't understand their shock; they had spoken of archangels before. Death had said he was different, but she couldn't imagine how. He looked the same as he'd looked the first time she'd seen him.

She kept staring at him and squinted to see if maybe she was truly missing something. There had to be something. She noticed a teasing glint in his eyes while he returned their stares. The way his eyes gleamed with sparks of bright emerald reminded her of his more playful side. She loved that gleam and didn't find it menacing.

He must have felt her stare and looked down to grin at her. She smiled up at him as he lowered his mouth to her ear. Someone let out a choked gasp, but she ignored it. "I told you that I am not the same with others," he whispered, letting his breath tickle her neck. "I also do not look the same as I do with you." His amusement with the situation was clear, but she still didn't understand what he was getting at. The room was too quiet. His smile widened when her baffled look did not fade.

In a lower voice that the others would not be able to make out, he said, "They see the Grim Reaper."

Her mouth fell open, and she quickly looked at the others. Their eyes were even wider than before. After scanning each one, she slowly turned back to him. Nothing seemed different about him; all she saw was her Death. There was no cloak or scythe. He did not have a skeletal face or anything that would suggest him being the Grim Reaper people often imagined.

He chuckled. "Do you want to see?" She nodded and watched him instantly become cloaked in black.

She gaped at him. He did not look like the classic version of a hooded man wearing a baggy black robe with an old scythe, but there was no denying that Death was the Grim Reaper.

A smooth black material hugged his powerful body. It wasn't skin tight, just enough to let his opponent know what they were up against. Almost every glorious muscle that she'd dreamt of seeing could be made out under his outfit. Every button and zipper on his leather jacket was gone and a large hood had formed over his head. It seemed no matter which way he turned, his face was never completely visible.

At one point, a spark of green from his glowing eyes allowed a superior smirk to show on his lips, but that was all you could see of his face.

Death grinned and shook his head for her not to worry about his reveal now and gently squeezed her shoulder before he looked back at the others. "She needs blood." An authoritative tone mixed with his words. "It is important that she stay nourished and not be allowed to grow unstable from her thirst."

The others remained quiet, but Arthur turned his head to look at the corner of the room. "David?"

Jane's gaze immediately darted to David's. Their eyes locked, and she felt her heart throb so painfully she nearly fell to the floor.

Death held her tighter, and she shut her eyes. She couldn't bear to see the pain in his blue eyes. She'd put it there. Her heart felt like it was being ripped to pieces.

She held her breath for a few seconds before exhaling slowly. She wanted to cry, scream, beg him for forgiveness and have him hold her.

She heard David sigh. "What?"

"What do you want to do?" Arthur asked.

Death spoke again before David could reply. "David, your blood will satisfy her most–"

Jane quickly opened her eyes and looked up at him. *No!* She could not ask that of David. She couldn't touch him after everything she'd done. Tears blurred her vision as she stared at the Death she recognized again. She hoped he could see her anguish. *Please don't let me hurt him again.*

"Jane." Death was warning her, but she shook her head and used her eyes to beg him to see this was too much. He had already told her she would need David, but she wasn't ready.

After he studied her for a moment, his firm look softened, and he caressed her head before pulling her back to his side. "Perhaps one of the others could get her some from your storage?" He suddenly turned his face toward Arthur. "Let her be," he said in the deadliest tone she'd ever heard him speak.

Arthur nodded before giving her an apologetic glance.

"I can get her something," Tristan said, pulling her attention away from Arthur.

Death glanced over and nodded to him. "Then get it. I think you may be useful for her training, too. Do not leave while she drinks."

Tristan glanced toward Arthur and received a swift nod. However, Tristan also seemed to want David's permission as he turned to him before moving.

David glanced at Tristan briefly then looked away with a small nod.

"All right," Tristan said. "I would enjoy the chance to train with her."

Death didn't give any sort of appreciative acknowledgment and pulled Jane closer to his side while he followed Tristan into the kitchen. He pulled out a chair and sat her sideways on his lap while he slid his hand up and down her arm. "Calm yourself. Do not let yourself get upset. I am with you."

He held the side of her face, sending those wonderful sparks into her skin and pulled her head to his shoulder.

Tristan offered the glass to Death when she continued to stare at her lap. "It will not taste as good as David's for her. But it's the best we can do."

Death took the glass without thanking him and pulled back from Jane a little bit. He tilted his head and observed her quietly for a moment. "Jane, you need to drink this. You are already growing too upset."

Jane looked away from him and took the glass of blood. She brought it up to her lips and watched Death give her an encouraging smile. It was vile, and she gagged. She didn't want this. It did not taste of David's sweetness. She wanted to spit it out.

Death quickly steadied her hand to prevent her from stopping. "Keep going, you can do this. You have to get used to it." She protested by shaking her head, but he was firm with her. "Drink."

Finally, she reached the bottom of the glass and shoved it back to Tristan. He quickly took the glass as she gagged and shook her head back and forth.

Death chuckled and wiped his thumb across her lips. "Don't be a baby—it can't be that bad."

Before Jane could think of responding, a loud bang sounded from the front of the house. She yelped and grabbed onto Death as they looked around for the source of the noise. The others had all been standing close to the kitchen, watching her, but now their attention was aimed at the entrance of the house.

Arthur grabbed Gawain's shoulder when he started moving toward the door. "Let him go," he said. "He needs time."

That's when Jane realized David was no longer there. Her eyes watered as she stared at the empty hall.

"*Shh . . .*" Death placed a soft kiss on her head. "Let's go outside with Tristan. I have a surprise for you."

She didn't care anymore. She deserved to suffer in this pain for hurting David. However, once she looked up and saw Death's hopeful expression, she nodded. It would be too much to hurt him as well.

Death helped her stand before leading her through the kitchen and out the back door. Tristan along with Gareth, Bors, Geraint, and Gawain followed them.

As Jane reached the middle of the yard, Death pulled her to a stop and cupped her cheek. She felt the knights watching them, but they remained quiet. She knew it must look strange to see the Grim Reaper touching her, but she no longer saw that image.

Death glanced at the men before returning his gaze to her. A single tear rested at the corner of her eyes, and she used all her strength to hold it back. He gave her a tender smile and caught her tear with his finger. "That's enough, Jane. I have someone special I want you to meet. He has been curious about you for quite some time. Do you want to meet him?" His deep voice was tender and powerful at the same time, as though energy was building inside him.

Nodding to him, she watched him smile, and he quickly pulled her back to his chest before wrapping his arms around her from behind. "Don't worry. You will like him."

Jane leaned against him. Whoever was coming was powerful. She noticed the others had all grown tense as they waited. Their eyes had paled in color, and their fangs were exposed.

She glanced up at Death. He showed no reaction to their agitation. He stared ahead, his eyes lighting up with emerald fire as he spoke in a more commanding tone. "Come, Sorrow."

Jane's heart pounded as the wind picked up and green flames erupted from the ground about twenty feet ahead of her. The sound of fire cracked and flashed, illuminating a huge silhouette.

It wasn't a man.

Standing tall on four legs, it stepped out of the green flames, snorting loudly. Jane jumped at the sound and tensed as it began approaching them, kicking up dirt with its hooves while shaking out its long mane. A deep nicker sounded as it got closer and lowered its massive head to her. Jane stared at the beast in awe. It was a magnificent pale-gray, almost white, horse. It was beautiful. She did not know much about horses, but she knew this one was larger than most she'd seen. Death was a giant at six foot seven, and his head barely reached the top of the horse's shoulder.

Death rubbed his muzzle affectionately. "Good boy. Jane, say hello to Sorrow."

Sorrow lifted his head and looked at her with intelligent eyes. They were the same bewitching emerald color as Death's. When she continued to stand there dumbfounded, Death raised her hand.

She gasped in fright as the animal quickly nuzzled her hand.

"You're fine," Death murmured. "He's saying hello."

Jane found herself smiling brightly as Sorrow took another step toward her. He nuzzled her neck, and she let out a nervous giggle.

Death chuckled and hugged her. "He likes you."

She reached up to pet Sorrow's neck. Just like Death's thick hair, his coat was soft as feathers beneath her fingers.

The pain in her chest eased, and for now, she felt peace with her angel. Her mind still haunted her with the terrible things she'd done to everyone, but she would keep going. She'd try to be the warrior they all expected her to be. Even if her heart never had the happiness she somehow knew could only be achieved with the vampire who she'd finally pushed away, she would fight to keep him and the others safe.

She might be hurting David now, but it was for the best. It was the only way she knew to keep him safe. She couldn't let her monster attack him again.

Being immortal didn't make her world all rainbows and sunshine. Having a handsome vampire knight save her didn't allow her to live happily ever after with him. The fact a powerful angel had been holding her hand throughout her moments of grief and pain didn't take away the horror that haunted her, or erase the sadness she'd lived with.

No, things were not fixed with her impressive abilities. Life wasn't perfect. It was dark and painful. It was complicated. Every choice had some consequence that, in her case, led to loss and tragedy.

"Hello, Sorrow," she said, feeling the exact emotion but accepting it as a part of herself she would never lose.

CHAPTER 26
SHE'S MINE

A forced smile spread across David's lips as he listened to the giggles and childish chatter coming from the house across from him. It had only been twenty minutes since he'd stormed out of the base camp, but it felt like hours.

He could deal with a lot, but after all the new developments, and with Jane wanting and needing another man, it had been too much to process. He needed some time to clear his head. He had no intention of starting a fight with Jane right there on Death's lap, but he feared he would snap if he had to watch that bastard touch her so easily.

When he left, he had no plans on where to go—he just needed to get away before he did something that would hurt Jane. It surprised him that his feet had carried him to her home.

Now he sat atop the roof where he'd first guarded Jane's home. He wasn't doing anything, simply studying the outside structure along with the countless corpses his men had dispatched. Jane had been the cause of the more decayed bodies. He smiled softly. She truly amazed him. So much of her past shaped her into the woman he loved, but the different sides in her were at constant battle with each other. He wanted to be the one to help her—the one she cried to when things were tearing her apart. He wanted to be the one she smiled and laughed with—the one she looked at with complete and utter devotion. He wanted to be the only man she loved.

He sighed, irritated with himself for acting and thinking so weakly. This wasn't him. He didn't walk away from fights. He didn't give up when a difficult opponent presented themselves. He came out of his battles victorious, and when obstacles blocked his way, he charged, crushing them until he achieved his goal. That's why he didn't understand this hesitation to fight Death.

Every part of him was ready to attack the arrogant angel. Every thought playing out in his mind ended with having the angel's blood dripping from his hands. He could almost feel the warm spray of blood across his face as he imagined ripping the angel's throat out.

But then her face would appear. She'd have the same fear in her hazel eyes when she begged him to save her from her demon. He'd heard the sorrow in her cries as she broke down for what she'd done and lost. Then he'd see her look at Death, the angel who so effortlessly did the impossible for her.

David ruffled his hair and shut his eyes. He needed to think rationally. He tried to imagine something soothing and in an instant, her face came to mind. Despite his inner turmoil over her, his body relaxed at the image of her. He even started to smile until dark eyes glared back at him.

He nearly growled as he remembered the threats that thing had issued, but he stopped himself from making any noise when laughter sounded again.

David dropped his focus to the house below him as Jane's daughter whispered to her brother. From what David had heard already, he figured out she had been playing with her dolls and was attempting to get Nathan to join her.

Nathan had been fairly quiet, and David wondered if that was a result of his autism or if he was just a quiet child. Whatever the reason for his less talkative nature, Natalie never stopped encouraging him to speak with her. She would prompt Nathan on what to say, and he would quickly repeat her words. They were complete opposites but a perfect match.

David sighed as footsteps approached him. He really didn't want company right now, but he thought it might distract him.

"David," Dagonet greeted and sat beside him.

David nodded at him before returning his watch over the house.

Dagonet stayed quiet for a few minutes but eventually spoke again. "Is everything all right, my prince?"

David shrugged. "Jane is well again. As is Gareth. His injury has healed, but he needs to rest a bit longer."

"That's good to hear, but I take it not everything is well."

Perhaps it wouldn't hurt to talk to someone about it. Dagonet was a fairly close companion, one that David knew would not share their private talk.

So, he decided to discuss his thoughts. "Jane has some sort of entity inside her. I guess it has been a part of her all along, but something triggered it to come out. It took over, and Jane wasn't able to fight it." He stopped, sighing and letting his head drop. "I could not overpower it. I had no hope of beating it. I was going to give it what it wanted because I could do nothing else." He looked back at the house. "But *he* could."

"Who?"

"Death. The fucking Angel of Death."

"But you said she was well," said Dagonet. "How—"

David chuckled. "She is well—he didn't kill her. He saved her from it because I could do nothing to help her. That thing inside her had me pinned like a mouse under a cat's paw. I could only watch as he drained her energy with a kiss. I suppose, in a way, I owe him for helping her. But I will not admit that to him.

"Apparently, they go way back. He was very cold, but his feelings for her were obvious—he adored her. And when she looked at him, you could see she reciprocated his feelings. She would not even look at me."

Dagonet shook his head. "David, I know you—you are not going to simply sit here and give her up. I know you have waited for this woman most of your life. Yes, there have been, and still are, obstacles in the way of your happiness together, but that does not mean you forfeit at the first challenge. You are the bravest and most feared of our kind. This does not sound like you. He's an opponent. Face him.

"Show her who her Other is. None of us may be able to defeat him, but you can prove to her that, even faced with Death, you are not afraid. Show her what every immortal knows: David is not one to be fucked with."

David chuckled, surprised to hear Dagonet's outburst. "Thank you. I suppose I needed someone to tell me to get over my self-pity."

Dagonet gave him a warm smile. "I am always happy to assist you, my prince. Now go. Get your woman back and bring her to meet me soon. If her daughter is anything to go by, and Gawain claims that the little one is a miniature clone of your Jane, I know she must be a goddess."

"She is. Amazing and beautiful. She's perfect for me." He smiled to himself, she really was perfect for him.

"And I am sure you are perfect for her, my prince. Now away. I have a home to guard."

David pulled himself up and looked back over to Jane's house. He hadn't given too much thought about her children. Now he was even more hopeful to see them, and he knew that being separated from her family was breaking Jane.

Perhaps Arthur was right, she simply needed someone to stay with her from her past. It had not gone unnoticed by him how badly she was hurting over the loss of her family. She was very skilled at hiding her pain, but he saw more than she realized.

He understood now she had already felt that darkness inside her. That's why she hardly ever spoke of her family—she was protecting them from herself. *Maybe that's what she's doing to me, too.*

"Do they cry for her?" he asked Dagonet, not taking his eyes off the home.

"Yes, every day."

David looked over at Dagonet and smiled. "Thank you for keeping them safe for her. I know it must be difficult for you, but I appreciate all that you have done."

Dagonet shook his head. "It is an honor to watch over them, my prince. And receiving a hug from Nathan meant the world to me." David smiled. He knew that would have a significant impact on the old vampire. It made him feel proud of Nathan for gifting the cursed man. "Go." Dagonet shooed, waving toward the edge of the roof.

David grinned and dropped down. He was done feeling sorry for himself. Dealing with Jane's marriage had been one thing, but Death wasn't going to just waltz in and take her from him. She may need the angel, but she needed him, too. He was going to make that clear to Jane and Death. He wasn't going anywhere.

✦✦✦

Jane stopped combing her fingers through Sorrow's mane, but he kept nuzzling her hand to prevent her from pulling it back. She smiled and resumed petting the giant horse.

"I know you miss your pets." Death placed his hand on the small of her back. "He has wondered about you for years. I thought it was time for the two of you to meet."

"He's wondered about me?" she asked. "How?"

"He is very intelligent, and he can understand most of my thoughts, which you are often in."

She smiled sadly as she thought about his absence from her life, as well as her family and pets.

"They are all fine, Jane," he said, as if he knew exactly what she was thinking. "All of them—your pets and family. Jason is still taking care of the animals, and your knights never leave their posts around your home."

Jane beamed up at him. "Thank you."

He shook his head. "It's not my doing. Thank your knights."

Jane smiled, rubbing Sorrow's nose. "Not about that, but I will thank them. I meant only that you always know what to say or do to make me feel better. I remember from before, too. I don't need to explain myself to you. I don't feel judged for who I am with you either. I know you'll accept my darkest secrets. Even if others say they will accept me, I'll never believe them. But you—"

"You're welcome." He kissed the top of her head. "Let's get to work on your training. Think back to any time you were using your abilities."

Jane stopped petting Sorrow and turned to face Death. She thought over the past events but quickly became frustrated. Looking over at her knights, she was saddened because David wasn't among them. She didn't blame him for leaving, but it hurt.

"Jane," said Death, startling her. "Do not worry over David right now; he will understand. Right now there are other matters you need to concentrate on. You need to get a grasp on your abilities if you want to protect him, the other knights, and your family. So focus.

"You've displayed the ability to manipulate matter and energy. I only want you to work on the basics: pushing and pulling. Once you master those, you can try more advanced attacks and defenses."

"Okay," she said, "but I don't really know how to do anything. I wasn't really aware."

He smiled. "I know, but you were before she came out. Something you were doing or thinking triggered your power. So try to remember what you were thinking right before she put you in the dark."

Jane bit her lip as she thought back to how she had pulled David down on her after her nightmare. She had been afraid she'd lost him. The dream had been so real, and she didn't believe he was really there. Once she accepted he was, she wanted him closer. On her. She felt her cheeks flush and dropped her gaze to the ground.

"Jane." Death's smooth voice slid over her skin like silk.

She didn't look up. "*Hm?*"

"Have you thought of something?" She could tell he was smiling.

"Yeah."

He chuckled. "Are you going to tell me?"

She knew Death wouldn't let up, so she answered him. He probably saw the entire thing anyway. "I was thinking about David."

Death lifted her chin with his finger and gave her a charming smile. "It's okay. Now try to remember exactly what you were thinking when you were able to pull him or objects to you."

She nodded and looked around. "What should I try it on?"

Death looked over at the group nearby. "Tristan, Jane needs your assistance."

"Sure," said Tristan as he stepped forward.

"Oh," she said, jumping up excited. "Is it like how Tristan does his fire?"

Tristan chuckled while Death answered. "No, Jane. Tristan can generate and control fire. He speeds up an object's atoms or the air particles until they ignite."

Jane frowned but suddenly jumped up and down, smiling. "He's like the Avatar!"

Tristan looked at her like she was crazy while Death laughed.

"Whatever you wish to believe, Jane," he said, smiling as she bounced in place. "Though I feel the Avatar is more impressive than Tristan."

"What the hell is the Avatar?" Tristan asked.

Death laughed again and waved his hand for Tristan to drop it. "It's an anime she likes."

Loud laughter filled the yard. When she turned her head, Jane saw Gawain and Gareth's smiles, and she was so happy that they weren't glaring at her or Death anymore that she grinned wider.

"All right, Jane," Death said, losing his playful tone. "Tristan can explain how he uses his power later. I want to figure out what's triggering your abilities. You need to think about whatever you were thinking and feeling before, and then try to pull Tristan to you."

Jane looked Tristan over. He was handsome, but he was no David. The desire she felt with David was nowhere to be found. She wondered if it would work when she simply focused the thought of pulling Tristan. Nothing happened.

"Jane, you need to concentrate." Death moved closer. "What was it you were thinking about anyway?"

Her face burned. How could she tell him she was thinking about having David's body all over hers?

He chuckled softly and lowered his voice. "Were you having naughty thoughts, Jane?" His tone was amused, and she was surprised he would tease her over her thoughts of David.

She shook her head quickly, and Death grinned then trailed his fingertips down her arm.

"I think you were," he murmured. She shook her head again, and his voice dropped even lower. "Do you think it would be better if you tried it on me instead? Could you have those thoughts about me, Sweet Jane?"

She gulped, staring at his glowing eyes before scanning him head to toe. Thank God he wasn't in his Grim Reaper form because she didn't know what she'd do seeing all the muscles that were hidden by his jacket and jeans.

A confident smirk formed on his lips when she finished her visual search of him. He knew he was perfect, and he knew she could think those same thoughts about him.

Jane nodded.

"Good girl. Now, just remember what you were thinking, and how you felt." His smooth voice almost made her moan from the tingles it caused to settle between her legs.

I'm going to Hell.

She looked into his glowing eyes and tried to remember what she was supposed to be doing. His sudden smile caused her to stare at his mouth—those perfect lips that had pressed against hers just like his hard body had.

Jane sighed. She'd been wrapped around him once before. Her fingers had been tangled in his hair, her breasts pressed against his firm chest, and her legs squeezed tightly around his waist as she pulled—

There it was. She could feel it, the rope that held him to her. It wasn't as strong as it had been with David, but it was there.

Death grinned. "I feel you, Sweet Jane."

✦✦✦

David quietly made his way through the base house. He knew Jane wasn't inside; he'd already heard her and a few of the others in the yard, but he wasn't quite ready to disturb her yet.

He stopped at the entrance to the dining room when he noticed Arthur, Kay, and Bedivere staring out the window.

"You still cannot break through?" Kay asked Arthur.

David stepped back, wanting to listen without bringing attention to himself.

"Not a single thought," Arthur said. "I tried to read her earlier, and he gave me the most powerful mental kick I've ever received."

Kay nodded. "I thought he was going to kill you when he told you to leave her alone."

Arthur chuckled. "I did as well."

"I do not understand how she can stand there with him," said Kay.

Bedivere rubbed his chin as he observed the scene outside. "It is strange, but you can see by his gentleness that he cares for her."

David stepped out. "He loves her."

They all turned their heads to look at him as he took a spot alongside Arthur. He didn't meet their stares. Instead, his gaze was already glued to Jane. She looked sexy, but he didn't really like that she was wearing so little. Then he reminded himself he'd put those shorts and tank tops in her drawer. This is what he got for wanting to see her in them. He shook his head.

"She's so casual with him," said Kay. "How does she not look frightened?"

"What do you mean?" he asked.

"David, he's the bloody Grim Reaper," said Kay. "How many people can ignore that?"

David looked at Arthur for a sign of understanding.

Arthur chuckled. "He sees a regular man. Though I cannot gather a clear image from his mind, I know he sees what looks like a human male."

David looked back at Death as if his appearance would suddenly change. "He looks completely normal to me—a bit of an ass, but he looks human for the most part.

"His power and ethereal features are similar to Michael and Gabriel's, so I know he is of divine origins. Why he dresses like a punk, I have no idea though." Arthur grinned, shaking his head while David went on. "I did not picture Jane as one to go for the whole biker look. Is her husband a biker?"

Arthur laughed. "No, her husband is not a biker. But I have a theory on why he looks human to you and not us."

David glanced at them. "He was telling her the truth? He looks like the Grim Reaper to everyone else?"

"He is the Grim Reaper," said Kay. "She's got to be the bravest soul I've ever seen to be so comfortable with him."

Arthur smiled at David. "You and Jane met Death when you were dying. Fate had destined your lives to be taken by him, and he came for you. However, Michael intervened before you could die, and Jane, well, I am not sure why he never took her. All the same, she was supposed to die, and he came for her. None of us have come so close to dying before, so he has never revealed himself to us. I expect that would be the only time one would be granted sight of God's most powerful angel."

Jane's groan and Death's laugh drew their attention away before anyone could respond to Arthur's theory. Death appeared to have stumbled a bit toward Jane, but she seemed frustrated with herself.

"It's all right, Jane," Death told her. "You did well."

David scowled when she pouted her lips at Death. Those were supposed to be his pouts. "Well, I did not remember his arrogant ass. But, now that you mention it, I do recall someone standing off to the side as

Michael spoke to me. He said nothing, only watched. It feels as if my soul recognizes him now. Actually, I believe I felt him when she was unconscious after her attack, too. The bastard watched her hurt and did nothing."

Arthur shrugged. "Well, he still did not take her, so he did something."

David glared at him. "Whose side are you on?"

Arthur held up his hands in defense. "Only pointing that out for you." David sighed and looked back out the window as Arthur said, "Now most people believe when we die, a hooded figure, decayed as our bodies will one day become, comes to carry our souls to the afterlife. I have often wondered over this myself. There are several stories throughout the world, and they all have variations of the Angel of Death. Most are shrouded figures that hide his identity. Obviously, those that saw his face, would not be around to describe him to a living soul after looking upon him. You and Jane are an exception. I am sure most of the cursed immortals have witnessed his true appearance as well, but the rest of us will only see what our minds conjure.

"I imagine, if we did not know he was Death, we may see a glamour many angels wear when in the presence of mortals. They hardly ever reveal their true identities to us because they are too divine to look upon. I am sure that Gabriel and Michael altered how we originally saw them. I know Gabriel had more divine features the second time I saw him. As far as us seeing the Grim Reaper and not a glamour, it may be because we knew the Angel of Death was upstairs. Perhaps his glamour won't work on us now."

"Well," David said, running his hand through his hair. "I'm not impressed. I would much rather go without seeing that fucking smirk on his face."

They chuckled before Bedivere turned to him. "David, you know you can take as much time as you need—"

He shook his head. "I'm fine. I only needed someone to tell me to stop feeling sorry for myself."

"What are you going to do?" Arthur asked.

He grinned. "I'm going to fight for her. She's mine."

"Well, there's the door," Arthur said, laughing.

David smiled wider and went outside to show Death he wasn't going anywhere.

✦✦✦

Jane groaned at the sight of Death's smile. She wasn't happy with her progress, and her audience made her feel even more humiliated. When they had started, she had definitely felt a hold on Death, but it wasn't strong enough to pull him. There'd been a moment she had made him stumble, a big step, but she wasn't a patient person. The fact she had already performed more impressive feats without knowing what she had been doing discouraged her.

At the sound of the back door opening, she watched Death's expression harden. It didn't take her long to understand why: David was back.

Anticipation and worry overwhelmed her thoughts, but she couldn't stop herself from turning to look at him.

He was just as glorious as the last time she'd seen him. His black hair blew in the slight breeze as he passed Sorrow. She admired how strong and confident he appeared, and she was happy he didn't seem as down as he had been.

His sapphire eyes suddenly connected with hers.

Jane gasped and her heart beat harder. She couldn't look away from him and felt nothing but the urge to have him with her. He was staring at her as if she was all he could see and there was no hate or anger.

Then he smiled.

Before she realized what had happened, his body collided with hers. She yelped, falling, but he caught her with one hand behind her back as his other hand smacked the ground. She looked up at him as he loomed over her. She had gripped his wide shoulders to steady herself and his thigh was between her legs.

David chuckled. "Well, that was fun." She couldn't speak. He smiled and, still holding them off the ground in a one-handed pushup position, pulled her closer. "I think you know how to use that ability now."

"Huh?" was her brilliant response.

He smiled wider.

"David." Death's voice was like a bucket of ice water down her back. "Glad to see you made yourself useful. You looked ridiculous flying through the air, by the way."

David chuckled and stood, pulling her up with him. "Well, it looked like you couldn't progress any further with her." He smiled, and she found the smug smirk on his lips incredibly attractive.

Jane knew they were taunting each other and was about to speak, but David's hand held the nape of her neck now, burning her skin. *My thighs are sweating.*

"I figured she might need a different partner to find what she needed." David's fingers slid back and forth behind her neck as his other hand spread out against the small of her back, pulling her closer. "I must have been right."

Death let out a low growl, and Sorrow snorted, stomping his hooves in the dirt. Jane tried to turn in her angel's direction, but David's soothing touch distracted her and he pulled her closer.

She sighed; she fit against him like a puzzle piece.

"Perhaps," Death said. "But I think she could use a break. She might benefit from watching some swordplay, though. What do you say? Feel like going a round with Death?"

David smiled, then lowered his face to softly kiss her forehead. She sighed again, not aware of how she swayed toward him. *This is nice.* She wanted to stay just like this.

David straightened. "Well, I came out all right the last time."

"Finally recalled your own near-*me* experience, I see." Death chuckled at his own joke. "Let's see if you fare better in this fight—because next time you receive a fatal wound, I might not find you worthy of a second chance. Or her heart."

"Death," she said, coming out of her blissful state. She didn't want David hurting further.

David smiled down at her. "God doesn't make mistakes. But He expects patience." Her mouth fell open. "Don't worry about me. I can handle whatever obstacles are thrown at me."

She stared at him, not really sure what to say.

"Jane," Death said. "Go watch with Tristan. Let's see what your boy's got in him." She slowly pulled away from David, feeling the heat slowly fade. Her eyes met Death's, and he smiled. "It's all right, Sweet Jane, I want to see him in a real fight. Go take a break."

She was going to argue, but she knew Death was agitated, and she needed to get away from David anyway. He was making her feel too much, and she felt like an absolute idiot for making him fly into her. She probably would have laughed seeing it, but the fact she did it made her want to hide. *Could I have been any more obvious?* She gave David a shy smile before quickly walking away.

As she stood beside Tristan, Gareth came to her side. He grinned and slung his arm over her shoulder, squeezing her gently, just like he had done when they first met. "Hello, darling."

She nearly cried from happiness. He was smiling like nothing was wrong. Her joy had to be put on hold, though, so she gave him a quick smile and turned just in time to see David pull his impressive sword.

Death had a dangerous glint in his eyes but so did David.

"This is going to be awesome," Gareth whispered excitedly to Tristan.

Jane shifted her gaze between both men and wasn't at all relieved when Death winked at her.

She looked at David who wore a confident smile.

"Don't worry, sweetheart," he said. "We'll behave."

Death chuckled darkly, then a huge scythe appeared in his hand. Jane gasped, admiring it as Death expertly twirled it before pointing it at David's sword. "Look, babe. Mine's bigger than his."

Jane glanced at David's sword. "Only a little bit. I like his."

David laughed, and she blushed hearing the others chuckling beside her.

I'm such a dumb girl!

Death chuckled and held out his scythe. It ignited in bright green flames and transformed into a sword, very similar to the one David owned.

"Wow," she whispered.

"I know," Death said as David shot him an annoyed look. "She likes mine, too."

"Death," she said, wanting to cover her face. She knew it was bright red.

He smirked. "I'm playing fair." She shook her head, seeing the teasing gleam in his eyes. He smirked and nodded to David. "Ready to fight for her?"

David twirled his sword and nodded. "Always."

CHAPTER 27
TWO GIANTS

A strong hand carefully unclenched Jane's fist. Her fingernails had already cut into her palm, but the wounds sealed within seconds. As she glanced up, she smiled softly at Gawain. His presence relieved some of her guilt but did little to soothe her anxiety for what was about to happen.

David and Death were circling each other, sizing each other up as they gripped their massive swords. The playful smiles did not hide their dislike for one another.

"I don't mind if you use your scythe," David said, not showing an ounce of fear for the angel who had a few inches of height on him.

Death grinned. "Let's show Jane how to fight with her sword, then we'll have some real fun."

David smiled and twirled his sword, giving his opponent a slight nod. "Let's hurry, then."

Death's dark chuckle echoed through the yard. No one moved or blinked. They all held their breath, waiting for the first strike to be delivered.

Her two protectors appeared relaxed as they matched each other, step for step. Their similar heights, build, and black hair, almost made them mirror images of each other. It was their eyes and smiles that ruined the illusion. David's sexy smile under the faint blue glow from his sapphire eyes were met with a more mischievous, cocky smirk shrouded in emerald light.

Jane darted her eyes back and forth. This was a bad idea.

David squeezed the grip of his sword, causing the muscles in his arm to flex. It was a sexy as hell sight, but she was too worried to swoon over it. She sucked in a worried breath, expecting him to strike. But he didn't.

Her angel met her gaze and smirked before licking his lips. His green eyes slid down her body, and she swore she felt his hands following the same path his eyes took. Her skin tingled in the most pleasant way, and she moaned without meaning to.

Death smiled at her, his emerald eyes flashing brightly, before he returned his attention to David.

She bit her quivering lip when David's fierce gaze connected with hers for the briefest of moments. So many emotions were exchanged between them and guilt overwhelmed her at the hurt she saw in the dark-blue depths of his sapphire eyes.

Death let out an unfriendly chuckle that sent chills down her spine. David showed no fear and bared his fangs at her angel.

Death swung his sword right at David's neck without any warning.

David quickly dodged the attack and aimed his own strike at Death's side.

Blocking the attack, Death looked David in the eye and grinned. "Oh, this is going to be fun."

David pushed off with his blade and laughed. The menacing gleam had not left either of their gazes, but they looked more excited about the challenge the other offered now.

This time, David attacked first. He moved swiftly, unleashing a devastating series of strikes. Each swing of his sword displayed the immense power he held. His speed and strength combined well with his fluid movements. His blade was an extension of him. This was something David was made to do well. He was meant to be the best.

Wearing an amused smile, Death blocked each strike David delivered. Had he not been who he was, Jane didn't doubt they would have resulted in injury or death. She believed David was the greatest of mankind's warriors, but David was fighting Death—and Death was the ultimate badass. No one beat Death.

Her angel's movements were more graceful than David's. Every attack and block appeared calculated, almost foreseen. He radiated confidence and power. There was no question in his mind whether he would win or lose because he didn't lose. He waited.

What worried her was that even waiting could result in devastating consequences for David.

As the fight continued, the differences in style became more apparent. Death's longer sweeps of his sword were delivered with incredible force. It shocked and awed Jane that David could block them at all. Clearly his physical strength could hold up against Death's, and she felt a burst of pride for her maker.

David's speed and ferocity made him frightening. Instead of the daunting calm that Death showed, he delivered brutal and forceful strikes. He was nothing like the sweet man who made sure she was okay all the time.

They were both beautiful displays of power and skill. Every time one would attack, the other would dodge or block it with impossible speed. They seemed evenly matched. At least, they were pretending to be.

Death's suddenly sliced David across the chest. Jane tightened her grip on Gawain's hand as she stared at the small drop of blood clinging to Death's blade.

David's wound healed quickly, but he didn't look happy about receiving the injury. Pale blue eyes shone under the moon's silver glow, and he retaliated with an onslaught of fierce, fast strikes. She smiled. David had been holding back, and his relentless series of attacks finally caught the back of Death's arm.

Her angel let out a spine-chilling hiss, and to Jane's horror Death's sword lengthened into the enchanted, nightmarish scythe he had originally summoned.

Death's eyes illuminated and shifted into a dangerous electric-green color while he twirled the deadly weapon in his hand.

The mayhem unfolding in front of her as they took turns going on the offensive terrified Jane.

This couldn't be happening. She could feel Death's fury pulsing through her veins. The somewhat harmless sparring match designed for her instruction had just turned into a deadly battle between two giants. They were going to destroy each other right before her eyes.

Death swung the scythe with devastating accuracy. His earlier attacks were nothing compared to the masterful assault he unleashed now. David appeared momentarily stunned by the abrupt change in weapon and direction the fight suddenly took, but he showed no fear when he exchanged blows with the powerful being opposite him. Instead of faltering, he became more violent with his attacks.

They were beasts and yielding wasn't an option for either male.

A shadow began to form behind Death's back in the shape of two gigantic, feathered wings. The ghostly wings remained in wraith-like form and stretched out as he delivered blow after blow to David.

David wasn't backing down and held his own, but neither outperformed the other.

David connected a quick blow from his sword's hilt to Death's chest, and just as quickly, Death returned with a devastating punch to David's face, sending a spray of blood through the air.

Jane panicked at the sight of the full-blown hate that shone in their bloodthirsty glares. They were ready to kill each other.

They swung at the same time, neither would be able to block the other. *Oh, God.*

Jane screamed, throwing her hands out. "Stop!"

Their strikes didn't hit, and both men were roughly shoved back by an invisible force. They both looked at each other, shocked, before turning their murderous gazes on her.

She didn't realize what she had done—or that she was still doing anything. She could barely concentrate on calming her heartbeat, let alone the pain shooting through her outstretched arms.

Both men snarled in her direction but their glares dissolved quickly. Somehow she felt them try to move toward her, but they stayed exactly where they were.

The knights didn't appear to be restrained but stood paralyzed by the onslaught of events all the same. Arthur, Bedivere, and Kay exited the house together and paused at the patio's edge.

Understanding and regret seemed to dawn on both Death and David as they stared at her. They looked back at each other and nodded, but she couldn't stop the fear rushing through her.

"Sweetheart," David said. "We're sorry. We got out of control, but we are done now. I promise we will stop fighting."

She believed him, but she couldn't stop whatever she was doing.

Death's soothing voice pulled her from David's eyes. "He's telling the truth, Sweet Jane. You need to let us go. Let us help you."

She didn't think it possible for her to stop Death. Yet, he was stuck in place, unable to break the hold she had over them. It felt like she was holding a wave of destruction back, and they were in its path.

A deafening roar filled her mind. It wanted to destroy them—destroy her angel and her vampire.

Her vision blurred as she looked back at David. The desire to protect him held against the horrible order. She whimpered as she tried to figure out how to let go and how to stop the rage building inside. A hate like she'd never imagined seemed to be directed at both men while two sides fought for control inside her.

Her mind was the arena, and her body the prize.

Death's jaw was clenched and his eyes burned brightly, but through all his anger, she could see him. The same man who always came when her world was falling apart, whose touch soothed the pain and loss that would never leave her. His love was so easy to see now.

She needed him. He would quiet the beast snarling for their blood.

The force building threatened to explode. Her arms shook painfully as a ringing sound reverberated in her ears. The edges of her vision darkened while a wicked feeling seemed to laugh at her for thinking Death could save her.

A faint glimpse of a sinister smile touched her mind when her gaze darted to David. She'd seen that smile too many sleepless nights before, and now it was there, on her lips.

She saw herself with David's blood smeared across her mouth. He tasted so sweet. It would be lovely to bleed him dry.

Jane screamed, her cry turning into a roar as her entire body trembled. The force inside her wanted out. It wanted chaos. It wanted to see her men suffer. It wanted her to suffer.

She cried. The power was terrifying but so alluring. It would be so easy to embrace it—to just stop fighting for once.

Let go. It's easy . . . Just give up.

That cruel smile stretched wider.

"Jane." David's voice halted the tempting thought of surrender.

She darted her eyes between her angel and her vampire, hearing a snarl in her mind when she focused on David.

"I don't know how to stop it," she told them.

Death shook his head quickly, but he still stayed stuck in place. "It's all right, baby girl. Let us come to you. We will help you."

Warmth surrounded her chest at the sight of his emerald eyes swirling. When sapphire eyes came into view, heat filled in that warmth. Both of their eyes were so different, yet so similar when they looked into hers. Love. Peace. Home.

The growling quieted. The violent tremors wracking her body weakened, and she felt a sudden disconnect from the two men.

They were beside her before her arms could fall, and, surprisingly, Death stepped back, allowing David to lift her in his arms.

"It's all right, sweetheart." David kissed her cheek. "I have you."

Death stood in front of them and caressed her hair, smiling as he did so.

Jane nodded to David, but the pulsing energy inside her continued to look for a way to rest.

She released her grip on his shirt and reached out to where Death stood.

He quickly took her hand and lifted it to his lips. "I'm here."

So much heat and peace between them.

Without warning, the surge of energy collapsed on itself.

David pulled her close as her body sagged. "It's okay."

She didn't want to let go of Death, she tried to keep her arm out, but she was so tired. She couldn't hold on.

"I'm here," Death repeated, his hand tightening around hers.

David glanced at her and Death's joined hands before he sighed. "Do you want him to hold you now?"

Death looked just as shocked as she felt, and she couldn't answer. She couldn't choose between them.

David wore no look of surrender as he smiled at her torn expression. He leaned down to kiss her cheek and then her forehead. "It's all right. Let Death hold you for now. I will still be here. I will always be here."

With one more quick kiss on her head from David, she was handed over to Death. She quickly sank into his embrace and accepted Death's innocent kisses to the side of her head. A sad smile touched her lips as he sighed in relief. She had scared him. She could overpower him. She was stronger than Death.

A tear slid down her cheek as she realized this. He had been just as helpless as David. She could have hurt both of them.

Death kissed her tear as he whispered, "I'm sorry. I'll find a way to stop this."

She smiled and shook her head. It felt heavy, and her eyes were closing on their own as fatigue washed down on her. Still, she managed to catch sight of her angel and vampire as they smirked at each other.

"Boys," she whispered and held her hand out for David this time. When he took her hand instantly, she sighed in relief. "Behave."

Death chuckled and nuzzled her head. “But Sweet Jane likes the bad boys.”

Although she smiled, her heart and mind were a disaster. Whatever was in her, wanting to destroy them all, and it wasn’t going away.

“Don’t worry.” Death brought his lips to her ear. “You have us both, Sweet Jane.”

CHAPTER 28
THREE

David smiled as Jane sparred with Death. They'd been working with her for three hours and not for one minute had the sparkle in her eyes dimmed. She was glowing.

She squeezed the sword in her hand and swung, her opponent's eyes igniting with green fire as she did so. Her attack went right for Death's side, but he blocked it.

David grinned, watching them. He knew what she was going to do.

With their blades still touching, Jane swiftly let go of her sword with one hand and released a burst of energy. It hit Death right in the stomach. He stumbled and missed her second swing that left him sword-less.

David laughed as Death stared at his useless weapon on the ground. Jane visibly shivered. She'd been trying to hide her reactions to him, but David had caught every blush that stained her cheeks, every gasp, and every time her gaze lingered on him while he trained with her. He definitely hadn't been knocked out of the game.

This time, she kept her eyes forward, a grin on her lips as she took in Death's stupefied expression. It truly amazed David to watch Jane and Death together. They were playful and comfortable with each other. Death hadn't lost the menacing gleam in his eyes whenever he looked at David or anyone else, but his gaze never failed to soften when it returned to Jane. David doubted she even realized how hostile her angel looked to everyone else.

Death narrowed his gaze at her, but there was no true malice in his look. "That was luck."

She laughed loudly now and received a threatening glare from the Angel of Death, but David saw a twinkle in his eyes that gave Death's true feelings away. Death was proud of her.

It was hard to accept, but watching her so free of sadness and worry, David didn't care that his rival was a part of her happiness. It also helped that he had his own close contact with her during her training. There was honestly nothing sexier than watching her battle. He knew Death felt the same way, especially when she briefly sparred with Tristan and slammed his friend to the ground, ready to deliver a lethal strike with her sword.

Her fangs were bared, and her eyes bright with gold and green. She was destruction in a beautiful package. He remembered the slaughter she'd been ready to unleash, her gorgeous chest heaving as she bent over in those tiny shorts. He and Death both got a good view, and he smiled thinking of how they both cut their gazes over to the other. They'd both thought the same thing: *damn.*

It probably took a lot of effort for Death to stand there while he went to help his comrade. David had pulled her body close to his to help calm her bloodlust, but he knew Death wanted to be the one to calm her. But they each held back their quarrel because they'd seen her falling apart when they had been ready to destroy each other.

For now, she needed them both, and David was ready to try his best to make sure she had that. Her smile and laughter made it easier to put up with Death's taunts.

David didn't know the extent of their past together, but if Death had been there for Jane in any way, he deserved respect and gratitude. Yes, David would set aside his feelings and put hers above his. Because it was clear to him now; she was setting aside her heart for both of them. She was suffering inside because she did not want to hurt anyone else. His job was to stand by her and help her through it all. If an arrogant angel had to hold her other hand, then so be it.

He smiled again as she giggled with Death. How the Angel of Death could pout like a child with her, David had no idea, but he could only assume it was because she had a bigger heart than anyone he'd ever met. Clearly she had power to destroy both him and Death, but her heart was strong enough to fight the darkness inside her. Their job was to strengthen her abilities and keep her from tearing herself apart.

So that's what David would do.

Already, they'd managed to guide her on using her basic powers. She wasn't consistent yet, but when she got it right, the results were devastating.

By no means was she on their level, but that was nothing time and experience couldn't remedy. David had already honed her skill with the sword and some hand to hand combat. Pinning her below him had been the highlight of his day. That is, until she countered him with the aid of her powers and wound up on top of him. He was forever prepared to lose to her if that was the outcome.

He refocused on the pair as Death's sour look vanished. The angel's eyes lit to a neon-green color as he grinned at Jane. She noticed, and her laughter came to an abrupt halt.

David knew Death wouldn't hurt her, but the angel seemed to enjoy defeating her with his more playful side. That smile was her warning, and Jane knew she was going to pay for laughing at him.

Death took a step in her direction, and she took two steps back. Death smirked.

"Oh, fuck," Jane whispered, nearly making David laugh. She had let out several curse words with Death. The fact Death showed no surprise made it clear that Jane had been hiding her sailor mouth.

Death made the tiniest movement, but she had already darted away by the time he lunged for her.

She screamed and ran over to David's side. He chuckled as he wrapped his arm around her shoulders. She had already used each of them as protection when she felt she was in over her head.

Death's eyes briefly darted to David's contact with Jane. "You're no fun, David."

David knew that translated to: *I hate you. Touch her any more than you are now, and you're dead.*

David kissed the top of her head and smiled, which for him translated: *Go fuck yourself. I saw you touch her ass.*

The angel's eyes glinted, but David swore he saw a faint smile as Death turned away, and his sword ignited in emerald flames before completely disappearing.

David didn't have to look down at Jane to know she was smiling and happy. She was amazed by Death's abilities, but she looked at him with equal appreciation for his strength and skill. It was a boost to his ego to see her smile when he held his own against Death.

"David," Jane said, tilting her face up.

"Yes?"

She blushed. "Can you show me more grappling moves? I want to pin you again."

David smiled. He was still in the game.

✦✦✦

Lucifer balled his hands into fists at his sides. He'd been watching the trio for some time now, and with every passing minute, his mood toward the playful scene darkened. Death had played him.

Jane's laugh pulled Lucifer's attention away from the angel she adored. He studied her face as she smiled with the two men. He watched her laugh uncontrollably as Death snatched her from the vampire and held her upside down.

Lucifer sneered, hearing Death laugh so comfortably. He didn't even know the angel was capable of a happy laugh. How had he been deceived so easily?

"The others have arrived, Lucifer."

He snarled at the intrusion but turned his head to look at the onyx-eyed immortal and nodded. "Good. Death will need to be lured from her side. His control over her is greater than the knight's. Be mindful of your actions and conceal our goal from your uncle, Hermes. I do not doubt he's lurking in the shadows for his master."

Hermes nodded. "Consider it done."

Another voice joined them. "What would you have me do?"

Lucifer didn't turn to acknowledge the new arrival. Instead, his gaze zeroed in on Death's fingers caressing Jane's arm. "Target the knights after Death leaves her. I'm sure you will enjoy toying with your old brethren, Lancelot."

Lancelot grinned. "Yes, I have grown tired of leading them on a chase."

Lucifer kept his eyes on Jane. He had not thought it possible to see so much happiness on her face.

"You let the girl get to you, didn't you?" asked Hermes.

Lucifer turned and glared at the vampire. "You haven't the slightest clue what I am thinking."

Hermes lowered his head. "I only meant to inform you others are aware you sought out her previous tormentors. They are worried about your intentions with the girl."

Lucifer snarled. "My intentions with her are my own. Now leave. You have your orders. See that your brother carries them out."

Hermes gave a small bow and sped off into the dark.

"He will be angry if you let this girl ruin his plans," said Lancelot.

Before Lancelot could blink, Lucifer grabbed him by the throat and lifted him. Lancelot's eyes bulged in their sockets as he grabbed at Lucifer's terrible hold.

"When?" Lancelot sputtered before the grip tightened around his throat, cutting off more words. "How?"

"Do not concern yourself in my affairs, dog. I gave you a job to do. Do it." He then dropped Lancelot to the ground and vanished.

✦✦✦

Death found his gaze zeroing back on David's fingers as they trailed along Jane's arm. She was barely holding back her blissful sigh. It disappointed him that she wanted to practice with David again, but he sure as hell wasn't going to whine.

He knew he could have found some excuse for her to come to him, and he considered it when David pressed his body against hers, putting her in a submission hold. Only, a silent call touched his mind.

Death tilted his head, and Jane quickly darted her eyes to him. The worry in those hazel eyes was difficult to bear, especially knowing what the call meant.

"What is it?" she asked, looking around for a threat.

He grinned to soothe her anxiety before it got out of control. "An old friend needs to see me."

Jane pulled out of David's hold and stepped toward him.

Death lifted his hand and caressed her cheek. "Don't worry."

She searched his face, her smile fading for the first time in hours. "You promised you wouldn't leave me."

"I have to go see what he wants. There are still duties I am responsible for." He shifted his gaze to David. "Your knight will take care of you while I am gone." He looked back to her. "I'll see you soon, I promise." He knew it hurt her, but she nodded, and he looked back at David. "May I have a moment alone with her?"

David's jaw tightened briefly, but he relaxed as Jane turned. "Of course. I will be inside when you need me."

Jane frowned as David left without another word, but she looked back at Death as he slid his fingers into her hair and pulled her closer. The sudden contact of their bodies made him sigh. He wrapped his other arm around her, and she moaned, whether she realized it or not.

He grinned and leaned down to kiss her cheek. It was hard to bend so low, but he managed, smiling wider because she was on the tips of her toes. "I'm very proud of you. You are learning so quickly. Then again, you are my girl—I expect nothing less."

She smiled softly, and her fingers flexed against his chest.

"Now, I want you to stay with David and continue your training." He slid his fingers along the small bit of exposed skin where her top had inched up.

She closed her eyes and exhaled softly as the unique sensation that occurred whenever they touched spread through his arm. She called it tingles, but he didn't know what to make of it. It felt alive as it passed from him to her, searching for something inside her.

He brushed his lips across the rapid pulse on her neck. Had he not supported her by tightening his hold, she would have fallen to her knees. Death chuckled and kissed her neck. "Did you hear me, Jane?"

She didn't answer.

He grinned and leaned back to wait until she opened her eyes. "I told you I am proud of you and that I want you to stay with David while you continue your training."

Jane blinked a few times. "Thank you, Death. I promise to keep training."

He needed to kiss her and lowered his face to hers. At the last second, though, she turned her head and his lips met her cheek.

He smiled against her skin. "You feel as though you're betraying all of us, don't you?"

"Yes," she whispered.

Death straightened as he pulled her head to his chest. "I'm sorry, baby girl." He kissed the top of her head.

"It's all right. I'm fine."

He grinned and leaned back, lifting her off the ground. "I know you're fine. You wouldn't be my girl if you weren't."

Jane shrieked from surprise when he suddenly tossed her over his shoulder and smacked her ass.

She yelped. "Death!"

"That's just a taste of your punishment if I find out you've been slacking off without me."

"Put me down," she screamed.

"No can do, babe." He laughed, walking her to the house. "David."

The knight opened the back door with a blank expression. Death smirked, watching David's gaze slide from Jane's rear to him. Instead of showing any rage, David simply shook his head while a faint smile teased the edge of his lips.

"Take care of this little monster, will you?" Death spanked her butt again but left his hand there. He wanted to see how much of this David would really take.

"We will always take care of her," Gawain said, storming out of the house, glaring at the placement of his hand.

Death smirked and squeezed her ass, setting off a series of threatening growls. "Of course you will, big brother," he said, not bothered with the hostile change in the atmosphere.

Jane smacked his back, and he chuckled at her hit as he lifted her off his shoulder. He'd seen the fire in her pretty eyes when he placed her on her feet; she was going to yell at him, so he quickly kissed her cheek and watched the reprimand die on her lips.

"Be careful," he said softly, nuzzling the side of her face with his.

Her cheek warmed, and she smiled, obviously forgetting any cross words she'd been prepared to give for him handling her so crudely. She wrapped her arms around his neck as she stood on her toes again, catching him before he could stand all the way. "Come back to me," she whispered.

"Always, Sweet Jane." He pressed one last kiss to her cheek and peeled her arms off his neck, nodding to David before he stepped out of her hold.

David quickly pulled her into his arms.

Death had to admit to himself, they looked good together. She didn't know it, but he saw how deeply she cared for David, and he knew he was going to regret leaving her. But he needed to go. At least she was with David and not Jason or Lucifer.

Death stared at her without saying anything. He knew, besides David and Jane, the others still saw a hooded man looking down to the girl they had formed an attachment to. So, with his veil, and only David to witness his true feelings, he let her see what he felt for her: *I love you.*

She nodded, and he saw it clearly in her beautiful hazel eyes: *And I love you.*

Sorrow stepped up to his side, shaking out his mane and stomping his hooves in an agitated gesture.

She slid her teary gaze to his horse briefly before looking back at him.

Death shushed him and pet Sorrow along his neck. "He does not like it when you are sad." She would understand he also meant the same for him.

Jane held her hand out. Sorrow took a few steps to reach her and nuzzled her palm. "I'll be fine," she said, sighing and looking back at him. "Goodbye, Sorrow."

CHAPTER 29
AWKWARD

Jane leaned her back against David's firm chest as they watched Death ride down the street. David's body heat and strength seemed to absorb some of the anguish that wanted to destroy her because her angel was leaving. Again.

She was lost. Empty. The farther away Death got, the hollower she felt. As stupid as it sounded, she felt less alive without Death.

He finally turned down another street and out of her sight completely. She wanted to scream or run after him, but she knew she couldn't. She knew Death would eventually have to leave for one reason or another; he always did, but she had hoped he would be with her longer.

Her chest hurt in a way it had never hurt before. It felt like a hole had been left, the edges singed with ice instead of fire. She felt the cry rise in her throat; it ached and fought to get out, but she merely closed her eyes and swallowed. She felt wrong. She felt like a part of her had been stolen.

Opening her eyes, she stared ahead, seeing nothing but the blurry vacant street. Pressure. So much pressure enveloped her. Her throat tightened, and her chest felt like it was collapsing. Something she should never part with had been taken.

"*Shh . . .*" David kissed her head and pulled her close to his body. Heat spread across her back and wrapped around her like a blanket. "Oh, Jane," he murmured, kissing her hair. She felt herself shaking, but she could only continue to stare at the spot where she'd last seen Death. "You can't let yourself get upset."

"I hurt," she said, not knowing she spoke until the words were out.

"I know." He hugged her tighter. "I am not him, but I'm here. I won't leave. I'll hold you until he comes back."

She closed her eyes, feeling the hot tears slide down her face. The heat he emitted settled in her chest, filling in the gaping wound Death's absence left her with. "I'm sorry, David."

"No, Jane." He turned her around and smiled. "You don't have to be sorry." He used his thumb to wipe her tears. "I'm the one who should apologize. I should not have reacted so negatively to your reunion with him. You could have had a more pleasant time if it were not for me."

"You didn't do anything wrong."

"I was scared for you," he said quickly. "First the entity threatened to take you, then I had to watch the Angel of Death kiss you. When I saw how you reacted to him, I doubted my trust in you. I felt betrayed realizing you knew him, and I was jealous you picked him without a second thought.

I should have let you explain instead of behaving like a child. You were in no state to process what had happened, and after everything I had been willing to do because of that entity, I should have known you needed to be away from me."

Jane hadn't expected him to say any of that. She knew he felt betrayed and hurt, but she couldn't believe he was worried over what had almost happened. It hadn't been his fault. "That's not why I needed to be away from you."

He continued caressing her cheek. "You're not afraid or angry that I would have—"

She shook her head to stop him. "No. I was afraid of what she'd do to you." She lowered her gaze. "And that you saw how pathetic I really am."

He was quiet for a few seconds. "Jane, look at me." She bit her lip to stop it from quivering and looked up. "She had me beat. There was nothing I could do to restrain her or any hope that I could defeat her. She overpowered me without lifting a finger. *Me*, Jane. I do not mean to sound arrogant, but I have never been defeated by an opponent before.

"Yes, I have had draws or outside factors that worked so my enemy could flee, but from the moment I became immortal, I have not fallen in a fair fight. Yet, she, or whatever she is, smiled as she forced my surrender. You continuously battle her—and I do not know how long it has been there, but the point is, you have not surrendered."

Jane shook her head. "I couldn't hold her back. I attacked Gareth and you. I was trapped in the dark. If it weren't for Death—"

"Sweetheart, you simply stumbled in battle." He smiled. "He helped weaken her, but he did not beat her; she is still there. I see you fighting her even when you do not realize it. If you were pathetic, she would have crushed us when she held us. Did you realize she was there?" She shook her head. "She was. I saw her in your eyes. We watched a battle raging inside you." He smoothed her hair back and smiled. "And we witnessed the moment you won. You are far from pathetic, Jane."

She didn't know what to say as she stared into his blue eyes. Without thinking, she pushed herself up onto her tippy-toes and wrapped her arms around his neck. She sighed as his arms quickly took their place around her waist, and he surprised her more by lifting her when he straightened.

Jane automatically wrapped her legs around his waist. It felt natural. In fact, she wasn't thinking about anything she was doing, when one of David's hands slid under her butt, and the other moved up her back to pull her closer.

So hot and inviting, she wanted to surround herself with him. She nuzzled her face in the crook of his neck, smiling as she breathed in his scent. "Thank you, David."

His right hand rubbed up and down her back. "For what?"

"I don't know—just everything," she said with an awkward shrug.

"You're welcome, sweetheart." He kissed her bare shoulder, and she shuddered at the brush of his hot lips on her skin. "Are you going to be okay with him gone? I'm sure he will be back as quickly as he can."

She hugged him and smiled when his hold on her tightened in response. "I'll be fine. It doesn't hurt so much now."

David pulled back, but the smile he wore slipped after he studied her face carefully. *So warm. So deliciously hot.* She leaned into his hand that he lifted to her cheek. "You're pale," he said. "Do you feel the need to feed?"

"I feel tired and weak. I'm sorry."

"Don't apologize. I will get you a blood ration."

"Is there something wrong with me? I mean, I just drank one before we came outside. You don't look as tired as I do."

"I have a lot of stamina." His gaze swept down her body that was still wrapped around him. "Don't worry. I'll help you increase yours."

"How are you going to do that?" she asked.

He chuckled. "Just practice."

"Oh."

"So innocent." He shook his head, grinning while he spoke. "I think your power drains more energy than we realize. Tristan reacts similarly after having a long battle, but your power exceeds his. We might need to increase your blood feedings. For all we know, your power could continuously syphon your energy away."

"That makes sense, I guess. I hate being a burden, though."

"Never, Jane." The way he said it really made it seem like she wasn't, and she was always awed because David wanted her around. "Let's go get you something to drink. The sun will be rising soon, and you can rest before we go out tonight."

Jane nodded, looking up at the stars.

"I don't want to take you into another fight with Lance's wolves," he said quickly, "but Tristan seems confident this is a small camp that became separated from the main group. At least under Lance's control, there is order. But without him directing them, they run wild."

"What if it's a trap like last time?"

He sighed and hugged her. "If Lance is there, I will only engage him if you are safe. Otherwise, I will be by your side. We still have a duty to mankind. If we let these wolves run loose, we put too many at risk."

"I understand." She always forgot they were doing a job. "And you're the best. Everyone is probably upset that you're hanging around with me. I'll go and do my part."

"I don't care what the others think. I'm sure they don't think that—they care about you—but even if they do, you are my priority." He squeezed her butt cheek, and she knew he hadn't done it intentionally by the way his eyes widened.

She blushed and tried to hide her face as he walked to the back door. He noticed her red face and laughed.

"Stop," she said, laughing as she turned away and rested her cheek on his shoulder.

"I didn't mean to squeeze." He chuckled as he stopped walking and gave her a little shake. She didn't look at him. "I swear it was unintentional."

"That's not what's wrong. I know you didn't mean it."

"Then what is it?"

She huffed. "You're carrying me like a baby." That wasn't the whole truth. She did feel stupid for the way she looked, but that wasn't why she was upset with herself. It was simply that she went from Death to David without knowing it.

"I'll put you down." He began to lower her to the ground.

"No!" She slapped her hand over her mouth.

They stared at each other in shock for a moment before he smiled. Jane wanted that smile to stay on his handsome face, so she pulled her hand down and smiled back.

"I like you holding me," she admitted the obvious. "You make me feel better. I just think it's wrong how much I want to be close to you . . . and Death."

Had her inclusion of Death hurt him, he showed no sign of it. He moved his hand to the back of her neck and pulled her to place a kiss on her forehead. "It's not wrong. Let me get you a drink now."

"Wait, David." She swallowed nervously. "Can I feed from you?"

David nodded without showing if her request affected him, and continued into the house. She relaxed. Maybe it wasn't a big deal. Hopefully, this time would go smoother than her previous feedings.

On their way through the house, they passed Tristan, and she swore she saw the knight move his eyebrows up and down suggestively. When she turned to look at David, he seemed to be fighting a smile, but his mouth stayed shut and he took a seat.

Unfortunately for Jane, Tristan didn't continue to wherever he had been going. Instead, he leaned up against the wall and crossed his arms while David rearranged her on his lap.

Her face was burning; she must look ridiculous. Perhaps Tristan wanted to get her back for tossing him over her shoulder during her training.

Tristan chuckled. "What are you kids up to?"

"She needs to feed again." David shrugged. "I think her power uses too much of her energy."

Tristan nodded. "It may become better for her in time, but she is more powerful than any immortal I've ever fought. It must be exhausting. Perhaps even the pull she emits uses energy?"

"I did not think of that," David said, and Jane's eyes widened as he caressed her bare thigh.

She stared at his hand, wondering if he knew he was turning her body into a furnace from that simple touch.

David's hand slid higher, making her eyes nearly pop out. "Now that you know how to use some of your abilities, Jane, do you sense the pull you give off?"

"Thumb," she blurted out as David's thumb went between her legs.

Tristan laughed, and David's hand moved down to her knee.

She wanted to roll out of the room, never to be seen again. *Thumb?*

David cleared his throat, but she didn't dare look up at either male.

"That's good," said Tristan. She could see him from the corner of her eye as he moved to leave the sitting room they were in. "Your blood will have a more lasting effect in her than a donor's. Uh . . . I have some information about the wolves if you want to come discuss it with me after you're done, David."

"Give me a few minutes." David lifted his hand to take hold of her chin and turned her so she could meet his gaze. "I am sorry."

She blushed and shook her head. "It's fine. I need to get used to you touching me. It just startled me."

He shook his head. "I should be more mindful with my actions around you. I know you do not wish to pursue anything between us. I apologize."

It was easy to pick up on his disappointment, and she didn't know how to tell him they couldn't be together. "David, I wish things were simpler."

He dismissed her apology. "We do not have to discuss this now. It is probably best we wait until you are at least fed before we talk."

"You're right." She glanced at his neck but looked away when her heart pounded.

"I should have continued drawing my blood for you. I can make sure I draw it from now on."

"No, this is fine," she said, realizing he was also worried about her feeding from him. "I promise I'll try to control myself more."

His thumb rubbed her bottom lip; she didn't even realize he was still holding her chin. With a small sigh, her lips parted a tiny bit, and she struggled not to suck his thumb into her mouth. She couldn't help but love the slight burning sensation their skin to skin contact created.

"I will not let you do anything you'll regret, Jane." His voice was slightly husky but it was a genuine promise. "Maybe you will be more comfortable taking from my wrist."

Her fangs had already extended. She stared at the inside of his wrist and wiggled on his lap. David pulled her back to his chest. She tried to turn back to face him, but he hushed her. "Here." He offered up his wrist and squeezed her with the arm around her waist. "Go on. I will stop you."

She was desperately trying to remain aware of what she was doing, but every part of her wanted him.

However, she tried to keep her mind focused and gave him a nod. Her lips brushed against his hot skin. She wanted to kiss, lick . . . suck.

David let out a strained hiss, but Jane wasn't swayed by it. She bit into his flesh. Nothing matched the complete ecstasy that came from David.

"*Mmm*." She moaned, rocking her body. David tightened his hold and exhaled. The taste of his blood and skin was addicting.

She didn't know how much time had passed before David dug his fingers into her hips. "That's enough, Jane."

She wanted to protest, but she obeyed and licked at his puncture wounds without considering how heavily David was breathing. After she finished licking up every drop of his delicious blood, she slumped back against his chest.

"Good girl," he said before softly kissing the back of her head.

Jane smiled, proud for fighting her desire, but David's uneven breaths caught her attention, and pulled her from her high. "David?"

He didn't answer, and she began to turn, but he quickly stopped her from shifting on his lap by gripping her hips tightly. "Don't move." He hissed as he rested his forehead against her shoulder.

"David?" Maybe she'd taken too much blood from him.

"I'm not hurt, baby."

Jane stayed still and listened to his breathing slowly become steady. It remained heavy, though. She was about to get help when she suddenly realized what was wrong.

She gasped at the feel of his erection against her backside, and she shivered as a delightful quiver settled between her thighs. She wanted to beg for him to come closer—to be inside her. It was wrong, but it felt so right.

It took all her mental strength to close her eyes and think of something other than David pushing her down on all fours, lifting her ass, and entering her from behind.

She moaned and delighted in his grip tightening on her hips. All she had to do was move a little more, and he would start relieving that ache. "David." Her voice shook.

"Quiet." The sharp tone of his voice did nothing but turn her on more. He pressed his forehead against her shoulder and flexed his fingers as he exhaled.

A bead of sweat rolled down her back. It was wrong to have these sorts of thoughts, but now she was desperate to see and feel more. She squeezed her eyes tighter and concentrated on her breathing, constantly listing off reasons as to why this was wrong. A little whisper deep within told her she was only hurting herself with her choice not to be with him. It promised David was right. *Just give in*, it said.

God, she wanted to listen to it, but she fought against her desire for him.

It took a few minutes, but they both steadied their breathing and sat in silence.

"Well, that was awkward," she said quietly.

David chuckled. "I am sorry. I already failed at my promise. I should have thought this feeding through more. You feel too good." He loosened his hold but slid his palms along her hips.

"It's fine, thank you," she said, laughing softly and tried not to love his touch. She knew he was unaware of what he was doing. "I was, um, kinda all over your—you know."

"I know." He chuckled, letting go of her hips and hugged her. "I would blame these shorts and tank top, but considering I'm the one who put them in your drawer, it is my fault you're wearing them."

"You only put tight clothes in there! Anything loose is yours."

His deep laugh made her smile. "I like to admire you." God, she almost swooned as he kissed her shoulder. "I still apologize. I will try, but you make it hard when you move like that."

Jane covered her face then fanned herself. "I'm embarrassed to move. Is it gone?"

"I hope not."

"David!" She hid her face in her hands. "You're awful. I thought you were supposed to be all proper."

He hugged her. "*It* is still there, but I am not as aroused. I take that back; I am very aroused, but I am in control."

Jane chuckled and leaned against him more. "Should I go get ready now?"

"Yes. That is probably best." He let out a groan and hugged her as he mumbled against her shoulder. "You should have new gear upstairs. Go take a bath and nap. After you get up, we can eat a meal together." He kissed her shoulder once more and gently lifted her off his lap as he stood up. The boyish look he gave her when she turned made her melt.

She didn't know why she did it, but she looked down at his crotch. "Holy shit," she whispered. Once she realized what she'd said and done, she snapped her head up and stared at him with wide eyes. She had not forgotten while she was under the control of her entity that she basically rode *that*. No wonder she had her first orgasm. She was sort of disappointed *she* didn't actually experience it.

David smirked as he took in her flushed cheeks.

"Bye!" She squeaked before she ran out of the room.

✦✦✦

David laughed at her silliness and went to the kitchen. She took a lot of blood from him, yet he was sure most of his blood was still in his dick.

He tried to adjust himself as he walked to the kitchen. David completely forgot there were others in the house, and he halted when five pairs of eyes stared at him as he entered the breakfast nook. He glared at each of them, then snatched the glass of blood from Gawain's hand. He chugged it down while their loud laughter filled the room.

"Shut up," was all he managed to say.

They laughed louder.

✦✦✦

The reflection in the mirror smiled back at Jane. A genuine smile. She wasn't used to seeing any sort of happiness in her eyes, but that is how they appeared: bright and sparkling. She noticed the brighter bits of green were faded, and her eyes were a more golden than she was used to.

"Weird," she muttered as she watched the gold dance around the green color, sparking whenever it managed to touch it.

She decided it wasn't wise to inspect her newer appearance, and quickly put her hair into a ponytail before she attached David's dagger to her waist. She felt much more confident in her ability to defend herself. This time she promised herself she'd be an asset to her knights.

David had faith in her, and Death claimed that she would be nothing but the best. She figured Death would always praise her, but their praise gave her a newer bit of confidence in herself. So she took in her reflection once more before heading out the door to search for David.

As soon as she started down the hall, it dawned on her David had only been staying in the room with her. Besides the meal he'd brought her, she hadn't seen much of him. He'd been doing things outside and across the street. She wondered if he had gotten a chance to clean up like she had. Maybe he had been waiting for her to leave the room.

The only way to find out was to ask him. Jane closed her eyes and took in a deep breath, instantly picking up his delicious scent down the hall.

She knew if she were caught right now as she crept along the wall like a ninja assassin, she'd die of embarrassment, but she had to amuse herself somehow. Anything to distract her from what had happened between them downstairs.

She'd always done this to Death when she was younger, but he never even flinched at her attempts to scare him.

So she crept along the wall and grinned when she discovered that David hadn't shut the door all the way. *Perfect.*

Jane positioned herself in front of the door and held her breath. Besides a rustling noise, there was no indication he'd heard her. She was careful not to give herself away as she lifted her foot and then she kicked the door wide open, slamming it into the wall as she jumped into the room with a roar.

Her battle cry quickly turned into a pathetic croak.

David stood there with a completely stunned expression on his handsome face. Laughs sounded from somewhere downstairs, but it was as if she hadn't heard a thing. She was too absorbed in the perfectness of a shirtless David.

The rustling she heard must have been him dressing, and when she had kicked the door open, he was midway through zipping his pants.

God, help me, she thought as her eyes ravaged every inch of muscle on his sculpted body. There were no thoughts on the fact he was watching her check him out so shamelessly. Not even when he finished zipping and buttoning his pants did she notice he'd just stood there, smiling. She was too entranced, watching the muscles in his arms flex from every tiny movement. She couldn't look away.

He reached for the T-shirt on the chair next to him. Jane swallowed, watching his abs contract from the small action and nearly collapsed when her eyes drifted down to the tempting v-cut leading into his pants. "Oh, wow," she whispered a little too dreamily.

David chuckled, which finally brought her attention to his elated face. At that moment, when his eyes practically laughed at her, she prayed for the ground to rip open and swallow her whole.

A smirk formed on his lips. "Don't be embarrassed for simply looking at what is yours."

Jane couldn't believe how much he sounded like Death right then. The teasing gleam didn't leave his sapphire eyes after he pulled his shirt over his head either.

He smiled and stepped in front of her. "I did not mean to embarrass you. Although, I admit, I am happy you like what you saw."

She gasped and shot her hand out to smack his chest, which he caught and laughed as he pulled her into a hug.

"Jane, I'll stop now. Do you forgive me?" He even gave her a sad puppy-dog look.

Who taught him that look?

"Fine," she said with a glare to try to hide her embarrassment.

"Thank you." His smile stretched wider as he let go of her hand.

She crossed her arms to make sure she didn't touch him or do something even more ridiculous and started toward the door. "He didn't even flinch. Stupid vampires and angels... not scared of anything. Muscles..."

✦✦✦

David stayed quiet as she continued her rant, and followed behind her. She stomped angrily down the stairs and completely ignored Arthur when she passed him in the hall.

Arthur held up his hand to stop David, but Jane continued around the corner and out of their sight.

"You shouldn't tease her." Arthur shook his head but smiled.

David shrugged. "She's not mad." Arthur raised an eyebrow at him. "She tried to scare me first."

His brother-in-law's amusement slipped away. "Be careful on your shift, okay? I have a bad feeling about letting you go out with her again."

David frowned, knowing that they had to return to more serious matters and nodded. As he rounded the corner, though, his smile returned.

There, he found Jane clinging to Gareth's back as she pinched his cheeks. His friends, Gawain, Tristan, Bors, and Geraint, held their stomachs as tears streamed down their smiling faces.

"Apologize," she hollered in Gareth's ear.

The knight in question laughed and gasped for air while his hands gripped her thighs to prevent her from falling.

"I'm sorry, Jane," Gareth finally wheezed out, laughing when she pinched harder. "I'm sorry. I didn't mean to say you want to kiss David's abs. Because I was mistaken—you want to lick them!"

Jane gasped, a mortified look spreading over her face. She quickly let go of one cheek before pinching the fuck out his friend's neck.

Gareth screamed out. A high-pitch, girl scream that David had never heard before.

The entire room went silent, and they blinked at Gareth's flushed face before erupting into louder laughs, Jane being the loudest with Gawain as she let go of Gareth in her fit of giggles.

Gareth, too stunned with his own reaction to keep his grip, didn't even notice her falling. But it hardly mattered, David rushed forward and caught her just before her back could meet the floor, and he pulled her up.

Still too absorbed in her laughter, she didn't even register she had nearly fallen.

David smiled, but his laughter wasn't from Gareth's humiliation. Her happy face did it for him. He planted a kiss to the top of her head and hugged her tight. He'd worry about the awkward and shitty parts of their relationship some other time.

CHAPTER 30
WEREWOLF 101

Scowling, Gareth stomped his way past Jane. She and many of the other knights were currently gearing up in the garage of their base camp. Nearly ten minutes had passed since she'd made Gareth scream, and he was still in a foul mood. It didn't help that Gawain continued to pick at him every chance he got either.

Gawain laughed. "Jane doesn't even scream like that."

Despite her efforts to stay quiet, a giggle escaped from Jane's tightly pressed lips.

David looked up at her and smiled. He was on a knee in front of her, adjusting her holsters. She grinned down at him but quickly clamped her mouth shut when Gareth glared at her.

Gareth roughly sheathed his sword as he kept his gaze locked with hers. "It's not even that funny, Jane."

David sighed, looking annoyed now. "Gareth." It was a warning, and everyone looked up that time.

Gawain butted in. "Aw, let them go at it, David. Cat Fight!"

"You ass," Gareth shouted.

"Gawain, that's enough," David said like he was the only grownup present.

Jane frowned watching Gareth grow more upset. "I'm sorry, Gareth."

He looked at her and calmed. "I'm not mad at you, darling." He winked at her but smacked Gawain hard on the head when he passed him.

David shook his head at his friends as he finished adjusting her belts. He didn't walk away from her to gather his things. Instead, he moved closer, cupping her cheeks with both hands.

She sighed and nuzzled her face against his incredibly warm hands while his eyes followed her every move. No man had ever looked at her the way David did, and she didn't know if she'd ever get used to him.

"You look beautiful," he told her before releasing her and pointing at her side. "You have more ammunition this time; we are all carrying more. Aim for the head or heart. Anything else is only going to piss them off and draw more to you."

"Are these silver bullets?" she asked, peeking at one clip.

"No. Arthur said we can expect the drop of new ammunition tomorrow night. You don't want to become dependent on silver weapons anyway. It's useful in a fight, but you need to be confident without tricks. Think about your powers for a moment; they are incredible and devastating, but if you are unable to use them, you can only rely on your skill as a fighter."

"What do you consider my skill as a fighter?"

"You're unpredictable," he said without hesitation. "Because of our creation, my skill was enhanced by Michael's. You gained my skill as well as some of his. You lack finesse, but the skill is there. Although, watching you spar, I would say you have your own style that flares up as well. You almost seem to predict your opponent's attacks or know that you will achieve your desired goal."

"Really?" She smiled.

He nodded, his eyes fixed on her smile as he continued speaking in that more serious way of his. "It's impressive. Though your focus often shifts when you worry or think too hard. When that happens, you leave yourself open. When you get angry, your force and speed increase, but your technique becomes sloppy. But when you're balanced, you are a beautiful and devastating force to behold."

A warm sensation spread through her chest. "So, I should try to stay focused and balanced."

"Yes. And follow my command. When I tell you to do something, trust me and do as I say. So, when I say try to avoid close combat, you do so unless it is necessary. Your lethality increases with your sword, but I want you to stay as far from the wolves as possible."

Her burst of giddiness dampened, and she pursed her lips. "So you're not confident I can handle myself?"

He sighed. "Sweetheart, I am not saying you are not capable—you are. I simply cannot stand the thought of you hurt again."

"But I want to help. I know I can do better this time."

"You did terrific last time, and you will do better this time." He reached up, caressing her cheek. "Just promise me, if you do engage in close combat and are surrounded, you will use your blast to get them off you. I don't care if it means you hit one of us. Don't worry about anything but saving yourself."

"I don't want to hurt one of you." She frowned.

"We will be fine," he said. "Death seemed confident that unless you lost control like last time, or aimed a direct hit at someone's heart, they'd survive the blasts you practiced. Remember, the last time you lost control, you had a blast radius of twenty feet with total destruction. Everyone else simply got knocked on their asses."

"All right, I won't hesitate."

"That's my girl."

My girl? That's what Death always called her. Guilt for every man in her life crushed her. And Jason . . . He thought she was dead, and she had been in the arms of two men. The worst part was he was not the one she immediately thought of as who she was devoted to. It was Death. The reality of knowing he was there this whole time, that all her memories were back in place, it was like she'd wronged him. Obviously, not, but that's how her mind was tormenting her for the moment. Yet, David was the one there with her, thinking she was the one for him, willing to do anything for her.

She lowered her head and stared at the ground. What was she going to do?

Jane looked over at David as he spoke to Gawain. She hadn't told him about Death's bet. She would either turn evil, neutral, or stay as pure as possible, which would technically give David the victory in their eyes. Death hadn't told her anything about the bet after they initially talked about it, but she was sure he didn't want David to know. David would probably lose his mind if he did. This was a mess.

"All right," David said. "The wolves we're after are camping out at an elementary school ten miles north. Lamorak has taken his team after the last trail we've found on Lance. It went south with the other scents, but I don't want to let our guard down. This could very well be another trap he's made, but we will only find out by getting this over with." He glanced over at her. "Arthur, Kay, and Bed will be staying behind with Dagonet and Lucan to watch your family."

She gave him a weak nod, trying not to let her mind go to scenarios of her family being attacked or an ambush on any of their groups.

"Are the other scents more wolves?" Gareth asked.

"No, they're rogues," said Tristan.

Jane looked to David. "What are rogues?"

"Cursed and Damned," he said. "But they are not like Dagonet and Lucan who fight beside us; they kill and turn humans to build small armies. Try not to worry about them right now—focus on the fight. If they do cross our path, though, we destroy them on sight."

"Okay," she said. She had yet to see a cursed vampire and didn't know what to expect.

"Any questions?" David looked around, getting no from everyone, except when he looked down at her. "What is it, sweetheart?"

She looked around feeling almost silly. "Don't the werewolves only change during a full moon?"

David grinned and shook his head. "They change every night, but Lance can change at will. I don't want you to be too overwhelmed because there are actually several categories the wolves fall into. I will explain more in time, but I don't believe we will run into the others here.

"Lance's wolves are all you need to worry about for now. They are similar to the types you may have seen in old werewolf movies. They lose their minds every night and transform whether they want to or not. The unique trait is that Lance controls them. He's the original of their particular kind."

The dumbfounded look on her face made Gawain laugh. Jane ignored him and asked another question. "What about the zombie looking ones?"

David frowned and looked at the others briefly. "We haven't figured everything out, but we believe he may have had some hand in the start of the plague. We will not know until we have more proof, but the coincidences the others noticed suggests he was a part of it. Perhaps a weapon to defeat us, in his eyes. But we have no other ideas besides he has infected wolves, and he can still control them. The positive side is we know that we can destroy them. For now, that will have to be enough."

"What if I get bit?"

"We're immune to their bite and the plague," he said confidently. "The infected wolves left several wounds on not just you, but the others during the fight—no one suffered extra side effects."

"But humans get infected from werewolf bites, right?"

"Yes, but most humans don't survive an attack. Their victims are eaten or dismembered, so there are no witnesses," David said as if this was completely normal. "Most that are alive have to be created by a disciplined individual, of which there are only two. Lance is one of the two."

"Why don't we just wait till daylight when they're in human form?"

They all shook their heads as David answered. "If we wait any longer, we could lose them, and they will take more lives that can be saved. The werewolves' curse is different from ours because they descend from Lucifer, so there are some differences between us. They appear human in every way during the day, so even with our senses, we cannot tell for sure who is a werewolf or human captive. They often keep humans for various vile reasons, so even running in and attacking an entire camp would run the risk of murdering an innocent, and our oaths forbade us from doing so."

Tristan smiled at her. "Trust us, Jane. You don't want to be responsible for the death of an innocent. Plus, it makes a death by your hand easier on your soul to bear."

Gareth nodded. "Just kick ass like you did before, and you'll be fine. If they turn into a wolf, they cannot be reasoned with. It's not a matter of the person they were, it's what they become and the destruction they will cause. If they hold any good in them, they do not want to live as they are anyway."

"I guess that's true," she said.

"It is, Jane," said David. "They are Lance's slaves. Most of their minds slip over time even if they are good men. Once they truly give over to darkness or madness, their punishment comes. If they don't, Lance tortures and kills them, and they are granted peace."

"Okay." She was worried about what killing something that was still alive. Zombies were already dead. She'd had that thought process ingrained from watching zombie movies and didn't give another thought about needing to destroy them because the person was already gone. When she'd first faced the werewolves, they were already monsters trying to kill her and the knights; she didn't think of them as people. But now it hit her that they were still people during the day. "Well, we'd better go."

Everyone nodded, and she turned to smile at David as he and Tristan lingered behind.

Gawain nudged her to follow him. "Did you think they howled at the moon, too?"

She scowled as she kept up with their long strides. "I didn't know! I'm trying to learn, but you guys make it complicated. For all I know, Lance could walk up to me and say 'Mine' and claim me as his mate like they do in books."

Gawain, Gareth, Bors, and Geraint stared at her with blank expressions before all roaring with laughter.

"Jane has her own vampire prince, but she's keeping her options open for a werewolf mate," Gareth said, wiping his eyes free of tears. "David," he hollered behind them. "You better come impress your girl with your alpha male qualities before she runs off with a sexy alpha werewolf!"

She covered her ears and refused to turn around as she heard David muttering something about showing her who the alpha male was, making the others laugh harder.

"Mate," Gawain growled, tickling her neck.

She pulled her hands off her ears and slapped his hand away. "Quit making fun." She turned around and met David's gaze. "David, make them stop."

Gareth and Gawain grinned at each other and both abruptly turned, dropping to their knees in front of David.

"He's using his alpha order, Jane," Gareth said. "Damn you, Alpha David!" He laughed as David knocked him over and approached her.

David caressed her hot cheeks, and for once his touch didn't burn her skin. "I promise, one day, when you give me a sign, I will toss you over my shoulder and declare you mine."

Her mouth fell open, and he winked before pulling his hand away and leading their group.

"Damn," Gareth muttered beside her. "How does David turn that shit into a pick-up line? Got her speechless—then just walked away. Fuck. He even rhymed!"

"Because I'm alpha," David said without turning around.

Gawain lifted his finger to her chin, shutting her mouth. Had that really just happened?

"Sorry, Alpha." Gareth laughed, jogging backward to catch up to David and Tristan. "I mean, *Ahh-woooooooo!*"

✦✦✦

Lance kicked a corpse out of his way. "Get this shit cleaned up."

"Sorry, Lancelot." A shirtless man ran forward with another man and dragged the dead body out of the hall.

"Sire," said another man. "The men are fearful of the female who fights with the knights. Five attempted to escape after receiving the last orders."

"David's bitch is a joke." Lance chuckled and took a bite out of an apple. "Where are the traitors?"

"They are bound."

Lance finished his apple and tossed it on the floor. "Let the dead feast on them. If they live long enough, I shall have more pets by nightfall." He walked through the hall until he stopped near a group of three naked women tied to a table. They cowered and tried to cover themselves, but he barely acknowledged them and glanced at the man behind him. "Where's my brunette?"

"Ill, Sire. She said she is with child."

Lance growled, his teeth sharpened for mere seconds before his face returned to its normal appearance. "Find her and bring her to me." He grabbed up a blonde woman from the group. They screamed and tried to hold onto her, but he kicked them away and dragged the one he'd chosen away by her hair.

"Yes, Sire." The man ran off.

"Please, just kill me," the blonde woman begged.

Lancelot smiled sweetly and caressed her cheek. "Be a good girl and I will consider throwing you to my men. They will be more than willing to fuck you to death."

He came to an empty room and threw her in as his name was called.

His servant walked up, clutching a brunette woman by her upper arm. "Here she is, Sire."

Lancelot shut the door on the crying blonde and walked up to the brunette. He grabbed her chin and turned her face. "You look like shit." Tears slipped from her eyes. "I did not desire offspring with you."

"I didn't mean to get pregnant," she said, crying. "I told you I wasn't on birth control."

He scoffed and roughly released her face. "I don't have time to deal with this. You were told to prevent this. I cannot travel with a pregnant whore." He looked at the other man. "Find the doctor and get her an abortion."

"No," the woman screamed, covering her belly. Lancelot didn't look at her as his servant spoke.

"The last doctor was killed during the battle with the knights."

Lancelot looked at the woman. "How far along are you?"

"I don't know. It's still early, but you can't kill my baby," she cried. "It's your baby, too!"

He grabbed her throat, choking her to stop her cries and looked at his servant. "See if someone can get it out of her."

"Unless we find a physician," the man said, "I do not know how we can abort the pregnancy. Unless you are knowledgeable, Sire."

The woman sputtered and her face turned red as Lancelot stared at her. "There is one way," he said before he squeezed his hand tighter around her neck. A series of cracks sounded, and he dropped her lifeless body to the ground. "Feed her to my pets."

"Yes, Sire." The man bent down to pick the dead woman up as Lancelot turned to enter the room.

However, Lancelot stopped and watched a group of three of his men carrying two small figures down the hall. He laughed. "Where'd you find these?"

"To the south," said one of the men.

Lance pointed to the door opposite the door he stood at. "Put them in there. They will be perfect bait for David's little whore." They obeyed, and he entered the room he'd left the blonde woman in.

From the hall, a few men paused and listened to the woman beg for him to stop. None of them flinched when a loud slap and scream echoed from the room. Some went about their way, others covered their ears, and some laughed or masturbated as they listened right outside the door.

Her cries went on for hours.

CHAPTER 31

FACES OF JANE

The pink and violet horizon of the Texas sky grew darker as Jane and the knights ran through the streets. The stars were not yet visible; there was only a cloudless, midnight-blue sky.

It had been so long since she was last outside; she had nearly forgotten that a zombie apocalypse was still taking place. That fact was impossible to forget now as she passed rotting corpses, wrecked or abandoned vehicles, and looted homes every few hundred feet.

There was so much loss and ruin. She felt horrible for every giggle and smile she'd allowed herself, sorrow for everything she'd lost and would never have back, and guilt for every moment of happiness she'd shared with Death and the knights.

A middle-aged man covered in flies and ants came into view. Jane crinkled her nose as she eyed where his neck had been ripped open and the massive hole in his stomach where intestines had spilled out onto the pavement.

As she quickly scanned his wounds, she noticed differences among his injuries. She hadn't realized she'd stopped running until David came to her side.

"It's from the wolves," he told her. "This man was attacked by an infected human. See?" He pointed at the ripped chunks on the man and then to a broken zombie corpse she hadn't seen. That body had been destroyed. "A wolf or wolves must have come along while he was already under attack. You see how the bites differentiate between ripping and razor like slices and tears?" She nodded as he went on. "The wolves are just as mindless as the undead humans. Sometimes they even forget to finish their meal."

She could smell it, then. The stench that came from the nightmarish wolves.

"Come on," David said, sliding his fingers down her arm until they touched her hand. "We're running out of time; sunset is minutes away. We need to get there before they head out for the night."

Jane snapped out of it and nodded. David gave her hand a quick squeeze before he let go.

The others took off without a word. David did not take the lead right away and stayed at her side. She knew she needed to stay focused, but as she passed a small figure on the side of the road, she gasped.

"You okay?" David reached out to take her hand and pulled her as she slowed to see it was a young girl. "Don't look."

Her eyes strained as she tore her gaze away. David gripped her hand tighter, and she held her breath as more children came into view. She couldn't help but search each one they passed for similarities to her children. She had forced herself not to think of them, and now she was terrified because she wasn't the only monster who could hurt them.

"Don't let yourself become upset," Tristan said over his shoulder while he ran just a few feet ahead of them. "Your emotions are more of a concern than the others. Those with abilities like ours need to have stronger minds."

Jane nodded again, trying to take his advice. She knew that if she let her thoughts linger on her family, she would become a mess.

"Jane," David said, squeezing her hand. "Remember what we talked about, okay? If you worry, you will become reckless. I need you focused on the fight and my orders. These children cannot be saved, but you can save others if you become the warrior I know you are. Show me the woman who destroyed monsters with only her fearless spirit and an M9 in her hand."

Jane kept her head forward, inhaling then exhaling as she cleared her mind. She didn't look to the side of the road or search the bodies they passed. These were not her children, but she could do what she'd done before and fight to protect them and others who were still out there. There were more than zombies to fear, and she had to do her part to keep innocent lives safe.

She bobbed her head in a sort of commitment to let her sorrow and worry slide away.

"Good girl," David said, letting go of her hand. "Just like that."

She wasn't looking at him, but she sensed his approval and delighted in it as he ran back to the front of their group.

Somehow, Jane was aware he wanted her near him, so she followed, staying close. The others grew tense, and she sniffed. A faint hiss left her mouth when strange scents reached her nose. She and the others turned their heads in unison to the west.

This scent was different than the one they'd been following. She snarled, not liking it one bit. The overwhelming urge to track down the new scent took over her thoughts, but David growled, and she turned toward him, not even questioning what she was doing.

Whatever scent she had caught continued to assault her nose, and the others were agitated by it too, increasing her building anxiety. They began baring their fangs, so she copied, letting out soft snarls when the smell grew more potent. *Threat*, her instincts told her, and she was ready to destroy it.

David let out a more threatening sound, and everyone, including her, released their attention on the foreign scents and raced toward their original goal.

Despite the obvious order to concentrate on finding the werewolf camp, she peeked at her leader. She knew he was the strongest here. He was feared and to be obeyed. The sudden urge to offer her blood and submit to him clouded her mind.

He cut a stern look at her. His gaze fell over her figure, and she wanted nothing more than to bite him and wrap herself around him. That single look had her ready to rip off her clothes. She couldn't even recall what had held her back from letting him take her.

"Enough," he growled. She shivered as goosebumps erupted across her arms. He bared his fangs and shook his head. "Control yourself, baby." His harsh tone became soothing, but firm at the same time. "You're giving over to the wrong instincts right now. Focus. We're almost there."

She turned away from his intense look. The rejection at least helped her regain her thoughts, as she remembered who she was and that she wasn't a wild animal who merely killed and fucked the strongest guy in the surrounding area.

Thankfully, she didn't have to berate herself for letting her hormones and instincts consume her, because the school finally came into view.

It was wrong to see a place normally populated with laughing children so empty of life. Cars were stuck in the same collisions they'd been abandoned in. One was even tipped over and smoldering while an ambulance with its doors open had a trail of dried blood and gore leading away, across the parking lot.

David held up his hand, and they all came to an abrupt stop. Tristan stood at his left while Gawain took his right. Jane stayed directly behind David while the remaining knights scattered around her.

"They're already shifting," Tristan said.

David nodded and searched the perimeter as agonized screams and the sick sound of bones breaking came from inside the school.

She'd never heard such a series of gruesome noises. Her eyes were wide and fixed on the school doors as she listened to the most horrifying cries of pain.

"How many, David?" Tristan asked.

"Sixteen," he replied quickly. "Including Lance. He might have more stashed elsewhere, but I do not think there are as many as before." David said nothing more, but the others spread out once he nodded.

Geraint, Bors, and Gareth went to the side of the school while Tristan and Gawain stayed with her and David.

The tortured cries ended abruptly, only to be replaced by growls, and the scraping of claws on tile floors.

Tristan and Gawain moved forward as David turned to her. "Jane, they're going to come out those doors any moment now. You stay with me, sweetheart." She nodded, and he bared his fangs before quickly pulling her to him. His aggressive action didn't hurt. She knew he was already struggling to have her be part of this fight because of Lancelot's presence. He kissed her forehead, and pulling back, looked into her eyes and said the words she craved but tortured her all the same. "I love you. Stay close."

She could only bob her head. There was no time to ponder over his love, although it pushed the bloodthirsty monster down and pulled the girl that David and Death adored back in full view.

David reached over and flicked the safety on her rifle just as a loud crash from inside the school sounded. He quickly grabbed her elbow and positioned her at his side. Giving her a tight smile, he turned to watch as the windows shattered at the main entrance.

They unleashed a hail of gunfire. The first three monsters let out ferocious roars before splitting up, and two others tore through the parking lot toward Gareth. Jane heard more glass shattering, but she was already firing at the two wolves approaching her new brother.

She moved away from David a bit but not far enough to be alone. She felt his gaze on her back, but he had his own target.

Gareth didn't stop firing until the first wolf reached him, then, faster than she thought possible, he pulled his sword and began hacking at the beast. Jane didn't stop her attack on the other wolf and smiled when it dropped to the ground without moving again. Gareth swung, delivering a powerful chop to the werewolf's neck, removing its massive head.

Two down.

She caught Gareth's gaze and smiled as he sent her a quick wink before taking off to help Bors and Geraint.

Tristan and Gawain had moved away from her and were battling three wolves together. David had also switched to his sword and took on four wolves by himself. A sense of pride filled her upon realizing he was completely capable of taking on more than the others.

While the knights held their own, the wolves growled and dodged the blades coming at them. It still shocked her that these bulky creatures were nearly as fast as they were.

Panic surged through her veins when Gareth, Geraint, and Bors suddenly chased after the four wolves they were fighting. It seemed foolish to leave, but she remembered the wolves would be killing innocent humans if they didn't stop them.

As they disappeared around the school, Jane looked away and froze at the sight of a figure strutting out of the broken entrance of the school.

Lancelot.

He was still in his human form, but that did not prevent the icy chill from crawling up her spine when his dark eyes settled on her.

David had yet to see him, and Lancelot continued watching her. She didn't know what to do, so she resumed firing her rifle whenever a wolf came in range.

The heavy smack on the pavement alerted her that at least one other wolf had been disposed of.

Thirteen.

David was still fighting off three huge wolves, and another lay a couple yards away. She caught his gaze and somehow understood he was issuing her an order: *don't leave.* Of course, she wasn't going anywhere, but a soft whimper made her turn back to Lancelot.

He wore a wicked grin and pulled something out from behind him. Jane's eyes widened in horror. He had a little boy, no older than five, clutched in his firm grip. She scanned the child's tearstained face, and her breath hitched as his terrified, hazel eyes met hers.

Lancelot suddenly grabbed the boy by his hair and lifted him in the air, causing a blood-curdling scream from the little boy.

Jane's heart pounded. She was scared, but fury drowned her fear, and she unsheathed her sword.

Lancelot smiled and curled his finger at her, taunting her to follow him. She hissed, enraged as he tucked the wailing boy under his arm and ran the other way. Two wolves she hadn't noticed followed him.

She took one step after them and David yelled, "No, Jane!"

She hesitated, but her rage was far too great now; there would be no reasoning with her. The deadly creature David had turned her into was awake and snarling.

The distraction she caused earned David a scratch across his back. He let out a terrifying growl and turned his attack back on the wolves. His hand shot out and grabbed the nearest one by the throat, and with incredible force, he threw its massive body into a nearby car. The windows exploded, spraying out shards of glass and buckling the tires from the powerful crash. A loud series of snaps most likely indicated a broken spine on the monster.

Without waiting, David hastened his attack. He delivered strike after strike to the next wolf on him. The monster roared and stumbled from each deadly blow it received, until it collapsed into a mutilated pile of flesh.

He was already busy slaughtering his final wolf when a noise from the street sounded.

All three sets of icy stares from her remaining vampires focused on her. *Stay*, they begged, but she shook her head at them.

"No," David hollered.

But Jane was already running, and six more wolves had been added to their fight with one successfully jumping on his back, preventing him from chasing after her.

Jane worried about him, but upon hearing his powerful roar, she knew he'd be okay. Even though a strong part of her told her to help him, she had to save the boy. Her protective instinct for the child was too great to ignore.

She didn't look back and ran faster. The distinct sound of flames and howls mixed with David's yells for her to come back, but she didn't stop.

The sound of the battle faded, but she heard the little boy's hysterical cries. She hissed and slid to a stop after rounding a building.

Lancelot stood there casually with the little boy dangling by his arm. "So you're the one who is causing so much trouble." Unlike the tender way her deadly vampires or Death looked at her, there was nothing but disgust in his dark gaze. "After all this time, I should have known David would be paired with a freak."

The lapdogs at his side growled and snapped their jaws. Jane wanted to growl back, but she bit her tongue and stared Lancelot down. "Put him down. You can take me." Bargaining herself was something she was very much prepared to do. All that she cared about was the little boy with hazel eyes. She'd give her life for him.

He laughed. "Foolish girl. You make it so easy; I was not prepared for you to come to me so soon."

The little boy reached out to her, and she shouted, "Please let him go! Do whatever you want to me."

"I should kill you right now," Lancelot said, his lip curling in disgusts. "But my master has plans for you." Her eyes widened, and he grinned. "Does David know of their little game?" She didn't answer, and he chuckled. "Then I will wait. It is no fun if he doesn't get to see you in the arms of another."

She bared her fangs. "I won't go with Lucifer."

"Are you sure?" He smirked. "There is much evil in you, I can almost taste it." He inhaled deeply. "Ah, that's what my master desires. I may as well be a good servant and draw that beautiful darkness out of you. All the more fun to watch David lose you this way. After all, he is Heaven's most beloved warrior–and you, well, you are simply undeserving of the noble knight."

Tears stung her eyes, but he didn't stop.

"You are not worthy of his pure heart. Remember that, whore. Because I know David, and I promise, when he sees what my master and I see in you, he will throw you away."

Lancelot's teeth suddenly elongated and sharpened. He grinned, looking very much like she'd imagine a shark would look if it were to smile at you, and she watched in terror as he savagely bit into the boy's neck. The little boy didn't even have time to scream before Lancelot tossed him away. His tiny body hit the ground hard as his blood spilled onto the pavement. "See you again soon, whore."

Jane was in shock, but she looked away in time to see Lancelot disappear down the street.

Bloodthirsty snarls forced her to return her attention to the scene in front of her. One of the wolves took a few steps in her direction, and one went to the boy.

"No," She screamed and threw out a burst of energy, just like she had practiced with Death. A low boom shook the ground and knocked both wolves back. It wasn't enough to injure them, but it distracted them and turned their focus solely on her.

Jane didn't fear them; she wanted their heads. She gripped her sword tight and charged.

The wolves stood no chance under her unforgiving blade. She snarled and hissed as her sword went right for the first one's leg. It fell to its knees, and she aimed a powerful kick at its torso, knocking it to its back.

Again and again, she sliced at it, cutting away the arms and head then stabbed her sword through its heart. Even though it was dead, she continued to roar out like a wild beast and cut him up further.

As black blood flew into the air and sprayed across her face, Jane heard a separate growl. Now she remembered the second wolf. She hadn't realized she'd used her power on it, but now, focused on his monstrous face, she grinned.

The monster growled again, and she hissed, but as she took a step, a sudden darkness blanketed her sight. She snarled and shook her head. The black faded but lingered around the edges of her vision as a faint whispering teased the back of her mind.

Taking another step, a faint wicked smile formed in her mind. "Leave me alone," she yelled and approached the werewolf.

Dark blood dripped from her blade as she raised her blade to the paralyzed wolf's neck.

It snapped its razor-sharp jaws, but she bared her fangs and slashed his jugular. Blood sprayed out like a broken hose across her body. The wolf whined and fought against her hold to no avail, and she laughed, closing her eyes as the blood covered her face and clothes.

The desire to torture him more excited her, and she moved her arm to cut into its belly. Only, before she could, a pair of muscular arms wrapped around her waist and dragged her back.

She thrashed and screamed out as her captor held her tight.

"Jane, I've got you," David cooed in her ear. His arms stayed wrapped tightly. "*Shh*, I'm here. I'm here, my love. Calm down."

The black that darkened her surroundings lifted, and she gradually regained her thoughts. Slowly, the bloodthirsty rage waned, and she relaxed in his hold.

David turned her around quickly. He wasted no time and began wiping the vile blood from her face, then pulled her to him. He hugged her and held her head to his firm chest. His heartbeat was fast but returned to a steadier pace as he breathed in her scent.

There was no way she would refuse him at that moment, and she wrapped her arms around his waist to return his embrace. Her own pounding heart slowed, and her hearing now settled on the soothing beat of David's heart.

"The same girl?" Gareth was talking to Tristan.

"I think this must be the brother," Tristan said.

Jane pulled out of David's hold as she remembered the boy, and she ran to where they all knelt. She quickly fell to the little boy's side.

He was still alive, but only just. The blood pumped slowly from his wound and oozed between her fingers as she tried to apply pressure.

Terrified hazel eyes opened to lock with hers, and Jane finally cried. Tears pooled in his eyes, but they did not fall.

Jane held his neck while Tristan pulled gauze out of his pack until he pushed her hand away to tend to the wound. The nameless little boy's lips moved, but blood spilled out of the corners of his mouth.

"*Shh* . . . You're going to be okay," she said, stopping him from speaking.

David knelt behind her and rubbed her back but said nothing.

"Mommy?" the little boy managed.

Jane sobbed and nodded. "Mommy's here, baby. It's going to be all right." The words were automatic. She knew he wasn't her son, but it didn't matter, and she leaned over to brush his soft brown hair away from his forehead. "It's okay," she whispered, placing a kiss on his head. "I'm here."

Her tears made it hard to see him as he gurgled blood, trying to breathe, until finally, she watched his pupils dilate, and the rapid rising of his tiny chest stilled.

"Jane," David whispered.

She didn't respond. All she could do was sit and stare at this lifeless, little body. The massive amount of blood loss had already turned his light complexion to a chalky white color.

David ran his hands up and down her arms to soothe her, but only one thing reached her mind: *Jack*, her baby brother. That's all she saw now.

"Sweetheart, he's gone."

Still, Jane kept her eyes fixed on the little boy and his blank hazel eyes that nearly matched her own. Her mind tortured her further by causing the little boy's face to morph into Nathan's. She was close to screaming and falling into madness as her own son's face became clearer.

"Please say something," said David. She finally turned away from the terrible sight to look at her vampire. David cradled her face in his hands. "I'm so sorry, Jane."

Her teary eyes wandered over his face then behind him. The rest of her knights had returned; none appeared to be injured. They all gazed down sadly at the small, broken body by her side. She noticed Gareth being handed a young girl's body. She was older than the little boy, maybe in her teens. *Still a child.*

The way he had to cradle her head made it obvious that her neck had been broken. Jane couldn't even bring herself to look at the girl's empty eyes after seeing Gareth's heartbroken look. So, she looked back at David.

She shook her head as she tried not to break down, but she couldn't hold it anymore. She wailed.

David quickly pulled her into his arms and stood up. When he turned to carry her away, she cried louder and tried to break out of his hold. He held her tighter and fixed her across him. "It's okay, sweetheart—we will not leave them behind."

She cried, in agony over her failure. "I couldn't save him."

David sighed and kissed her head. "I know. I'm sorry I did not get to you faster. You did everything that you could, and you kept them from hurting him further."

"Nathan," she blurted out. "Where are Nathan and Natalie?"

"They're safe, my love. Arthur is keeping them safe for you." He walked faster and kissed her hair. "Stay with me, Jane. Don't lose yourself."

She shut her eyes and cried. So many thoughts bombarded her mind. Failure, fear, shame, guilt, worthlessness. Lancelot's words cut into her heart like a jagged knife, and she hugged David. Lancelot was right; she was evil and unworthy. She didn't deserve him. He would throw her away when he saw her.

"Talk to me, baby," David murmured in her ear as he began to jog with her. "Are you still with me?"

Tears soaked her face, and she shook her head. "He's right."

"Who?" He nuzzled her but looked around to find his bearings and ran down a new street. "Did Lance say something to you?" She didn't answer him. He heaved a heavy sigh. "Whatever he told you isn't true. He's trying to get in your head to make you doubt yourself."

"It's true, though."

"What's true?" he asked.

She stayed quiet.

"Dammit, Jane." He sighed when she flinched. "Forgive me—I didn't mean to yell. Please tell me what he said."

She couldn't say anything. There was too much sadness and guilt over everything that had happened. She realized now how much she had enjoyed slaughtering that wolf. Lancelot was right about her; she was evil inside, and she was a whore. She didn't have to have sex with anyone to be one; she was jumping from male to male, and she wouldn't stop no matter how wrong she knew it was.

David's hot lips touched her temple. "Don't doubt me. Even if there is some truth to anything that comes out of Lance's mouth, it doesn't matter. You are still amazing and beautiful, and nothing can stop me from loving you."

It only hurt to hear him say that. She wanted him to love her, but she knew once he saw through his feelings, he would leave. They all left eventually.

David kissed her temple, murmuring he loved her, that she fought her best, that the boy's death wasn't her fault, and that Lance was a liar. But she couldn't accept it. If Lucifer himself saw the darkness in her; if he was willing to make a bet with Death for her, he obviously had a reason to, and she wondered if her so-called entity was really something separate from her. For all she knew, Death was telling her what he thought would hurt her less.

Then the thought came to her that Death must not have planned on winning now. He had walked away, left her without any reassurance that he was going to make sure Lucifer didn't win her. Why? Because he saw what Lucifer and Lancelot did: a demon.

"Jane," David whispered. "You can tell me anything."

"I want to see my children," she said, not sure why she'd blurted that out. Now that she had said it, though, she needed to confirm they were safe with her own eyes. "Please, David."

"I'll figure something out." He kissed her temple. "Just don't let anything he said get to you. Believe in me, okay?"

Jane wrapped her arms around David's neck and curled into him, only now realizing she was shaking.

David pulled back to look into her eyes. He was looking at her like she was a bomb ready to explode. "It's finally eating you up to be away from them, isn't it?" She stayed quiet, and he spoke again. "Jane, if I take you to your home, you have to understand that you cannot go inside. I have sat there; you can hear them, but there is no way to see inside."

"David." Gawain's warning tone didn't go unnoticed as he ran up beside them.

David glared at him. "She needs this. It will keep destroying her if we keep her away."

Gawain looked from David to her. "You are not in control of yourself, Jane. Can you not feel—"

David snarled and pulled her against him. "She's fine!"

Gawain stared at them and shook his head. "This is a mistake."

"I only want to make sure they're okay," she said.

Gawain sighed. "You say that now, but it will be different for you once you get there. Wait until you are calm. You do not see how you look right now. Did you look at what you did to that wolf?"

She covered her face as David stopped walking and raised his voice. "She fought in hopes of saving that child."

"David, you know that's not what you saw," Gawain muttered sadly, and she cried. "I adore you, Jane, but you are not in control of yourself. You are a threat to your children if you go near them now."

"Leave," David snarled. "Get the fuck away from us unless you want to anger me more."

Jane sobbed, she felt Gawain would always back her up. But even he saw how evil she was, and it broke her heart.

"David, calm down," said Tristan. "You will not help the situation if you grow upset yourself."

David breathed out harshly and hugged her, but she could not feel any comfort. She remembered how monstrous she looked in the mirror that first night. That was still her. That was before Lucifer.

"Enough of this, David," Gareth snapped. "You know you are not thinking rationally. Let us bury the children and then we can discuss helping Jane see that her son and daughter are safe. Now let's get back to camp. She is growing more unstable with our arguing."

Jane lifted her head and snarled, baring her fangs at the young knight.

David quickly pulled her head to his chest and turned them away from the knights' surprised gazes. "*Shh . . .*" He kissed her forehead over and over. "Jane, my Jane, stay with me. I'm sorry. I'm sorry."

She didn't know what she thought anymore, but as he pulled back and searched her face with concerned eyes, she cried, feeling incredibly exhausted.

"I see you," he said. "Just stay. Let me see your pretty eyes—your beautiful face. Not hers."

She whimpered and let him hold her close. "I'm sorry."

He sighed and spoke to the knights still standing behind him. "Go. We will be there soon."

"Are you sure?" Gawain asked David. In her mind, she could almost hear the silent addition: *she might hurt you.*

"I'm sure," David replied, sounding much calmer than he had been. There were a few sighs followed by footsteps leading away.

"What are we doing?" she asked as David continued to stand there.

He started walking in the opposite direction from where the knights had gone. "We're going somewhere where we can calm down together."

She glanced around as he picked up his pace and tightened her grip as he entered a wooded area. "David, you should listen to them," she murmured, staring at the side of his face. "I'm not safe."

He spoke quietly as he navigated carefully though the brush. "I don't care if it is not safe to be around you—I will still love you. And I will help you fight whatever threatens to destroy you. Even if you're the one who is destroying you."

She sniffed, wrapping her arm around him as she buried her face against his neck.

David quickly rearranged her so that her legs were around his waist. He didn't stop walking, and in the darkness, she let her emotions free.

His shirt was soaked in her tears, but he merely rubbed her back or murmured sweet words.

She didn't deserve him. He was too perfect. An urge to protect him from everything that she was overwhelmed her, but his hand spreading heat along her back where he rubbed her beckoned her to just stay.

"We are almost there," he said, sliding his forearm under her butt so he could push a branch away with his other hand. "Don't fall asleep yet." He sniffed the air, then turned a different way. "It's up here."

"What is?" She turned her head as they walked out into a clearing and gasped, her tears finally coming to a stop.

"Take a swim with me." He kissed her cheek and carried her closer to the creek. "There's no one around for miles. It's just us. We can wash away some of this blood and go back later."

It wasn't a magical lagoon or anything, but it was pretty. It reminded her of a creek she'd gone to as a child with her family. The water was shallow, but there was a small waterfall that flowed into a deeper area. "You want to swim?"

He glanced at the water. "I want to be with you and pretend there's nothing wrong for just a little while. I want it to just be us, no one else."

At that moment, that's all she wanted too. "Okay."

David smiled and lowered her onto a boulder. He helped her remove her sword and holsters. Once she was free of weapons, he stepped back and removed his own, placing them on the ground next to hers.

When he was done, he started untying her boots. She felt her body growing hotter but stayed quiet, watching him concentrate on what he was doing. He said nothing as he pulled her boots and socks off. He turned and leaned against the rock she was on and bent over to untie his boots.

Jane bit her lip, admiring his wide back. She could see his muscles flexing through his shirt and remembered when she'd seen him shirtless.

"Do you want me to close my eyes?"

She melted under his tender gaze. "I—"

He grinned and pushed himself away from the rock, then quickly tugged his shirt over his head. Her mouth fell open, and he went for his pants. "Close your mouth, Jane."

She snapped her mouth shut and glared at his smiling face.

He chuckled and pushed down his black pants, leaving him in a pair of black boxer-briefs. "Don't run off. Take off whatever you want and come in, okay? Don't make yourself uncomfortable. We are just going to rinse off and relax for a while."

"Okay," she whispered, trying to only look at his face.

"Okay," he said, turning to walk to the water. He jumped into the deeper end without hesitation and swam closer to the waterfall where he seemed to be able to stand. "Hurry up."

She watched him stick his arm under the running water, then looked down at herself. She'd completely forgotten that she practically bathed in the blood of those two werewolves. It had dried on her clothes and arms.

She gasped, noticing red blood from the little boy staining her fingers. Her breath sped up, and her eyes burned.

"You coming?"

She looked up to see David in the water. He had his back to her, but she could tell he wanted to turn. He was still a gentleman even though he'd seen her almost completely naked before.

Jane smiled sadly and tugged off her shirt. "I'm coming."

CHAPTER 32
LOVE

Jane wasn't the greatest swimmer, and she was disappointed when she realized her new immortality hadn't improved her ability to look graceful in the water. Her small stature didn't help either because she couldn't stand in the rushing water where David was.

"Do you need help?" He chuckled, turning around once she was close to him. She was ready to refuse, but all that went out the door when his fingers slid around her hand, and he pulled her close to him. David smiled, sliding his hand down her side and guided her legs around his waist. With on hand holding her thigh, he asked, "Is this okay?"

She nodded, her breath hitching as she asked him, "Do I look bad?"

"No." He dipped his hand in the water and reached up to rub her face. "You look sad."

"I don't look like her?"

He looked at her eyes and shook his head, his dark hair that had been slicked back from the water fell across his forehead. "I see you, Jane."

She smiled and went to push his hair back when she noticed her hands dripping with blood. "Oh!" She dunked them in the water over and over until David stopped her.

"Relax." He carried her closer to the waterfall. "This is not your blood this time." He held her arm under the flowing water. "It's not the blood from one of our comrades–"

She cut him off. "But it is from the little boy I failed to save."

He gave her a stern look. "It's from the child you ran off to save by yourself. I have no doubt you would have given your life for him if it meant he could be saved."

She sighed and looked at the flowing water as he cleaned her hand in it. "Why are you so good?"

He chuckled and turned them so he could wash her other hand. "I'm only this way for you."

She smiled and looked back at him. "I think you must always be good, though. Not like me."

Those blue eyes pierced her. "Do you always see yourself so negatively?"

"Don't you?" she snapped. He didn't respond, so she went on. "What did you and the others see? Why was Gawain so worried? I'll tell you why. He saw what I am. Evil."

"Baby, you are not evil." He lifted his hand and held the back of her neck so she couldn't look away. "You are everything right in my world—everything I've waited my entire life for."

Jane could barely concentrate with him touching her, but she managed to respond. "I know you think I'm your soul mate and some savior of mankind who will end the darkness in the world, but I don't think I'm any of those things. And I think, deep down, you know that, too." Her eyes watered. "If you knew what was after me, what I see in my head, you'd agree." Her lips trembled, and she whined, "And you would leave me; you'd regret ever meeting me."

David pulled her head to his shoulder. "No, I cherish the night I found you and every moment since then. I would never leave you, and I do not think any of that."

She whimpered against his shoulder. "You don't know what's happening."

"What's happening?"

She squeezed her eyes tight as sobs wracked her body. There was no way she could tell him about Lucifer. There was no way she could tell him how much she loved and needed Death, but desired to have him all to herself, too. She couldn't say how awful she felt for being in his arms right now when her husband mourned her death alongside her children.

"Jane," he murmured, taking them out to the calmer water. "Tell me what's happening."

"I can't." She wrapped her arms around his neck. "Don't ask me to tell you."

He sighed and slid his hand up and down her back. "I won't make you tell me, but I am here. I promise I won't judge you or run away. I know we are not together, but I won't turn my back on you."

"You should," she whispered.

David leaned back and looked her in the eye. "You're right. I should. I should have left when I saw you were married and again when I saw your heart belonged to another."

Her eyes widened at his words and her heart threatened to shatter.

"But I stayed," he said in the most tender way. "I'm going to stay. So let's stop discussing what I should and should not do. Because no matter what happens, I will still be here whether your heart is mine or another's."

She frowned, unable to speak and stayed still as he leaned forward to kiss her cheek. He left his lips there and smiled as he waded deeper into the water. Jane leaned her cheek against his lips and held on to him as he slowly turned them in circles.

He was so warm. She completely melted against him and looked up at the cloudy sky. "David?" She lightly scratched his scalp.

"Yes?"

She shivered and closed her eyes as she listened to the soothing sounds of the splashing water and crickets chirping.

"Jane?"

She opened her eyes and moved her lips to his ear. "What if we pretended there was only us."

"It is only us out here."

"No. I mean, what if we pretend there is no one else between us? Right now I'm not married. I'm not evil. I never met Death . . . I'm the woman you were looking for, and when I saw you, I knew."

"I don't understand what that would achieve." He rubbed her back a little harder, and she grinned as she kissed his neck.

"Jane?"

She kissed his jaw. "It would achieve us."

He gripped her waist hard. "No, Jane. You're not thinking clearly."

"I am," she whispered, kissing his jaw again, then his cheek. "I need you."

David used one hand to hold her back. "Please don't say things like this. This isn't you."

She shook her head and pulled him closer. "This is me." He groaned as she got herself close enough to kiss his cheek again. "I'm not her."

"This is only you *here*. Now. As soon as we finish or leave, you will regret everything we shared, and you will push me away." He sighed and held her cheek again. "I love you, Jane. But I know you do not love me." His thumb rubbed a tear that suddenly fell. "Don't take advantage of my feelings for you."

"But I do love you."

David's eyes darted between hers. "Please don't say that unless you mean it, Jane."

She held her hand over his. "I do mean it," she said quickly. "I've been stupid. I don't want to deny it anymore. I love you, David. I need you. I want you. No one e—" Before she could finish, his mouth covered hers.

Without hesitating, she kissed him back. His hand slid into her hair and tugged so he could angle her better for his kiss. He sighed and sucked her lip before pushing her mouth open. Their tongues touched, and she couldn't hold her moan back. His kiss tasted even better than his blood.

David's chest rumbled, and he pulled her face even closer, kissing her harder—possessively. She was his and no one else's, that's what his kiss said. A sound of acceptance hummed from her mouth to his, and he grinned in triumph against her lips.

"I love you," he said, kissing her again. "So much, Jane." He still had one hand tangled in her hair, but his other had gripped her butt cheek. His lips trailed across her jaw, and he gently sucked her neck.

Jane gasped, trying to touch him wherever she could, but she only managed to grab the back of his head. He lifted her slightly to kiss down her neck. Being exposed above the water had her shivering, but his fiery kisses and licks down her neck had her warming quickly.

His fangs scraped her neck and collar bone, and he pushed one strap of her bra down and kissed across her shoulder. Releasing her hair, he cupped her breast, squeezing once before pulling her bra down more.

"David." She moaned as his hot mouth instantly covered her nipple. He growled and lifted her higher, still kissing and sucking. Her entire body was shaking.

"Tell me again," he said, placing a wet kiss between her breasts. "Tell me you love me."

"I love you, David." Her breathing was coming so fast. "I love you. I want you to have me."

He bared his fangs but gently kissed her other breast as he shoved her bra down. "No one else?"

She shook her head and reached for his face to make him look up at her. "Just you."

He smiled and claimed her lips again, pulling her naked breasts against his chest as he began walking out of the water.

A cold solid surface met Jane's back. She hissed and opened her eyes, realizing he held her against a boulder.

He kissed her harder, making her go dizzy. Both of his hands slid down the back of her panties and palmed her ass. She felt his erection pressing against her and moaned as his lips went down the column of her throat. "You're sure?"

"Yes." She was, breathless, and she yelped as her panties were ripped right off.

He lifted his face and grinned, pulling her lips back to his, then adjusted her legs. The back of her ankles met his bare ass, and she moaned loudly as his erection nudged her core. She nearly came undone right there, but she had to look.

She peeked down and gasped.

David chuckled and nuzzled her cheek. "I was made for you, my love." He kissed the corner of her mouth. "I'll fit."

Jane nodded, gasping every time he teased her with his dick. "Oh, God, David." She clawed at his shoulders, needing him to be inside her.

"I love you, Jane."

Her breath sped up. "I love you, David."

He smiled and with a single thrust, he was inside her . . .

"Jane."

A cold sensation flitted across her lips and down her jaw.

"Wake up, sweetheart."

Jane's eyes flew open as she gasped. She looked around, confused with her surroundings. She was in the bed at their base camp, covered with a thick blanket. Her damp hair stuck to parts of her face, and she quickly moved them to look down at herself.

She was wearing David's shirt, and besides the tingling and wetness between her legs, there was no indication from her body that she'd been intimate with him.

"Are you all right?" he asked, feeling her forehead. "You were moaning and moving quite a bit. I thought you were having a nightmare again."

"When did we get here?" she asked, looking around the room.

"We came back a few hours ago. You fell asleep on my shoulder when we were in the water. Did you forget?"

"At the creek?" she asked, trying to figure out what was real.

"Yes. I cleaned some of the blood off you, then we talked for a short while, and you fell asleep. You woke up when I placed you on the rocks long enough to let me slide my shirt over you, but you fell back to sleep quickly. I brought you here and put you in bed." He touched her cheek. "Did you have a bad dream? Did you forget what happened?"

"What happened?" she asked harshly. "Did we—?"

He frowned. "Did we what?"

Jane pushed his hand away and covered her face. "Nothing. I'm sorry. I got confused." A tear quickly fell, but she wiped it away as her mind and heart screamed at each other. "It wasn't real," she whispered, thankful but full of emptiness at the same time. "It was just a dream."

CHAPTER 33

MORNING GLORY

The flower painting on the wall blurred as Jane struggled to contain her tears. Yes, she was practically crying again! But she was running out of fight, and she was so tired of everything continuously knocking her down. It had been this way for too long.

David had excused himself for a few minutes, but he was back now and she felt utterly humiliated and guilty in his presence. Most of all, she was sad because he was so amazing and waiting for her, and she'd never be worthy of him.

She refused to look at him, keeping her head turned away as he sat beside her on the bed. She was still in his shirt, and she hugged her knees to ensure she didn't touch him. After all, she'd been acting like a bimbo around him.

"Do you want to talk?" Poor guy was stressing so hard over her.

"There's nothing to talk about." She wiped away another tear.

He sighed and scooted close enough that she could feel his body heat warming up her right side. "Are you sad over what we talked about at the creek? Or because we swam together? I know it was probably wrong to swim in our underwear, but I promise I did not touch you inappropriately after you fell asleep."

She let out a bitter laugh and covered her face just in case he could see her. "I know you didn't, David. You did nothing wrong. You never do anything wrong."

"Is that bad?"

She wanted to hug him. "No. It's not bad."

He reached around and pulled her so she'd lean against him. She cried silently and let him pull her onto his lap. She even laid her head against his chest as he hugged her, warming every bit of her body. "Did you have a bad dream?" he asked.

"It wasn't a bad dream; it was a very nice dream." She reached up and wiped her tears again, wondering how she could make so many. "It was nice because I'm evil inside."

"I don't understand."

"Because I shouldn't like it." She breathed in his scent and calmed a little. "I'm horrible for liking it so much."

He began to comb his fingers through her hair. "I wish you could see yourself the way I do."

"You don't know me, David."

His voice was softer. "I want to, but you will not let me."

She sighed and closed her eyes. Her mind wouldn't rest. Everything with him felt so right, but she knew it was wrong. It was wrong to care for him so deeply when she loved Death, and she felt even worse because she realized Jason wasn't even the main reason she felt guilty for being with David. What did that make her if she put Death above Jason? Was she putting David above her husband, too? Did she love David as well? She'd confessed she did in her dream.

"Would it help if you talked to someone else?" he asked. When she shook her head, he made another suggestion. "What about Death? Do you know how to reach him?"

She smiled sadly. David really would do anything if it meant she could be better. "He left me."

"Only because he had to, Jane."

Staring off, she felt herself drifting into darkness. "Did you know I saw myself after I changed?"

"You mean as an immortal?"

"I mean, when I lose control. My eyes, they turn black."

"Oh." He hugged her. "I did not know you had seen yourself."

"I was too afraid to tell anyone. The boys had said only Cursed and Damned had black eyes. Oh, and demons or fallen angels. But I had them, too. Even before—"

"Before what?"

Lucifer, she thought but continued to talk about her experience. "I had looked through the bathroom window and watched you leave with Arthur, then I saw my home. At first I had been devastated, then all I wanted was their blood. I wanted to kill my children, David. I *was* going to kill them. But I had caught sight of my reflection and hissed like I was staring at an enemy. Then the monster copied me. And only then did I realize I was the monster and what I'd almost done.

"When I thought of my children again, I watched my eyes flood with blackness and the most evil thoughts filled my mind. I can't think of my children without wanting to harm them. What kind of mother can't think of her own children without wanting to kill them?"

"That's not you, Jane."

"Then who is it?" She chuckled sadly. "If I were possessed, Death would be able to call them out or they'd flee from him. So what does that say about me?"

"It says you are fighting something more powerful than even Death has faced."

"You don't understand," she whispered.

"Because you refuse to let me help you, Jane," he said, frustrated. "You refuse to explain anything to me."

She pushed herself out of his arms and crawled to the edge of the bed. "I need to take a real shower. If you hear anything, stay away."

"I'm sorry. I did not mean to sound harsh." His apologetic tone made her tummy squeeze. "I'm worried."

"I know." She climbed off the bed and pulled the shirt to cover her butt as she walked to the bathroom.

"You need to feed," he called out.

She stopped walking and stared at the floor as she listened to him get off the bed.

He placed a hand on her left shoulder before sliding it down her arm and across her waist, caging her against his body. His heat and muscles pressed against her back as he offered his other arm up to her mouth. "Drink."

"I don't want to."

He held her tighter but pulled his wrist away. She only had time to blink before his bleeding wrist was pressed against her lips. "Drink."

She cried but could not resist him. Just like she could not resist anything about him or Death. They offered, she accepted, and like always, she desired more than she should.

A chill swept across her as she sucked, and she instantly imagined David using his free hand to shove her panties down before he sat on the bed and pulled her on his—

Jane moaned, and David growled when she tried to pull his hand down between her legs.

"Stop!" He tugged her tighter. Her left arm was trapped, but she fought to free herself.

If he wasn't going to give her what she wanted, she was going to take it.

"Jane!"

She pulled her mouth from his wrist and hissed, but he used both of his arms to keep her from getting out of his hold.

"Jane," he said softer. She stilled in his hold. "There you go." He nuzzled the top of her head. "Good girl."

She'd done it again. "I'm sorry."

"This is normal behavior for new immortals. It's okay. I'll stop you."

She shook her head. He didn't know she wanted more than his blood. That is, until she heard him inhale the scent she emitted.

He tensed and hissed as his hand spread out across her stomach. His fingers flexed, making her whimper, and he finally exhaled, relaxing his grip. "I'm sorry. I didn't mean to hurt you."

"I know you don't want to hurt me, David—and you didn't." She pushed his hands away and went to the bathroom again. "But please get it through your head that I don't want to hurt you either. And that's all I'll do."

"Jane . . ."

"I'll see you downstairs," she said, shutting the door before he could say another word.

✦✦✦

A wooden plank lay beneath each body and had ropes attached at each corner. Jane glanced at the huge pile of dirt off to the side and saddened at the thought of it crushing the little boy.

Of course, he was dead would not be hurt from the weight of the dirt, but she still worried if he would be scared down in the dark hole. The knights had lined the bottom with flat rocks; she supposed it was the only improvement they could provide to the makeshift grave.

Jane briefly scanned the taller figure lying next to the boy's body. She remembered a young girl Gareth seemed to know. Rather coldly, though, she didn't care for her or her significance to Gareth. Jane knew that was cruel of her, but she didn't feel a sliver of sympathy. She only cared that the little boy would not be alone in the dark now. Because she'd failed him.

She gazed at the boy again. Something about seeing the body of the dead always stuck with Jane. She'd been to several funerals, and she always felt it necessary to see their face one last time. So she knelt down beside him and carefully undid the covering over his face.

She pulled the sheet away and let out a soft sob. Someone had cleaned his face and combed his hair. They had also wrapped a blue handkerchief around the fatal wound on his neck. She caressed his pale cheek. He really did look like her brother, and her son.

She brushed the stray hairs from his face before leaning over and kissing his forehead. "I'm sorry." She leaned back, securing the wraps before smoothing out the wrinkles as best she could.

When she sat there staring at the sheet, David reached down and pulled her up. He kissed her head, then walked forward with Gawain, Gareth, and Tristan.

Jane only then realized all the knights were there, and they all watched her with sad and worried gazes. She looked away from them and back to David. He and the others picked up the ends of rope that had been attached to the wooden plank and lowered the boy.

As his body disappeared into the shadows, an empty feeling spread through her stomach. An unnatural, empty feeling.

The wooden plank hit the bottom, the knights discarded the ends of the ropes and repeated the process with the girl.

This was what always happened. Everyone wound up here because of her. She always failed. Her best was never enough. She was never enough. She either destroyed or let things get destroyed because she was too weak to make a difference.

With the hollowness spreading through her chest, she glanced at Gawain and Gareth. They weren't looking at her as they shoveled dirt over the bodies, but she knew they were disgusted with her. She'd lost control and hurt them again. She had tried to be happy and good, but she wasn't good. They all thought she was something she wasn't. They all believed she'd save the world and be David's soul mate, but she wasn't.

She could feel the fire simmering deep inside her. Like a sleeping volcano, it was waiting for her to erupt. How many of them would be in her path when she did? How many would she put in their graves? Would it be only Gawain and Gareth? Would they be able to keep her children safe from her? Would David fall at her hand because he refused to leave?

David grabbed her hand and placed something in her palm then put his arm over her shoulder and pulled her against his side. She didn't fight him. All she could do was stare at what he'd placed in her hand. He'd given her a flower from a morning glory vine.

Jane stayed still in his arms and let a slow breath out. She'd always found the simple flower so beautiful. They reminded her of fairies, of magic she had believed in when she was still innocent.

This was sad magic, though. It always closed when the light left to shield itself from the dark. Then it reopened in the morning light, only to wither and close again when the heat became too much. It could not stand too much light or dark.

The sound of dirt being shoveled made her look away from the delicate violet petals. She watched the knights tossing dirt down into the hole and without thinking, she tossed David's flower in as well.

Her lips trembled when she could no longer see it. She remembered how the flowers she'd placed over her family's caskets disappeared in almost the same way under the dirt. She remembered how Wendy loved blue morning glories and that she liked the violet ones. She had been trying to get a pair to grow in her flower garden, but they wouldn't. They never would. She'd never see her flowers. She'd never see her parents or Wendy, just like she would never see this little boy or her flower again. Just like she'd never see her family.

Excruciating pain spread from her burning eyes down her tightening throat and into her throbbing chest. She'd never see any of them. Her babies would forget her. Jason would remember for a while, but he would forget her like he did everything else. Even her pets would go on without her. She always thought, at least, they relied on her, but she stood corrected.

No one needed her. They were better off without her.

If she tried to have anything, just like her flower tried to have the sun, she'd perish. Or also like her flower, spread like an untamable weed, smothering every living thing around her so she could have all the light to herself. Just like she knew it was wrong to try to be happy with David and Death, the flower knew it was wrong to stay in the sun—but she and her flower stayed because they were greedy. They craved the light when they had no right to bask in its warmth. They were doomed to a stinted period of good but shunned to only look from the shadows.

She feared what waited inside her. If she broke, what would happen? If she tried one last time to be anything great, and she failed, what horror would she unleash?

No one could stop her. She would be like the morning glory vine, able to spread out where she was not wanted, smothering, strangling, killing all life that deserved to be there, and not even the sun would be able to stop her once she lost herself.

She did not want to see what she would do. She wished everything would stop. It needed to or she would fall to a depth she could not return from.

She pressed her lips together and swallowed the cry that needed to come out.

She would never have David or Death—not the way she wanted to. She wasn't good enough for either of them. They were light and warmth, and they held her steady between them. But she couldn't keep doing this to David. If she became the one to destroy him, she would never be able to come back from the dark.

Make it stop, she silently prayed to whoever would listen.

As

You

Wish.

A chill, a familiar chill, crawled its way to her heart and encased it. It was going to do more than stop it all, though. She felt it. It was a menacing thing with a task to carry out.

So, instead, she shut off on her own. It was like she was sitting in a house, and one by one, the lights went out.

It hurt to feel. It hurt to remember. It hurt to want what she couldn't have—what she didn't deserve. She didn't want to hurt anymore. She didn't want to cry over her many losses or feel her heart pulled in different directions. She was tired of fighting. Tired of not being enough. Just tired.

So, when the lights flickered and died, she hid in the dark.

✦✦✦

David shuddered as a cold sensation slid across his arm. He wasn't bonded to Jane in the same sense that she and Death were, but he could still read her well, and what he saw on her empty expression made his chest ache. "Jane?"

"What?" The hollowness of her voice caused a sick feeling to stir in his stomach.

He tried not to panic and lowered his hand from her shoulder to caress her arm; she always reacted to his touch. She tensed under his fingertips, giving him hope she could feel him, but she made no other reaction. "Sweetheart, do you want to discuss our visit to your home?"

There was no spark in her eyes as she looked up. The green and golden-brown fire didn't swirl around each other; they were a solid olive color. Pretty but not alive.

She didn't utter a word or show anxiety of any sort. She simply gave him a single nod and pulled out of his hold to walk back inside. He watched her close the door behind her and turned to see that everyone had witnessed her strange departure.

Arthur gestured toward the house. "Go to her. Something is wrong. Her thoughts are—" He shook his head, looking frustrated. "Just go."

David didn't have to be told twice, but he didn't know what awaited him. Her emotions made her volatile. She either radiated happiness, drowned in sorrow, or roared like a raging inferno. Yet, what he saw as he entered the sitting room was nothing like he expected. "Jane?"

✦✦✦

Death opened his eyes to a silent and colorless world. The grass and shrubs, all varying shades of gray, extended for miles. An occasional small tree or flower would pop up on the empty fields, but even they were void of color.

This place held no surprises for him. He'd traveled to this ashen realm many times throughout his existence. After all, he knew that as deserted as it seemed, life flourished at the heart of this world.

He turned around to view the mass behind him and, without waiting, walked toward the enormous lake.

The mirror stillness of the water's surface caught you eye, at first. Once you truly looked into the depths of the black and gray water the reflection of a magnificent and brightly colored tree on the opposite shore stole all its wonder. Various sizes of leaves and buds spread over the gigantic branches. Some new and vibrant in color while others were withered, clinging desperately to their stems. All joined, though.

Death finally arrived at the edge of the bank. He glanced into the clear water and found not just the impressive tree's reflection, but also, stars. Billions of stars surrounding a lone planet.

Earth.

For a small moment, he paused to admire the beauty it created. Never had he truly cared about Earth or its inhabitants. His role as the Angel of Death did not allow him to care. Duty brought him to the humans, nothing more. Unlike Heaven's angels who adored humanity as dearly as their Father, or the Fallen and Demons who hated them, Death felt nothing. That is, until the night he found Jane.

He chose not to question why Jane was the only being he attached to and continued his journey.

At last, he caught sight of the lone figure circling the tree. The angel occasionally reached up and plucked a leaf or bud from a branch to toss it into the lake. The man was his mentor, but Death had more power than him, even here.

Death finally came to a stop but did not speak. Instead, he turned to watch the discarded leaves disappear into the dark depths of the lake. He already knew which leaves were to be plucked, even before the angel at his side. There were so many now, floating aimlessly in the darkness. Waiting.

"Hello, Death."

"You know why I have come." Death still didn't look at him. "Tell me what you know and try to keep your opinions to a minimum. I'm in a hurry."

"I am sure you are. You never could stand being away from her." His mentor smiled. "All right. I will tell you what I have learned. You will not like it."

"Speak now."

The man sighed but did as he was told. "Lucifer is commanding most of the cursed immortals. Many of the Greeks and southern clans, as well as several other nations to the east, follow him. The few who still hold good hearts have fled to avoid confrontation. There is no telling what they will do, though.

"Along with Lancelot and Fallen, several demon armies aid him. I am sure you are aware of Hermes and Ares being nearby?" Death nodded. "Well, they are changing humans who have yet to be claimed by the plague."

"They're creating an army," Death said.

The man nodded. "Yes. Nyx tells me Thanatos and Mania have been spotted in various towns near your female." Death eyed him but stayed quiet. "Nyx has failed to locate Pestilence, and the others have not been successful in locating the rest of Hell's Lieutenants." Death made an irritated noise and waited for him to continue. "Most of us do not place blame on your brother. Nor should you. Be patient; we will know who is behind this when we find him.

"Pestilence aside, Nyx also reports Lycaon is being hunted in Germany by the Norse. This is not Lucifer's doing, Death. He is following orders." That had Death's attention. "I do not think Lucifer desires any of this, but you know him, his own jealousy and pride cause him to make foolish choices. Although this is someone else's bidding, he will attempt to destroy Arthur and his knights, including Jane. You should never have bargained the girl with him."

Death looked away from the disappointed expression on his mentor's face. He knew that to be true, but he didn't want to admit his faults regarding Jane's well-being to anyone.

She always forgave him, though. She welcomed him back with open arms, just like she did every time he failed her. He smiled to himself as he thought over their recent reunion until he heard a light laugh.

"It amazes me what the love of a woman will do to a man—mortal or not."

"Anything else?" Death asked, not willing to discuss Jane.

"This is more than even you can handle alone."

"I will bring down Lucifer," Death said, clenching his fist. "He will not win her, and any other fool who so much as thinks about harming Jane, will beg for my mercy when I come for their life."

A sad smile formed on his mentor's lips as he lay his hand on Death's shoulder. "I am not Father; I do not know why you have attached to this woman, but I fear your bond with her is not meant to be. They say she is the mate of the knight. He has been alone for centuries, and all have wondered why. Then it turns out the very soul destined to be his has already fallen in love with you. Why would you interfere with a union as destined as theirs?"

Death sighed and looked up at the tree behind them. "Call me if you locate my brother." He looked back at his mentor. "As always, I appreciate your council."

"Did you ever question why she had no guardian?" Death paused before he could take a step, but he did not respond to the question. "This is only the beginning. Be cautious with the girl; I fear she is not what she seems."

Death turned and glanced at a leaf on the tree. It had wilted, but a flowery vine had erupted from the stem. The flower, a morning glory mixed with gold and green, was closed, but he knew it was beautiful. He closed his eyes, exhaling as he prepared to depart to his next location. "Goodbye, Azrael."

CHAPTER 34
VIOLIN

For a few seconds, David could only stare into the dark sitting room. Jane hadn't turned any lights on, but he could make out her silhouette where she sat cross-legged on the floor with her back against the base of a sofa. She wasn't doing anything, simply staring at the wall across from her.

"Jane." He flicked on the light and went to stand in front of her, but she didn't acknowledge his presence. Her normally expressive eyes were completely empty. She was a shell of the person he loved.

What had happened? He'd never been around such an emotional person as Jane. Everything about being with her was so natural for him; he loved she was so delicate and caring, but this was wrong, and he had no idea how to help her. She'd been so happy and carefree before they fought the wolves. He had mentally prepared himself to comfort his sad soul mate, but this, this was not sadness. He would have preferred her tears and blubbering over the empty person sitting there.

A part of him said he should leave Jane behind him; he wasn't the one she chose, after all. She didn't even believe he was her soul mate, and she had two other men she held in higher regard than him. He'd never be the one she relied on. It didn't matter that he was the one who stood by her now, she would always need another.

Walk away. Wash your hands of her. She's too great a burden. These thoughts made perfect sense, but his heart wouldn't listen. It roared until every one of those cowardly thoughts went silent.

He may not be the man she loved, but he wasn't walking away from her.

More nervous than he'd been around her in a while, he sat beside her. He glanced at the wall to see if maybe there was something of interest, but it was blank. "Why are you on the floor, Jane?"

She didn't acknowledge him at all and kept staring at nothing. He glanced at her hand resting on her lap and reached over to hold it. Sadly, she still didn't react to his presence or even his touch. It felt like he held a useless appendage and there was no owner to guide it.

He wanted to grab her and kiss her until she felt something again, but he knew that would be disastrous, too. So, he placed her hand in both of his, and lifted it to his lips. He kissed her fingers and a jolt of electricity stung his lips. She even jerked, proving he'd not been the only one to feel it, but when he looked back to her face, his heart ached. Whatever she'd felt had already faded. She sat there, but he could not see the woman he loved.

"We are all going to go with you in a bit." He waited for any indication she'd heard or cared. She did nothing. "We will meet Dagonet in a few hours at the post he has maintained. It will be close to six by then, and perhaps they may be awake. You can easily hear everything inside from there; we can stay as long as you like. But like I told you, you will not be able to see inside. In time, we can come up with a way for you to safely watch them." Jane didn't respond to his plan. The excitement and playfully intense love she radiated were gone. "What do you think?"

She stayed quiet and still.

"Please say something," he begged. "Where are you, my love?"

Finally, she turned away from her staring contest with the wall. No emerald or gold glinted in the depths of her hazel eyes. Though he was heartbroken, he smiled as best he could and watched her slip further away.

"I'll go wait in my room." She got up and walked away.

David still held her hand in his and watched it fall limp at her side once she moved out of his reach. He felt helpless. No matter how much he wanted to follow her upstairs, his mind screamed at him to wait. So, he did.

He didn't know how long he sat there, but Arthur was suddenly speaking to him. "You know, David, Jane is a very special person."

"I know," David replied as he continued to stare out at nothing in particular.

"I was able to learn more about her and Death."

At the mention of Death, he became more aware of his brother-in-law and gave him his full attention.

"I was right about him sparing her life," Arthur said. "He came to her during her family's car crash because she was meant to die that night, but he didn't take her. He has been with her as often as possible, protecting her the best way he knows how and comforting her when no one is there to hold her. Unfortunately, he wasn't always able to remain with her, and evil pursued her."

David nodded, absorbing the information. "That doesn't explain what I witnessed between them." He suddenly grew angry, afraid Death had added to her abuse.

Arthur read his thoughts, stopping him losing his composure. "He kept their relationship innocent, merely helping her fall asleep because she wasn't comforted after her parents died. Visiting her on her birthday when no one celebrated with her—that kind of thing. She was the one who pushed for a relationship."

That didn't help David relax.

His brother-in-law chuckled. "Relax. She was a young and infatuated with the only man who had been there for her. She confessed on her seventeenth birthday, and he turned her down. When she grew sad, he gave her the gift she asked for . . .

"I feel it wrong to share what they did, but I will say that was when he realized they could not stay the same as they'd always been. So he wiped her memories in hopes she would have a normal life. He has remained with her, just not where she could see him."

This was not what David expected. "I figured it had to be when she was a child or when she attempted to end her life," he said, staring down at the floor while he pondered this information. "I did not think he could do something so honorable."

"I believe he only does so for her," Arthur said, a slight smile as he continued. "He's quite the big softy when it comes to her, but I think he and Jane know his actions with her are, at times, inappropriate. She allows it because it's been all she's ever had. Her husband never comforted her as Death has. He hasn't given her the affection she needs to feel loved. Death doesn't hold back."

David glared at the floor. The more he heard about Jason, the more he wanted to beat the man. He was considering letting Death share the fight with him.

Arthur sighed, his jaw clenching though he spoke calmly. "Her husband failed her, but she is loyal. That's why she seems to halt her relationship with you. She is so loyal, she now feels she has been betraying Death with Jason."

"What?" David furrowed his brow, trying to understand why she would think such a thing.

"Brother, she regained memories about their past, and she is trying to fit together the life she really had with him alongside the one where he was absent. It's overwhelming for her. Unfortunately, you are the last to arrive for her heart. She's trying to do what she thinks is right by all of you and it's tearing her apart."

"I know I should not be so affectionate with her," David muttered as his own actions with a married woman hit him. "It was just difficult to cast her aside. She is my Other, and when I thought she was going to die . . ."

"I know." Arthur nodded. "This is similar for him, I believe. I could not read his mind, but I gathered he was incredibly fearful about her future. He's not going to hold back any longer, and she may struggle refusing him."

"Great," David muttered.

Arthur laughed softly. "It is even harder for her to resist you. She is quite strong if you think about her resistance to you. Take it as a compliment, not a sign you are lesser in her heart."

David sighed. "It's her heart I worry about. Even though she cries often, I see her as one of the bravest and strongest souls I've ever met."

"Yes, she is." Arthur agreed. "She has had every opportunity, especially with that entity inside her, to embrace darkness, but she lets herself suffer instead of inflicting pain on others. It might seem foolish, but to her, she either destroys herself or unleashes it on others. Even what she has done to you and your brothers is a failure to keep her darker side back."

"Is that why she's like this now?" David asked.

"Yes. This is her mind protecting itself. I doubt that she is even aware of how or what she is doing; I am not aware of how she did it. She was drowning in fear, sorrow, and confusion. Then some inner part of her mind, or perhaps something that I cannot begin to comprehend, acted by shutting off every emotion. It's a defense mechanism. She knew she could not bear losing you or anyone else and feared what she would unleash if she did. She especially fears being the one responsible for harming you or her children. She sees no good when she looks at herself and only greatness when she thinks of you."

Warmth spread through his chest. "She is worried about me?"

Arthur smiled. "Brother, she has placed you on a very high pedestal. Only, she feels unworthy to look upon you and nowhere in her mind does she feel she deserves you."

His chest and throat tightened. "Isn't that for me to decide?"

"Perhaps you should remind her of that."

"How?" David scowled. "She does not react when I speak to her."

"I think you will be able to reach her," Arthur said calmly "She has many tactics that she's used to help her function, but she has never shut off before. Something else was happening—I am baffled as to what it was."

Yes, something wasn't natural about what she'd just done. Not that anything about her was unfolding naturally, other than his feelings for her. "Why hasn't Death come to help her?"

"I don't know," Arthur answered. "His abilities prevent me from understanding all he intends with her. I only know he has done something that impacts her, but she forgave him. I simply cannot see what it is that he's done."

David thought for a moment. "She kept saying I don't know what's happening . . . Do you think he did something to her? Or told her something about the entity that he didn't tell us?"

"Your guess is as good as mine, brother. All I know is she has been worried, but she's not angry with him. This emotional shutdown might have cut off their connection because when I try to read her now, there is almost nothing. There were literally no thoughts in her mind as you sat here talking to her. It's fascinating, but it makes my heart weep.

"She is able to think and remember, but there is no emotional response. She's there, just being kept safe. I can only compare it to watching herself move on autopilot from the outside. She knows things are happening, but she is seeing everything as though they have no relevance to her. Even her children, she knows she has them and is supposed to care, but she feels nothing."

The crushing feeling in his chest worsened. "Did she choose this?"

Arthur sighed, nodding. "She begged for it all to stop, and she sat still when everything severed within."

This didn't seem like Jane, he thought. "She wanted to fight—I don't believe she'd give up."

"She didn't give up," Arthur said quickly. "She did what she believes is necessary to save everyone."

He could only stare at Arthur for a few seconds. It made sense. She had feared darkness within, and Death had been the only one to stop her. Now her angel was gone, and she wasn't ready to battle it. Her first chance to fight, she'd begun to give over to the wickedness and failed a child that likely reminded her of her son. He'd failed as an Other to make her see that she could rely on him because she didn't know how to cope with her attraction to him.

"Exactly," Arthur said to his thoughts. "She needs the angel, or she needs to see you can share such a dangerous burden with her. I think she just needs a bit of help to hold herself up so she can fight, but she is afraid—so afraid to destroy all of us."

"How do I bring her back?"

Arthur thought for a moment then smiled. "Show her what she stands to lose. Love her. She will see her fear is nothing compared to what you offer her."

"Brother, you know she isn't ready to accept me romantically. If ever. And I am the last one to be considered."

"Last to arrive—not the last," Arthur said, a teasing gleam in his eyes. "Trust me, David. You are very high in her thoughts. Prove to her you are different from Jason and Death. All her life, those she loves, including Death, have left her or let her down in some way. Be the one who doesn't."

Arthur hesitated before he added, "You know, she reminds me of a violin. She's sad but beautiful. Powerful and fragile—all at once. No matter how dark, sad or light, she will always enchant us. So lovely."

It was a beautiful way to envision her. "She is lovely. Thank you, brother."

"You're welcome." Arthur patted his shoulder. "Go check on her. We will meet you at the house in a few hours."

"Do you know what she is doing now?" he asked, watching Arthur stand.

Absolute sorrow filled Arthur's gaze. "Staring at the floor."

David took a deep breath as he got up. "We'll see you in a few hours."

He watched Arthur walk away and then made his way upstairs. He was afraid of what he would see, and his heart broke when he pushed the door open.

Just as Arthur said, she was staring at the floor. She was against the far wall, sitting on the floor again. Just staring. The empty look on her face almost made him want to cry.

"Hey, baby." He joined her on the floor, and just like she'd done downstairs, she didn't react to him. He took her hand anyway, growing more devastated by how lifeless and cold she felt. "Whenever you want to come back, I'll be here." He lifted her hand and kissed it. "You're not alone, Jane. I'm here."

CHAPTER 35
KNIGHTS & PENGUINS

"Jane, this is Dagonet," Arthur said, gesturing to the middle-aged man beside him. "He and another guard have been watching over your family since we arrived here."

Dagonet glanced at David before nodding to her. "Pleasure to meet you, Jane."

The words came out almost robotically for her. "You as well."

David's hand enclosed around hers. She lifted her gaze to him, waiting for him to tell her what to do next, but he wasn't looking at her.

Dagonet spoke again. "It has been an honor to guard your home, Jane. I owe David a great deal, yet I am not often given the opportunity to show my gratitude to him. To protect the family of his Other has given me more peace than I ever hoped for. I might add, your children are wonderful. It's incredible to see the amount of love and care they must have received growing up."

"Thank you," she said, unsure why he felt it necessary to speak so long. "Which way are we going?"

Dagonet gestured toward the stairs behind him. "Upstairs. I will show you."

She followed behind him and entered a large bedroom very similar to the one she had at the base camp. She somewhat noticed some of the knights gathered in the room, but she didn't see a reason to acknowledge them as she stepped close to the large window.

As Jane peered down at the home she'd left behind, she wondered if it was wrong to not feel anything. The thought, and any others trying to manifest disappeared quickly, and she found herself staring at the dinosaur sheet partially visible through a few boards on a window.

"Penguin!" a happy voice cheered from within her home.

Jane didn't respond in any way.

"Penguin," they yelled again, and this time, little giggles erupted from the speaker.

Jane knew the voice. She knew it was her son talking, but she felt nothing toward him. It occurred to her how strange that seemed, but she found her thoughts fading to the back of her mind before she could think any more.

"Nathan, you have to be quiet," the sweeter, softer voice of her daughter scolded.

"Penguin," he said again.

"No, Nathan. The penguin movie is over. Come play with me."

"Play," he repeated.

"Here," she said. "You can be the good knight."

"Good might."

"Knight," she corrected him. "I'll be the evil prince who steals the princess. You save her because you're a prince, too." Jane tilted her head as she listened, not sure why she felt a light pressure against her chest. "No, Nathan—listen: I'll save you, princess . . . You say: no, you won't."

"No won't."

Natalie went on, altering her voice so it was deeper. "I'm going to keep the princess in my dungeon forever . . . Say: I will save her."

"Save," Nathan muttered.

Jane heard everything they were saying but other than the increasing pressure on her chest, their words and roles in her life were nothing more than white noise. A meaningless afterthought.

Even as she suddenly reflected on her earlier actions and wondered if she'd hurt David's feelings or if her dismissal of Dagonet's words and the knights came off rude, she couldn't feel any true concern. No hate, no love—just nothing.

Though, every so often, as if her name was called in the distance, she returned to wondering if this was all wrong, if she was supposed to stop this. Who called and what they wanted was unclear, but it hardly mattered; she was unable to respond anyway.

"Jane?" David called softly. "Are you all right?"

She blinked a few times, uneasy in his presence. He loved her, she knew, but what that felt like she couldn't grasp. It made it uncomfortable to be around him. Like she knew he was going to attempt dragging her out of the darkness where she was supposed to stay.

A deeper voice spoke from within her house. "What are you guys doing awake?"

"Jason," she said to no one, just an automatic uttering of his name.

"It's too early for you to be playing," he told their kids. "You need to go back to sleep."

She felt David's stare for a few seconds, but she ignored him and listened to her family's conversation. It was slightly bothersome to know she was supposed to love them, yet not feel a single ounce of emotion for them.

"We're not tired," Natalie whined. "And I'm hungry."

"But I am tired," Jason said. "You played all night. Can't you be quiet and sleep for another hour?"

"I don't know how," Natalie said.

"How did Jane stay sane with this?" Jason muttered.

Jane tilted her head to the side. She remembered the nights she'd gotten little sleep and had to wake early even though she was tired. Jason always slept through it all.

"Mommy?" asked Nathan.

Jane held her breath as Jason spoke to him.

"Oh, bubby," he whispered. "Mommy had to go, remember?"

David rubbed his thumb on the back of her hand. She looked down, not remembering when he had grabbed hold of it.

Nathan cried again. "Mommy!"

"*Shh*, Nathan," Jason hushed. "Mommy had to go to the doctor. They made her feel better, but she can't come home."

"Yeah, Nathan." Natalie joined in. "You want Mommy to feel better, right?"

"Mommy," he hollered.

Jane's breath suddenly rushed out as the pressure on her chest felt like a full-blown kick had been thrown through it. She looked around, panicked. It had taken so long for Nathan to even call her Mommy, and now he was screaming it as loud as he could.

Memories, both painful and joyous, roared like a freight train as they forced their way into the conscious part of her mind. All at once, they pulled her under the massive weight of every emotion she'd ever experienced.

Every. Single. One.

They yanked and held her under them until she couldn't breathe.

She tried to suck in air and looked down to where David's and her hands were joined. The warmth there grew incredibly hot as it spread up her arm.

"Baby," David whispered.

No! She didn't want this again. She would lose him. *Them!* All of them.

She'd destroy them.

It was too much. So much sorrow and fear. David's thumb caressed the back of her hand. So much love.

Her breathing grew harsher. She was stuck in a vortex of memories and emotion. She wasn't strong enough. She couldn't fight. She couldn't fail again. They'd die. She'd kill them.

Like a trapped animal, she searched the room, looking for a way to escape. The concern from the knights and Arthur was overwhelming. They weren't supposed to care. They were supposed to hate her—want nothing to do with her.

She raised a hand to her head. Everything hurt. She couldn't take anymore. Why couldn't he see that? Why did everyone think it was so easy to just keep going?

I don't want to feel anymore, she thought more violently than she expected.

She looked up at David, then back at her home where Nathan continued to cry. Jason continued his attempt to comfort their son while Natalie finally succumbed to her sorrow.

Shallower breaths escaped Jane as she listened. Their cries for her spun around her mind. She shouldn't have had to leave them. She should be the one comforting them. She should be there. She should have been good enough for them.

David stepped closer to her, but she felt so angry with him that she roughly shook his hand off hers. The knights looked at her with shock, but she glared solely at David.

Her fury vanished when she stared into his eyes. No. She wasn't mad at him; he hadn't done anything wrong. But the only way to keep the darkness from escaping was to hide it with anger. She wanted to cry but kept her furious gaze fixed on him. He looked so worried.

I'm sorry.

"Jane, it's okay," he said with all the love a man could ever give a girl. "We are here with you. It's all right to be sad."

She closed her eyes before letting out a slow breath. She wouldn't let herself hurt them.

No more. Hide.

Save them.

✦✦✦

David watched Jane breathing heavily with her eyes closed. No one spoke. No one moved except for Arthur who was clutching his head like he was experiencing the worst headache of his life. It was Jane causing it; she was in pain and Arthur was too connected with her to escape whatever she had suddenly experienced after hearing Nathan cry for her.

They all knew the risk of bringing her here, but he hadn't expected to be on the receiving end of her rage. It hurt, but he'd seen the apology in her eyes. She did care for him; she was protecting him, and he needed to stay strong for her as he looked for a way to support her.

Monsters came in all forms, and Jane's was one who looked at her in her reflection. He couldn't fight it the way he did other evil, so he'd let her beat him down so she didn't attack herself.

Finally, Jane's breathing evened, and she opened her eyes.

Empty.

Dull amber colored eyes greeted him. No green; no specks of gold fire dancing for the emerald flames that sparked from time to time. No olive-green when it swallowed the golden-brown during her sorrow. She was gone.

"I'm going to be downstairs." She didn't wait for a response, and left the room.

He stared at her retreating figure in agony. His brothers all looked from the now empty door to him, but he didn't know what to say.

"Follow her before she goes anywhere else," Arthur said coldly.

David broke out of his frozen state and walked past the others to go find her. He knew she hadn't left, but he hurried down the stairs as his senses picked up a new presence in the house.

Rage consumed him as he rounded the corner and found a man in a black cloak standing close to Jane. At first David thought it was Death, but he was leaner in build and though his hair was black and styled in the same messy spiked up style Death's hair was, his skin was pale. Very pale.

"Oh, Jane," the man said, cupping her cheek. "What has happened to you?"

David saw red. Jane's back was to him, so he rushed forward and yanked her away, shoving her behind him as he quickly enclosed his hand around the intruder's throat.

Snarling, David lifted the man off the ground. "Who are you?" He tightened his grip. "And where in the hell did you come from?"

The man let out a choked laugh, and David loosened his grip only enough so the man could answer him.

"Interesting choice of words there." He gasped and tried to free himself.

David slammed the man's back against the wall. "You have five seconds before I rip your fucking throat out."

"I do not mean you nor Jane any harm. I'm a friend."

The fact this stranger knew her name enraged him. "Leave her out of this and answer me or you will meet your death."

The man laughed sharply before responding. "Death would do worse than kill me if I ever harmed her. I would know, he's my master, after all."

"Speak your name," David shouted, his patience nearly at its end.

A painful smile worked its way on the man's pale lips. "I am Hades."

CHAPTER 36
OBLIVION

Arthur quickly moved forward and placed a hand on David's shoulder. "He's telling the truth. Let him go, David. He won't harm her."

David looked to Arthur and back at Hades before dropping him to the floor. He watched the so-called God of the Underworld stumble as he let out a growl and walked back to Jane. He cupped her face and checked her for injuries. Once satisfied she wasn't harmed, he studied her eyes. The beautiful green and brown colors he loved were absent. His Jane was still missing.

He sighed, not sure if he felt relieved because she didn't seem upset over him attacking a stranger for simply talking to her. It should have had some reaction, but she seemed completely unfazed by the uproar. David pulled her to his chest and wrapped his arms around her as he placed a quick kiss to her head.

She stood with her arms limp at her sides as he held her. She looked around her from time to time but didn't seem to really take in anything further than a physical examination before she went back to staring off at nothing.

Hades watched them quietly before he spoke again. "What happened to her?"

David mentally told Arthur to deal with things for a minute.

"She's fine," Arthur told Hades. "She's just under a lot of stress. How did you get in here without us knowing?"

Hades grinned, his smile somewhat familiar. "You learn a few things when you work for Death."

"Stop wasting our time." Gawain stormed up to Hades. "What do you want?"

Bowing his head, Hades answered calmly. "Death is my master. He gave me orders to gather those loyal to us after I informed him Ares and Hermes were close by. I had been looking for him, and that's when I noticed Hermes watching your camp. At the time, Jane and Death were outside together. He wasn't happy. He said he'd deal with it, but I haven't seen him since then.

"His last orders to me were to have my niece find the rogues your knights have been scouting." He looked at Jane. "When is the last time Death was with her?"

"He left two days ago," Arthur answered. "Do you know where he went?"

Hades shook his head. "He left me at the same time. I have a feeling he went to visit the angel Azrael. There is chaos in the different realms, not just Earth, and he may have received news that took him elsewhere."

Arthur glanced at David, then back to Hades. "Do you have a way to send for him?"

"Yes," Hades said, scanning Jane. "She should, as well. If he can sense her, of course."

David sighed and hugged Jane. She wasn't feeling anything, and that meant Death had no idea she needed help.

"Does he have a telepathic link to her?" Arthur asked.

Hades shrugged. "He doesn't speak about her to anyone. I have known of her, though nothing other than a female must be on his mind."

Arthur paced, continuously darting his gaze to Jane though he continued with Hades. "Do you have a telepathic link to him, then?"

"My bond allows me to send a distress signal." He laughed lightly. "He rarely comes. I doubt he will care since he does not know I'm with her. Should I try anyway?"

Arthur sighed. "No. If he has business, let him attend to it. We can discuss why you came here."

Hades relaxed, his tone shifting to one of a warrior preparing for battle. "I met with one of my niece's scouts. They attacked the rogues and suffered losses. The rogues are using new weaponry none of them have seen before."

"And Ares and Hermes?" Arthur asked.

"I was tracking Hermes, but I think he knew I was following him. He led me to the south, then I lost all traces of him. When I came back here, I picked up signs he had joined with Ares. The problem is they are traveling faster than I am capable on my own, and they can hide themselves. Though, with the pattern they've continued, I fear they are planning out an attack on your knights."

Gawain scoffed. "Are we supposed to believe you're here to warn us? This sounds like a trap you Olympians schemed up."

"Have you ever seen me among the Olympians, Knight?" Hades' pale eyes flashed as his features sharpened. "Since the age when men worshiped my brother, I have been Death's servant. If you doubt me, ask your king to inform you what he has been digging out of my mind."

Arthur held up a hand to Gawain. "He is a loyal servant of Death. We will trust him for now. After all, Death will do worse if he betrays us."

"Yes, he would." Hades expression softened as his attention fell on Jane. "I have seen first-hand what he does to those who bring her harm, and I have no desire to be on the receiving end of his wrath."

"I thought he didn't speak of her," Gawain said, giving Hades an accusatory glare.

"You don't understand–Death feels nothing for anyone," Hades told him before his eyes drifted toward Jane. "But I was there when he skinned a demon alive—a demon who cried her name before Death ripped out his tongue for even speaking it. Actions speak louder than words. She is all he sees, feels, desires."

As David listened, his respect for Death rose. He knew why Death would torture a demon. The angel really loved her. So much that he would hide her from his own servants and stop another being from even knowing about her existence.

Arthur watched no reaction on Jane's face and changed the subject. "What were you planning to do with the rogues?"

"I want to attack before they increase in numbers," Hades told him. "If they join with Ares and Hermes, we are all in danger. I hoped we could combine forces, eliminate the rogues, then focus on my nephews."

"How far are the rogues?" Arthur asked. "Do you have any information on Lancelot?"

"The rogues will take half a day to reach," Hades informed them. "Last I heard on Lancelot was he headed north."

David glanced down at Jane. She was at least focused on Hades but there was none of the excitement his Jane would no doubt display at being in the presence of a *god*.

"If we leave now, we will reach their camp by sunset." Hades took a step in David and Jane's direction. "I think it unwise to let Jane come."

David held her tighter. There was no way he was leaving her.

Arthur sighed. "David, he's probably right. Jane is in no state to fight or travel right now. You will only be distracted if she is there. Plus, she has yet to engage other vampires. We don't want to have a repeat of the first time she fought the wolves."

David let out a harsh breath before he pulled back and tilted her face up. She stared at him without fear, anger or sadness. He rubbed her cold cheek, then pulled her back to his chest as he returned his gaze to Arthur and Hades. "She fought bravely in her first and second battles."

"I did not mean she was not brave," Arthur said. "Like you, I do not wish to see her like that again. What's happening in her head is not safe."

They all glanced down at her, but she didn't seem to care they were talking about her.

"She doesn't care," Arthur said, responding to David's thoughts. "She is only watching. She cannot come with us."

David swallowed, wondering if Arthur meant she would never return. He pushed her hair aside and cupped one side of her face so she'd look up. She did, but his baby wasn't looking back at him. "I need a moment with her," he told the others.

Arthur gestured with a nod for everyone to leave. "Take your time. We will prepare what we need to leave. She will be safe here, David. Dagonet and Lucan will keep an eye on her, and we will be back before you know it."

David gave them a stiff nod while he eyed Hades, who had yet to take his eyes off Jane.

Hades smiled softly at Jane and walked up to them. "It's lovely to finally meet you, Jane. You have no idea how much you mean to Death, young beauty. You are so loved. Never forget or doubt his or your knight's love for you."

David was surprised to see a flicker of emerald color spread through her eyes, but it faded before he could begin to hope.

"Don't give up," Hades told her. "You are stronger than you think." He stared at her for a few seconds before sighing and leaving the same way the others had gone.

"Let me feed you, sweetheart," David said, looking back down after a few short moments. She didn't respond, so he took her hand and led her into a bedroom nearby.

✦✦✦

Jane knew David was leaving with Hades and the others. She knew was upset about leaving her, or perhaps he was upset about everything that had happened earlier.

She had already gotten over the incident upstairs. She'd brushed the thing aside.

A tingling sensation manifested as David brushed his fingers along her jaw. He paused and watched her. His hand remained, slowly warming her skin with tiny sparks bursting where he touched her.

"Sweetheart," he said, trailing his finger and those sparks along her jawline. It felt nice now, not like a fire threatening to engulf her. "Are you going to be all right if I go?"

She ignored the sudden desire to lean into his hand. "Yes."

"Come here." He pulled her to sit sideways on his lap and offered his wrist. "Drink. I don't want anything happening while I am gone." All her focus went to the pulse. "Go on, sweetheart."

She pulled his arm to her mouth and bit without thinking. Sweet blood poured down her throat, and a faint current hummed between them. She remembered she had loved connecting with him this way, and now she felt herself wanting to connect with him in every way.

It will hurt when he's gone . . .

Jane immediately stopped sucking and let go of his arm. She glanced around the room, almost expecting to find someone in there with them.

He will let you down like they all do, another thought whispered.

Her head throbbed. She hadn't meant to think of connecting with him, but the electric shock of his touch and blood made something powerful rise inside her. Heat pulsed in her chest and she realized its rhythm matched his heartbeat. Every beat, something roared and pounded as if it was trapped behind a door.

She glanced at David. He was so handsome.

There was the urge to feel more of him, but she didn't want this. She couldn't want anything without . . .

As his blue eyes drifted over her, the despair washing down on her shifted. The spark ignited, giving her a painful sting, then slowly burned her heart.

Why was he doing this? Didn't he know she would ruin him?

The burning feeling she once craved from him would consume her. She would do something she'd never be able to take back. Then he'd leave. One way or another, he'd leave, and she'd be in agony.

She looked back at his worried stare and forced all thoughts and feelings away. She didn't know how she could do it while looking into those eyes of his, but she did.

Perhaps it as the icy prick to her wrist and sliding into her veins that did it. The sensation reminded her of receiving pain medication intravenously.

The cold liquid feeling crawled up her arm, chasing the fire that had spread until it cornered and smothered it in lovely ice.

She sighed and embraced the numbing anesthetic.

David sighed and cupped her face as he shook his head. "No," he said. "No, Jane, come back to me. I saw you." He forced her to stare at him. "Look at me; stop looking through me and listen to me. I know you don't want to feel any more pain, and you're afraid to lose me. Believe me, I wish I could take away all your pain. I can't, though. But I swear I will be with you through it all." He smoothed her hair back. "You don't have to worry about me leaving; I will be with you. Always."

She blinked once.

David sighed as his eyes fell to her pink lips. He lowered his face to hers until their lips were almost touching. His breath even swept across her lips. "Baby, where are you?" His thumb rubbed her cheek. "Even your body feels cold and empty. Where are you, Jane?"

He moved closer but stopped and glanced up at her eyes. For a few seconds, he stared at her, then leaned forward and kissed her cheek. He pulled back enough to rest his forehead against hers. "I love you."

It was like a damn match lit in her chest again. *Please not again.*

"I will always love you," he went on. "And I will wait for you. But wherever you are hiding, listen to me—I am here. I will always be here. You don't have to face your battles alone. I can be with you. I want to be there to hold you through whatever you face. Please let me have that chance. Why can't you see I'm not like them?"

She let out a harsh breath, and he pulled back to see watery eyes.

"There you are." He caressed her hair, his blue eyes glowing as he touched her as much as possible. "Stay, Jane. Just stay."

"You should go," she said, not showing any distress, though her lungs felt like they were engulfed in flames while her eyes burned right along with them.

"No, baby, I saw you." His eyes darted between hers, though his hope appeared to dim.

That was what she needed. She needed him to give up on her. So, she fixed her gaze over his shoulder and told him, "The others are waiting for you."

He tried to get her to look at him, tilting her chin, but she refused to meet his stare.

Eventually, he sighed and leaned forward, kissing her forehead. "I love you," he murmured, leaving his lips against her skin, feeding the inferno burning her from the inside. "I'll be back. I am only going to help the others, but I will be back. Just stay here."

She nodded and pulled out of his hold.

"Get Dagonet if you need anything."

She nodded again and tried her best to keep her face neutral.

He hesitated then blurted, "We can go to the creek."

"No," she replied in an instant, her panic skyrocketing. "I'm fine." *I'm not fine!*

His jaw clenched, and the muscles in his arms jumped. "It's okay to not be fine, Jane," he said, lowering his eyes to hers when she stood there frozen. "I'm strong enough to hold your hand through all this. I want to."

"Just go." She stepped farther away from him. "I'll be okay."

He looked up at the ceiling briefly before he looked back to her. He didn't say anything else and left.

Jane opened and closed her mouth over and over as she stared at the closed door. She couldn't get enough air.

Tears gathered, ready to pour down her face as she listened to him talking to someone. She tried to cry out for him to come back—to not leave her, but she couldn't make a sound.

As their footsteps faded and the front door shut, she frantically looked all around the room as if she could find protection or something to save her—anything to fix whatever was being ripped from her chest.

Rip them apart, something whispered to her mind.

She mutely sobbed and shook her head at the menacing thought. *No. Please no.*

Nothing will stop you, it said. *No one can stop you.*

She finally stumbled back to the bed and sat down, still looking for something that could make it better.

Nothing will help. Nothing here, at least.

She needed to hide again. She nodded to herself as she thought this. Hide inside her mind—where nothing hurt. She had to get there again. And this time, she'd build stronger walls to keep David and the others out.

Yes. Hide inside. You could hurt him. Is that what you want?

She shook her head. No, they couldn't come close again. She didn't want to hurt him.

It would be so horrible.

Please stop, she begged the thoughts to go away.

David would have to give up after a while. She just had to make it so she couldn't hear him. That way he would lose hope. He was too good for her.

He is too good for you. Let him go. You keep saying you will . . . Do it.

All Jane could do was open her mouth as a silent cry went unnoticed. So, she accepted the silence and surrendered to the chill now seeking out the warmth David had left behind.

Her rapidly beating heart slowed, and her breathing became effortless as she continued to stare at the wall in front of her, emptying her mind. The cold, numbing sensation crept in, stronger now.

Minute after minute passed, and each second of those minutes, she slipped further into oblivion.

She would gladly sit there undisturbed until she rotted, but a flicker of white light suddenly warmed the side of her face.

Not bothered, she merely tilted her head to get a better look at the man standing before her. She didn't think she recognized him, but something about him seemed familiar enough.

He stayed quiet and watched her, his face just as inexpressive as hers. Slowly, though, a malicious smile crept up on his handsome face.

She did not react, and his gray eyes seemed to gleam with satisfaction at this. Still, he said nothing, but after smiling almost cruelly for a short moment, his gaze softened. She still did not react, and he kept quiet as he gazed into her eyes.

He gracefully knelt in front of her before reaching out with his right hand to touch her cheek.

She didn't move—didn't flinch when his cold fingers slid down around her jaw. She stared at his neatly combed blond hair and perfect features.

He rubbed her lips with his thumb. "Hello, Jane." Her lips parted on their own, and he gave her a brilliant smile. "I am Lucifer."

She should've been afraid, but she wasn't. In fact, she felt safe in his presence.

His beauty and smile promised her something. Somehow, even without knowing what it was exactly, she wanted that promise.

"Hello," she said.

He smiled again. "I will not hurt you. I only want to talk." When she nodded, he continued. "I know what you're feeling, Jane. You are afraid of hurting again. You have been hurt so much, haven't you?"

"Yes. I don't want to hurt anymore. I can't—I can't do it anymore." Even though her voice gave no hint of emotion, she could tell he saw her desperation. The way he stared at her, she felt he had found where she was hiding.

"I know," he said. "I am sorry you were hurt. I promise you I was never aware of your sufferings."

Jane tilted her head as she searched his face. "I believe you."

He smoothed her hair back, smiling. It was fake, but a breathtaking smile nonetheless.

"Thank you, Jane," he said, as his gaze moved between her eyes. She wondered why he looked genuinely touched by her trust. "I know Death has told you of our wager; you have nothing to fear from me. I only seek to give you all you have ever desired, and I know what it is you desire more than anything: to keep your loved ones safe, and to not be tortured inside your mind."

She nodded.

"I can keep you from feeling that pain again," he said. "I can help you forget it all. Isn't that what you want?" His cold fingers trailed down her neck, spreading a numbing sensation.

Yes, that's what she wanted. It hurt too much to not have her family. To not have Death by her side. To not return David's love.

She nodded, and his smile grew.

"I will make it go away," he told her. "And then they will be safe. But you must come to me. I cannot help you here. You must get away from them. Will you do that?"

He could give her what she wanted, but David's smile surfaced in her mind, and her lip trembled. She wanted him to come back.

Lucifer was there, though, and he quickly pulled her into his arms. "*Shh* . . . I will make it go away." His alluring voice softened as he tilted her face up. He did not explain, and she stayed still as he lowered his mouth to the corner of hers.

Ice. Lovely ice spread out from his kiss, smothering all the warmth that lingered without her knowing.

David's face and loving smile slowly faded from her mind, Death's sweet kisses and comfort vanished from her soul, Natalie and Nathan's laughter, and her commitment to Jason—all of it—banished from her entire being.

Sweet oblivion.

Lucifer pulled back and studied her for a few quiet seconds before his eyes glinted with silver, and he grinned. "That's better now, isn't it?"

"Yes," said Jane, though she hardly felt aware of what happened around her now.

"It is temporary unless you come to me. Will you come to me, Jane?"

"Yes."

"Good. It's not far from here. You must go alone. I cannot take you because this is something you must do on your own. But I will be waiting for you at the cemetery nearby. Do you know which one I mean?"

Somehow she did, and she nodded.

"That is where I can take you to a place where you will never feel pain again. I will take it all away. You only have to wait until the guard comes to check on you, then you must slip out the window after he leaves."

"Okay."

"That's a good girl. Come to me, and I will make everything better. Nothing will ever hurt you again. No more pain. No more sadness or fear. Nothing. You will feel nothing."

Jane stared up at him. "Nothing," she said softly.

With a victorious smile, he lowered his head and pressed his lips against hers. She didn't kiss back, but it hardly seemed to matter to him.

He pulled away from her mouth and looked over his shoulder. "The guard is coming. Dismiss him, then do as I have instructed."

Jane nodded back, and he pulled her face to his once again, kissing her harder this time. Still, she remained frozen, and still, he didn't appear to care.

After he stopped kissing her, he kept his lips close. "I will be waiting. It's almost over, Jane." Another chilly kiss. "Come to me."

CHAPTER 37

DAGONET'S TALE

Get away from the guards . . . That's all Jane could think while she continued to stare at the empty space where Lucifer had been standing. Lucifer. He would help her. He would make it all better. Nothing else mattered, just getting to him.

There was a light knock on the door.

"Yes?" She hardly recognized the sound of her detached voice.

The door opened slowly to reveal Dagonet, the guard she somewhat remembered meeting. He smiled before he took a single step into the room. She knew he must be a kind man, but all she saw when she looked at him was an obstacle on her quest to join Lucifer.

"Hello again," he said. "I wanted to make sure you were holding up all right—I'm about to take up my post again."

It was then she remembered where she was: the house neighboring her old home and her family.

Not a single ounce of emotion manifested at the thought of them.

"I'm fine," she said.

He frowned and stepped into the room. "Are you sure?"

She stared back, unaffected by his concern. "Yes, I'm sure. You can return to your post. I'll come find you if I need anything."

"You know, Jane. I have suffered similar losses to those that you have experienced. Obviously you have suffered in ways I have not, but I do understand what it's like to lose one's family."

"I'm fine, honestly."

He ignored her clear refusal to have this conversation. "I don't mean to be impolite, but you are not fine. Closing yourself off like this is dangerous. I know it hurts to feel so much pain; I really do, but you will regret what you are doing right now."

Jane looked at the man in front of her curiously. He looked much different from her knights. Physically, he appeared to be older, but she was certain that wasn't the case. Then she realized she couldn't look away from his black eyes. A Damned.

Despite her mind screaming to get away from him, she asked, "What happened to you?"

He smiled and sat next to her. "I was one of Guinevere's, David's sister, guards. At the time, I did not know that Arthur and his knights were immortals. No one did. There were rumors when he dismissed many from court—he only kept a few he deemed worthy to sit at his round table, which happened to be the few foreigners Kay, his adopted brother, had been sent to locate.

"After Arthur wed Guinevere, the king showed interest in David's skills. Since David's older brother had taken the throne at their kingdom, Arthur used Guinevere as a reason to invite David into his elite group of knights. David accepted, honored to be allowed a seat at Arthur's Round Table.

"Others came with David, court resumed, and Arthur's strange behavior and appearance were forgotten. After all, the kingdom prospered, and his chosen knights were honorable and brave.

"It all changed a single night. Arthur requested I go to Guinevere's chambers. I left my wife and newborn son because my duty was to my queen." He sighed and rubbed his face. "I took my post. I knew my queen was very stressed; she couldn't stop pacing, but she asked about my son."

His tone softened as a smile came over his face. "His name was Matthew. He was only one month old, but I loved him as if I had always done so. As I began telling her more about how he was growing each day, she panicked and told me to return home. I did not understand the sudden change in her, but she ordered me to leave her—to go to my wife and son, and bring them back with me. I realized, then, the threat was already inside the castle walls.

"I ran as fast as I could to reach our home. There were people screaming in the streets. Our forces were engaged at every turn, but I ignored my duty as a soldier and ran to my family. When I arrived, I knew I had been too late. My home had been ransacked.

"I called out for Meghan, but she did not answer. I heard Matthew, though. His cries were weak and fading, but I ran to our room where I could hear him. That is where I found Meghan, face down in a puddle of her own blood. I could tell she had fought her attackers, but she was already dead."

He paused, rubbing the moisture from his dark eyes as he cleared his throat. "After I realized Meghan was gone, I focused on finding Matthew. He had stopped crying, but I heard a strangled noise coming from the side of our bed. His neck had been ripped open."

He blew out a hard breath and hesitated for a few seconds before speaking again. "I lifted him into my arms and did my best to apply pressure to the wound on his neck. He was so small. I knew with the amount of blood on the floor that my son was going to die in my arms. Still, I yelled out for someone to help me. My shout startled him, and when I looked down, he had opened his blue eyes. *My eyes*. He had my eyes."

Dagonet smiled sadly. "I told him that I loved him—that he brought so much joy to my life and to not be frightened anymore because Papa was with him now."

Jane sat quietly still and watched a tear as it slowly slid down his cheek.

"His breathing stopped. My wife and son were gone. I could not accept what had happened yet, and I began to rock him, humming the lullaby that Meghan always sang to him. I did not hear others as they reentered my home. When I did, it was too late.

"I did not know it at the time—did not even know of the madness of the creatures who shared this planet with us, but a cursed vampire—two actually, attacked with strength and speed I could not begin to comprehend.

"I fought, but I did not care if I died. My family was gone, I wanted to join them. However, they had other plans. They had nearly drained me, and I unknowingly drank their cursed blood. That is what the attack had been about—taking Arthur's army.

"Anyhow, I had taken enough for the change when David and Arthur came to my aid. They killed the two immortals with ease, and that was when I realized my king and prince were not who I had believed them to be.

"I begged for them to kill me, but David argued and stopped Arthur from carrying out my last wish. I changed, and they kept me in their service after locking me away for ten years. I never wanted to take a life the way those beasts had taken my family; David helped me with that. He instructed me on how to feed without taking a life. He helped me see my curse as a way to help rid the world of the evil that took everything I held dear. I owe him everything."

The smile he wore was one of gratitude and acceptance. "There will be a day I pass, finally, and though I remain cursed to darkness, and I will spend eternity in Hell because of my forbidden creation, I will die knowing I have saved others from the fate my Meghan and Matthew befell. Until that day, I will remain one of the Damned. A man whose heart stopped but whose soul remained chained to his immortal body." He smiled sadly, and she did not react.

"Thank you for sharing this with me," Jane said. "And I'm sorry you've lost and suffered."

He put a cold hand over hers where it rested on her lap and squeezed it gently. "Thank you, Jane. I want you to understand there are others who know pain like you. It may not match your sufferings, but I do understand most of it. I know you are different, though. I know you are more powerful and dangerous than any of the rest of us.

"Along with all the sorrow and loss you are dealing with, I imagine you must be terrified. It must seem like there is no hope—that you are all alone. I, too, have struggled with loneliness. The others, my fellow knights, they are always there, but there is a loneliness and sadness that they have yet to know.

"I know what it's like to look at a good man like David and fear you will never live up to his hopes for you. He sacrificed years of his time to train and strengthen me against the darkness inside me, and not once did he look down upon me. Arthur did not trust me—he could see my dark thoughts. But David, even with Arthur's warnings, he never gave up on me. He will not give up on you."

Jane's eyes watered, and she had no words to say to him.

He spoke again. "Pushing him away—pushing all of it away—will ruin you. Do not carry on like this. Feeling even the worst of pain and sadness is better than feeling nothing. With pain, you have happiness and love. David, your children, husband, and knights, they cherish every beat of your heart.

"Whatever frightens you, let David stand beside you as you fight against it. He will not think badly of you. He is not frightened of the evil lurking inside you. Believe me, that man has never gone into a battle afraid. But when he came to me—telling me about you—I saw fear in him for the first time."

"I know," she said. "I attacked him and Gareth. I'm a monster."

The old knight shook his head and chuckled softly. "No, dear girl. He was not afraid *of* you or the creature that hides within you." He lifted his hand to turn her chin so she would be forced to meet his gaze. "He feared he would lose you to it. He feared he was not enough to give you power over that darkness. Out of all the monsters he has fought, do not let it be *you* who takes you from him."

Dagonet smiled and let go of her chin. "You are everything he has ever dreamed of. He will not disappoint you, and you can do nothing for him to think badly of you. Even your children, though he does not realize it himself, are a blessing to him. He will not let harm come to them. He will give his life if it means keeping them safe for you. Whether you are here matters not; they will be protected.

"I, myself, will not leave my duty to them—even if Arthur asks me to. So do not worry, you are not the only one taking care of them now."

"Thank you," she whispered.

"You deserve to have happiness," he said. "And David deserves to be at your side for it."

Her breath caught in her throat. She needed to leave. His speech and his description of David's feelings for her were too much to deal with. Whatever Lucifer did to her must have come to an end. He had said it wouldn't last.

"Again, thank you." A pathetic excuse for a grateful smile formed on her face. "What you've said means a lot to me. But I promise I'll be fine."

"All right, Jane," he said with a sigh. "I am here, though, should you desire to speak to someone who will not judge you. I know the others do not, but it seems like almost everyone is when you feel this way about yourself. But do not doubt David. He may not understand completely, but he would give anything if it meant he could help you."

She nodded, and he patted her hand before he left the room.

Jane blew out a breath and stood up. For a moment, she stared out the window and thought over what he said. She wanted to believe in his words, but she knew no matter what, eventually, she would lose them all.

Tears slipped from her eyes as she looked down at her home. No more voices called out; they must have gone back to sleep, but she could hear their heartbeats. It both broke her heart as much as it relieved her.

She covered her mouth to suppress her cry, realizing everything that she had done now. To her family, to David and the knights. To herself.

It was too late. She could feel the hatred inside. It was building and burning as her sorrow returned. Lucifer's magic had worn off, and she knew she was not strong enough to keep any of them safe. No matter what Dagonet said, she could not overcome the fear of destroying them.

Her only hope was to let Lucifer numb her. She would let him take her away. She would become nothing so they could have a chance, so they could have everything. Everything but her.

CHAPTER 38

THE VIRGIN GODDESS

David couldn't shake off the urge to return to Jane. He still didn't know why he left her at all.

"Do not worry, Sir David." Hades came up beside him. "If there is serious harm upon her, Death will come."

David eyed the vampire wearing a black cloak. Hades had said it was a gift from Death that protected him from the sun. It covered him well, but David could still make out his pale blue eyes and ivory skin.

Hades continued. "Whatever happened to her recently eludes me, but he has always been able to pull her out of darkness. She may not realize how often he was there with her, and though I know he wishes he had done more, I cannot see anyone else doing what he has for her."

David's jaw tightened at this. He felt he should be the only one to bring her out of darkness, not Death. "I thought you didn't know much about her."

"I've heard him speaking to himself." Hades shrugged, grimacing. "He didn't have to say her name or list off all she was suffering for me to gather she was going through hell, or that he had wished he had done more to comfort her."

Nodding, David accepted the reminder that Death had been there first. She wasn't going to accept help when even her angel was gone. "I just have a bad feeling about leaving her," he told Hades.

The immortal laughed lightly. "Well, new romances are like that."

"Jane and I are not in that type of relationship," David said tersely. "I think your master holds that title."

Hades gave him a dismissive look. "Death would not be so temperamental if he was in a romantic relationship with her."

David almost smiled at him. "I do not take Death as the type to not be temperamental."

"He should be unable to feel any emotion," Hades said matter of factly. "Do not get me wrong; he has always appeared cruel and arrogant, but it is simply his nature to be uncaring. It is human nature to be offended when someone does not display their concern. If you are not kissing someone's ass, you are considered unkind.

"I am sure you can relate. I've heard rumors of your unpleasant nature, though if one inquired more to the story, it is clear the matter or persons involved are of no immediate importance to you."

"It is usually regarding a female, I know," David muttered.

"Exactly. You have had no interest in one, except for the possibility of meeting your Other. Your lack of enthusiasm for another female results in you being labeled insensitive. It is the same for Death. However, where you are capable of feeling anger or happiness, he does not—and that is purely a result of his making. He takes life because it is his purpose, nothing more. He is neutral. If he were to feel any emotion toward a soul, it would become complicated, wouldn't you agree?"

"I suppose it would complicate his duty," David admitted.

"Undoubtedly. It might not matter when it comes to him seeing her, I'm afraid."

"Well, she does have a unique charm that draws you in."

Hades nodded, agreeing. "It's not only her personality either. She emits a physical pull for some reason."

"You feel it as well?"

"Not as much as I did before. It is as though she is not quite there herself."

"She isn't," David whispered.

"I suppose it was only a matter of time before she finally had enough. With him gone, perhaps she becomes unstable as well?"

David grunted. In his opinion, Jane should rely on him for stability. All the other wives did. *But she's not my wife.*

"I apologize," Hades said softly. "I suppose it bothers you to hear about their attachment to one another."

David didn't reply and, after several more minutes, Hades pointed toward a large house at the edge of an empty field. They all nodded and slowed to make their way toward it.

"It's fine," David finally said. "I have to accept his presence in her life, along with her family's. Understanding their relationship helps me cope with the fact I am not significant in her heart."

"Of course you are," Hades said quickly. "And Death knows that." David paused before entering the front door as Hades grinned. "Hang in there, bud. Everything happens for a reason."

David chuckled, following him into the house. "I truly hope so. Who are we meeting here exactly?"

As the words left his mouth, a feminine voice spoke from the sitting room. "Hello, David. It's always a pleasure to see you." A petite, green-eyed brunette came closer. Her dark brown hair was pulled back into a French braid, and the short black hunting dress she wore showed off her fit body.

"Artemis," David greeted, keeping his tone polite. He didn't have a problem with the woman, who many still identified as a virgin goddess rather than a vampire, but he felt foolish for not realizing sooner she was the niece Hades had spoken of.

"Oh, boy," Gawain muttered under his breath before heading to the next room.

David glared at the empty doorway his best friend escaped through.

"It has been too long." She looked up at him with eager eyes and an enchanting smile. "How have you been?"

David darted his eyes to Hades, and thankfully, he seemed to understand David's silent plea for help.

"David has found his Other," Hades blurted out.

"Really?" Artemis asked, a brief hurt look flashing across her face.

David took a step back to gain some breathing room. "Yes," he said with a smile as he realized that was nothing but the truth. He found his Jane.

Her eyes narrowed at him. "Well, where is she?"

David frowned at the nastiness in her tone and felt an instant urge to defend Jane.

Hades jumped in again, though. "She's busy." His harsh tone caused her to quickly shrink back and lower her head. All the friendliness from moments ago was gone. "I'm sure David would like to return to her quickly, so let us go over the information you've gathered."

"Yes, Uncle," she said softly and left the room without another word.

David sighed and gave Hades a grateful look.

A light laugh slipped out of the vampire's mouth, and he gave David a slap on the back—his friendly demeanor returned once again. "Even the most chaste and noble women can fall victim to the green-eyed monster." David chuckled as Hades went on. "I cherish my niece, but she should not behave in such a way. Am I correct in assuming she has no claim over you?"

David quickly stopped his laughing and shook his head. "No, of course not. I mean, there were times when I questioned my Other's existence, and entertained the idea of settling for someone else, but I couldn't. My heart told me she was out there." He smiled and looked in the direction he knew Jane was until Hades' loud laugh broke his reverie.

"You're a good man, Sir David." Hades' grin stretched wide over his face. "Come. Let's get this over with so you can get back to the young beauty."

✦✦✦

David pushed a branch out of his way and glanced around the makeshift camp. Thirty men and at least a dozen women were scattered around the run-down site. Battered tents and smoldering campfires were all they had for shelter besides the abandoned barn they surrounded.

"This is ridiculous." Gawain squatted next to David. "They could have taken these out themselves."

David side eyed him and shrugged. "Artemis says their new weaponry has cost her many losses. She's in over her head. We should be careful."

"I am always careful," Gawain said. David gave him a disbelieving look. "All right, not always. But I do not see why we are necessary."

"She has lost men, Gawain."

"She will lose her pretty face if she sneers one more time Jane is mentioned in her presence," Gawain snapped. "I have no problem hitting a woman if she is foolish enough to threaten Jane. It was enough she mocked her absence. I should knock her on her stuck-up ass."

"No, you shouldn't," David said, smiling. "But I do not think she means anything by her comments."

Gawain snorted, shaking his head. "David, you're a fool. You have been the most sought-after male of our kind. These women are going to flip when they find out about Jane."

"I do not know why. I have never given any of them false hope." He didn't like dealing with women. He was polite until they tried to be more forward.

Gawain chuckled. "Tell that to Artemis and Melody. It doesn't matter you feel nothing for them. In their minds, they are the best choice for you, and it is only a matter of time before you see that. But as I said—I have no problem hitting a woman who messes with Jane. She's like the baby sister I always wanted."

"Shut up, you will not."

"Yeah, maybe not," Gawain admitted with a grin. "I'll sic Elle and Gwen on 'em."

They both laughed softly as David received a signal from Arthur in his earpiece. "They spotted Ares and Hermes," he told Gawain, losing his smile. "We have to move now."

Gawain nodded and moved into position. While David began to signal they were ready, an arrow suddenly shot into the camp and plunged directly into a man's chest.

The rogues reacted quickly, unleashing a near instant assault of gunfire. The knights, as well as Artemis' team of Hades and five other vampires, did not let that stop them from rushing in for the attack.

The rogues fired their weapons recklessly as they darted in various directions. They hissed and snarled like wild animals, not displaying any trace of their humanity. David knew their new instincts had taken over. They were soulless monsters.

David, the knights, and Hades all came in for hand to hand while Artemis and her team stayed back to cut off any fleeing.

Cries of pain sounded in all directions. David blocked all of it out and grabbed a brown-haired male preparing to attack Gawain. David squeezed his throat and slammed him onto the ground. The sickening crack of a spine didn't bother him, and he swung his sword, removing the man's head completely.

He didn't wait before moving to the next. Swinging swiftly, he dismembered another vampire and already had another lying in his wake. He cut them in half.

Blood sprayed across his chest as he ripped his sword from his fifth victim's throat. The vampire's head dangled from his neck while he swayed on his feet. David merely shoved the lifeless body to the ground, out of his way.

David would have continued without letting anything stop him, but he had trained himself to recognize distress from his team, which is why he hesitated at the sound of a grunt.

He turned his head and saw Tristan holding his leg as blood spread down his pants. Tristan collapsed with a groan.

"Shit," David said, rushing to his side.

Tristan nodded over David's shoulder, not too concerned over his injury. David wasn't either and turned to grab the approaching man roughly by the hair, completely ripping his head off without a second thought. Blood squirted out of his neck like an out of control hose. He tossed the mutilated head to the side in disgust and turned back to Tristan.

"Silver?" David asked.

Tristan nodded and stopped David from helping him up. "Don't. I can't stand. It's already spreading through my system. It burns, and it's moving through my bloodstream." He smiled. "It's not fatal."

David nodded and handed Tristan his spare gun. The battle was nearing its end when he spotted Ares running off.

He looked to the trees and found Artemis letting loose arrow after arrow. She had told them she would focus on the females—the men always had a hard time killing women, cursed or not.

"Artemis," he shouted, getting her attention instantly. "Ares." She nodded and jumped from her spot on the tree to chase him. That wasn't what he intended for her to do.

"Dammit, David," Tristan scolded. "She's going to get herself killed. Go. I'll be fine."

David stood and followed her. He could barely make out her silhouette ahead. She was fast, not as fast as himself, but she still had a head start.

The wind blew through his hair and branches smacked his bloody arms as he raced through the trees. He could hear others following. He didn't know if they were friends or enemies, but his goal was to get to Artemis before she tried to take on her brother; she'd be no match for him.

Her scream had him speeding up, and he burst through the tree line to find her fighting off three rogues. Ares was nowhere to be found.

Artemis was wounded, and David didn't hesitate to turn his attention to her three attackers. They were unarmed, so it was no effort to slay them.

Swinging his sword, he ran it through the first cursed vampire. He was only wearing a pair of ripped jeans and covered in blood. He was very emaciated; nearly every bone was protruding from his pale skin.

David ignored his strange appearance and ripped the sword from the lifeless vampire's chest. He turned in time to see Gawain removing the heads of another two who had joined the attack. With a final swing, David decapitated the other two he first spotted. Easy.

He bent down to extend a hand to Artemis. She smiled up at him, too brightly for his liking, and swayed a bit when she got to her feet. She fell toward him, and he caught her around the waist.

"Oh, thank you, David." She leaned against him. "I do not think I would have survived without your help."

Gawain rolled his eyes before leaving them to check the other bodies. David examined the cut on her side. It exposed part of her toned stomach but wasn't deep at all. She tried to lean into him for more unneeded support.

It was then that David realized he was still holding her and quickly let go. "It doesn't look that bad."

She batted her dark eyelashes up at him. "Are you sure? It really hurts."

David sighed, trying to think of a nice way to dismiss her when Hades came marching out of the woods.

"Artemis! What the hell was that? Why would you run off by yourself? You could have been killed." Hades came to a halt in front of the pair. Except for the fact that he looked as if he'd bathed in a tub of blood, he didn't appear to be injured.

"I apologize, Uncle. David yelled that Ares was getting away, and I wanted to ensure he did not."

She tried to step closer to David, but Hades yelled out again. "Silly, infatuated girl." Hades glared at her and grabbed her arm to keep her still. "You knew he meant for you to take a shot at him—not to run off by yourself. Ares is not an idiot, and you are no match for him. You're trying to show off and nearly got yourself killed. This could have been a trap!"

She glared up at Hades while David and the others dropped their gazes to the floor at her scolding.

Hades sighed. "Go get cleaned up. We kept one alive for questioning and Ares is long gone by now. Hermes got away as well. We will not find them tonight."

"Yes, Uncle." She bowed before speeding off toward the camp.

David felt bad. "It was my fault. I should not have made her think she should take him on by herself."

Hades raised a hand, silencing him before he could say more. "This is not your fault. She made a foolish mistake because she is trying to impress you. She's one of the best fighters I know, but she stands no chance against Ares. Thank you for keeping her safe. I am in your debt."

David nodded and began to follow behind the others who had joined them. They were gathering up the bodies to take back to the barn.

"Let's hurry up," said Gawain. "This looks to only be a feeding and weapons exchange camp. Their meals are piled in the barn, waiting to be burned."

David shook his head at their savagery and arrived back where the remainder of their group had begun to clean up. He walked up to Tristan who was being treated by Bedivere. "Are you all right, Tristan?"

"Yes, it will heal in time." Tristan grimaced as he looked at his bandaged leg. "It's silver nitrate. I won't be able to get it out of my system easily."

"Who uses that?" David asked.

"Rogues do." Arthur said as he came to inspect Tristan's wound. He sighed and rubbed his neck nervously before looking at David. "The rogue we captured isn't talking, but there's more you should know about. They have maps that show our camp."

David quickly stood up as Arthur gave him a worried look.

"They have pictures of Jane and her home," Arthur said. "They know about her, David."

CHAPTER 39
MANIA

Jane stopped walking and listened carefully as she scanned the dark street. A fluttering noise breezed past her. She turned around quickly but saw nothing.

She didn't have any weapons with her. It had taken her all day to leave because of a high amount of zombie activity that kept the two guards active. They were efficient and alert, checking on her frequently. She'd decided to wait until one went to rest, but that wasn't until dusk when Lucan went for a nap.

Dagonet had tried to persuade her to join him for his watch, but she'd told him she felt tired. He tried to insist she come sleep in the room closest to where he'd be on watch, but she refused, stating she'd rather be away from all the activity for a while. He was hesitant to leave, but his duty to guard her home was greater than babysitting her.

Even though he left her alone, it still took all day and as more time passed, more sensations assaulted her. She kept pushing what she could back, but it wasn't like before. Now it felt like she needed Lucifer in order to achieve the calm, unfeeling state again.

Glancing behind herself once more, she decided to stop thinking about everything and get to Lucifer. He would stop the ache in her heart. The ache that was there because David's face and smile wouldn't leave her mind. Her vampire haunted her, and now his image was accompanied by her children. They were standing with David, holding his hands, as he told her to stay—that they needed and loved her.

A tear quickly slipped from her eye, but she wiped it away and kept walking as the same fluttering noise from earlier returned. It was closer.

Jane whirled around with a gasp and looked all around the seemingly empty street. A spine-tingling chill crawled up her back, and she stiffened as she listened to flapping sounds circling above her in the dark sky. Even with her perfect sight, she couldn't see anything. But something was there.

More rustling sounds along with faint scrapes and whispers echoed around her. She looked away from the sky and glanced back toward the direction she'd come from. Images of Natalie and Nathan at various stages of their lives rapidly flashed in her mind again. She pressed her hand against her chest as a stabbing sensation pierced her heart, almost knocking her to her knees.

She wished the numbness hadn't faded. The haze that had fallen over the past few hours prevented her from fully embracing the bonds she had with her family and the knights, but she still felt a connection. It was just out of her grasp, but it was there. Only it felt as if a glass wall stood between her and everyone else.

Through her tears, she stared in the direction of her home and imagined David standing on one side of the glass with her family standing behind him. He pressed his hand against the clear barrier, and she held her hand on the other side. Close, but not touching.

She didn't even know she had actually held her hand out, as if she were really pressing her hand against a wall, until goosebumps rose and spread up her arm. Hundreds of sinister whispers erupted all around her. There was no mistaking it now, she was surrounded.

She took one last look at the road that would lead her home, then turned and ran the other way. There was no going back now. She'd brought this on herself. She would make sure whatever was after her, came only for her. As long as it didn't go to them, she'd let it come. She just had to get farther away first.

Jane ran as fast as she could. The cemetery was close; that meant Lucifer was close. She still had every intention to go to him; he would help her keep them safe. He would make it easier to breathe when her heart broke all the way.

Her chest throbbed, and letting out a quiet sob, she came to a stop. Placing her palm over her heart, she pressed hard, hoping it would stop the pain somehow. She closed her eyes, panting as she tried to gather herself.

For several seconds, she stayed like that until the pain became tolerable. When she finally opened her eyes, panic replaced the pain.

A hundred feet away, two figures stood side by side, blocking her path. The first was obviously male. He was tall, easily eye level with David, though he didn't appear as built as him. Jane eyed the black cloak the stranger wore. It was arranged awkwardly, but she didn't analyze it too carefully before she darted her eyes to the second, shorter figure.

This one was female and close to her height, only more petite. Even in the dark, Jane could see her pale doll-like face and wild tendrils of black hair sprouting all around her head. They reminded Jane of the snakes on Medusa's head.

The pair said nothing, and neither did Jane. They just stood there staring back at her, not making any threatening movements. She might have thought she had a chance if it weren't for their glowing, red eyes and wicked smiles.

"This is the one?" the female asked, gesturing with her hands in Jane's direction. "She's not even pretty."

The male chuckled, a deep, dark laugh. "You're not a man, Nia." His blood red gaze trailed up and down Jane's body, and he winked. "She's fucking hot."

Regardless of all the times Jane had silly daydreams about a mysterious man saying such things about her, she wasn't flattered. Her heart pounded away in her chest now. These two were something more than vampires.

"Who are you?" she asked them.

"Ooh, she's a brave one." The female let out a wicked giggle. "This will be fun."

The male glared at his companion before glancing back at Jane. "My apologies. I am Thanatos—this is Mania. You need to come with us."

Jane shook her head. "No. I have to be somewhere. Please let me pass."

Mania snorted. "You hear that, Than? She has somewhere to be."

"Nia," Thanatos snapped, but looked back at Jane with a charming smile. "Forgive her; she has no manners. We know you are heading to Lucifer. We have come to escort you to him. He had to attend matters elsewhere and sent us in his place."

The fluttering sounds around her grew louder again.

Jane took a step back. "Thank you, but I can wait for him to come back."

His smile dropped. "I did not give you a choice, beautiful."

Mania giggled. The sound cut and dragged across her skin like tiny shards of glass. Then loud thumps began to smack the pavement. Jane frantically looked around her to see other figures closing in on her.

The thuds continued to fall. Her heart was beating so fast, she thought it might explode. There were hundreds of them. Jane started to step back again, but they'd already surrounded her. She looked to the closest figure, and her blood turned to ice.

Demons.

Their black and gray skin was tight along their lean bodies. Twisted horns adorned their heads. Her eyes widened as she caught sight of their wings. They were thin and membrane-like, reminding her of a bat's wings. That's what she'd been hearing. They'd been stalking her since she left the house.

When she saw some with feathered wings landing, she nearly cried out in joy because she figured they were angels. They had to be.

Her joy didn't come. Their wings were black, and their eyes—she looked between a group of them—were black, too. *The Fallen.*

"Oh, my God," she whispered.

"God can't help you now." Mania giggled.

"I will not tell you again. Come with us now." Thanatos' voice held none of the niceties from before.

Jane looked back at him. Total fear consumed her as she watched the blackness she had assumed was his cloak expand. He had huge, black feathered wings. He was a fallen angel, and he was working with demons to capture her.

The unsettling cackling from Mania drew Jane's shocked stare, and she stood petrified at the sight of Mania's leathery wings protruding from her small frame. Jane could now see her crazed, childlike features in the moonlight.

Her pulse hummed in her ears, mixing with the sound of hundreds of wings flapping. She knew they were probably going to kill her now. That is, until a memory of her first conversation with Gawain came to mind. He had told her angels and demons could not directly harm her. They could only influence her.

"You can't touch me," Jane said. "I know you can't."

Mania laughed. "You think that because we cannot touch you, physically, you're safe?" Jane's smile fell. "Silly girl. I will make you kill yourself."

The swarm rushed her and laughed at her obvious fright when she screamed.

Images, not of Jane's making, began to bombard her mind. She saw herself crying as she slit her wrist, then her dead body lying in a puddle of her own blood.

She clutched her head as their demonic whispers intensified, becoming a horrifying roar. Their words didn't make sense. English words mixed with languages she didn't recognize, and then they shifted to terrifying howls.

"No," Jane yelled, falling to her knees. "Stop. Please!"

They grew louder and forced more images into her head. First, she saw David and the knights lying lifeless at her feet as their vacant eyes stared upward.

Tears slid down her face as more flashes tormented her. Natalie and Nathan sobbed—then they were on the ground, their throats were ripped from their tiny necks. Blood covered their soft baby skin.

The wind blew wildly through her hair as they circled her faster and faster. She cried as each heartbreaking image crossed her mind.

All of Lucifer's anesthetic was gone now. Her pain had multiplied times a thousand. She wailed again in sorrow, but when she saw a glimpse of Mania in the distance—smiling—laughing at her torment, her sorrow abruptly shifted. Rage.

Jane stood from the crouched position she'd fallen to and glared in Mania's direction. "You can't touch me. But maybe I can touch you."

Mania laughed. "What are you going to do, stupid girl?"

Thanatos said nothing and only tilted his head as he watched her struggling to stand. Mania's confidence only fueled Jane's anger, and she grinned when she mentally shoved away the sick images of her feeding on her children before she shot herself. It felt like hornets' stings as they tried to force the images back in, but she pushed on, using every ounce of strength she had left.

"What are you waiting for?" Mania shouted at her minions. "Get her!"

With a thunderous onslaught of horrific screeches, they swarmed her. But Jane lifted her hands out in front of her and screamed.

Blue light exploded out of her in all directions. Any demons within fifty feet of her fell to the ground, screaming in agony as their bodies broke from her explosion of energy. Only a few looked to be completely dead, and the others were unfortunately starting to stand again.

It's not enough. She'd used all she had, but she wasn't strong enough.

Despite it not being enough, Thanatos stared at her in complete shock while Mania stomped her feet like a temperamental child. "How did she do that?"

Thanatos didn't reply, but slowly, a wicked grin formed on his lips. He glanced around as the other demons became more hostile, and the stench of fear tainted the air. "Don't worry. She will not be doing that again. Will you, Jane?" Sweat trickled down Jane's neck and her lip quivered. He chuckled softly. "That's what I thought."

Jane darted her head around in a panic. The demon horde seemed to regain their confidence, taking steps closer and closer to her.

She glanced back at Thanatos. He winked, then looked at his partner. "Do what you do best, Nia. She won't last long." Looking back into Jane's nervous gaze, he smiled. "I must be off now. Do not worry, beautiful. I will make sure we meet again."

With that, he vanished and Mania's insane cackling grew. "That's better. He always cramps my style. You know, I wish I would have heard about you before. I would have enjoyed watching you slowly lose your mind. Oh, well." She sighed wistfully. "I shall simply have to cherish these last moments of your pathetic life."

More images were forced into her mind. Jane screamed, and her knees shook. She could hardly stand; nor could she escape her tormented mind. She was forced to watch herself as she stood over her sleeping children, and she cried in horror as she watched herself point a gun at their peaceful faces and fired twice. "No!" She screamed when the blood sprayed across her face.

Mania's laughter began to mix with her anguished cries, enough to remind Jane it wasn't real.

Finding a last bit of strength, she focused on making a mental wall. She ignored the hundreds of beating wings and whispers surrounding her and strained, putting everything she had in her to force an invisible barrier around herself.

The new image of David with his arms around an unknown, naked brunette blurred and began to fade. Though she knew she was still doomed, she smiled weakly at an enraged Mania. *I'll go down, but I'm going to put up a fight.*

Tremendous force pressed in on her, squeezing her bones and stealing her breath. Her body shook as she struggled to push the wall out farther, and with every push, another, harder push came back at her.

"You won't be able to hold that forever, sweetie." Mania taunted. "You're only prolonging the inevitable."

Jane's face twisted in pain. There were too many. Her hands trembled, and liquid began to ooze out of her ears. She groaned as the pressure became unbearable while Mania's insane laughs mixed horrifyingly with the demonic chants.

Her legs trembled; she was close to buckling under the weight of their mental attack. She could see them moving in again. "No," she cried. They were within ten feet of her now. The swarm smiled, excited as they prepared to break her, and finally, Jane collapsed.

Tears and sweat drenched her entire body. The chanting and faint flickers of images forced their way into her mind again. She squeezed her eyes shut, but she knew it was over.

A loud crash landed right in front of her, shaking the ground. She screamed, expecting something to grab her. But nothing did.

Instead, a terrifying roar shook the sky. Jane snapped her eyes open and breathed in the rich scent of leather and cologne. Death.

A murderous gleam lit his emerald eyes as he swung his scythe at the demons directly around her. Ten of the disfigured beasts fell at his feet and disintegrated into a pile of ash.

His deadly growl caused the hundreds of demons surrounding to hiss and move back. But they didn't retreat. Jane looked around frantically while Death kept his electric-green glare on them.

She looked back to see Mania quickly vanish in a poof of smoke.

Another dangerous noise sounded from Death's chest, a warning.

Surprisingly, a few dared to step closer, but they quickly dropped to the ground as they cried out in agony. Jane's eyes widened, watching as their flesh began to decay.

The growls and hisses from her attackers grew louder, but they stepped back to wait him out. Death scoffed and turned to look down at her.

The deadly look on his face dropped. "Jane." He reached down and pulled her to him, cupping her cheek as he gazed into her eyes. "What's happened to you?" He smoothed the sweaty hair out of her face. His eyes burned brightly as he pulled his hand back and looked at the blood coating his fingers.

She cried as she stared into his eyes. She was exhausted and terrified, but relieved that he was holding her. He held her, but it seemed like he, too, stood on one side of the glass wall around her. She knew he was there, but it wasn't enough.

More tortured cries sounded around her. She tried to turn to see what was happening, but he held her face.

"Don't look," he said softly, not looking away from her eyes.

She nodded as he kept up his scrutinizing search of her face. He trailed his fingertips across her cheek and down her jaw. *Tingles.* She sighed and closed her eyes.

"Look at me, Sweet Jane."

She obeyed and found him staring at her.

"You need to go to your family," he said. "Go to David." She shook her head, but he gripped her tighter, raising his voice when he spoke again. "Yes, Jane . . . Stop this. You are stronger than this."

"I'm not."

His fierce look vanished, and he cupped her cheek. She could barely hear the screams from the demons around her as he lowered his face within an inch of hers.

All she saw was his beautiful face, and he smiled that smile that had always remained out of reach in her dreams. "You are." He brushed his nose against hers, and she shivered from the sparks that spread from the small contact. "Do you feel it—me?"

She whimpered and nodded. *Please come back.*

"Remember how much I love you, Sweet Jane." He kissed her cheek. She gasped at the electric shocks left by his lips. "Remember how much David loves you. Remember Nathan and Natalie." He pulled back slightly to smile at her. "Come back, baby girl. I am with you. I will always come back for you." Giving her no time to respond, he covered her mouth with his.

The eruption of sparks overwhelmed her. All thoughts of fear and sadness were smothered. The glass wall splintered before finally shattering into a million pieces. All his strength and love called to her in the dark room she'd hidden herself in and demanded she come out.

His lips moved with hers, so loving and delicate. Memories of him holding her and the loving way he always cared for her came forward. She wanted to cry as much as she wanted to kiss him harder.

Death didn't let her cry. He licked her lip and then pushed her mouth open. His soft kiss turned to a more powerful, hungry one as he explored her mouth with his tongue. She felt he was showing that he would protect her—always be strong for her. That he'd always come when she needed him.

Her heart filled up. The emptiness was replaced with his unique warmth as electricity sizzled throughout her body. His muscles flexed around her until he slowed down his kiss, ending it completely when he pulled back.

She slowly opened her eyes and found him smiling as he returned her gaze. He pressed his lips to hers and whispered, "There you are, Sweet Jane."

She smiled but cried. "I'm sorry, Death."

His head shook. "It's okay. But I need you to go now. Your hold won't last on them much longer." He glanced around at the waiting enemy with a frightening glare.

She looked around. He had distracted her so much that she had completely forgotten about them.

His words registered, and she realized the demons appeared to be immobilized. A few dozen closest to them looked almost dead as flesh and bone withered away.

"I'm doing that?"

Death chuckled and delightful shocks danced across her skin as he caressed her cheek. "No. You're holding them. I'm doing that." He motioned with his eyes to the writhing demons. "I told you that you were strong." He wore a proud smile. "You won't last much longer, though. Go to David. Why the fuck you're not with him, I don't know, but go—tell them you must prepare your family to leave. Go with the knights, Jane. None of you are safe anymore. They're after you."

"Who?"

"I don't know everything yet, but I'll explain when I can. For now, you must leave. I will deal with this."

Jane shook her head, gripping his jacket. "I'm not leaving you!"

He smiled and kissed her again. "You have to, angel. I'll catch up, but you must do as I say. Go to David. Tell him what has happened and that you want your family. He won't refuse you. I will be there before you know it."

She whimpered at the thought of leaving him here. There were still hundreds of them, and they looked ready to rip him apart even with the terror in their dark eyes. They were ready to go down fighting. She already knew he could be hurt after watching him spar with David. His blood was as red as hers.

"Sorrow," Death said, staring over her shoulder.

The magnificent horse emerged from his emerald flames in the ground and stepped close. Jane looked between the horse and Death. He pulled her in for another quick kiss and pressed his forehead to hers. "Sorrow will take you to David. Do not come back for me, and do not go anywhere else."

"Death," she said, still not wanting to leave him.

"Do as I say, Jane." He kissed her again and lifted her on the horse's back. "Take her to David."

The horse nodded with a snort. Death smiled at Jane's sad face. "I love you," she told him in a pathetic whimper. And she did. She loved him so very much, and she felt every bit of their love passing between them.

He smiled wider. "And I love you. Drop your hold now."

Sorrow started to walk away, but she turned to face Death. She feared he would get hurt.

He nodded to her, and she watched his scythe appear in his hands again while he gave her a playful grin.

She shook her head as Sorrow picked up pace. "No. I can't leave you."

He laughed, a dark, terrorizing laugh. "Drop your hold, Jane."

She yelled back, feeling blood drip from her nose. "No!"

His smile dropped. "Do it now!" His thunderous roar shook the ground, and she nodded quickly, letting go. The hisses and snarls increased while her hair blew around her face wildly, but she watched Death smile again.

Never taking his eyes from hers, his scythe lit up and split into two smaller, fiery versions of his deadly weapon. Their wicked blades burned blue from the hellish fire he had called forward.

Her eyes widened as she watched his jeans and jacket darken. Now, the blackest of fabrics hugged his muscular body, and a hood covered his head. She still saw his glowing emerald eyes through the darkness his hood cast over his face.

"You forget, babe"—he turned to face the swarm then looked over his shoulder one last time—"I'm Death."

CHAPTER 40

EXPLANATIONS

Fury and dread consumed David's heart as Jane's home came into view. His panic reached new heights when he saw Dagonet and Lucan arguing outside. She was already gone.

David came to a stop in front of them, yelling, unable to contain his rage. "Where is she?"

Dagonet sighed. "My prince, I'm sorry. I checked on her often, spoke with her even, but she slipped out the window sometime after I returned to my watch."

All rational thoughts left David's mind, and he grabbed his old friend by the throat, lifting him off the ground. "Where is she?"

Gawain and Hades finally arrived. They pulled at his hands, but he shook them off. He glared at the old vampire but dropped him to the ground.

Dagonet rubbed his throat and coughed. "I do not know. She left false trails, but I didn't want to leave my post. Lucan searched, but he has been unsuccessful in finding the right path."

David snarled at the useless answer. It took all his restraint not to kill his old friend.

"David, calm down," Arthur said, walking up to put himself between them.

It only pissed David off to hear Arthur's authoritative tone mix with his words. He would kill anyone who hurt her.

Arthur gave him a stern look. "We'll find her. You need to think clearly. Your anger will not help you find her any faster."

David could barely keep from baring his fangs as he gave out orders. "Gawain, Hades, come with me now." He began making his way around the house to locate her trail when a soft cry made him stop. They all looked around in the direction of the sound.

Hades pointed down the street. "There!"

David's rage vanished, and he immediately ran toward the enormous horse barreling down the street. Sorrow reared back, neighing loudly as he stomped at David's quick approach but allowed him to come near. David didn't care about the horse. He would have punched him if it tried to keep him away.

Jane's bloody face and tangled hair finally came into view, and his eyes widened as she sobbed, spotting him, too.

David quickly pulled her from the horse and hugged her trembling body. "Oh, thank God."

"I'm so sorry." She tried hugging him, but her hands fell to her sides, and she simply cried.

He squeezed her, softly kissing her head. "*Shh*. It's all right."

He was so relieved when she melted into his embrace. She was acting like his Jane again.

She cried harder. "I'm sorry."

He hugged her but quickly pulled back to inspect her bloody face. "What happened to you? Where are you hurt?" He turned her head from side to side and looked her over carefully but found no open wounds.

"I'm fine. This came from my nose and ears." She pointed to her bloody nose. Her energy seemed to suddenly fade. So much so that he had to support her weight.

He lifted her into his arms and began carrying her to the house. "I've got you. Tell me what happened, Jane." He smoothed her tangled hair out of her face and tried wiping the blood from her face while her eyes started shutting.

"Death saved me," she said, bobbing her head as she fought to keep her eyes open.

Arthur held the door for him, and they entered the living room. David quickly sat down with her in his arms as Gawain handed him a wet cloth.

David wiped the drying blood from her face. He was overwhelmed that she was finally showing emotion, but he was worried about her physical state. She was pale and weak. "Sweetheart, look at me. I need to know what happened."

Jane held his pleading gaze. "I couldn't hold them back anymore. He saved me–told Sorrow to bring me back to you . . . He said I need to stay with you and get my family." Her eyes fluttered shut, but David gently shook her to wake her up. "Not safe," she whispered. "They're coming for me. I couldn't hold them–they want me . . . Inside my head. It hurt." Her eyes shut and her breathing slowed.

"David, feed her," Hades said, panic visible in his eyes from where he hovered nearby. "She's completely drained of energy. Whatever she did, she's used up almost all of it."

David nodded and grabbed hold of her face. "Jane, wake up. You need to feed again."

She barely opened her eyes but nodded and took David's wrist. She bit down, drinking slowly at first. His panic was still too present to enjoy her touch, but apparently, not enough for Jane.

Though her eyes stayed closed, she moaned loudly and tugged him close to her.

David look around, slightly embarrassed. It earned him grins from Gawain and Arthur while a teasing glint merely appeared in Hades' eyes.

Finally, after lots of moaning from Jane, she slowed her pace and opened her eyes. David smiled as she let go and felt so relieved when that beautiful blush spread over her cheeks and hazel eyes stared up at him, shimmering with all the colors he loved so much.

She leaned against him as Hades knelt in front of them and addressed her. "Jane, are you feeling better now?"

"Yes." She returned her attention to David. "Thank you." Her smile made him forget everyone else.

Hades interrupted their staring contest with a small cough and an amused grin before turning more serious. "Jane, you need to tell us what happened. Where is Death?"

She froze and pulled away from David completely before she suddenly jumped up.

David stood up. "Jane, calm down. Just tell us what happened."

Her eyes moved around. Panic and sadness flooded her gaze as she met every pair of concerned eyes and when her gaze settled on Dagonet, her lips quivered.

"Jane," David said, trying to get her away from whatever saddened her over Dagonet. "Don't be afraid. We need to know what happened."

She held his gaze and nodded. "I was going to meet Lucifer."

Well, he wasn't expecting that.

A slew of curses in languages that even David couldn't understand spilled out of Hades' mouth but all David could focus on was her eyes. So colorful once more but what shocked him was the amount of fear she looked at him with.

David had never been more pissed off in his entire life than he was at this moment. His muscles felt ready to explode. "Jane," he said, barely holding his temper in check. "I need you to tell us everything." He stared at her frightened eyes. "I'm not mad at you. I will not be angry with you over whatever you tell me—but I will be furious if you keep things from me now. No more hiding what's hurting you or what you're afraid of. Do you understand?" Some of his anger slipped away as he watched her flinch. He didn't want to be harsh with her. Ever.

"I'll tell you everything." Her voice shook, but she held his fierce stare.

He knew he looked threatening, but she didn't break eye contact even though her lips trembled and her eyes reddened more. She looked at him as though she were seeing him for the last time, just like she had done before she told him about her past. He knew she was preparing herself to lose him from whatever she was about to say.

This was the start—showing her he was different. So, he exhaled and held out his hand. "Come here." To his relief, she ran right into his arms, shaking as she tried to hold her cries in. He wrapped his arms around her, breathing her in as he hugged her.

"I'll tell you," she whispered.

He kissed the top of her head. "And I will still be here when you finish." Small fingers dug into his sides as she pulled him to her more. He smiled—it was like she was trying to hold on to him. "Go on, Jane. Every detail you can recall."

And she did. She told them everything.

He had hugged her, rocked her—placed kisses even when he wanted to yell at her for thinking some of the things she had been. But he didn't.

When tears slid down her cheeks, he wiped them away. When she seemed too ashamed and tried to pull away, he hugged her tighter. When her body shook, and she spoke of the fallen angels and demons along with their mental attack, he kissed her forehead and promised her those things they made her see would never happen.

And when she recounted the use of her power, he smiled down at her in awe.

His amazement faded when she explained her powers had not been enough and annoyance along with relief rose up in him as she talked about Death arriving. He watched her eyes light up as she spoke of her angel and how he pulled her from her own personal hell. Death had saved her again, and David already knew how Death would bring her back: a kiss.

It hurt. It felt like a fatal wound to the chest, but he kissed her forehead when watery, hazel eyes stared at him. She had not wanted to tell him this, but she did.

"David," she said, pulling his attention away from thinking about her and Death kissing, and onto her alone. "I want my family to come with us. We need to listen to Death—it's not safe. I won't leave them."

He searched her face and knew there was no way he could get her to leave. She'd do whatever it took to get them away from danger. Honestly, he was happy she was so protective of them again.

"Arthur." David looked away from her. "We must bring them with us."

Arthur exhaled but nodded. "There will be strict rules, but we will talk to Jason."

Excitement lit up Jane's face. "Really?"

"Really," David said. "I will have to be with you because it is still too dangerous for you. We will all have to watch you carefully around all mortals. You understand, don't you?"

Jane nodded eagerly with that beautiful smile that he loved to see on her lips. "Yes, I understand. Thank you, David." She hugged him back, hearing the others laugh. She pulled back to look at Arthur. "Thank you."

"You are welcome," Arthur told her.

Her eyes drifted to Hades, and she asked him, "Will he be all right? He made me drop the hold I had on those things and forced me to leave."

Hades laughed off her fear. "Of course he'll be fine. He's Death."

Jane frowned and looked to David for reassurance. He thought it was cute that she would ask him if the Angel of Death would be safe. "I'm sure he'll be fine."

"Okay," she whispered before looking around. "What happened with you?"

Arthur answered her. "Tristan was injured, but he will recover. David can tell you later."

"Oh. Well, when can we go?"

Arthur sighed but answered her. "I will call for our crew to head in. It will take a day for them to get here. Why don't you shower as we all get cleaned up to meet your family?"

"That sounds great," she said, almost tugging David's hand to run out, but Arthur stopped them.

Arthur lowered his face to look her directly in the eye. "Whatever reservations you have about your contact with David needs to be set aside from here on out." She looked to him and bit her lip as Arthur added, "You two are not a mistake. You are not a mistake."

"I'm sorry," she whispered.

Arthur shook his head and smiled. "No, my dear. You are only trying to do what you think is best by everyone else. For now, though, you need to do what's best for you."

Jane looked around and when her gaze landed on Dagonet, she lowered her head. "Dagonet, I'm so sorry."

His old friend walked up to them and lifted her head with his finger. "Apology accepted, Jane . . . if you promise to remember our chat."

Jane suddenly hugged Dagonet. "I will remember. Thank you for telling me. I wish you could have them back."

Dagonet smiled sadly and patted her back. "I do as well. For now, I will find peace in knowing I kept your children safe for you." They split apart. "My prince." Dagonet bowed to David before walking away.

Jane grabbed his hand, making him smile as she addressed the others. "We'll go get cleaned up, if that's okay?"

Arthur waved them off, and David chuckled at her excitement. His Jane was back.

"David?" Jane looked up at him as they crossed the street. "Do you really think Death is fine?"

The worry in her eyes crushed his annoyance about the angel he loathed.

"Yes, sweetheart. He will be fine. Like Hades said, he's Death." She laughed after he said this, and looked away quickly. "What's funny?" he asked, unable to stop smiling as she radiated happiness.

"Nothing," she said. "He just said the same thing."

David laughed. "Arrogant prick."

"David," she reprimanded, but a smile still played at her pretty lips.

He shrugged a shoulder. "I am only stating the truth."

"Just be nice." She pushed the door open to their base.

He smiled, figuring he was off the hook when she giggled again. Before she started up the stairs, he made her stop.

Jane frowned and stepped down.

He still stood taller than her, and he smiled because of that before taking her face in his hands. "I'm glad you are okay. But promise me you will never leave again. Please don't put me through that again."

Her eyes watered suddenly, and she nodded.

He placed a kiss on her forehead and lowered his hands to hold her waist. "You have no idea how scared I've been for you. I already thought I'd lost you inside yourself, but coming back, finding you gone . . . And then realizing you'd left on your own—"

"I'm sorry," she whispered, wrapping her arms around his neck.

"I know," he said, sliding a hand across her back. "It's just, everything is about to change. I don't want you getting upset and thinking you should leave or choose between any of us. I will understand the choices you're about to make. No matter what, I will never be angry with you. I will always love you."

She tensed but did not move away from him, so he tried to explain his feelings for her. He hoped that if she understood how he felt about her, maybe she would be able to handle things better. "I know it must seem absurd for me to say those words to you so soon," he said, "but I do. I have waited too long for you to come into my life for me to hide my love for you. I will wait, though. Even if what I want with you never comes, I will wait."

She blinked to keep her tears in but one escaped.

"Don't cry for this," he told her. "I only want you to know you never have to feel pressured. I want you to know nothing will ever change how I feel. But I will understand when you do not choose me." David pulled back and took her face again as he leaned down. All he had to do was press his lips against hers for her to know how much she was meant to be with him. He smiled when she held her breath, but instead of kissing her waiting lips like he so badly wanted to, he kissed the tear on her cheek.

He left his lips against her sweet skin, breathing in deeply for a few moments. "I love you, baby." He knew that he would not be able to call her that in front of her husband and needed to let her hear his adoration of her a little while longer. She was his baby, his feisty kitten when she slept, his sweetheart. His Jane. They just weren't ready for each other, and he finally understood how hard it must be for her to war with her heart over all the love she had to share.

She sobbed softly and leaned her face into his hand.

"It's okay." He pulled back and dropped his hands to her waist again. "No more crying about this, all right? We are going to see your family. This is a good thing, and we will all be there to help you. I won't leave your side unless Death is on the other side."

"I know," she said. She lifted her hand to touch the side of his face.

Oh, how he loved when she showed simple affection like this. He wanted to pull her to him, but he stayed still and let her caress his cheek as her eyes seemed to take in every detail of his face. She always appeared to be in awe of him but so sad when she stared at him for too long.

Those hazel eyes he loved finally met his while her soft hand stayed on his cheek. "David," she said, looking conflicted for a moment but more confident when she spoke again. "It wasn't just Death who brought me back."

He was unsure if she meant he had something to do with her recovery, but when she stayed quiet, as if waiting for him to understand, he smiled.

Her eyes watered, and she laughed sadly as her fingers twitched before moving to touch the curve of his lips. He closed his mouth but still smiled. She focused on it and lightly trailed her fingers across his mouth. "This," she said, staring at his lips for a few more seconds before she looked up to meet his eyes. "You." She smiled, lowering her hand. After pulling his from her waist, she held it, moving her fingers over his and then pressed their palms together. "I saw you."

David looked down at their touching hands and then at her. She looked so sad as she held all her attention on their hands. She didn't do anything else, just kept them pressed flat against each other, looking at them as though it broke her heart somehow.

He moved his fingers so that they could slide between hers until their hands were clasped together.

Jane looked up, as if she was amazed by what he'd just done. "Thank you, David."

He smiled and brought their hands to his lips. "Always, Jane."

CHAPTER 41
HIS MOON

The reflection staring back at Jane wasn't what she was really seeing. As she had often found herself in the past, she was lost in her chaotic thoughts—overthinking every little thing that happened. Doubting herself and regretting her choices was something she had never been able to overcome. Every decision, every word she said—they were all second guessed. This behavior could drive a person mad, and Jane knew all too well how dangerous this path could be for her. It was part of why she had shut off before.

She knew focusing on reuniting with Jason and her children was more important than analyzing things that could not be undone. So, she closed her eyes and breathed out the anxiety she felt over everything. She accepted that David and Death were with her. They both promised to stand by her, and she needed to let them if she wanted to save her family.

Opening her eyes, she once again found herself looking at the girl in the mirror. *Still a monster,* she thought. She tried recalling how her reflection appeared when she was still human because now that she was really looking, she could see how much smoother her skin was and the faint silver shimmer she emitted.

Gawain had said humans would not see her as clearly as they saw each other because of their heightened eyesight. Hopefully she would not seem as different to her family as she did to herself.

She leaned forward to look at her hazel eyes. Each color shone more vibrantly. She glanced back at her face and smiled, tilting her head to see the difference from a human smile. Her canines only appeared slightly elongated, but she knew they were sharper and more prominent than they originally were.

"Beautiful," a deep voice spoke from behind her.

She gasped and turned to see the man she undoubtedly loved standing there in all his magnificent glory. Smiling, she ran into Death's arms as he held them out for her. "You're okay," she whispered, clutching his jacket.

He chuckled and slid his fingers into her hair. "I told you I would be. Did you doubt me?"

Jane pulled back, smiling even more. "No. I just can't believe you're here. Are you hurt?"

"Hurt?" He snorted. "Are you trying to insult me?"

She grinned at his playful smile. "No. I didn't mean I don't think you're capable; I know you are. Thank you for saving me again."

It melted her heart to see so much love in his eyes. He rubbed her lips with his thumb. They tingled, and that strange but addicting warmth sank into her skin. The way it spread throughout her body, almost searching for something inside her; she loved and hated it, but could not help but want more of the sensation.

"I will always be there, Jane." He didn't take his eyes off her lips. "Just don't run off again."

"I won't." Her words sounded more breathless than she intended to. "I'm sorry for everything."

He lifted his gaze to meet hers. "There's nothing to be sorry for. You were very brave. I'm proud of you."

She realized he didn't know about Lucifer, about anything that happened since he left her. "You don't know what I did, though."

He tilted his head, frowning "Have I ever been angry with you?"

"No."

"I know that you finally fell apart," he said softly. "That's nothing to be ashamed of. Everyone falls, but not everyone gets back up. The fact that you did means everything. Don't worry about anything else."

"Do you know what I did, though?"

He cupped her cheek and shook his head no.

She tore her gaze from him and looked to the side. "I didn't want to feel any more pain, so I stopped it all. I don't even know how I did it. It was like I was still there but not. I knew what was going on, but I couldn't do anything, couldn't feel any of it. I didn't want to . . . . I was so tired, Death."

She looked back up to see him nod. He was being patient with her like he had always been. "David and the knights left me behind because of how I made myself."

He didn't look happy about her being left but stayed quiet.

"Death, I met Lucifer," she said as his eyes darkened. "He promised to make it go away for me—to take me somewhere where it would stop. I let him do something to me. It's my fault all this happened because I didn't want to hurt any of you. I was afraid, and you weren't here. I didn't want to hurt anyone. It hurt so much. And David—I was hurting him. I'm so sorry."

Death said nothing. He only stared down at her, the green color of his eyes shifted every few seconds from a deep emerald color to burning, electric-green fire.

She grew more worried. "De—"

He cut his name off with his lips. He kissed her, desperately, as though she could vanish from his arms at any moment. He didn't deepen it, just pressed kiss after kiss to her lips. He stopped but kept his lips hovering over hers, sending intense sparks across them at every tiny brush.

So badly she felt the urge to pull his lips back to hers. Something deep inside her craved, no, needed his kiss.

"Don't ever do that again," he whispered. "You have no idea what it would have meant for you to go with him."

The true fear in his voice had her trembling with sadness. "I won't," she said. "I promise. I'm sorry."

He kissed her quickly, then a throat cleared from the doorway.

Jane jumped and looked over to see David standing there. He smiled even though his eyes held a mixture of sorrow and anger. Her gaze fell to the floor in hopes that when she looked up, time might reverse so that David would have never witnessed her kisses with Death.

Death pulled Jane against his side. "Hello, David. I'm glad to see she made it back to you."

Jane glanced up, surprised to see David smile.

"Death," he greeted with a slight nod. "Thank you for coming to her aid and sending her back. She explained all that happened—we are preparing to leave after we gather her family. I hoped you would return in time so you could join me. I think it's best we both make sure all goes well when she sees them again."

Jane stared at them in shock of their calm exchange. It eased some of her guilt, and she looked up at Death, hopeful that he would agree.

"Pulling out the big guns, I see." Death's eyes stayed focused on her pouting lip, and he smiled, squeezing her closer. "Fine. I will come chaperone your little visit."

Jane beamed up at him and smiled brightly to David.

"One of us should always be with her," Death told David. "Don't hesitate to drag her out of there if she gets upset. Jason is not going to take it well when he sees us with her. If he gets angry, she's going to be furious. We cannot let her get to a destructive point because of him."

Death lowered his gaze to hers. "Don't give me that look, baby girl. You know how volatile your emotions make you. And you know how bad Jason can make you feel."

"Death," she said, looking at David briefly.

The angel shrugged. "David needs to know before he meets him anyway. Just because you didn't see me doesn't mean I was not present for some of your bad moments together." He stopped, letting that sink in. "You may think you can hide shit, but everyone can see how wrong things are between you and your husband. He's a prick."

David cleared his throat, but Jane didn't look up. She could only stare down at the floor. "Perhaps now is not the time—"

"I would not say this if it were not necessary," he told David, before focusing on her again. "Jane, you are a powerful immortal. You are a threat to even the deadliest of creatures in many realms. Your power—the darkness in you—and the fact you're newly made on top of your temper makes you a ticking time bomb. I won't hesitate in knocking your sexy ass out if I think you are a danger to anyone. David should be prepared to do the same. I will not let you make a mistake that will drive you insane."

She didn't even react to how he worded things. All she focused on was him saying how dangerous she truly was, and just how much he seemed to know about her and Jason's marriage. "Do whatever you think is best," she told them.

"I always try to." Death pushed some of her hair behind her ear. "Angry with me, Sweet Jane?" His smile, and the fact he now slid the back of his fingers down her jaw, soothed the harsh blow his honest words had delivered. He was only being honest, as always.

"You know I can never be mad at you," she said, smiling at the little tingles before he pulled his hand away. "It's probably some spell you cast over me."

He didn't reply. Instead, he tossed her a mischievous wink and looked away when David spoke.

"Don't worry, sweetheart," David said. "I promise everything will work out. We are on a schedule, though. Gawain, Arthur, and Dagonet are coming with us while the others break down camp. So, let's go get your family."

She was getting her family back! She smiled at both of them, completely forgetting about Death's speech with all the warmth spreading inside her. They were doing so much for her, and she felt complete standing there between them as they both smiled down at her.

Death chuckled when she kept looking between them, and finally grabbed her hand to pull her out of the room.

Since she was behind Death, and he followed David, she got the chance to appreciate how big and powerful they both were. The best part was they were working together for her.

David met Death's gaze. You didn't need to hear them speak to know they were forming an alliance—teaming up against whatever threatened her, including Jason.

They glanced down at her and then looked back at each other. They both had that possessive gleam in their eye, but they nodded to each other.

✦✦✦

The delightful tingles traveling up and down the side of her arm almost distracted her from the anxiety she felt while she and Death waited for David to return.

Her vampire had gone to speak with Arthur and Dagonet, saying he wanted to make sure everything was set before bringing her over to see Jason.

Jane glanced to the spot beside her on the couch. Death's massive size looked ridiculous sitting there in a living room with his head tilted back against the couch while he stared up at the ceiling.

He had one arm draped over her shoulder as his fingers glided over the upper part of her arm. He'd even gone as far as tossing his muscular legs, ankles crossed, on the glass coffee table. She eyed the glass, wondering how it managed to not give under his weight. And to think, if one of the knights saw him, they'd see the Grim Reaper lounging on a couch with her.

She shook her head and looked back to the doorway.

"Staring at the doorway won't make him come back any sooner. You need to relax, babe." He didn't even look away from the ceiling, but she realized he was very aware of just how tense she was. "You're starting to stress me out."

"And what are you accomplishing, staring at the ceiling?"

His fingers slowed, but then slid up her arm, over her shoulder, and then barely extended to touch her jaw. She shivered, and his lip twitched with a hint of a smile. "Trying to distract myself from the memory of my lips on yours."

She looked into his eyes, which had lowered slightly to look at her. "We shouldn't do that, Death."

"*Hm.*" He let his finger graze her jaw once more before his eyes moved to her mouth. "Do you know how many times I have imagined kissing you since your birthday kiss?"

"No."

He responded instantly. "Every night when I first see the moon in the night's sky, and every morning before the sun hides it."

She had to stare at him in silence for a minute. "Why, then?"

He looked back at the ceiling. "I think it has something to do with how I visited you every night before I took your memory of us. When I saw the moon, I knew you were waiting for me. And when it disappeared behind the blue sky, I knew I had to leave."

"Hello and goodbye kisses."

"Good night and good morning." He corrected, smiling a little now while he kept his gaze on the ceiling. "You are my moon—all that I see in the dark sky."

She smiled, too, and leaned back to join him in staring upwards. "That's kinda romantic, Death." She chuckled and leaned against him more. "I did not expect that."

"I'm not romantic," he said, chuckling. "I imagined more than just kissing when I saw the moon. Loving you as you're completely naked under the moonlight is definitely one of my favorite recurring fantasies."

"Pervert." She smiled wider, enjoying the sound of his laugh.

"You love it."

"I do, actually. And I love the moon part."

"I know you love it." He chuckled. "Naughty girl. Next full moon: you, me—butt naked."

She laughed and let her head roll to the side. He copied her, giving her a smile that was *hers,* and hers alone.

"I love you," she whispered.

"And I love you," he replied instantly. God, she loved his voice.

"But we—"

"I know." He let out a breath. "But I will kiss you when I wish. Unless you tell me to stop, of course."

"You'll force me to kiss you?"

"I didn't say that. I said unless you tell me to stop, I will kiss you when I want. I cannot help it anymore." He eyed her seriously. "Are you telling me to stop?"

The response of yes should have been instant, but she could only stare at his gorgeous face in silence, and David chose that moment to walk through the doorway with Arthur right behind him.

Jane and Death slowly looked in David's direction, but neither moved to sit up straight yet.

David eyed where Death's hand rested on Jane's shoulder before looking back at a smiling Death. Surprisingly, though, Death chuckled and removed his arm before lifting his legs off the table to sit up. David smiled, that is, until Death grabbed hold of her right hand. Jane didn't really pay attention to Death—she was waiting for David to tell her how things went.

Death chuckled again and David grunted before he looked away.

"What's funny?" she asked Death.

He squeezed her hand, smiling. "Nothing." He looked to David and Arthur. "How did Dagonet's conversation with Jason go?"

They took a seat on the opposite couch as Arthur started. "So far—good. He's aware that we intend to relocate and bring them with us. He knows I have news for him, but not that you're alive or that you have been with us the entire time.

"There's not really a delicate way to handle this situation, I'm afraid. To keep him calm and still willing to come, I will explain we gave you a treatment to save you from the virus. And the only reason we kept the information was because of how dangerous and uncertain your recovery was. After all, losing you a second time wouldn't help any of them."

"That makes sense," she said, happy that it was partially true—they weren't sure of anything about her.

"I'll make up something about your appearance," Arthur said, searching her face. "As well as your similarities with us now. I'm sure he will already be happy to hear you're alive and want to go directly to you, but I need you both to understand the dangers here. So I will tell him you're unstable, which you are, and that you may always be this way, but that we are taking measures to ensure their safety.

"Since David and Death are the only two who can overpower you, it will not be a lie when I inform him of this. He'll have to accept that any member of your family alone with you is not permitted; one of them must always be at your side."

Jane swallowed and leaned forward as Death gently squeezed her hand. "He won't like that."

Arthur sighed and rubbed his tired face. "Probably not. But we have no choice. None of us are exaggerating the danger, Jane. You could injure or kill your family in the blink of an eye. You know that's your worst fear."

"I know," she said, looking down at Death's hand as it held hers. His tanned skin was so beautiful next to her pale hand.

Arthur spoke again. "This will be overwhelming for Jason. I would not be surprised if he ends up angry. I will explain the urgency of our departure and that whether he agrees or not, you will be coming with us. And you wish to bring your children. He can come or stay; it matters not to me."

"Brother," David said, shaking his head at Arthur. "They are a family. We will not split them up."

Arthur looked at Jane. "It is not my desire to separate your family, but I think you know why I care so little for Jason's wishes."

Death squeezed her hand, and David's eye color lightened a bit as he stared at her with an expectant look. She breathed out, relieved that David didn't seem to know what Arthur and Death knew.

"What's he talking about, Jane?" David asked.

"Now is not the time," Death told him, earning an annoyed glare from David. "She knows to let us handle Jason." He turned to her and grabbed her chin to turn her face toward his. The cool and warm sensation of his touch relaxed her. "Don't you, Sweet Jane?"

"I trust you to handle Jason," she told him.

Death gave her a serious look. "You should never have been treated that way. You are worth everything, and you should never think the way you do about yourself because of him." Her eyes watered.

"Those were his faults and weaknesses," he said. "Not because you had failed him in some way. Do you understand me?" He rubbed her trembling lip as she nodded. "That's my girl. Let us deal with him." He leaned forward and kissed her head, then let go of her face to stand.

He turned to help her up, too, and she looked to see David staring at them. She sighed and rubbed her forehead as she smiled. Even with them all working together, she knew it wasn't going to be simple with Jason. It wasn't ever her intention to let David know some of the things he'd found out about her and Jason, but she wasn't ready to tell him these things.

David stayed quiet as Death shook his head at him, a silent order to not talk about anything else.

David smiled back at her. "We'll deal with him together."

Jane glanced around, meeting each of their confident gazes and took a deep breath. "Okay."

CHAPTER 42
JASON
VS
JANE'S IMMORTALS

"Mr. Winters, it's Gawain again. May we come in?"

Jason moved to the window and made room for it to be opened as he spoke. "I've already packed some things, but I have a little more I need to get—just some things that belonged to my wife—stuff I'm not ready to part with." He spotted Gawain first, then a larger, more intimidating man behind him. He smiled politely, but the man simply nodded and climbed through the window.

"We understand," Gawain said. "And it's no problem. We can help you gather what you need here shortly." He gestured to the other man. "Let me introduce my commander, Arthur."

Jason reached out to shake Arthur's hand, but he did not return the greeting, so Jason lowered his hand to his side.

"Mr. Winters," said Arthur, "I have some matters to discuss with you before we depart."

"Please call me Jason."

Arthur nodded. "All right—Jason—when my men approached you, they told you we came across your wife. I'm sure she relayed her initial meeting with a few of my men?" Jason nodded and Arthur resumed, "And you were then told about us finding her after she fled from your home with the virus—"

Jason nodded. "Yes. Jane told me about running into three men, and Gawain told me about her asking you to help us before she died."

"She did not die," Arthur said bluntly. "She's alive, and you will be reunited with her shortly."

Jason couldn't think. "What? I—I don't understand—"

Arthur sighed and glanced around the room briefly. "We had a way to keep her from succumbing to death and stopped the effects of the plague."

"Jane's alive?" He didn't know how to describe the feeling attempting to grow inside himself.

"Yes, very much so," Arthur said. "Let me explain a few things before you get your hopes up."

Jason's racing heart nearly came to an abrupt stop at the thoughts of her being crippled or worse. "Oh, God, is she—"

Arthur held up his hand. "She is healthy." Jason let out a breath. "However, there are some side effects of the treatment."

"What kind?" Jason knew Jane wouldn't want to be disfigured or a burden.

"Dangerous side effects," Arthur said without any kindness. "It was either that or let her change. If we allowed that, we would have been forced to eliminate her."

Jason grabbed his head. "So what's wrong with her now? Why did you let them lie to me about her? Why didn't she come home?"

"Nothing is wrong with her. I did not order my men to lie, I ordered them to omit information for the safety of your family and wife. She has been with us—I have her waiting close by. But before I allow her near you or your children, you will listen to what I have to say. Do you understand?"

Jason didn't like this guy now, but he nodded.

"Do you notice my physical differences from you? Gawain and Dagonet, as well?"

Jason nodded, shifting his eyes between them. He wasn't going to list them, but he wasn't blind.

"We underwent the same treatment as Jane," Arthur said slowly. "Only, we've had time to adjust to life as we are now—Jane has not. She is, and may always be, unstable and unsafe to be around. The control we have harnessed has not come quickly, and it will not for her. In fact, she is a great deal more dangerous than most of us.

"Do not misunderstand, she is the same person, but the treatment has permanently changed her physically, mentally, and emotionally. At any moment, she could easily lose control of herself and harm you or your children."

"What do you mean?" Jason glared at the two men. "What did you do to her?"

Gawain held out his hands to calm him. "Jason, we saved her. That's what matters, is it not?"

"Yes, that's what matters! But you're saying she's dangerous? That I can't trust her with our children?"

"No, you cannot trust her with them or yourself." Arthur's calmness over everything he was saying only irritated Jason. "Actually, she is a threat to everyone, including us. Which brings me to the next part. There are only two who can control her—well, more appropriately, help her maintain control. If needed, they can overpower her, physically."

"What?" Jason began to pace the room. "This is a joke. Jane is a tiny thing. Are you even sure we're talking about the same woman?"

"Yes, the woman I speak of is Jane," Arthur said. "I would not joke about such things. Now, listen to what I say. These two men are stronger than anyone you will ever meet, and it is only they who will be able to keep Jane from doing something that could devastate everyone."

"Two men?" The words burned Jason's throat.

Arthur settled a threatening stare on Jason as he said, "Jealousy is expected, but I will not tolerate unpleasant behavior from you."

"Me?" Jason yelled.

"It's simple, Jason: Piss me off, I will remove you from contact with her. Piss either of those men off, you're playing with death." Arthur chuckled. "Anger or upset your wife–and death will be a gift she grants you herself. Need I say more?"

"I want to talk to her," Jason said. "Now."

"You will speak to her when I say," Arthur said calmly. "Now you know we agreed to relocate you; that is true. However, we will be relocating to my home in Canada."

"I'm not going to Canada." Jason spat. "I want to see Jane. I will discuss with her where we go."

"Jane comes with us," Arthur said. "That is not up for discussion."

"Like hell she will!"

"Mr. Winters, I advise you to take a seat and reconsider how you speak to me. I do not have to bring you with us, but Jane wants all of you to come. Your home is under threat; she knows this, and she will not allow her children to be left behind for slaughter."

Jason breathed out angrily but sat anyway.

Arthur continued, "You have the choice to stay, if you wish. If you come, you will abide by my rules. I will not be questioned. Do we have an understanding?"

These people had his wife all this time, and now they were taking her while ordering him around like he was below them. He had no choice, though. He wasn't a fool. They were armed, dangerous, and they had Jane.

"I'll come."

✦✦✦

Jane and her two immortals stood outside the window Arthur and Gawain had entered earlier. They hadn't spoken, only listened in silence to the conversation happening. Death hugged her when she covered her eyes to keep from letting them see how upset Jason and Arthur's conversation was making her.

David hadn't look happy either, as he cast an annoyed look at Death when Jason started to argue with Arthur about them needing to be with her.

"I can't believe he's so angry," she whispered into Death's chest. "I thought he would be happy I'm alive."

Death leaned back to look at her. "He is, Jane. This is shocking for him. Arthur is just telling him how it is. I won't have a problem doing the same." He smirked and nodded to David. "I've been waiting for the chance to fuck with this bastard."

"He's not that bad," Jane said as David chuckled. "Please behave. I just want to see my family and get out of here."

Death sighed. "Sorry, babe. Just for your sexy ass, I'll play nice."

"Leave her ass out of your thoughts," David said.

Death snickered at David's glare and lowered one hand to hover over her bottom. "You're right—these sweet cheeks should be in my hand."

"Death," Jane scolded, turning out of his hold and smacking his hand.

David stepped close to Death. "I can't kill you. But touch her ass—or any part of her she does not wish you to—and I will rip off your damned arm."

Jane gasped and looked between them, watching Death smirk while his eyes burned so brightly they cast a green glow across David's face.

"And what if she never tells me not to? What if she likes it?" Death's smirk grew. "She does, by the way."

David smiled, and it was about the most frightening look she'd ever seen on his handsome face. "Then I will rip off both your arms."

Death laughed, truly laughed, and Jane took that chance to push herself between both men. "Please don't fight."

Both men glanced down at her, and shocking her, they both grinned.

"This is the only way I can tolerate him," said David.

Her mouth fell open, and she looked to Death.

"We're men," was all her angel said.

"Okay." She rubbed her temples and mentally counted to ten. "Just hands off my ass, and no ripping limbs from anyone."

Death chuckled at her. "You're no fun."

David laughed, too, and turned back to the window and stuck his head in. "I think we should go say hello, now."

Jane looked between the both of them, but rushed back into Death's arms quickly.

"See?" Death chuckled again as David turned away.

"She has to sleep sometime," David muttered, climbing through the window.

"That's right, Sweet Jane," Death whispered in her ear as he placed his hands on her waist from behind to help lift her. "When the cat's away, the big bad wolves will play."

Jane turned to glare at him. "That's not how the saying goes."

"Do we look like mice?" He lifted her up as David chuckled and held his hands out for hers.

David pulled her through the window and snuck a quick kiss to her temple, which made her face hotter than any Texas sun ever had.

"I saw that." Death glared at David as he squeezed a part of the window frame hard enough to make the wood splinter under his hands.

At first, she thought he was angry at David, but his glare at the window while he bent down to pull himself through made her realize he wasn't angry with them. She giggled and walked to help pull him through.

Finally, he got through and stood, dusting off his jacket. "Shut up. I'm not used to taking doors, let alone a fucking window."

David laughed quietly. "No one said you had to come through the window."

Death flipped David off, shoving him in the chest, not hard, but enough to make him move, and pulled Jane back to his side.

David let the exchange go with a smile, and Jane grinned, happy to see them not exhibiting any true malice against one another. Her vampire caught her eye and winked, and she felt as if David knew she needed Death more than him at the moment. *Perfect.*

He confirmed her thoughts when he moved closer and cupped her cheek with one hand. "I know he has to be close enough to touch you if you lose control." This made her smile more; he really did understand—and he wasn't letting the fact Death had more power bother him anymore. "But I will be right here."

"I know," she said, smiling as Death took her hand.

The angel smirked at David's quick glance to their hands. "Lead the way, Mr. Perfect—I'll take her in her rear."

They walked through the house, halting when Arthur's voice rang out.

"Jason, this is David, my second in command. David, this is Jason."

Jane stared at David's tense shoulders and then noticed how one of his hands had balled into a fist.

"Jason," said David.

"David," said Jason. "May I see *my* wife now? Or did you plan on giving me a lecture as well?"

Jane's eyes widened at Jason's harsh tone. She could barely breathe from all the tension in the atmosphere and judging by the rigidness in David's posture, her vampire was ready to cut that tension, and Jason's claim on her.

Death pulled her close and turned her face to look at him. "Let us handle him." He pecked her cheek, then straightened, taking her hand in his.

She nodded and looked down at his hand. Apparently, Death planned on staking his claim, too. *Oh, great.*

David turned slightly and called out to her. "Jane, you may come in now."

Death squeezed her hand. "Showtime," he said, pulling her behind him and letting Jason get a view of him first.

Jane immediately panicked, wondering if Jason would react the same way the knights had when they first met him, but noticing a quick exchange of nods between Arthur and Death, she hoped her angel had some trick up his sleeve.

Jason certainly looked unsure as he eyed Death, but he didn't look as shocked as the knights had been. He stood tall despite the fact the man holding her hand was taller, more built, and definitely not hiding his glowing eyes.

"Jane?" Jason called out, snapping her thoughts away from Death.

Death stopped and carefully pulled her out from behind him but kept a firm grip on her hand. She was shaking, but she moved around slowly and looked up at a pair of brown eyes.

"Jason." Her eyes watered at the sight of his shocked face.

"I can't believe you're alive," Jason whispered. "Are you hurt? Are you okay? My God, you're really alive!"

"I'm fine," she told him quickly. "They've taken good care of me." She glanced at Death, then David, smiling when David moved a tiny bit closer to them.

At that moment, Jason's gaze fell on Death's hand holding hers, then snapped up to glare at her angel. "Who are you?"

Jane frowned at Jason, forgetting their reunion for now.

Death, however, smiled innocently. "Jason, it's a pleasure to finally meet you in person. I'm Ryder."

Ryder? Jane looked around the room, noticing the confused expressions from David and Gawain. Then she felt stupid for expecting him to walk up to her husband and introduce himself as the Angel of Death.

Jason's bravado slipped at the sound of Death's voice. She had talked to him so often and felt bliss at his smooth tone, but she knew the power hidden in his words must intimidate anyone he spoke to.

Once again, though, Jason looked down at hers and Death's joined hands. "Jane." He held out his hand for her. "Please come here."

Without thinking, she looked to David for approval. If he was okay with it, it should be safe.

He smiled and nodded. "It's okay. We are right here."

She didn't move, though, and glanced up at Death.

"Go on, babe. I'm not going anywhere."

Jason glared at the exchange between all three of them but softened as she prepared to step away.

Her chest ached when she moved away from her immortals. She tried to breathe evenly and barely controlled flinching when Jason's fingers touched her cheek. She smiled, but inside she wanted to move away from his slightly warm touch. There were no shocks, no tingles, no addicting fire from his skin on hers. She smiled sadly, and she felt horrible because her husband's touch was not the one she craved.

The last time she'd felt cared for by him was when she was dying. She couldn't recall the last loving gesture she'd received from him before that time.

"It's you," Jason said. "You're really here."

"It's me." She nodded. "I'm so glad that you're all safe."

Jason shook his head before yanking her into a tight hug. Tears filled his eyes and he pulled back, cupping her face in his hands, looking between her eyes as though he still couldn't believe she was there. "I thought I'd never see you again," he whispered, running his fingers through her hair.

Without warning, Jason pulled her face to his and kissed her. "God," he said against her unresponsive lips. "I love you so much, Jane. I thought I lost you."

He kissed her over and over, but Jane could only stand there in shock. She wanted to cry for the fact she should be happy to be home with him, but she wasn't. It didn't feel like home anymore. Jason had never been who she felt peace or protection with, and it had been so long since he'd given her a real kiss.

Home, she thought, quickly shifting her eyes to David's but then looked forward so she wouldn't get sucked in by those turbulent, blue orbs staring at her.

When Jason seemed to realize she wasn't responding, he pulled back. She couldn't look him in the eye and looked away from his gaze. He gripped her face a little harder. "What's wrong?"

She still kept her eyes away from his while Jason glanced around the room.

Death kept a blank expression, but David's was unmistakable. He was absolutely furious. His icy glare settled on Jane's turned head. She still avoided looking at Jason but slowly made eye contact with David and almost smiled when his rage vanished.

"What was that?" Jason yelled as he roughly pulled her face back toward his.

"Jason." She stared wide-eyed at the hate in his dark eyes.

"Don't fucking *Jason* me!" His voice grew louder and more enraged with each word. "You left us! I've been losing my mind thinking you're dead—I thought you died, Jane! But no—you've been with these people—these *men*—while I've been taking care of our children!"

Both David and Death moved closer, but Jason ignored them and continued yelling in her face. "You have no idea how hard it's been—how awful I've felt thinking you were dead. Do you have any idea what you've put me through? What our kids have been dealing with?"

Her heart throbbed painfully. She hadn't meant to hurt him so badly. She hadn't meant to forget about them. She had only pushed them far enough out of her active thoughts so she wouldn't break. Jane whimpered and tried to look away from him. She hated herself for leaving them—for not dying like she was supposed to.

Jason looked away from her to glare at David. "Is it because of him that you didn't want to come back?" He looked back at her, and Jane gaped as she stared between both violent-looking males. Rage flitted across Jason's face. "It is, isn't it? Was this the plan all along? When you first met him? Pretend to be sick so you could be with him?"

Jane shook her head, frantically. "That's not what happened, Jason. I never talked to him that first night. And it hasn't been easy for me! I wanted to come back from the very beginning—I just couldn't. You don't understand what's happened. Give me a chance to explain."

Jason gave her a dirty look. "Bullshit, Jane. I always knew if you got the chance, you would spread your legs for the first man who looked at you."

She gasped at the same moment David let out a dangerous snarl and yanked her so she was behind his back.

Before Jane could comprehend being shoved behind David, Death had also gotten in front of her, and she watched him squeeze David's shoulder. *Hard.* She figured this was Death calming or simply restraining David, but it had to hurt.

David didn't flinch.

No one spoke for a full minute, simply watching the angry stare-down.

Jason didn't see the true threat, apparently, and when he looked down at David still holding Jane's wrist, he snapped. "Get your hands off my goddamned wife, you son of a bitch!"

Blood! All she wanted was Jason's blood. Nothing made sense or mattered, and she moved.

Death didn't react fast enough. In an instant, she was standing between David and Jason, hissing and preparing to rip off his head.

David still had a hold of her wrist, though, and he held her back.

"Don't talk to him that way!" She tried to hit Jason, but David secured his arms around her waist, keeping her from tackling her husband to the ground. "You have no idea who he is. I'll kill you," she shouted, thrashing in David's arms. "I'll let him kill you. How can you say that about me? I hate you!"

Death moved in front of her. "David, take her out of here. Gawain, go with him. I will be with her in a moment to help calm her."

David didn't argue, and she faintly realized he'd been whispering in her ear to relax. But she kept her bloodthirsty gaze on Jason as she let him drag her out of the room.

✦✦✦

Once she was out of the room, Death turned his attention to Jason. "Talk to her like that one more time, and we're going to have ourselves a serious problem." Jason visibly swallowed before Death spoke again. "She has been through hell and back. Do not think for one moment she has been having the time of her life. She knows that it has been difficult for you—we all do. But it has been a living nightmare for her."

"That man"—Death jabbed his finger toward the archway where David had taken Jane—"is the best man that I have ever seen, and he saved your wife. You owe him as much as you owe these men who have been guarding your home and bringing you supplies.

"As for me, I'm not afraid to tell you I love her. You, nor anyone else, will destroy what she and I share. And I don't give a fuck what you think about that. Try to keep her from me, and I will break your goddamned neck.

"You can try and test me all you want, boy, but you will show those two the respect they deserve. And if you hurt her again—and I'm not simply talking about this shit you just displayed." He smiled in a terrifying way. "Yeah, I know all about the shit you've put her through. You've let her break and fall down again and again, ignoring or kicking her every time she tried to get back up."

Jason's eyes widened.

"There it is," Death said, sniffing deeply. "You should fear me. I promise when you fuck up—and I know you will—I will enjoy watching you beg for your life when I take it in my hands." He smiled and stood tall. "Do I make myself clear?"

Jason nodded quickly. "I shouldn't have said that to her. It's just overwhelming to see her again."

Death eyed him before taking a step back. "Arthur will discuss the plans regarding your departure. I don't expect there to be any problems with his offer. But in case you feel like throwing a tantrum—remember this—the kids go with Jane whether you like it or not." He didn't wait for Jason to reply and left the room. It only took a moment for him to find Jane clinging to David down the hall.

He made eye contact with David who carefully moved Jane so she could be pulled into his embrace.

"*Shh . . .*" Death squeezed her trembling body and kissed the top of her head. "It's fine now. You did really well."

She shook her head. "I almost killed him!"

Death chuckled. "No, you didn't. I wouldn't have let you."

Any further discussion on what had just happened came to a halt when a voice down the hall drew all their attention. "Mommy?"

CHAPTER 43

GOOD NIGHT

Jane fell to her knees at the sight of her son standing at the end of the hall.

"Mommy," he said with his eyes wide.

She nodded, crying. "It's mommy, bubby."

David knelt down beside her, smiling at her little boy while Death squatted behind her, rubbing her back.

Nathan ran to Jane, and she quickly pulled him into a hug. Tears streamed down her face as Nathan smiled and cried, "Mommy" repeatedly into her shoulder.

Gawain's voice joined Nathan's, and Jane looked up to see him carrying Natalie. Her little curls were all tangled and her sleepy face had failed to register the new occupants in the room.

"Look, Natalie," said Gawain, "you're missing all the fun. Don't you want to see who I've brought to you today?"

"I'm sleepy." Natalie yawned, still oblivious to the three adults staring at her.

"Just like her mother," Death whispered softly in Jane's ear.

"Mommy home!" Nathan chirped.

At her brother's words, Natalie's eyes flew open and connected right with Jane's. The small girl blinked a couple times but stayed quiet.

Gawain whispered in her ear. "She's real, Natalie. Mommy's home." The knight placed her down on the floor and finally Natalie sprang toward Jane as she held her arm out.

Jane cried tears of happiness, unable to form words while Natalie cried touching her face as if to confirm she was really there.

Jane couldn't believe she held her children in her arms again. They smelled so much more like their baby smell than she ever recalled. Between the tingles from Death's touch against her back, the heat from David beside her, and the softness of her children in her arms—Jane felt peace.

It took nearly five minutes for their cries to quiet down. Jane looked at David and gave him the happiest smile she could give, hoping her gratitude showed on her face. She was with them again because of him.

David reached out and gently caressed her cheek with the back of his fingers, using his thumb to wipe away some of her tears as he nodded.

She leaned into his hand for only a second before she tried to hold the kids away. Nathan, however, wouldn't budge and clung tightly to her neck. She sighed, already knowing he was not going to let go anytime soon. "I want you guys to meet some very important people."

Finally, both children looked up, registering the two enormous men next to her.

First she gestured to David. "Nathan, Natalie, this is David. He saved me when I got sick. He cured the sickness mommy had." She smiled at David. "I care about him a whole lot."

They looked at David as if he were a superhero.

He chuckled and held out his hand to Nathan. "Hello, Nathan." David waited for him to take his hand, but Nathan only stared at the hand being offered.

Jane smiled at David's adorableness when he shot her a pleading look, and she took Nathan's hand to place in David's. She prompted her son. "Say: Hello, David."

Nathan looked to his mom and copied, "Hello, David."

David grinned. "It's nice to finally meet you, little man." He let go of his hand and turned to Natalie. "Hello, Natalie. It's a pleasure to meet you as well. You're just as beautiful as your mommy." Jane blushed and Natalie hid her face. David chuckled and took her little hand before kissing the back of it.

Jane laughed at her daughter's obvious captivation with David and continued her introductions. "And this is Ryder," she said, gesturing toward Death. "I met him when I was a little girl. He came back to me." She held Death's gaze. "He's always been there for me. I would not be here without him." She looked back at her children. "He's my angel."

"Like a real angel?" Natalie asked, looking a little stunned as she stared at Death while Nathan seemed less interested.

"Do you believe in angels?" Death asked her.

Natalie nodded, blushing more than she was before, and Jane wondered just who her children saw when they looked at him. "Mommy said they're real. But she also says we're angels."

"You don't have wings." Death didn't show an ounce of emotion as he spoke to her daughter. It baffled Jane completely to see him so stone-faced.

"Neither do you," Natalie pointed out, making David chuckle.

Death didn't even smile, but he did turn his head to look at his shoulder. "Maybe I'm using magic to hide them." He looked back at the girl, still without a hint of warmth in his gaze.

"Dea—" Jane stopped and corrected herself. "I mean, Ryder." He moved his eyes to her and only then did she see his green eyes warm. She had never noticed it before, but now she recalled he looked at everyone without an ounce of feeling. Except her.

"What?" he asked.

She gazed at his face, her eyes moving over every perfect feature about him before looking at David. He gave her a sympathetic smile, and she looked back to Death. "You have to be sweeter with her."

He tilted his head a little as if he didn't comprehend the request, then looked back at her daughter. Once more the warm glow in his eyes dimmed.

Despite the cold change in his expression, Natalie smiled at him. "Your magic hides them?"

"Maybe," he said. "Or maybe I'm not an angel."

"Mommy doesn't lie." Natalie retorted, and Jane sighed. Natalie was impossible to argue with.

Death looked at Jane, his lips curving upward a tiny bit. "*Hm.* I'm sure she's lied about a thing or two before." He looked back at Natalie, again, completely neutral. "So, what do you think? Am I a real angel? Or just some sexy guy your mom can't stop staring at?"

Jane slapped her forehead as Natalie and Nathan giggled. She pulled her hand away, glaring at Death.

"What? I'm sexy," he said.

David chuckled and turned to speak to her daughter. "I think there are different kinds of angels, princess. You're still your mommy's angel."

"Oh," said Natalie. "But I don't have wings."

David grinned. "I think that's because you're a special kind of angel. The other angels might be jealous because you're already so pretty."

Natalie smiled brightly and turned back to Death. "Is that why you don't have wings? Because you're so pretty the other angels will be jealous?"

"Like mother, like daughter," Death said, dropping the smile he'd given Jane when he turned his gaze back to her daughter. "But don't call me pretty again. Only Sweet Jane can call me pretty."

Natalie giggled at that exact moment Arthur and Jason walked around the corner.

All smiles, even her children's, disappeared at the sight of the two unhappy men.

Jane nodded to Gawain, signaling to take Natalie. He did. She then whispered into Nathan's ear that she wanted him to go with David. Surprisingly, her son held out his arms for David without protest.

David stood and quickly pulled him from her arms. Jane was temporarily captivated by the sight of him holding her son so naturally, but Death standing up behind her and sliding one hand around her waist to lift her up, snapped her out of her dreaming.

Finally, standing, she glared at her husband. Jason's hostility toward Death and David wasn't something she was willing to accept. They were her protectors. Her lifesavers. Despite their abilities to protect themselves, she couldn't stop herself from needing to defend them.

"Jane," Arthur said. "Jason has agreed to come with us. We'll start packing what's important to you and head over to the base. Our plane will arrive in seven hours."

Jason sighed and took one step closer. "I'm sorry, Jane."

"Don't apologize to me," she said, feeling a fiery rage simmering under her skin. Death pulled her back flush against his body.

He leaned down and whispered in her ear. "David is a big boy. Let's just play nice. Remember, your children are watching."

Jason eyed Death's hold on her but said nothing as Jane barely picked up on the action. She had always cuddled with Death; it felt natural to have him so close anyway. But right now, she wanted to make sure David was okay.

She looked at her vampire and received a nod from him, a silent confirmation all was well, and she huffed before looking back to Jason. "Thank you." She barely contained the hiss wanting to slip out of her mouth. "I'll handle getting my things and checking over the kids' belongings."

"Can we talk for a minute?" Jason asked.

"I have nothing to say to you right now." That time her sharp tone was unavoidable. "You made it clear to everyone how you see me. I can't be around you without doing something I'll regret. You have no idea how—" Jane let out a frustrated growl as her temper started to get the best of her and quickly walked toward the kid's room, thankful Death let her go without a fuss.

She couldn't even look at Jason without hearing his words. It hurt that he'd apparently always thought she'd do that, but the worst part was, in a way, she had. She had crawled right on David's lap, accepted his sweet words and touches, and eagerly accepted more affection from Death.

She had, indeed, spread her legs for David and Death. She'd done it all while Jason believed she was dead.

Jane let out a frustrated growl and walked faster.

✦✦✦

Death eyed David as neither of them moved to follow Jane. "David, go with her. She's angry, but she needs you."

David glared at him, but threw a more violent look at Jason before he left to find Jane.

Death chuckled and looked back to see Gawain also standing there, glaring at Jason. He shook his head. *I must do everything around here.*

"Come," Death held out his arms for Natalie, who was looking between everyone confused. Just like Jane had always been, she eagerly went to him, blushing also like her mother. "Let's go help your sexy mom pack your things and put a smile back on her face."

Jason opened his mouth likely to say something, but Death grinned in a way he knew terrified everyone. Jason shut his mouth.

Death snickered and muttered to himself as he situated Natalie better. "Pussy. No idea why I thought I could leave her in your hands."

"What's that supposed to mean?" Jason asked.

Death made his eyes glow brighter and smiled when Natalie touched his cheek, not afraid of the violent stare he gave her father. *Just like Jane,* he mused.

He decided since Jason had hurt Jane, which he had more than she let on to everyone here, he'd return the favor. It seemed only fair for Jason to realize he's not as great as he thought himself to be.

"Tell me, Jason, do you ever wonder why you believed Jane when her classmates called her a liar?" Death's lips pulled back, revealing a more frightening smile. "Ever think about your confrontation with her uncle—the threats you made to him? Not something you would normally do, am I right? Do you reflect on your earliest memories with her and realize it was all one big blur?"

Jason's mouth opened and closed a few times. "How do you—"

He cut him off. "It's a shame the only moments she admires about you are not really your own doing." Death smirked at Jason's shocked face. "Don't worry, she's clueless. You can go on holding how you *saved* her as a pass for what you have done to her, but you know the truth.

"One day, though, all secrets will come to light. One day, she will stop trying to please you no matter how much it hurts her. I suggest you use the time given to you to become a real man in her eyes. It would be far better if she could hold on to something truly worthy of you instead of realizing it was all a lie." Death glanced at Arthur, not reacting to the faint smile the legendary king wore, then left to find Jane.

✦✦✦

The cold leather under Jane's cheek normally brought her so much peace; it meant Death was with her. Only, this time, it meant goodbye.

She hugged him tighter where they stood alone in the master bedroom of the base camp. David had gone to occupy her kids so she could say her goodbyes.

"I don't want you to go," she whispered.

"I have to. I'll meet you soon, though. You won't even miss me."

She looked up at him, trying to soak up his beautiful smile and touch as he rubbed her cheek. "Will you tell me what you've been doing and what happened with the demons when you come back?"

He grinned, a bit of a menacing glee lighting in his emerald eyes as he spoke. "Yes, if you promise to stay strong, and stay with David. No running off, and you must enjoy being reunited with your family. I did not behave myself just so you could feel like shit the entire time you're back with that dick."

"Death." She huffed as she played with his leather jacket. "Please be nicer about Jason. It's because you left that I even looked at him."

He shrugged. "That may be, but he is a dick all on his own."

"Whatever," she said, chuckling. "Thanks for behaving. And I promise to stay close to David while I enjoy my family."

"And no running off," he restated.

She smiled. "I won't run away again. But please come back to me quickly. You don't understand how I feel without you."

"I'll do my best, and I do understand." He caressed her cheek.

"You do?"

He nodded. "Incomplete. I feel it, too."

She nodded as her eyes watered. "It hurts."

"I know, angel," he murmured but suddenly grinned and grabbed her butt. "Back to serious business, though. If you run off, I'm smacking this mouthwatering ass until it's as red as your face when I turn you on." He squeezed, and she yelped, feeling her face burn. "*Hm . . .*" He squeezed again. "I never knew you were into that. Good to know."

"Death." She leveled him with a serious look. "Let go."

He didn't. "Are you running off again? I can take your sweet ass with me. Fuck David and Jason. You were mine first."

She laughed. She loved that he always tried to put her in a better mood. "Would you really take me if I asked?"

He stared at her for a few seconds. "Maybe. Do you want to come with me?"

Her mouth hung open, and she realized maybe that meant going with him forever. "Do you mean like for the bet?"

"If you want it to be." His face showed no sign of hope, but she could see the desire in his eyes.

"I can't leave my children, Death," she said quickly. She wanted to go with him so badly, but she couldn't.

"Then stay." He didn't say it coldly, but it stung her heart nonetheless.

"I'll stay."

"And?" He tapped her ass, making her laugh even though she wanted to cry.

"And I will not run off."

"That's my girl." He sighed, squeezing her butt once more before sliding his hand up to the small of her back, *under* her shirt.

She tried not to moan but still let out a small noise of approval. "But we should talk about the bet when you come back. And about David." She bit her lip, nervous about how much closer she'd become with the knight. It was impossible to not feel guilty about David and even Jason when she was with Death.

He nodded as his gaze swept over her face until it settled on her lips. "As long as you stay away from Luc, there is nothing to worry about. And I know your feelings for David have grown."

She waited for him to say more, but he only continued to stare at her mouth.

"I'm going to kiss you, Jane."

Her pulse sped up. This was wrong. Jason was very much back in her life, and there was still David. All she had to do was tell him no.

"I'm not asking." Barely brushing them together, he whispered, "My Sweet Jane. These lips will always be mine. You know they are mine. Don't you?"

She needed this. So she smiled and closed her eyes as she felt his lips turn up as well.

Softly, he pressed their lips together. The tingles made her lips feel fuzzy, and she loved it.

She sighed and gripped his shoulders while Death let out a deep purring noise and pulled her closer, molding their bodies together. He was so tall, but he always made their kiss and closeness seem effortless.

He swept his tongue over the seam of her lips, prompting her to open her mouth. She did quickly, moaning as he nipped them once before slipping his tongue inside, sending warmth throughout her body.

Without realizing it, her hands came around the back of his neck and slid up into his hair. She whimpered and pressed her body closer to his. He liked that, apparently, and deepened his kiss until her lungs began to burn.

Our goodbye kiss.

He finally let her breathe but sucked her lip gently, humming as they both enjoyed the sweetness of each other's taste. Releasing her lip, he then pressed one more brief kiss to her tender lips and pulled away. They both smiled sadly at each other.

She hated this. Her eyes and inside of her nose stung while she tried to keep her tears at bay. Her panic rose, and she gripped him tighter.

Death sighed and rested his forehead against hers, putting off his inevitable departure.

She struggled to form words. "I love you."

"And I love you. I will never stop." He kissed her nose. "Be happy, baby girl. I will see you again." He kissed her lips softly and then let his gaze drift toward the window where they could see the moon glowing in the dark sky.

She saw it and whined before looking back at him.

"Good night, Sweet Jane. My moon."

Gone.

She sobbed, finally letting her tears free, and stared at the empty space in front of her. Hugging herself tightly, she prayed the torn sensation her body instantly suffered would let up.

David called from the doorway. "Jane."

She looked over and couldn't contain her sadness as she cried. "He left again."

"I know." He held out his arms. She ran into them and let him hold her together. "He'll be back, but we have to go now. Everyone is waiting." He kissed her forehead. "Be brave, Jane. No more tears."

She nodded and smiled as he wiped away the rest of her tears.

"Good girl," he said, dropping his hand to take hers. He looked around the room and smiled. "Let's go."

Jane smiled and looked back at the room, her eyes catching sight of the moon. "Good night," she whispered and let David pull her away.

CHAPTER 44
GODS & MONSTERS

Jane didn't stop walking as she glanced at the SUV driving behind her. It was her car, and it was carrying her family as it slowly wove between stalled vehicles and corpses littering the roads.

Lucan, the guard she'd not met, had hot-wired another vehicle and taken her pets, along with most of her family's belongings, to the plane waiting for them.

Dagonet waved to her from the driver's seat of her car. She smiled but quickly turned forward when Gawain and Gareth, who were flanking the SUV, motioned for her to turn around.

"Are you sure you do not want to ride with them?" David asked. He was walking beside her.

She shook her head and kept her eyes on the van in front of them. Tristan was driving this one since his leg was still injured. Arthur, Bedivere, and Kay, were walking in front of it. The other knights were behind her family's vehicle.

David nudged her shoulder with his elbow, and she finally responded to him. "I'm sure. I can't be around him right now. I think he's afraid of me, and the kids are asleep anyway."

David lifted his rifle and released a shot. "He's afraid of me, not you." He casually shot another zombie and smirked back at her. "I can smell his fear. He only emits it when he looks at me."

She chuckled because he seemed very pleased with himself. "I was the one who almost killed him, not you."

David grinned. "As dangerous and angry as you were, sweetheart, you are always a beautiful sight. I'm certain I was not the only man captivated by your fury."

She tried not to smile but failed. "Is that your way of saying I'm cute when I'm angry?"

"You blushing right now is cute." He gave her a sexy smile. "Watching the woman I love defend me while proving she would kill for me is definitely one of the sexiest moments I have ever witnessed. So, no, I am not saying you are cute when you are angry. You are breathtakingly beautiful when you are angry."

Jane's face was on fire as she listened to the group of knights laughing around them.

"In other words, Jane," Gareth said, chuckling. "You turn our big boy David on when you're angry."

The group laughed louder while David simply smiled at her before he glanced away. The others followed his lead and raised their rifles, firing shots. Jane shot her own target and tried to stop thinking about David so much. Jason was right behind them, and she'd just said a very passionate goodbye to Death. She didn't know how she was supposed to act around anyone now.

After eliminating the zombies, they all hesitated moving forward and sniffed the air.

"David," Arthur called but said nothing else.

"I'm not sure what they are yet," David said, scanning the perimeter. "They're blocking their scents somehow, but I hear them. There are too many to count. Hundreds."

Arthur walked to Tristan's window and spoke to him quickly as David jogged to Dagonet's door and spoke to him.

Jane's breathing sped up as she glanced at the others. No more smiles, no more vibrant green or blue eyes. Their beautiful eyes were replaced with frightening pale glares while their fangs pressed against their lips.

David ran back to her side and began adjusting her belts, adding more magazines. "We have to move faster, Jane."

"What's happening?" She kept her eyes on the perimeter as the men began tossing extra ammo around.

"These are silver." David showed her one magazine for her rifle. "It won't work like the nitrate the rogues used, but it will burn and prevent them from healing."

"Who, David?"

He stood up and cupped her face. "I cannot tell what they are. It might be Lance or Ares and Hermes with other rogues. They're hunting us."

"I thought Hades left to go after them with his niece," she whispered, leaning into his palm.

"He did," he said, annoyed. "They are using methods I'm not familiar with to hide themselves. They might have been waiting for them and Death to leave before attacking. I need you to concentrate, okay? We will get your family on the plane."

Arthur walked up beside her and patted her back. "The small airstrip we found is only two miles away; we'll get them there. We're almost ready to move out." She looked toward her family as Arthur addressed where her thoughts were about to head. "Jason has still not grasped what we are, Jane, but if we are attacked, there is no more hiding."

"I know." She didn't look away from Jason after she locked eyes with him. He was sitting in the passenger seat next to Dagonet.

Arthur nodded and spoke into his communication piece, "Lucan, we're surrounded. Have the plane prepped for departure and get Tor and Jasper armed at the door. Order them not to leave the plane, though. Once the family is secure, you are clear to leave if we cannot make it."

"Affirmative," was the muffled reply.

"Arthur," she whispered, awed by the sacrifice he was willing to make for her family.

He smiled. "Your children will not fall into evil hands. If we must, we will hold them off until the plane can leave with them."

"Jane as well," David said quickly. He still held her face and gently guided her to look at him again. "Get on the plane, baby. You leave with them if you have to. I'll find you. I'm sure Death will come for you."

She shook her head. "No. I'm not leaving you."

"Jane." David's warning tone did not sway her.

"Don't argue with me, David." She placed one hand over his. "I'm not leaving you."

He smiled that gorgeous smile of his and leaned forward to kiss her forehead. "I will not leave you either."

"If you cannot make it," Arthur addressed everyone as David removed his hands from her face. "Proceed to one of the other designated LZs. Our communications have been cut off with the other teams, but we will reach out every fifteen minutes. After twenty-four hours, if you do not make contact, we will return home."

The knights nodded and moved back into position around the two vehicles.

✦✦✦

Jason watched David take Jane's hand as the others moved away, then he leaned down and whispered in her ear. There was no way to tell what exchanged between them, but Jason clearly saw the love in David's eyes whenever he stared at her, and he'd seen a similar look in Jane's eyes when she received that look from the soldier.

She had blushed and laughed with David every chance she got. Earlier, Jason had assumed Ryder was the one she was cozier with, but he must have been mistaken because there was no denying Jane had feelings for David as well. Her eyes sparkled with something he'd never seen in her before when she looked at both men, but David was the one with her now.

Dagonet snapped his fingers in front of Jason's face, which stopped him from brooding at the pair for the moment. "If something happens, you get out and run. I will carry Nathan while one of the others will carry Natalie for you. My only goal is to get the children on the plane. If you fall, I will not hesitate to leave you behind."

His words were honest, not malicious in any way, and Jason could respect that. "That's all I want. Thank you."

Jason glanced back at his sleeping children but met Dagonet's stare when he turned forward. The others seemed to be preparing to start moving again.

"He loves her more than you can imagine," Dagonet said abruptly. "It is neither of their faults what they feel for one another. They were destined to meet, and they are destined to love one another."

Jason was surprised by the bold statements and turned back to see David shaking his head at Jane as he flipped the safety on her rifle. She pouted and received a kiss on the temple as David gently pushed her back to her spot.

Jason ground his teeth together. "I don't believe in destiny."

Dagonet chuckled and put the car in gear. "Whether or not you believe in destiny, it exists, and they share one of the most important fates of our world."

Jason scoffed, and the car began to move. "You believe what you like, but Jane is my wife. Our marriage is important to her; she won't walk away from me."

"She is loyal and takes her commitment in marriage to you seriously," Dagonet said, turning the wheel but not looking at him. "So my question to you is, did you honor her when she was at her lowest–when she needed you most?" Jason stared at the side of Dagonet's face in shock. "Have you loved and cherished every moment with her? Have you proven your love to her or taken her presence for granted?" Dagonet chuckled. "A good and loving husband would not feel the way you are feeling at this moment, and she would not crave his affection if she had been given it in the first place. You see her happy–something I have gathered she has not been in some time–but you are angry to see her that way."

"Because she shouldn't be that way with another man!"

Dagonet nodded. "True. She should not, and I have a feeling she feels tremendous guilt–"

"She should feel guilty," Jason retorted, furious this man would lecture him. "This is unacceptable."

"Have you ever seen her stare at nothing?" Dagonet asked softly.

Jason frowned and looked back out the window. "What does that have to do with anything?"

"Just humor me, because I have." He inclined his head toward David and Jane. "So has he."

Jason stared at Jane, remembering all the times he'd notice her zoned out or crying. He'd tried to help in the beginning, but she simply wouldn't get better. "She has a shitty past, and she holds onto it–keeping herself sad instead of moving on."

Dagonet chuckled. "I suppose it seems that way to most who have not experienced significant sadness and horror."

"She's not the only person to go through bad things."

"No. But she is your wife." Dagonet glanced at him before looking at the road. "Have you been there for her when it consumes her?"

"Yes," Jason snapped, not knowing why he was letting all of this out in front of this man. "I was a teenage boy, and I suddenly had all this pressure to take care of her. I love her, but she's not easy to put up with. But that still doesn't mean *this* is okay. I haven't cheated on her."

Dagonet stayed relaxed. "Put up with her, you say. What does that entail?"

"I'm through with this conversation."

"Have you talked to her—really talked to her? Do you even recall the last time she confided in you? The last time you touched her in a way that displayed love a husband should have for his wife, so she would know it is okay to seek comfort from you?"

Jason sighed. He was done, but Dagonet kept talking anyway.

"In the little time he has known her, David has not *put up* with her. He has been a pillar of strength and undying love at her side while she's been separated from you. And I swear to you, they were not lying when they said she's been through hell. She's still there, and David is holding her so she doesn't slip away.

"Ryder may have played a more active role in pulling her out of the dark, but it is David who has stayed. In the condition I witnessed her in, and what I have heard from others, she is not a woman who has been cared for properly. She does not know what it means to be loved unconditionally because she hasn't been by you."

Dagonet pointed at David. "You cannot tell, but he is monitoring her every movement, placing himself where she is vulnerable to attack. You are witnessing true love, yet you put the marriage you failed at as a husband above her heart and happiness. When you put your needs and desires above your wife, you fail her.

"As a husband, you do not choose when you will be there for your wife or which parts you love about her—you are all in. And you think of her before yourself. Remember that when you watch him put her first."

"I don't have to listen to this."

Dagonet sighed. "No. You do not. But you will remember it."

✦✦✦

David stayed close to Jane's side as low growls started erupting around them. He made sure he kept himself between her and any opening for a potential attack. She still had a lot to learn.

Several shots suddenly rang out. David raised his rifle and fired along with the others, but the damage had been done.

Jane yelled out and ran to the smoking SUV before he could stop her. He followed as the knights closed in around them, unleashing cover fire. Dread consumed him, hearing the children screaming inside the car.

"*Shh* . . . Mommy's here." Jane took Natalie out of her seat as Dagonet jumped out to unbuckle Nathan.

David came behind her, relieved to see no one was hurt. Only the tires and engine had been shot.

Jane pulled Natalie out and checked Jason. "Are you hit?"

Jason stared at her without answering, and David knew why; her instincts had revealed what she was to her family.

"Jane, give her to Jason," David whispered in her ear. "He sees what you are."

Jane looked at him horrified and touched her fangs as Natalie screamed in her face and shoved her little hands against her chest.

David pulled the little girl from her, and as he went to hand her to Jason, Tristan intercepted him. "I can get the baby on the plane."

David nodded and placed Natalie in Tristan's arms. Dagonet ran around, and Jane went to embrace her son but held back and covered her mouth, which revealed her fangs as the roar of gunfire made the children cry louder.

"Sweetheart, you need to focus," David grabbed the sides of Jane's face. "You are what I've made you. You're like me." He smoothed her hair back. "We are warriors for good and it's time to fight. Protect them." He watched that switch flip in her, the moment she went from doubting and hating herself, to seeing her purpose. Her eyes burned brightly with gold and emerald. "There you are."

"Jason," she said, and he let her go. "Follow Dagonet and Tristan. Don't look back. Get on the plane."

"Jane, where are you going?" Jason asked, grabbing her wrist.

She smiled, showing her fangs and causing Jason to let go as gunfire burst around them. "I'm going to make sure you get on that plane. Now go."

Jane ran to David's side, following him as they rejoined their group. He would rather she'd gone to the plane with her family, but he knew she was a fighter.

"They're toying with us," Gawain shouted over his shoulder.

David and Jane began shooting at the tree line and buildings surrounding them. Gawain was right, they were shooting around them, entertaining themselves.

He glanced at Jane and bared his fangs as a different possibility for the attack manifested: separate and capture someone from their group. *They want Jane.*

He wanted to embrace the carnage that would soon surround them, but David couldn't lose himself to bloodlust. He had to make sure she and her family made it to safety.

Four wolves bursting through the trees broke him from his thoughts.

The knights opened fire, shifting their attack to the threat, and as soon as they did, more wolves poured out of the darkness. The flashing bursts of enemy gunfire made it nearly impossible to make out anything: the wolves were not alone.

Thanks to the knights' silver ammunition, the werewolves dropped much quicker than they had during their previous fights, but there were still too many charging in.

David took his eyes off his targets to check on Jane. She was focused, darting her eyes around frantically, but he could see she desperately tried to keep her sights on Dagonet and Tristan.

"Let's go," Arthur said, and they took off.

David unsheathed his sword and ran out in front of Jane when she didn't notice three wolves coming directly at her. He wasn't letting them get close to her. Not this time.

He cut them down, smiling when she didn't hesitate moving closer to Jason and the men carrying her screaming children while never ceasing her assault.

That's my girl, he thought, briefly smiling before turning to attack more coming their way.

✦✦✦

Jason had already known something was off about Jane's companions, and though he'd been shocked by her behavior at their home, he hadn't feared her. That all changed when she got Natalie out of the car.

The angles of her face had sharpened, and she had fangs pressed against her lips. They had been telling the truth about her: she was dangerous. She was a monster.

It scared him to think of what she could do, but her deadly features were nothing compared to the beasts running at them now.

These things were moving too fast to make out what they were exactly, but he knew they were out to kill them. The fact the intimidating men he traveled with were no longer casual with their killings—as they'd been with the zombies—Jason knew they were in trouble.

He ran around a car and looked behind him to see Jane. She was not the same. Curing her was not all they'd done to her. He barely recognized her now with the wicked grin touching the corners of her mouth as she fired her rifle.

Unlike the soldiers, whose eyes all paled in color, hers were vibrant and constantly changing color. She hissed, baring her fangs as she shot and killed a huge beast.

Jason's heart plummeted. His wife was a vampire.

Her roaring voice made him realize he'd stopped running. "Jason, fucking go!"

He needed to get away from her—from these men. He stared at her deadly gaze for a moment, and then at David who fought close by her. He swung a huge sword with so much force entire torsos and heads were sent flying through the air.

Jason had never seen a man so powerful before. Movies with all their magic were no comparison to the beings darting around him, especially David. He had the strength and speed of a god. They all did. Jason could barely keep up with their movements. Even Jane moved like a lethal feline as she pulled her gun and fired multiple rounds with expert precision before swiftly exchanging her weapon for a sword he hadn't noticed she had.

Jason stumbled, falling over something. He scrambled off the hairy creature twitching as it died below him. "What the fuck?" he shouted, staring into the black eyes of a wolf-like head. "A werewolf?"

"Hurry," Dagonet yelled, firing several shots before turning to leave him there.

Jason stood, and though his mind screamed to run away from Jane, that she was not the woman he married—that she was a monster, he ignored it and followed Dagonet.

Yells and grunts from the soldiers worried him that the monsters he'd chosen to follow were not doing well.

He looked around as he ran, flinching and ducking when flashes of gunfire came from all sides. He spotted Jane again. She still fought next to David, taking on five creatures by herself. Any urge to run to her aid vanished as he watched David reach out with his hand to rip the jaws from two werewolves in front of him.

His wife didn't look to be in much trouble anyway. Her own battle cry, sounding more beast than human, and the perfect way in which she handled the sword proved she did not need him. Her blade cut whatever was available to her: arms, necks, legs.

Jason looked ahead, relieved when the plane came into view. He ran through a gate. They were almost there, but they still had to cut across the airfield, and more attackers were joining the battle.

At first, Jason couldn't make out these new figures, but he knew these were not werewolves. In fact, he would guess they moved almost exactly like Jane and the team of soldiers. *More vampires.*

Orders and shouts were all around him, but he didn't understand any of them. Some of the men had started to help others who were bleeding. His rescuers were losing.

Jason pushed himself, running faster and breathing easier when he noticed Tristan had reached the plane with Natalie still in his arms.

"Nathan!" Jane's scream turned his blood cold.

✦✦✦

David turned, his eyes widening at what he saw. "Run, Jane!"

She shook her head as tears fell down her cheeks, and she shouted, "Help them!"

Before David could argue with her, an enormous blast sounded, and a hue of blue light shot out of her outstretched hands.

He smiled as he watched her arms shake with the power she still held out. "Hold on to it, baby. Just keep running—I'll guide you."

She didn't respond to him; her bright eyes stayed glued to the mayhem behind them. He grabbed her by the waist of her pants and tugged, guiding her so she could concentrate on what she was doing. Any who had already made it past her invisible wall became the focus of his injured team, but he continued leading Jane, still cutting down any that tried to come close.

"Nathan." Her strained whisper seemed to be the only thing he could hear in all the mayhem. He turned his head to look in the direction where they'd been looking before she used her attack.

There, he saw Dagonet on his knees, still holding a screaming Nathan.

"No," Jane screamed out in horror. "David, help him."

He was hesitant about leaving her, but he raced to Dagonet anyway. Arthur and Gawain were already surrounding him to take out the shooters.

Gawain let out a shout of pain but didn't let up his attack.

David knelt down and looked to see Jason running up beside him. He looked back at Dagonet and turned him to his back, afraid to see the condition of the little boy.

Both he and Jason let out a breath upon seeing Nathan safe. But silvery liquid leaking out of the large holes in Dagonet's body filled David's heart with sorrow.

Nathan cried and Jason quickly pulled him from Dagonet's protective grip.

"Hang on," David told Dagonet. "I'll get you to the plane." He tried applying pressure, but there were too many wounds to cover. The dried grass already looked to be soaked in inky blood.

Dagonet shook his head. "I will not make it, my prince. Get the boy to the plane. Do not let her lose them."

David held his friend's bloody hand and nodded to Dagonet as he smiled up at him. His inky eyes faded to a crystal blue suddenly, startling David, until a serene smile formed on Dagonet's lips.

Nathan stared down at his savior. "Dragony?"

"Be a good boy, Nathan," said Dagonet. "I'm okay. Be a good boy. Be brave for your mother."

David squeezed his hand and watched his friend's body stiffen, and his now visible pupils dilated so much that they covered his eyes in black once more. He was gone.

David sighed and looked to find Jane's arms trembling under the strain of her power as she held a protective wall around them. He surveyed the other side and watched the hundreds of cursed vampires and werewolves who had united to kill them.

Hazel eyes met his, and he watched blood drip from Jane's nose. He knew she wanted him to ensure Nathan's safety now. So, he turned away from his love and held his hands out for her son. "Give him here and start running." Jason looked at him with hate, but David wasn't in the mood. He took Nathan as carefully as possible. "Run. She won't last much longer. Go before we're all killed."

Jason looked to his son but took off toward the plane. David pulled Nathan tight and turned to see Gawain and Arthur guarding Jane now. The knights had pulled in around her decreasing shield.

Lucan knelt beside Dagonet. "Damn," he said.

"Take his body," David told him. "We won't leave him."

Lucan nodded and hoisted their fallen comrade onto his shoulders before running off. David turned back to Jane. Her sad eyes met his, and she nodded, telling him to leave her. It went against everything in him, but he held Nathan and turned to head for the safety of the plane.

✦✦✦

"Did David make it to the plane?" Jane shouted, not daring to turn her head to look at anyone, afraid of seeing something that would destroy her soul.

"Not yet, Jane," said Kay. "He will."

She nodded and felt more blood dripping from her nose. "I can't hold it. Go without me."

"You can hold it." Arthur snapped, grabbing her belt loop.

"Don't touch me yet," she screamed. He let go. "I can't hold it."

She gasped when dozens of the werewolves and vampires started pressing against her wall. They were holding up the deceased bodies of their own army of monsters to use as shields. They then started beating at the barrier, making her arms nearly give out with each blow.

She screamed out, pushing more energy into her wall. "YOU HAVE TO GO!"

✦✦✦

David spotted the guards at the door of the plane. They were helping Jason, who was now limping and clutching a shoulder. Jason made it, though, and he was already moving to a screaming Natalie who Tristan had been holding back.

Two blurs of white fur bolted out of the plane, and David realized Jane's dogs had escaped their kennels and were now running in her direction.

He stopped, turning his head to look, hoping they wouldn't distract her but a sharp pain pierced his shoulder before he could turn all the way. He grunted and pulled Nathan against him, forgetting the dogs. He felt more shots tear through the muscles in his back. He didn't want to frighten Nathan, so he gritted his teeth and started running again.

The fiery pain that spread out from each hit made it clear to him that he was in serious trouble.

Roaring as pain exploded across his side again, he glanced down at the pair of brown eyes staring up at him.

The guards opened fire to cover him, but David knew already it was too late for him. He'd been shot more than Dagonet. His insides were burning from the silver. "I've got you, little man," David said, feeling the little boy shaking against him. "Close your eyes."

Energy left his body quickly and he nearly collapsed from the pain and blood loss. He had to make sure Nathan was safe, though. He had to do this for Jane. She trusted him to keep her child safe. If he died, he would do it for her.

✦✦✦

"Spooky five miles out . . ." Jane heard the strange words echo through Arthur's earpiece.

"Affirm," said Arthur.

The roar of gunfire and thunder broke up the rest of his message.

"Proceed . . . Red smoke . . . Close . . ."

"Arthur?" Jane yelled.

She heard him say more, but she didn't understand him. Her attention shifted to the blinding red flares the knights began to throw toward her barrier. "I CAN'T HOLD IT!"

✦✦✦

David stumbled but kept Nathan shielded as he got shot again. He roared out his pain but refused to let the little boy receive the same fate he was sure to have.

Blurry shapes and light were all he could see now until a hand reached out for him. "Come on. Stand up you bastard."

David opened his tired eyes and if he had the strength, he would have said something to his rival.

Jason tugged, wincing from whatever injury he himself had sustained. "I should leave you," Jason said, struggling with him for those last five steps up the ramp and into the plane.

David didn't have the energy to reply and was relieved when he felt his body being lowered onto the floor of the plane.

He blinked at the blinding light overhead and felt Nathan being removed from his grip.

"Where's Jane?" David asked.

"She's still out there," Jason said.

David's blood felt warm under his fingers when his arms were free of the little boy. He looked into Jason's eyes and to Nathan with a sense of peace. Nathan was safe. He was with his father, and so was Natalie. Jane had her family back.

He knew Jane would stay alive for them. He knew she wouldn't let herself be killed out there—she was stronger than him. Not to mention, she had the Angel of Death wrapped around her little finger.

David smiled to himself. "I love her," he said, not caring what Jason thought. "Tell her it's okay . . . Death is okay." He could see Jason frowning and closed his eyes as he hissed from the pain still boiling inside him. "It's okay to love him. Let her be happy."

"Daddy," Natalie cried. "Help him, Daddy."

✦✦✦

"Drop the shield, Jane," someone yelled.

She felt the wind picking up from somewhere.

"Grab her!"

Jane squinted from the flickering red light as she tried to focus on the monstrous figures beating against her wall.

"Now, Jane!"

She didn't know what they wanted her to do. She could barely hear herself hyperventilating as she was.

"Dammit," someone else yelled over the whirring sounds all around them.

Several sets of arms quickly wrapped around her body and pulled her to the ground, causing her to drop control of her force field.

Blasts louder than she'd ever heard in her entire life shook the ground and bursts of blinding light lit up the airfield as several different aircrafts—at least two helicopters and one plane—unleashed hell on the horde in front of them.

The air seemed to tremble from the cannon fire as the gunship circled above, delivering a constant assault from their cannons and Gatling guns. While the plane continued its pylon turn, two military helicopters hovered above the ground where she and the knights had been standing, massacring their attackers.

The deafening screams and blasts had her covering her ears just as someone lifted her off the ground. Her hair whipped around her face as the person carrying her started to run to the plane, that judging by the louder whirring sound and dust kicking up, was preparing for take-off.

The deep banging sound from the cannons shot off in rounds of ten, sending debris and body parts flying through the air. Total chaos.

"Are they with us?" She didn't even know why she was asking as she watched the werewolf and vampire army trying to escape.

"They're our human allies," said Lamorak, who she realized was the person running with her. "Aw, shit."

"What?" She saw Bedivere run inside the plane, yelling out for Arthur to keep her back.

"Where's David?" she asked. Lamorak sat her down and pointed across the plane. "David!"

✦✦✦

David smiled at the sound of Natalie's soft voice, and although he could hear the muffled sound of explosions, and the whirring of the plane's engine, he thought he heard Jane calling him.

David looked over and saw Nathan staring down at him through teary eyes, and then he moved his gaze over to the adorable little girl who resembled the woman he had been dreaming of for centuries.

"Jane," he said.

"NO!"

He swore now he could hear Jane, but he kept staring at Natalie and Nathan, seeing the features of the woman he loved staring back at him through them.

"No, David!"

Jane's voice sounded closer, but everything had become so dark. He wished he could see her face one last time. So, he sighed and closed his eyes to see the beautiful, hazel eyes that blessed his dreams during so many lonely nights.

"Look at me, David." The voice sounded like her, but he couldn't open his eyes. She probably wasn't even there.

"I love you," he said anyway.

"I know you do." Her voice was shaking. "Please look at me. Don't leave me."

He wanted to stay with her, but he knew he couldn't. "Stay with Death, baby."

"No!" Her voice was stronger.

"He loves you. It's okay."

"No, David." Her voice was growing softer. He wanted to make sure she knew it was okay to go with Death.

"My love." He heard her cries for him to wake up. "Be happy." It took everything he had left to open his mouth. "I love you."

He had no more control over his body, but he saw her come closer, lighting up the darkness like the moon brightens the night sky.

His angel, his Jane. She smiled at him in the dark.

He smiled back . . .

✦✦✦

Jane pressed down on one of David's many wounds. His body was cold but the blood seeping through her fingers was still hot. "Please." She cried. "Please, God. Bedivere, will he be okay?"

Bedivere looked up but said nothing as he returned his attention to David's wounds.

Gawain dropped down behind her and held on to her as the plane began to move. Several of the other knights grabbed David's body and the bolted-down benches to keep him from rolling as the plane lifted off.

She shook back and forth while tears poured down her face. "David, wake up!" She patted his cheek once the plane leveled out.

He didn't respond and they all watched his color grow paler.

Bedivere and other men she did not recognize began to work on him, but she refused to leave. She did notice her family was strapped on a bench while another person applied bandages to Jason.

They made eye contact briefly, but she looked back to David as blood poured out of his mouth.

She cried, wiping it away. "Don't, David. Don't . . . I—" She didn't even know what she was going to tell him.

She looked at the man closest to her. "Draw my blood for him."

"Jane you're too weak," Bedivere said without looking up.

"Take my blood now!"

Tristan came up behind her and ripped her sleeve to prep her arm.

She looked back at David and held her arm out for Tristan. Silver liquid like she'd never seen before seeped from each bloody hole on David's back. There was no way to remove it like Bedivere had done to her.

This couldn't be happening. He was her warrior—always strong, unbreakable. "My David," she whispered.

She held his hand in hers tightly. They propped him on his side, ripping his shirt and exposing his back. It revealed numerous bullet holes across his beautiful skin. He had been Nathan's shield.

Jane stopped paying attention to what they did to him and watched her tears dripping onto their joined hands.

She couldn't lose him.

"Jane," said Bedivere.

She looked up and saw defeat in his eyes. Shaking her head, she tore her eyes away to stare at Arthur. His pale-blue gaze held nothing but despair.

Her lips trembled and she screamed. "No, fix him! He's strong. I can't lose him. Arthur!" She sobbed, shaking as she lifted his hand to her face. "He's my David. He's my David."

Gawain tried to pull her away. "Come away, Jane."

She pushed him back with a growl. "No! I won't lose him."

"Jane, there is nothing else to be done," Bedivere said. "His wounds are too great and the silver is in his system. He's practically human. I'm sorry."

Again they tried to pull her away, but she screamed. "Don't touch me!" She breathed heavily and held herself in front of him as if it would protect David somehow.

The knights, some with tears in their eyes, nodded and moved away.

After they left her, she turned back to David. She squeezed his cold hand tightly and kissed his bloody knuckles. It was the first time she knowingly kissed a part of him. "I won't lose you," she repeated over and over, kissing his fingers, touching his cold cheek with her trembling hands. "You said you'd always be here—that you wouldn't leave me. You said I didn't have to be alone. So don't leave me here. If you die—" She stopped talking and kissed his fingers again.

CHAPTER 45
TARTARUS

Death's thunderous roar shook the dark Texas sky as he slammed the fallen angel onto the asphalt. He growled, tightening his hold on his victim's neck, watching the green fire from his eyes light up the angel's face. "Where is my brother, Thanatos?"

His former general thrashed in vain as chaos unfolded around them. Death ignored the battle between light and dark, grabbing one of Thanatos' raven wings and snapping it in half.

Thanatos roared in pain. "Why would I know where he is?"

Death smirked, squeezing Thanatos' intact wing. "Do not play me for a fool, Fallen. I know you were involved in the attack on Jane. The only reason I'm not ripping you apart right now is because of your mother and what little respect I once held for you as my general. That doesn't mean I won't enjoy knocking you off that invisible throne you've placed yourself on. Now tell me where my brother is."

"You thought you hid her well, didn't you?" The ruby color of Thanatos' eyes sparked as he chuckled. "I can see why you would keep her to yourself—sexy little thing, isn't she? Does she taste as sweet as your name for her suggests?"

Death punched him in the face, shutting him up. "If you come near her again, I will make you beg me to take your life. Now tell me what I want to hear."

The clashing of swords filled the silence as Thanatos glanced around. The gathering of vampires and Fallen was no match for the small army Death had brought with him.

Thanatos turned back to Death. "If you wanted her to stay secret, you really should have controlled your emotions. All anyone has to do is mention her, and you look ready to destroy the world."

Death snarled as he restrained himself from ripping Thanatos in half.

Thanatos smirked. "The love you have for her will be her downfall."

"What do you know?" Death seethed.

"More than you ever will. As far as your brother is concerned, where is the one place all of you never think to look?"

"Tartarus?" Death growled.

"It is the one place Light rarely ventures, but I would not worry about your brother. You should be much more concerned with Jane." Thanatos smiled as Death's rage soared to new heights. "They haven't told you yet, have they? She will fall, Death—and you will stand by and watch as she cries for you."

"Tell me what you know," he yelled, punching Thanatos' smiling face again and again.

"Sorry, handsome," a sickeningly sweet voice whispered in his ear just as fiery pain exploded across his back.

Death roared, letting go of Thanatos as he reached for the source of pain, a dagger embedded near his shoulder blade. Once he realized he couldn't pull it out easily, he glanced around and found his attacker. "Mania, you bitch!"

She cackled, waving at him before disappearing.

A low laugh pulled his gaze back to the angel below him. Thanatos smiled, then also vanished.

"Fucking bitch." Death finally got a grip on the dagger and ripped it from his shoulder. He snarled at the cursed blade as he tossed it on the ground before reaching to feel the wound on his back.

"Be still," Hades said, shoving his hands away. "Damn, she got you good."

"No shit." Death moved away from Hades, not allowing him to inspect the wound further. "Did we keep any to question?"

Hades shook his head. "No, I thought you were keeping Than. We killed the last of ours. The arrival of the Keres threw me off."

"What, can you no longer handle those flying harpies in your old age?" Death looked around the bloody battlefield. He already knew he'd find forty-eight dead immortals. Still, he briefly inspected the various states of slaughter of Fallen and vampires before shifting his gaze back to Hades, who was covered from head to toe in blood and glaring at him. Death chuckled, rotating his shoulder. "Did I hurt your feelings?"

Hades wiped some of the filth from his face as he glared at Death. "I am one of the few who can kill those flying whores."

Death motioned to his blood-soaked attire. "You are also one of the few who cannot stay clean . . . Do you have any manners?"

"Bathing in the slaughter is part of the fun." Hades grinned, glancing at the carnage. "We haven't had this much action in a long time. I'm just enjoying the moment while it lasts."

"There is more death to come, Hades," Death said, walking toward the three angels waiting for him. He eyed the two males towering over a female in their group as their snowy wings flapped, removing the splatters of their battle.

The dark-skinned male, Moros, nodded to Death. "Are you all right?"

"I'm fine." Death rubbed his burning shoulder. "The little whore just snuck up on me."

"I heard what Than said about Pestilence," Moros said. "We will follow you, but you should send your vampires to Arthur. The knights will need to fight together against the Cursed Ones, especially with Keres. Darkness has grown with the plague."

Death glanced at Hades, not bothering to say the order.

Hades was already in agreement. "We will return to them at once."

"Just watch over Jane," Death said, staring him in the eye.

"Of course, Master." Hades bowed his head.

"Thank you for honoring my mother's wishes, Death," said a female voice behind him. "I know my brother is not worthy in your eyes, so I thank you for sparing him. I will follow you to retrieve yours now."

"Your brother is a piece of shit, Nemesis," Death said, pinning his gaze on her. "It's time you and your mother realize that."

Her eyes strained with sadness as she banished her blade. "Yes, Master."

A male, who apart from his blond hair and blue eyes bore an uncanny likeness to Thanatos, placed his arm over her shoulder. "Do not be so harsh with her. Our brother is not the brother at fault."

"Hypnos," Death said, struggling to not attack him. "When I want your opinion, I'll ask for it. And I suggest you avoid speaking to me until I am calm—all I see is your twin when I look at you."

"So, Tartarus?" Hades said, pulling Death's attention away from Hypnos.

"So it seems," Death said, still tense as Jane's frantic state reached out to him through their bond. He knew why she was panicking.

"I feel foolish for not suspecting that sooner." Hades went on. "Are you sure you only need the four of you?"

Death chuckled as three pairs of irritated glares shot to Hades, but they quickly returned their attention to him when he spoke. "Do any of you know what Than was talking about?"

"There are only whispers," Moros said. "They involve your female—but it is unclear what is happening. There is a great amount of death coming from her direction. Do you still sense her?"

Death nodded and rubbed his chest. "She is in distress, but her life is not in danger—only the others."

"Should you go to her?" Hades asked him. "She has only just recovered from her last episode—"

Death stopped him. "If I want to keep her safe, I must find out what Than was speaking about."

"But you said the others are in danger."

"And?" Death glared at Hades. "Learn your place, slave. If their lives matter to you, you can return to them. You never should have left them anyway. I don't give a shit if you and Arthur thought it best for Jane not to meet this little tramp." He pointed at Artemis. "If you had mentioned your niece was a jealous whore, I would have simply sent her away. Then perhaps the others would not be in the danger they are in."

"I apologize for not consulting you." Hades lowered his head, but Death could see his fury at the insult to Artemis. "Are they in battle now?"

"Yes. And a member of their party has fallen," Death said. "Another is—"

"One of the knights?" Artemis asked, panicked. "Is it David?"

Death slid his gaze from Hades to her, smiling when she shrank back in fear. "The prince has received a fatal wound."

"Is he . . . ?" Hades asked, not finishing his question.

"Dead?" Death said, not looking at Hades but chuckling as he watched Artemis tear up. "No . . . But dying?" Death grinned. "Most definitely."

Artemis covered her mouth as she sobbed.

"Is there anything you can do, Master?" Hades asked, glancing at the three angels and the vampires all staring in shock at the news about David. "Surely, your young beauty will expect you to come."

"I will not save David," Death said quickly. "He has been on borrowed time since his change, just as Jane and many others. His fate is already determined."

Hades nodded and looked down at the ground. "Should we return to them?"

Death closed his eyes and studied his bond with Jane. "They have already departed—I sense her moving farther away." He opened his eyes and glared at Hades. "Now you can enjoy crossing this goddamned country on foot."

Hades opened his mouth.

Death cut him off before he could reply. "Just get there and tell them what we've learned here about Fallen and demons working with Cursed. This war is only beginning." He turned to Artemis and approached her, snarling when she cowered. "And if you so much as roll your eyes at my girl, I will rip your fucking throat out."

She paled and bowed her head. "I did not know who she was, Master."

"Do you know who she is now?" Death sneered.

Artemis nodded. "She is my master's most cherished soul."

"And?" Death asked.

Artemis whined but kept her head bowed. "And she was Sir David's Other."

Death inhaled deeply. "Even with him dying, I can smell your jealousy over them, vampire. How did it feel, *hm*? Finding out the knight truly had no intentions with you? Did it cut your bitter heart to see him smile at the simple thought of her?"

Artemis whimpered.

"Do you realize she is all that I feel?" he asked.

"I do now, Master," she cried.

"Do you know I smile for her?"

"No, Master. I cannot see your face."

He chuckled. "You want to, though. Don't you?"

Artemis cried but did not answer.

"Did you know my father made me His most beautiful creation?"

Artemis nodded.

"And did you know a mortal only gets to see my true face when they are about to die?"

"I have been told this, yes," said Artemis.

Death leaned down close, knowing all she saw was his hood and glowing eyes. "She sees me," he whispered. "She has touched my face; she has stared into my eyes as I have confessed my love to her. She has kissed my lips."

Artemis dropped her head lower.

"I still smell your jealousy, vampire. Get over it now. I do not want to smell your stink in my presence again."

"She knows her place, Death." Hades walked between them and pushed Artemis behind him. "I will take responsibility for her actions, and Jane will be kept safe."

"She better be." Death shifted his attention to Hades. "Do not disappoint me."

"I will give my life for hers, Master."

"Good," Death said. "I'll see you soon."

"Death?" Moros called.

Death waved him off. "I feel it."

"They are saving the vampire prince again?" Nemesis asked, looking in the same direction where he sensed Jane.

"No. They are not permitted to save him," Death said. "But they are there."

Hades coughed. "Master, she will be devastated. Perhaps you should go—"

Death glared at him. "I have something I must do. I suggest you begin your journey to Arthur's kingdom now."

"Shall I give her a message, Master?" Hades asked. "I realize it is hard for you to understand loss, but she will be broken when she loses him. She will need your comfort and will not understand why you have not come to her."

Death stared at him for a moment. "Tell her whatever you like."

Hades shook his head but gestured with a wave of his hand for his teams to depart.

Moros walked closer as they watched the vampires leave. "He is right, Death. She will desire your presence."

"I know what she desires," he said. "She desires the vampire."

"You are jealous?" Hypnos asked. "So you will let him die, let her weep alone, so she will desire only you?"

"I will not explain my choices to any of you," Death said, glaring at Hypnos. "Do not question me regarding Jane. She is my business, not yours. Now find me the newest gate to Tartarus. I will rejoin you after I take care of something."

They all bowed, illuminating in white light before disappearing.

"You are foolish."

Death sighed and did not turn as he responded to the angel behind him. "Nyx."

"Death," she said, walking to stand beside him.

He had not taken his eyes off the distance where he knew Jane was, but he could see the fabric of Nyx's black dress and her long black hair blowing in the breeze.

"She fought well. Her power is immeasurable. If only she would release it."

"I know," he said. "Did you see her battle?"

"Of course. It occurred in the night—you know I see all that happens in the dark."

"How did David fall?"

"Protecting her child. The boy."

Death nodded. He knew David's injury was fatal, but, unless he had been present or David finally died, he would not know the events leading up to such an injury. "And Jane?"

"She held the attack back long enough for help to come. But it was already too late for the prince and their comrade." He said nothing as she added, "Do you abandon her because she loves him?"

He chuckled and ignored her question. "Do you have news for me?"

Nyx sighed. "She loves you as well. She will always love you."

"Do you have news?" He was not willing to discuss Jane any further.

Nyx let out another sigh. "You did not heed your call. I have come to retrieve you in Michael's place."

"I have something I must see to." He had felt Michael's summons during his fight with Thanatos, but he ignored it. "What did he want?"

"He was warning you because he learned Gabriel had been sent to retrieve Lucifer on the night Jane left to meet him. Lucifer has seen Father again, and Michael believes you are the better option than our fallen brother, so he wanted you informed."

"Where is Luc now?"

"Gabriel returned him to Earth moments after the vampire prince was wounded."

Death nodded. "Anything else?"

"Yes." She placed a hand on his shoulder. "Father wishes to see you now."

"Is it about Jane?"

"Yes. Be prepared for the worst news of your incredibly long existence."

He lifted his gaze to the moon as his heart felt all of Jane's sorrow surrounding him. "Forgive me, Sweet Jane."

Nyx squeezed his shoulder as he exhaled, letting night take him.

CHAPTER 46
TINGLES

An hour passed. No more tears fell from Jane's eyes, but the pain inside her heart continued to grow.

David suddenly coughed and began to make choking noises as blood lined his lips. His body shook, and she sobbed because no one even came closer. Some of them held their heads in their hands while others watched with tears in their eyes. It was too late.

"Please, no." She cried, wiping the blood and holding him still. "Don't leave me."

David's body went rigid, and more blood spilled out of his mouth.

"Please, God," she cried, squeezing her eyes shut because a blinding, white light filled the cabin of the plane.

She tried to open her eyes, but a second burst of light forced her to keep them shut while two sets of footsteps walked closer.

The words were not spoken aloud, but she heard them clearly in her mind: "*You're not alone, Jane.*"

A gentle caress slid across Jane's cheek. Tingles. She sobbed because they were not the same as Death's. They were warmer than the unique sensation Death's touch gave her. With him, she could never decide if he was warm or cold. His touch constantly danced between both.

Jane forced her eyes open once the brightness dimmed. The two figures wearing black suits looked down at her. Though they held no emotion on their ethereal faces and appeared almost as dangerous as her own angel, she felt no fear in their presence.

Death, where are you? she mentally screamed. It did not matter she wasn't afraid of these beings; she wanted Death, and she didn't understand why he'd leave her if this was going to happen.

"Help him," she said, shifting her teary gaze between them. "Please. I'll do anything you ask."

They didn't respond, and she noticed all the knights were kneeling with their heads bowed.

Tingles slid across her cheek again, and she faced the blond male with blue eyes who was standing in front of her. His eyes reminded her of David's.

As he pulled his hand away from her cheek and looked at her tears on his fingers, Jane assessed the brunet male standing behind him. He seemed even more emotionless than the blond, but she still didn't feel threatened. She believed they were there to help.

The blond male returned her gaze, and the voice she'd heard in her head earlier rang through her mind again. *"I am Michael. He is Gabriel."*

"Just fix him." She took in David's pale face. "Please!"

Michael turned to Gabriel and nodded.

She stayed still as Gabriel knelt beside her. He said nothing but grabbed her hand and pulled her to sit next to David. He held their hands over a wound on David's back. She expected something miraculous to occur, but nothing did.

Jane stared back at him, unsure of what he wanted her to do. "I don't understand."

Shocking her, Gabriel smiled and cupped her cheek as a different, louder voice sounded in her mind. *"Remove the silver."*

Jane shook off the ringing sound his words left in her head as she began panicking at the realization David's body no longer emitted his beautiful heat. "I don't know what to do. Please help him."

Michael touched her shoulder, and the original voice filled her mind, *"You can. You will."*

David began to cough and his body convulsed.

"Help him," she screamed.

Gabriel squeezed her hand he still held. *"Concentrate, Jane."*

She winced at the powerful voice in her head.

"We cannot save him again, but you can."

"I can't." She tried to pull away.

He kept her hands in place and continued speaking to her mind. *"Do you feel it? The silver is there–call it to your hand."*

Jane darted her eyes to the large holes littering his back, and more tears blurred her sight as she tried to think of how she pulled things to her before. The sight of his blood was all she could see, though.

"I can't save him. I'm not good." Jane shook her head back and forth at the thought of losing him–of never seeing his beautiful smile again or hearing him say he loved her. "I'm not strong."

"Enough, Jane," Gabriel's mental voice roared, making her squeeze her eyes shut and grit her teeth.

She fought against the force that seemed to crush her when his words entered her mind and nodded as she opened her eyes. David was so pale. If it wasn't for the weak breaths he took, she would think he was already gone.

"He needs you to be brave and fight your fears." Michael's voice soothed her painful thoughts. *"You are strong. You are everything."*

Jane kept crying as she studied David's face and remembered how he looked at her, telling her he needed her to be brave. She blew out a breath as she held her hands over his wound.

A fiery sensation seeped into her skin where Gabriel's hands touched her, and she breathed in, letting her eyes close as the burn spread.

Gabriel's voice pushed into her thoughts. *"Think of the silver, its texture—how it drips from his wounds."*

Jane began to imagine the silvery liquid. She remembered how it felt on her fingers and how it looked on the rags that had been thrown to the ground after trying to stop David's bleeding.

Gabriel's tone was still firm. *"Do you feel it?"*

"Yes," she said, not opening her eyes.

"Call it to your hand," he prompted, more calmly. *"Imagine pulling it through his veins, out of his body."*

The first thing she envisioned was a syringe that could draw it all together, and when she pictured herself pulling back on the syringe's plunger, a sudden connection to all parts of David's body switched on inside her. She could feel every part of him: his skin, muscles—his organs. She felt the air in his lungs as if it were in hers.

She breathed in and heard him inhale until she slowly let out her breath. Tears slid down her lips, and she licked them, remembering the faint salty taste of David's skin whenever she fed from him.

She bit her lip even though her fangs pierced her skin. She needed blood, too, but she swallowed her own to hold off her hunger.

"Relax." Gabriel's words gently caressed her mind. *"Breathe."*

She did, inhaling and exhaling slowly, once again syncing her body with David's. His chest rose and fell with each breath she took, relaxing her to a more meditative state. She focused on his heartbeat and practically felt it beating in her hand. She could almost see a scan of his entire body in her mind, and she watched his heart pumping blood, carrying the toxic silver with it.

Again, she pictured a syringe in her hand and, only seeing the silver, she began to pull.

"You have it," Gabriel praised. *"Slowly, now, gather it in your hand. Once it is out and he feeds, the injuries will heal with fresh tissue."*

She nodded, still visualizing the silver rolling through David's veins, leaving behind only healthy blood.

A hand squeezed her shoulder as Michael's voice entered her mind. *"Open your eyes, Jane."*

She did and stared in amazement at the undulating ball of liquid silver in her hand. Michael nodded to someone, and she looked away from the ball to see Arthur holding a bucket out for her.

"Release it here," Michael instructed, his words warming her thoughts with praise.

Gabriel pulled his hand from hers, and Jane released the silver into the bucket Arthur held out for her.

Not wasting a second more on what she'd just done, Jane turned back to inspect David's wounds. They were already coming together, though most of his skin would not fully close over the bullet holes, and blood began to replace the silvery substance that oozed from the wounds.

Her lip trembled, fearing her efforts were for nothing. He needed blood.

She averted her gaze from the awful bullet wounds on his body and focused on his face. He was still unconscious and extremely pale. She held her hand against his cold cheek and watched him still struggling to breathe.

Michael moved closer, placing his hand over hers. His hand glowed and warmth spread through her hand to David. *"It is time to wake, David,"* Michael's voice resonated through her mind.

She briefly looked at Michael before glancing back in time to see David squeezing his eyes tight as he winced in pain.

"David," she said softly, rubbing her thumb over his cheek.

He must have heard her, because his eyes opened quickly. He blinked several times, staring at her as more tears fell from her eyes. She couldn't explain what she felt right then, only that it was an overwhelming combination of warmth, joy, and sadness.

"Jane." David's voice was hoarse, but she thought it the most wonderful sound and cried as she dropped her head to his chest.

"Baby, don't cry," he said, placing his hand behind her head.

She touched his face. She couldn't believe he was talking to her. He still appeared to be in terrible pain, and yet he smiled anyway.

"You came back to me," she whispered, sighing as he cupped her cheek and rubbed her tears away with his thumb. "I thought you left me."

"Never. I will never leave you."

She turned her face against his hand and cried.

At that moment, David seemed to finally notice the two angels standing close. Jane watched him look between the two before returning to her.

"They helped me," she said.

David held eye contact with Michael for a moment, and she watched him nodding, but they never spoke aloud.

Gabriel's words suddenly thundered throughout her mind. *"Jane?"*

She glanced over at him and felt he was keeping their mental conversation separate from the one David and Michael were having.

"It is crucial that you do not discuss Death and Lucifer's wager. I have placed a stronger block in your mind to prevent Arthur from knowing all that Death disclosed to you, and also to protect you from my fallen brother."

Jane didn't know if she could communicate mentally, but she tried pushing her thoughts out to only him. *Why didn't Death come?*

Gabriel smiled softly as his response came, *"I cannot answer that, child. All I will say is do not forget your faith. He is always with you."*

"Who?" she asked aloud this time, earning questioning looks from David and Michael.

"You know, Jane," was Gabriel's parting thought as he suddenly glowed with white light and vanished.

"Who did he mean?" she asked Michael.

"I know not," Michael spoke gently to her mind. *"My message for you is simply to believe. Believe in yourself. Believe in David. Darkness will always find you–it grows inside you already."* He smiled sadly. *"But never forget your heart shines brightly. Look for it, believe in it, and you will find your way home."* He placed a hand on her cheek and the other on David's. *"It gives me joy to see you have found one another. Cherish your moments together."*

David grabbed one of her hands, and they smiled as light filled the cabin of the plane. Michael was gone.

Arthur and Bedivere rushed to David's side.

"David, you need to feed," Bedivere said, inspecting the wounds that were still trying to heal themselves. "The transfusion isn't enough."

Jane pulled her hand from David's and roughly started wiping her tears from her face. She smiled when he reached up to help her.

"Don't cry, baby. I'm fine."

She hiccupped and nodded. "I'm trying to stop."

He chuckled but winced in pain as he tried to get comfortable.

Jane gasped and held his shoulders as he breathed out harshly. "You need to feed. Take it from me, okay?"

"Jane, you've given too much," said Bedivere. "You need to feed as well."

"I feel fine. Please, David–I need you to be okay."

Despite the pain he must have been feeling, David shook his head. "No, Jane." He held her cheek. "I'll be okay."

"No," she shouted. She could feel everyone watching her, but she kept her eyes on Bedivere since he was the one who suggested she not feed David.

David quickly grabbed her face, turning her so she would look into his eyes instead. "All right, Jane. I will feed from you, but I want you to drink double the donor blood after. Do you understand?"

She couldn't respond. She couldn't think about anything but making sure he was okay, and that they didn't want to let her help him.

"My love." David's soothing tone broke into her violent thoughts. "You're losing control. Do you hear me? I need you to stay with me."

She blinked a few times, not realizing she wasn't really seeing him anymore.

"There you are," he said, staring at her eyes. He smiled, rubbing her cheek with his thumb. "There are those hazel eyes I love."

"David," Arthur whispered.

Jane couldn't stop herself from hissing at Arthur. She didn't want him to oppose her helping David, too.

"*Shh . . .*" David pulled her face back to him as he addressed Arthur. "Leave us, brother. Keep the others away and prepare her several donor bags."

"David, Jason is watching," Arthur said as Jane blinked away the blurry, red haze in her sight. "Give me a moment to at least distract him and have a curtain put up to block her family from seeing you two like this."

Arthur's words finally registered, and Jane turned her head as both she and David looked at Jason.

David continued to stare, but Jane turned away from her husband. She'd seen that both her children were asleep, but it was clear Jason had been watching her the entire time. She didn't know what she felt. Shame, she guessed, but she couldn't stop herself from needing to remain close to David.

"It's all right, Jane," said David. "Arthur will talk to him."

She knew she should probably go check on her family, but once she focused on the paleness of David's face and how he had begun to break into a cold sweat, nothing else mattered but him.

Arthur sighed and walked toward Jason, and Jane scooted closer to David.

"You smiled at me," he said as she wiped the sweat on his forehead. "I could see your smile in the dark . . . So beautiful, my love."

Gawain arrived and began to situate a divider around them.

"Let me feed you." She sighed as he held her face again. She could feel a hint of his heat.

"Okay," he said as she lowered her neck for him. David licked where he intended to feed, chuckling before he pressed a soft kiss to her neck. "Thank you for saving me, baby."

"I will always try to save you." She brought her hand up to hold his head.

"*Mm*." He rubbed his lips across her skin. "That's my job, though. Now, relax, my love. I want you to enjoy this as much as I will."

She gasped and welcomed the complete ecstasy from having David's mouth on her neck.

Continued in book two of the Gods & Monsters trilogy:

THE FALLEN QUEEN

THE FALLEN QUEEN

Book Two – Gods & Monsters

Even immortality can be filled with tragedy.

The plague was just the beginning. While Jane's impressive powers allowed her to secure her family's safety, new trials on her heart, mind, and soul will begin. Thrust among the most wicked creatures, Jane will learn more truths about the myths and monsters of her world as well as the extent of the power she holds. Unfortunately, it is the source of her power that is her darkest rival. And, this time, Death won't be there to save her or those she loves.

But Jane is far from alone. While David remains loyal at her side, whispers of Lucifer's presence strengthen. And one thing is certain about his interest in her; he desires to see her fall. Perhaps that has been Jane's destiny all along.

After all, how else can darkness end if she, the most evil monster of them all, remains?

Thank you for reading.
Please consider posting a review on Amazon and/or Goodreads.

ACKNOWLEDGEMENTS

I had never given any thought about writing a story before. It was my best friend who planted the seed. Tifani passed away in March 2010 from cervical cancer. But she is the reason I took the broken pieces of my heart and soul and turned them into something magical.

Tifani, you are not here for me to hand you this book, and I cannot see you smile because I managed to bring all of our favorite fantasies to life on the page, but I know your star will shine a little brighter every time this story is read. I love you, always.

✧

I have been blessed to meet some wonderful people as a writer. One of those amazing people happens to be author Ashley Claudy. We became friends shortly after becoming fans of each other, and I cannot thank God enough that our friendship blossomed into what it is today.

Honestly, and I know you always tell me I would have eventually gotten here, but I know this book is in my hands because of you. Thank you for being such an incredible friend. Thank you for listening to me, pushing me, encouraging me, for drawing stick Janie's on the laps of sexy men. Haha. I cherish you and our friendship so very much. I'm so thankful I had you throughout this process, and I'm so happy you're a daily part of my life. I love you.

✧

To my babies: Tristan, Keira, and Evangeline—you three are my heart. Thank you for understanding when Mommy was stressing out. Thank you for listening when I talked about my story and characters, and for not being too concerned when Mommy repeatedly admitted Death was her soul mate. It's okay—Daddy knows all about him.

Siah... Babe, I love you. You are my rock. I would not be able to make my characters so lovely if I didn't experience the love you gift me with. Thank you for pushing me when I wanted to give up, and every ten minutes I doubted myself. Thank you for sticking up for me when I was laughed at, for being a wonderful father—for buying me Dr. Pepper and fries when I'd forget to eat while I was writing. Thank you for reading even though you don't like to read... I could go on and on, so I will just say one more time, thank you and I love you.

✧

I'd like to say a huge thank you to my two beta teams: The Fearsome 14 and The Captain Queen's Dreaded Beta Team. Ashley Claudy, Shawn Gunnin, Kristi Faehse, Zeyba Haider, Kaitlyn Zantello, Elaine Stipe, Sheila Krieger, Dinah Jellema, Desiree Grana Feliu, Kelly Mahmud, Kat Walker, Emily Vaughan, Katie Foley, Laura Rincon, Leah Blundell, Jéssica Reis, Fabia Ali, Uness Denniston, Sadhbh Ni Fhlaithbheartaigh, Aisha GK,

Zahlé Eloff, Emily Croft, Éabha Puirséil, Maria Reyes, Shane Rana, Ailen Mondejar, Amanda Brandow, Zatunia DC, I love each and every one of you. You are so much more than my betas—you are my friends, and I will never forget your hard work, kindness, and encouragement. You have all been such an incredible support. You ladies are my warriors. Thank you for being on this journey with me.

I'd also like to thank my old co-workers who became my friends. We drifted apart after I left, but I cannot thank you enough for the support you guys gave when I was falling apart. Thank you for listening me go on and on about my stories, for those who read my horrible first drafts and said, one day, you'll be a published author, and I shrugged, not believing I could do it. Thank you for being there when I reach out to you. Love you.

Finally, thank you to my wonderful readers. You guys are my cheer section. I never expected support and to have had it from so many people all across the world has been an incredible experience. Thank you.

I do want to say an extra thank you to the readers who've read G&M over and over—every version—and you still send me praise that makes me truly feel like your Captain Queen. You guys are incredible.

Kisses from your Captain Queen,
Janie Marie

ABOUT THE AUTHOR

Janie Marie is a native Texan, and she resides in her hometown north of Austin, Texas with her husband and three children.

Much of her life experiences—good and a lot of bad—are where she has chosen to draw inspiration from to create her characters and stories. It's important to her to create the kind of characters she needs or needed at one point in time because she wanted to create something only the saddest souls would recognize as brave and strong.

Be ready for raw, emotional tales, as Janie never holds back. With her darkest thoughts she found light is still possible, that the sad girl can sometimes glow the brightest.

Because she is beauty surrounded by darkness.

Visit Janie Marie's website to find links to her social media. She is most active with her fans inside her private Facebook group and Instagram. You can also sign up for her mailing list to receive important book news and exclusive bonus chapters that Janie will randomly publish.

www.janiemariebooks.com

CPSIA information can be obtained
at www.ICGtesting.com
Printed in the USA
LVHW092232020621
689219LV00016B/97